I0738291

# THE

# INDIVISIBLE

## AND THE

# VOID

Copyright © 2019 D.M. Wozniak
ISBN: 978-0-578-44715-5

All rights reserved. No part of this book may be reproduced or transmitted in any form or by any means, electronic or mechanical, including photocopying, recording, or any information storage and retrieval system, without prior written permission of the author. Your support of authors' rights is appreciated.

All characters in this compilation are fictitious. Any resemblance to actual persons, living or dead, is purely coincidental.


Cover design by Kathryn Rosa Miller
www.kathrynrosamiller.com

# THE
# INDIVISIBLE
# AND THE
# VOID

## AGE OF AXION
## BOOK ONE

## D.M. WOZNIAK

The fundamental notion that any voider's power relies upon is this: Everything in our creation is made of infinitesimal building blocks, called the indivisible. There is nothing else besides the indivisible and the void.

**– Master Voider Democryos**

I cannot bear to put the words Dear Love down on this parchment, but the formality of your name betrays the years of happiness we had together. I want to remember you as being more than just my teacher. You were my lover, too.

Dem will suffice, then.

If it helps, think of this goodbye as my graduation. As you always taught me beneath your layered charm, the indivisibles move about randomly. There is great disorder to the natural world, and the power of a voidstone holds no permanent sway.

Things fall apart, Dem. I've fallen in love with someone else, and we are indivisible no more.

**– A letter written by the Lady Marine to Democryos**

# PART ONE


# THE GIRL FROM SCORPIONTAIL

# A LETTER FROM THE LADY MARINE

I let go of the parchment as I would a voidstone—with deliberate finality. Because it's either a little piece of me that dies right now or all of me.

Despite my heartache, I choose not to die today.

Similar to that of releasing a voidstone, the sensation is one of slowing down, falling. If I were to explain it to a non-voider, I'd compare it to riding the king's steed, or captaining a nine-mast ship, and then going from that ecstatic blur to a crawl in the mud, your body weighed down with pockets full of stones.

For when you hold a voidstone, everything changes. You no longer see people, things, or places. You no longer see the world. You see what the world *is made of*, moving around with the ferocity of creation.

You see the indivisible and the void.

The letter hits the marble floor of my room, and I realize that for the last five years, I've been living in an ecstatic blur. The five years that Marine and I were together were a dream. But now the dream is gone.

The letter folds in upon itself where she previously creased it. I see the line in the last paragraph clearly: "Things fall apart, Dem."

Perhaps Marine is right. And I almost wonder if part of me always knew this, in the deep recesses of my mind.

When we met, she was so young. I remind myself that she is *still* young, but five years ago she was almost half my age, at twenty-one. A first-year student at the university, and my opposite in every way, she was pragmatic and adventurous, the daughter of a wealthy landowner from Giriya. For some reason, she pursued me. She didn't have to. She was smart enough to get by on her own merits. She had the gift. In fact, she was so strong, I am confident that she would have experienced voideath on her own, had she not received proper training at the university. But in the end, she admitted to me that she would rather have luxury than a diploma. Fame rather than function. And I was an aging bachelor susceptible to perfection.

The first time I saw her, with her golden hair in a tidy ponytail and her eyes the color of Xi Bay, I knew that I was powerless. Whatever she wanted, she would have.

But now, the Lady Marine apparently wants someone else.

Is it because I am too old and idealistic for her? Her passionate youth always pushed at the edges. Years ago, she admitted to smoking hilma once. She dove naked off the cliffs of Northinglight. On occasion, she would touch her voidstone when we made love. Her entire body would shudder.

Perhaps it has nothing to do with my age, but rather my responsibilities. I have simply been too wrapped up in my teaching. The king has been pushing me to train the students hard, to get them ready for war. There were nights upon end where I stayed in the lab or classroom, leaving Marine here, alone.

*Or was she alone?*

My hands form fists as I think of the possibilities.

Closing my eyes, I remind myself that the love between us *was* real. But when I open them and see the letter on the floor, I admit the bitter truth: this love was temporary. It had a beginning and an end.

In some ways, it was no different from the first lecture I gave to all my students.

*Voiders don't create or destroy. We only change. We manipulate what is already there. And many times this change is brief. If you hold on to the power of the voidstone for too long, you risk voideath. So you must always let go, and when you do, things tend to go back to the way they were. It may take a fullbell, or it may take days, but eventually, the world returns to normal. You cannot change things forever.*

The same is true when it comes to love.

These are the words that I have said to many a student. After a student became enraptured and subsequently forgotten by some daughter of a prosperous merchant, they would come running to me. I would tell them that they were the subject of a morbid curiosity, for the wealthy like to experience things. It comes either out of boredom or the perception of power. Loving a voider is one of these experiences. I would remind my students of my first lecture, and give them encouragement, telling them to focus on their studies and leave everything else behind. Because they are the lucky ones. They have the gift. And this gift is better than all the money and beauty in the world.

Except I am not a simple student.

I am Master Voider Democryos.

This is the reason I cannot let her go. Not until I know the truth. One does not simply leave a man possessing my power with nothing more than a cryptic letter.

I, alone, understand how the world was built. And so I, alone, must understand why it has been destroyed.

A gentle tapping on the door brings me out of my thoughts.

"Elrich, come in," I say, recognizing the knock of my first footman.

"Morning, Lord Democryos."

He opens the door as I bend to pick up Marine's letter and place it back neatly on my pillow, folded in thirds. I don't look at the lanky young man, but I smell the coffee in the room and hear him place the silver tray on my desk. Usually, he's talking by now, relaying the day's agenda. But not today.

*He knows.*

This makes my anger swell. The rumors must be all over the citadel by now. The kitchen, four stories below, was probably alive and buzzing with hearsay well before sunrise.

I take a deep breath.

Elrich is a good man. He takes his job seriously, and can always be relied upon. There are not many people like him in the world. Even the king lacks this characteristic. Of course, the king's responsibilities are far broader than that of a first footman, but still, the king doesn't seem to fill his role like Elrich fills his. Like a perfectly tailored suit, Elrich and his station are meant to be. It's not that the king can't fill his place—he understands what needs to be done, and he has blood right. It's more a lack of caring.

The room is flooded with summer light as Elrich draws the silk damask curtains.

"How was the graduation ceremony?" he eventually says, weakly.

My mind flashes to yesterday: My final morning speech addressing the graduating voiders. The elaborate outdoor ceremony midday with King Andrej X. The final dinner banquet. Out of everything that transpired, only one thing stays with me—a sunspot in my vision. The Lady Marine, in a canary-yellow dress that hugged her every curve. She was distant, and at the time I attributed it to her wishing she had stayed in her studies instead of coming to live with me. Years ago, I had been adamant about that. I could not be both her teacher and her lover—she had to pick. And this year would have been her graduation. The students leaving for war were her friends—the same students who were once her classmates.

Last night had been humid. After dinner, when I went outside, I caught her standing in the fountain, her high-heeled shoes left on the stone railing. She was running water through her golden hair, and her face was wet in the moonlight. Now I wonder if there were tears there, as well.

I ignore Elrich as I walk to my desk and pour myself a cup of coffee, not caring that I should wait until he does it for me.

"How long have you known?" I ask him.

As if considering his answer, my first footman walks over to the armoire and retrieves one of my black flaxen cloaks. He hangs it on the brass post with a clang.

"Since this morning, my lord. Anna relayed the troubling news." After an awkward pause he adds, "You have my sincerest condolences."

His guarded response is darkly amusing. He is not calling her a whore to make me feel better, since he doesn't know how angry I am at her. But he is not denying the fact either.

I hear the soft sound of him brushing the fabric of my cloak. But as I leave the room, walking beyond the drawn curtains and onto the covered stone balcony, the sound of his work is covered by layers of summer. Chirping birds, nesting impossibly high on the tower's walls. Women in the king's choir having morning practice. The din of commerce in the square far below. From this height, the commoners look as small as game tokens.

Anna is Marine's lady maid—she would naturally have been the first to know. The woman has never been known to keep a secret. No wonder everyone has heard by now. Marine did not sleep with me last night. She must have awoken in her separate bedchamber fullbells ago and summoned Anna to help her prepare for the journey.

Whatever journey that was.

I look out at the kingdom, with its rolling hills glowing in the morning sun and sparkling with dew that has not yet burned off. And I realize that I have not been asking myself the correct questions. Ever since I found the letter, I have been focused on the *why*. But I will never know why she left me, not until I ask her. For me to ask her, I need to find her first.

"Elrich, get over here," I bark.

Elrich puts down the brush and walks over to me, nervously.

"My lord?"

"Whom did she leave with?"

He shakes his head. "I do not know. I asked the lady's maid the same question this morning, anticipating that you would want to know. Lady Marine left the citadel by herself while it was still dark, against Anna's strong counsel."

I take a sip of coffee while I think.

"What was she wearing?" I ask.

"Her white blouse and tan riding pants, my lord." Elrich clears his throat before continuing. "Anna already sent a footman down to the stables. There are no horses missing."

I look sideways at him, and he looks down at the floor. His skin is flushed redder than usual at the cheeks, and a strand of strawberry-blond hair has fallen across his forehead. As I glare at him, a single droplet of sweat falls off his brow and hits the black stone tiles between us.

Talking about such things is apparently hard on him. The man is trembling, walking on eggshells.

Everything in life is relative. At this moment, I would relish the chance to switch places with him.

Is he the master voider of the citadel who has just been publicly humiliated in front of the entire court? No. He is an unknown servant who gets paid a handsome wage for doing something anyone can do. In truth, he has not a single care in the world. His burden is made of straw.

Elrich swallows. "My lord, did you wish for me to summon the captain?"

"What for?"

"To arrange a search party."

A bitter smile crosses my face, as I slowly shake my head. "No. She left on her own. She wasn't taken from me.

I am not about to sap the king's resources, which are already thinned due to the war, looking for a girl who no longer desires the pleasure of my company."

This is a half-truth. What I don't tell him is that I am not about to make this humiliation worse by having hundreds of men scour the countryside in my name. I will find her on my own, since I have the power of hundreds of men.

Elrich takes this as an end to the conversation, and he rushes back to retrieve my undergarments. I extend my arms in anticipation, and he places a silk shirt on me and changes the subject.

"If I may kindly suggest then, the weather today looks splendid, and an afternoon ride may be exactly what you need. The fresh air will do you good. Your only obligation today is dinner with the king, at sevenbell."

But I am not ready to end the conversation. Not by a king's mile.

Elrich steps away, only to return with my black flaxen cloak.

"Back to the lab this morning?" he innocently asks me, but I shake my head.

"Lady Marine's bedchamber," I answer, feeling the weight upon my shoulders.

# A BLACK SUBSTANCE

I let Elrich unlock Marine's door with his gold skeleton key, even though I could do it just as easily by fingering the voidstone hung about my neck.

Let him feel useful.

"You can leave now," I utter.

When the door shuts behind me and I hear his long strides fade down the hall, I let out a sigh and then breathe in deeply.

I can still smell her.

Her bedchamber has always been more luxuriant than mine, as it should be. I never spend much time in my room. I am always busy in the library, laboratory, or classrooms. My room is for sleeping and dressing, and little else. Marine would come to me sometimes, in the middle of the night, but more often I would come here, for her. To be embraced in her world of pink.

Layered rugs in blushes, creams, and golds cover the floor, hiding the white marble tile. A sitting room with floral settees lies between the entrance and her actual bedroom—a semi-private place where she would entertain her closest friends, where the young, beautiful women could talk beyond the earshot and gaze of men.

I pass through this room like a ghost, heading straight for her bed as I try to remember the last time I was here. A week ago. The days leading up to the graduation are now part of the tapestry—a blur.

Now I wonder, if I had come to her this past week and showered her with attention, would things be any different?

Somehow I doubt it. Our problems go back further.

Gathering the white silk bedsheets to my face, I once again breathe in her scent deeply.

There's nothing exotic about it. I smell her hyacinth-infused soap, but it is weak, barely there. Yet it intoxicates me. The smell of her sweat should repulse me. Any other person's would. But hers is achingly familiar.

With one hand, I tear back the sheets to the foot of the bed while touching the voidstone with my other and channeling its power.

The world of white, pink, and cream disappears, and the black void takes its place.

The soft, feminine silence of the room also changes. The voices fill my head.

Of course, they're not actual people speaking to me, but I've always thought of them as such. When I was a child, my teacher used an analogy that has always stuck with me.

*Imagine there is a terrible storm. The violent wind enters the mouth of the cavern and whips around, echoing off the jagged walls, creating dozens of copies, each different in pitch and strength. Now imagine that you are a scared child, and within this dark cave, every once in a while, the wind is speaking to you.*

Under the influence of the voidstone, I still see the bedsheets, but they are not white. There is no color here besides black and nonblack. Only shape and movement and the voices swirl around me. The fibers are woven tightly by expert hands—massive, humming ropes, overlapping themselves repeatedly. Over, under, over, under. They fill my vision as I move between them. The ropes surround me now, vibrating like guitar strings. I am in a maze that goes left, right, up, and down. Which way do I go? I could go inside one of the ropes, or stay between them, swimming in this blackness. If I went inside, the movement would increase and the ropes would cease to be, becoming points of nonblack that collided in tight, random angles.

The indivisible. This is as far as one can go.

Something catches my attention. I stay where I am.

Far away, over the landscape of humming ropes, the lattice is suspended within some medium. Everywhere else is blackness. But here, I can distinguish an ocean of nonblack that is made of indivisibles different from the rope. I go in further and stop once I discover what it means. The millions of tails and heads. The infestation repulses me, and I let go of the stone.

*A man has been here.*

The stain clearly isn't mine. We have not been intimate in over a week, and the idea that Marine's bedsheets have not been washed in that time is ridiculous.

*Almost as ridiculous a notion as her being faithful to me.*

I just stand there in the silence of the room as the realization hits me. The letter was one thing, but this stain is indelible. I finger the voidstone absently. Not the smooth black surface of it, shaped like the pit of a peach, but the gold setting of the necklace itself. This will not draw its power. The only voices in my head, for the moment, are my own.

When I eventually look up, I stare at my reflection, caught within Marine's massive gold-framed mirror, which is leaning against the wall. I don't look like an old man, although suddenly I feel like one. My brown eyes are partially sunken in. My short beard and hair are still more brown than gray, but they seem to be getting grayer every day. As for my body, it is in good shape for its forty-three years. I stand straight and strong, framed in my luxurious black cloak made from the finest flax.

Despite the war raging far to the south, here in the citadel we are immune. Most men my age have taken to daily wine and feasting and have let their bodies go to shame. Take the king, a man of less than thirty years who can hardly walk up a flight of stairs.

Not me. I have always kept both my mind and body honed, since that is the proper thing to do. Anything less is a sign of weakness. My studies have kept my mind sharp, while a younger wife ensured that my body didn't lag.

*Why wasn't I enough for her?*

Touching the smooth black surface of my voidstone, I shatter the mirror to pieces.

I let out a sharp breath, letting go.

*What are you doing?*

This is not acceptable—no matter how devastated I feel, I must not lose control. Working voidance under emotion is dangerous. Anger, especially, leads to overconsumption. It leads to voideath.

Taking a deep breath to steady myself, I wipe the corner of my eye and walk around the room.

Miscellaneous items lie everywhere. Marine was not a tidy woman. Vials of perfumed oils, orchid vases, makeup cases, feather plumes, and jewelry litter her immense marble-top vanity. In the center rests her wedding ring, and I stand for a moment looking at it before moving on. Her cream nightgown lies in a pile on the floor, next to the bed. Candelabras rest in odd places, too close to the curtains.

She actually preferred it this way, and often told the maids not to clean every day. Now I realize this touch of chaos suited her exuberance. She treated all the things around her like she treated me when we made love—a little bit out of control and a little bit as if I didn't matter. A frame to her picture.

But this room is in tatters, even for her.

I imagine her, awash in candlelight, fullbells ago, frantically packing for her midnight trip.

*How long has she been planning this?*

She didn't take much, and seemingly left in a hurry. Rifling through her wardrobe, I see her clothes are still here. Her lingerie, gowns, shoes—all of it.

But her voidstone, diminutive and lined with diamonds, is gone. She never wore it to bed. Instead, she always rested it on the headboard's turned bedpost, keeping it within arm's reach.

Walking into her bathroom, I open the shutters to let in the sunlight. Here there are no rugs. Only hard stone, and a large clawfoot tub still full of tepid water and rose petals.

A soiled towel rests against the sink.

I pick it up by one of the clean sections and bring it to my face. The smears covering the white cloth are black, and sticky. There is a strong smell to it that I cannot place.

Walking back to her vanity, I check her makeup. The only thing that it could be is eyeshadow, but I quickly use my voidstone to compare the two substances—they don't match. They are made of different indivisibles.

Running footsteps pause outside the bedroom door. After a moment, a knock follows.

"What is it?" I ask.

"Lord Democryos, may I enter? It's Anna."

"Of course," I say. I wonder if she can hear the sarcasm in my voice.

She opens the door and cautiously makes her way through the parlor into the bedchamber, holding her full black skirt to prevent herself from tripping. She looks at the shards of mirror covering the floor and then back to me with wide eyes.

"I—" she stammers. "I heard the noise from down the hall, my lord."

I wave the soiled towel in the general direction of the damage. "That is of no importance," I say. Then I extend the towel in front of me. "But *this* is."

"My lord?"

"What is on this?"

"I—" Anna curls a blonde lock behind her ear, a confused expression on her face.

"This was left by the Lady Marine," I say between clenched teeth. "In her bathroom."

"That is her washing linen."

"I know it's her washing linen. What is *on* it?" I ask, more loudly this time.

She looks at me as if I am asking the stupidest question in the world. "I do not know, my lord."

Although her expression makes me even angrier, I can see that she is telling the truth. But there are lies of omission, too.

My eyes narrow. "You assisted her this morning."

Anna looks down at the shattered mirror and takes a step or two around the shards, as if calculating the extent of the damage. But I know she is only buying time. She didn't expect to run into me this morning, here in Marine's bedchamber. Her steps resemble those of a caged animal testing the limits of a new confinement.

She starts to cry, wringing her hands in her black dress, and I sense that she is about to tell me something.

"Talk," I say.

"There was a man here, in her bedchamber."

I nod once, waiting for her to continue.

"I am so sorry, my lord. He told me that if I said anything he would hurt my family. I wanted to let Elrich know, so he could warn you. But my little Liuka. And my husband, Bartha. He said that people would come for them unless I was quiet. Unless I kept his secret." She wipes her face. "I am so sorry!"

"Who was he?" I scream.

She shakes her head. "His face was veiled, my lord."

"What does that mean?"

"I never saw him!" She seems at a loss for words. "A cloud always hung about his face. It made him blurry."

"You mean something physical?"

She shakes her head. "Something in the air."

*Voidance.*

There are so many things I could ask her, but one word cuts deeper than the rest.

"Always?" I snarl.

"My lord?"

"You said *always*." I swallow. "A cloud *always* hung about his face. How long has this been going on?"

She closes her eyes tightly, as if trying to remember the ugly truth, or maybe trying desperately not to reveal it.

"Months, my lord," she eventually whispers. "Since the rainy season ended."

My mouth hangs open, ready to ask another question, but my chest expands and contracts rapidly, preventing me from doing so. I force myself to inhale slowly through my nostrils. My body softens. I push all my emotions and visions of Marine into the back of my mind and focus on what's in front of me. Anna looks at me as though I am another mirror that might shatter.

I have seen the baby Liuka, and the oaf Bartha. I know the love this woman has for them. Part of me envies the tidy family they have begun together. Perhaps there is something indivisible left in this world after all.

*The man behind the veil threatened them.*

I realize, repulsed with myself, I was close to doing the same. When Anna first hesitated, I was half-prepared to threaten voidance as a way to pull the truth out of her. But the truth is already evident. It's all over Marine's bedsheets.

Before self-loathing fully consumes me, I tell myself there is an important distinction. In the end, my threats to Anna would have been empty. I could never harm this gentle woman—instilling fear in her would have been my only crime. But that is a crime nonetheless.

*Can the same be said for this mysterious veiled man?*

"My lord," she says, as if reading my mind. "Please do not say anything. He could still hurt—"

I cut her off with a wave of my hand, the soiled towel still clutched in it. "I will not betray your trust, Anna. But you should have come to me. There is no man in this world—veiled or not—that you need to fear. If this thief shows himself again, he is the one who will know fear."

She closes her eyes as if she were an effulgent, praying.

Meanwhile, I keep a small sample of the sticky black substance to take back to my lab. Touching my voidstone, I create a perfect square about one finger's length and drop the rest of the towel at my feet.

"Is there anything else you wish to tell me?" I ask her, as I carefully fold the swatch and place it in my cloak pocket.

She goes into more detail. She was awoken and asked to carry a single case of clothes down for Marine. A spare pair of boots. Her journal, ink vial, and quills. Marine was alone and in a hurry. She could have done all of this by herself, but only Anna knew the way from the servants' entrance of the Royal House to the Southern Gate of the First Ring, where fewer guards patrolled.

One thing becomes clear: Anna didn't know anything about Marine's decision to leave prior to last night. And quite possibly, neither did Marine.

"I will clean up this mess, my lord," she assures me, already on her knees, carefully picking up the larger shards and placing them into a silver bucket from the bathroom. As she works, her tears fall inside of it, clinking like rain on a soldier's armor.

I nod distantly, slowly spinning in place. I look upon all this luxury, so rare with an entire war going on to the south. Most people live and die without seeing such opulence, even in times of peace. Quite the life, even for the daughter of a Giriyan landowner.

*Marine threw it all away.*

Which means that whatever she is after must be greater than all of this.

# THE SECOND RING

It's much worse than I feared.

Everyone on the wide black cobblestone street is avoiding me. Merchants gaze downward over their barrels of wares, unconcerned with making a sale. Passersby huddle in urgent, forced discussion behind arborvitae. Wrinkled men too old for war sit mutely underneath the green awning of a corner cafe, gazing at me with glassy eyes from behind a storm cloud of tobacco smoke. Above them, women peek out at me from under the thin undershirts they hang to dry in the breeze.

Only the children approach me, asking to see my voidstone, or for me to show them a sign. They are too innocent to understand the nature of disgrace.

I ignore them all.

Only near the arched Southern Gate of the First Ring does an adult acknowledge me, though I doubt he has good intent.

"Greetings, Democryos," bellows the head effulgent. "Be nothing," he adds—the idiotic, common effulgency greeting.

His temple sits just inside the First Ring, almost within the shadow of the impossibly high wall, and right off Xi Bay Road. Its towering plaster spire gleams in the midday sun, as do his robes.

The large bald man walks down red-brick steps toward the road with his arms out at his sides. His skin is impossibly smooth, like all effulgents'. Not a patch of his body is covered in hair. No eyebrows, no beard, no arm hair—nothing.

"Your Effulgency," I say. I don't stop walking. I am intent on reaching the archway in the distance while keeping a keen lookout for anything out of place. Anything that would lead me to Marine's whereabouts. This is the way she went last night, from what Anna had said, but for the thousandth time today, I feel I am on a fool's errand.

Surprisingly, he matches my stride. I hear the exertion on his breath.

"Congratulations on your graduating class," he says. "The ceremony yesterday was impressive. I hope the students bring a quick end to the war."

I know this man all too well—he is my peer in many ways, reporting to the king in very much the same fashion that I do. He, however, has nothing to offer the king but a few of his younger effulgents and graycloaks to lead soldiers in prayer on foreign battlefields before they die wretched deaths. And to deliver bouquets of flowery language, like the one he's producing for me now.

"You can spare me the bullshit," I mumble.

The older man lets out a deep laugh. "I know we may not see eye to eye on most things, but I actually mean the words I say. Anything to stop this war is a good thing."

I wait for him to reveal his true reason for approaching me. These compliments are but one of his devices.

"My point is," he continues, "just because I see you as evil doesn't mean we cannot work together on a common cause."

I shoot him a glance, but do not stop.

"Well, *you* are not evil, to be clear. But the black arcana you proselytize is, just as swinging a sword to kill another is evil. War is evil. This is what I wanted to tell the students yesterday in my final blessing to them. But I couldn't with the king there. His lordship would have my head."

"That would be a shame."

Soon we reach the sheltering archway of the Southern Gate. Beneath it, everything becomes cool and dark. I stop and look sideways at him, hoping to end the discussion.

"What do you want?"

He catches his breath. Beyond that, I hear soft rattling as he fidgets with a set of ivory beads in his hand.

"I heard what happened."

I don't say anything. Based on his prior compliments, I was half-expecting him to ask me for a favor. Something to do with the king or the war. Certainly not Marine.

"And I just wanted to add that if you need someone to talk to—for guidance, or counseling—I am here."

"How can you possibly offer me guidance?" I instinctively answer. "You don't even share a bed with a woman."

It's bright enough in the tunnel to see his self-deprecating smile.

"That's true," he answers, "but I do know how hard it is to let go of one's possessions."

It takes me a moment to understand his jab, and when I do, I feel my brow furrow. "She's not my possession," I say, raising my voice.

A passing family turns our way briefly. They walk next to their old horse, which is carrying burlap bags of goods through the tunnel. I'm immediately embarrassed about losing my composure in public. They walk on, and the head effulgent and I are again left in relative privacy.

I had not intended to make a mockery of the situation by asking strangers if they had seen my wife the night before. But this effulgent might be able to help. He's already brought up the bitter conversation, and as we're standing within the moderate shelter of the tunnel, it doesn't seem harmful to ask.

"Did you see anything early this morning?" I ask him quietly.

The holy man tilts his head.

"Before sunrise," I add. "The Lady Marine may have passed this way. Possibly with another man. I heard she took Xi Bay Road."

The effulgent looks at me with a mix of sympathy and disgust, and I have the urge to put my hands around his throat and press him up against the tunnel wall. "Oh, my son," he says deeply. "Is *that* why you are walking here in this neighborhood? You are looking for *her*?"

"Never mind," I mumble as I walk away, realizing it was a stupid idea. Anything involving an effulgent is a stupid idea.

The hairless man stays where he is, but after I've put some distance between us, he calls out to me, his baritone voice echoing off the damp stone.

"That is the problem with you voiders! You think that you can use people! Just like you use the poor souls in your stones!"

I pick up my pace and contemplate filling this entire tunnel with a windstorm.

The effulgents—they're all the same. Deep down, they hate voiders. Their writings proclaim that we're evil—that living beings are trapped in every voidstone, but of course they have no proof of such nonsense. They wrap their ignorance in false compassion and pretend to invite us into the light. But secretly, they wish they had such power themselves. They are hypocrites.

Warm sunlight hits me, and I raise my face. I've exited through the tunnel and am now on the other side of the wall.

The Second Ring.

I'm still within the safety of the citadel, but it's markedly less dense here. Gone are the paved surfaces and stone facades of the First Ring. Buildings exist, but they only dot the grassy, rolling landscape, offering a much-needed change of pace. Groves of pine and oak are the towers here, and somewhere to the east must be the river.

The gravel road leads into the distance, so narrow here that I need to step off its path as a horse and carriage pass by. My boots make shallow prints in the fine sand.

An entire countryside lies before me.

It will be impossible to locate her. Even if this was the way she came—even if she exited through the Southern Gate and I am now following her exact footprints—what am I supposed to do? I trace her moonlit journey in my mind. Permutations of the past. Most likely, by now, she is on horseback. Elrich said he checked the stables, but that just meant those at the Royal House. Marine could have walked a few king's miles down Xi Bay Road and paid off a stable boy or innkeeper for a horse. Or maybe she walked all this way and visited one of the farms in the Second Ring.

The bell tower of the effulgency temple starts ringing out the time. Even though the tower is on the other side of the thick wall, the tip of the spire peeks through, mocking me.

It's threebell.

In four fullbells I need to be at dinner with the king. That is not something one is late for. Not even a master voider plays with that sort of fire.

The problem is that I have no idea where Marine was going. From here, though there are not many options, each would take days to explore. This gravel road continues for many miles to the Outer Wall. That entrance is gated and staffed with a guardhouse. If she'd gone that way, the guards would have noticed, but she could have paid them to stay silent. Besides, it would take me a fullbell to reach it, which would put me late for dinner. Unless I could procure a carriage.

But then what?

Past the Outer Wall, Wainwright is the nearest village to the south. I suppose I could travel there tomorrow and see if she passed through. Wainwright is known for superb parchment production. I have one nearly empty box of it in my lab.

I begin walking south again, though slower now, without a destination. I won't reach the Outer Wall, nor Wainwright. At least not today.

But walking helps me think.

The man she was seeing covered himself in a veil. *A cloud always hung about his face. It made him blurry.* That is what Anna said.

So he was a voider, too.

He used a simple trick any first-year student learns: speeding up the indivisibles in the air surrounding the subject. This creates disturbances. A haziness. This morning, the sun shone off the black road that led me here, creating the same illusion. Perhaps in a non-voider's eyes, this made his face appear veiled.

Did he and Marine rendezvous here? In the Second Ring?

And if so, where would two voiders supposedly in love go?

*Anywhere they wanted to.*

A large covered wagon approaches from the south, and I step off the gravel again, well past the sandy roadside, to escape the dust. I wipe the sweat off my brow and realize I am thirsty and exhausted. The sun has been beating down on me for most of the day as I foolishly follow the footprints of a ghost. And while my flaxen cloak is incredibly lightweight, its black color absorbs much of the summer heat.

A grove of tall pines stands behind me, its shade refreshing. I decide to go in deeper and lie down on the bed of dry needles that blanket the ground. Some rest will do me good before I head home. But when I lean my hand on a nearby trunk for support, I curse loudly and inspect my palm.

It's covered in tree sap.

I moan in utter annoyance.

There's no way to get this grime off using natural means, at least until I return home.

I collapse on the needles with my soiled hand laid out in front of me, and I touch the voidstone with the other. This use of voidance will only tire me more, but the thought of traveling through the crowded citadel with sap on my hand is more than I can bear.

In the world of black and nonblack, I work on separating the indivisibles from each other. Instead of weaving between the humming ropes of Marine's bedsheets, I navigate rounded honeycomb structures that form a road almost like the black one I took here, except this one covers the mountainous terrain of my palm. Massive trees, not unlike the pines hanging over me, jut out every so often. They are the hairs on my skin. The more I enter the area with the sap, the more the honeycombs take over.

I stop.

*I've seen these honeycombs before.*

I let go, and the world around me snaps back as I fervently search my cloak's pockets. I find it and pull it out then peel the square of white fabric apart to reveal the black substance.

Marine's soiled linen.

Though the color of the grime is different from that of the sap on my palm, it's clear they're both honeycombs, and when I get as close as I can, the indivisibles are nearly the same.

My heart races as I finish cleaning my hand. When I release the stone, I look at the shaved remains of the sap, crystallized and hardened, that lie on the pine needles between my legs. I know then why the colors are different: the raw sap is amber, while the substance on the towel is black—one can become the other.

I recall my studies from years ago, back when the king's father ruled. He had asked me for help because the fleet was taking on leaks. We developed the end product to waterproof the hulls of large ships. Without it, the king's navy would have sunk into the abyss.

I started by making a herringbone pattern of cuts on the trunk, and then collected the sap in a pot at the base of the tree. When the sap finished flowing, the tree was chopped down and burned. The resulting black powder was added to the boiling pine resin.

This is what creates the black pitch.

Perhaps it's because I've overused the voidstone. Perhaps it's because of the heat. Or perhaps it's because of this newfound revelation. Whatever the cause, I lie on my back and stare into the blue-green heights of the pines above me. They sway in the breeze, sounding like the wind in the void.

Before Marine left, she was around a shipyard. And I can think of only one reason for a woman of her caliber to be in a place like that. Preparations for a journey.

*Marine took a ship.*

# VOIDREAMING

There's a knock on my bedchamber door, but I already know who it is. I can hear the large man breathing through his mouth like a fireplace bellows. No wonder Submaster Herrophilus hates visiting me. I'm in the topmost floor of the Royal House—a hard climb, even for someone who's in shape.

"Come in."

Herrophilus storms in, barely fitting through the doorframe.

"How is it coming?" I ask him, referring to the new hospital being built in the lake district—the first of its kind outside the reaches of the citadel.

He nods. "Very well, but that is not the reason I am here. I have made a fortunate find." Clearing his throat, he turns around, facing the open door and dark hallway beyond.

"Well, what are you waiting for?" he booms, his chest heaving, his face glistening with sweat. "Show yourselves to the master voider."

A young man and woman enter. Both wear tan and white riding clothes.

"This is Anaxarchis and Marine," the submaster says to me between breaths, as he extends a hand in their direction. "I plucked them from the Northern town of Giriya, by the lake."

"Why were you in Giriya?" I ask.

"I found them on my way back from the hospital site. My wagon hit a hole in the road and needed repair."

"You didn't think to fix it with voidance?"

"I did," he answers defensively. "But the balance was off, so I stopped by the wheelwright in Giriya, which is owned by this boy's father. The moment I saw him, I thought that he might have the gift."

"Why?"

He shrugs. "I don't know. You know how it is. When you've been doing field admissions for so long, you just sort of get a hunch with some people."

I nod as he motions toward the boy. "I asked him to do the touch test. At first, he was too nervous."

I glance at the boy. I suppose, technically, he is a man, but he's small—maybe five feet tall. The same height as the girl. He looks sheepishly at the floor.

"And then this one comes in," Herrophilus says, glaring at the girl. "She's the boy's second cousin. Once she heard what was going on, she walked right up to me and grabbed my stone. Impulsive little brat. Father owns half of Giriya and she's been raised to think the same. Did the touch test without my even asking permission."

I switch my attention to the young blonde woman in front of me. Her white cotton shirt is tied in a tight knot at the side of her waist. She's gathering a ponytail in her hands and biting a jeweled hair ring that is the same color as her sea-blue eyes.

"This seemed to give the boy here enough courage to do the same." He laughs. "Can you believe it? Two voiders in the same lake town."

"Are there any other voiders in your family?" I ask both of them. "Any history of voidance?"

Anaxarchis shakes his head while continuing to look at the floor, but Marine stares intently at me. Unlike the boy, she does not seem intimidated. She seems intrigued.

She finishes tying up her hair. "No. My family has enough power in Giriya without resorting to the black arcana."

Herrophilus gasps in disbelief and then raises his hand to strike her in the face, but I catch his arm before it connects.

"Such insolence cannot be tolerated!" he yells.

I give him a patient, understanding nod as I release his wrist.

Still, he turns to the girl, a vein protruding from his reddened forehead. "You are speaking to the master voider, girl. Watch your tongue."

Marine ignores him. She looks around my luxurious room calmly. Without hesitation, she walks over to my desk, pulls one of my books off the shelf, and opens it.

"My submaster is right," I say to her back. "You don't seem to respect or appreciate the opportunity we're giving you. My library isn't a Giriyan fishmarket, you know—"

"Is this Asima's complete writings of Xiland?" she interrupts, looking at me excitedly while her blonde ponytail whips behind her like one of Anna's feather dusters.

Herrophilus gasps. "Put that back!"

Instead of complying, she rifles through the leather-bound book, finding a page illustrated with a map. She places a slender finger on it, as if tracing where she currently is and planning how to get to the place she wants to be.

Herrophilus yells again, and she jumps, reluctantly setting the volume back down on my desk.

"It is one of ten volumes," I say. "My scribes are working on copying the later ones."

"Have you been to Xi Bay?"

I nod.

"I've heard it's more beautiful than anything," she says dreamily.

"Almost anything."

I approach her, and I see her swallow nervously.

Her blue eyes dart down to my chest, where my voidstone is resting at the bottom of my necklace, before meeting my gaze again.

"Is that why you agreed to come to the citadel with the submaster? Just to learn about the Southern lands?"

She shakes her head. "It's more than just that."

"Explain, then."

She bites her lip, as if contemplating how much truth to share, but then she suddenly opens up, her voice getting quicker and louder with each passing word.

"Giriya is a small town full of small-minded people. Your submaster is right in the sense that my family owns most of it. I could live my entire life there without worry. Marry some fat fishmonger. Give him a net-full of babies. But that's not my dream. I was meant for more."

"Then start acting like it," warns Herrophilus.

She ignores him. She's been talking too fast and must catch her breath. Meanwhile, I pick the book up off my desk and place it back in her hands.

"When you're done reading it, come see me," I say. "We will discuss it together."

She nods once excitedly while slowly looking around the room at the gilded mirrors, trident candelabrum, and damask curtains blowing in the breeze from the balcony. And for the first time, a content, appreciative smile crosses her face. Her body softens too, as if she has finally let her guard down.

I try not to focus on how incredibly beautiful she is.

"Thank you," she says, motioning to the book in her hands.

I nod. "We may be a far cry from Giriya, but I feel that you'll be glad you joined us."

"I already am," she says without hesitation. "I was never meant for that place. I was never meant for the ordinary."

"No," I agree. "I don't suppose you were."

# DINNER WITH THE KING

I fell asleep underneath the pines.

My desperate search for Marine's ship after that was cut short. Covered in dust and sweat, I had no choice but to head back to the Royal House. I drew a cold bath myself, since Elrich was out fetching my boots from the cobbler. I quickly changed into new undergarments and threw on a fresh flaxen cloak and arrived on time, panting and exhausted, just before sevenbell.

That was a fullbell ago.

Ever since, I have been pacing alone in this cavernous dining room. It's King Andrej X's twisted sense of power at work. I'm sure that he believes he is exerting dominance over me by having me wait, but all he is doing is making the two of us hungry.

*Even in his absence, he makes me miss his father.*

I've been in this room countless times, but never alone. I could spend days here, admiring the luxurious details without having to split my attention between them and a person. And after the day I've had, I find it calming to be surrounded by such delicate silence.

The walls are gold leaf, reflecting the burnished candlelight. Most of it comes from the center chandelier, which has precisely fifty candles. I've counted them twice. Five gold candelabras sit on the wooden dining table that crosses the entire room. It's polished so well that it resembles a mirror. Fifty chairs surround it. I wonder if the matching number of chairs and candles is a coincidence.

Below the table lies an ornate rug, equally as large, featuring yellow stars, orange fish, and tangled white nets, all against a field of brilliant blue. I touch my voidstone for a moment just to make sure it is woven and not a painting. It must be from the archipelago—they are known for such work.

Turning my attention back to the wall, I study the framed portraits. They flank a fireplace so large I could easily walk into it. The painting I admire the most is of King Andrej IX—the father, who died five years ago. It depicts the moment right after a bow hunt when he downed an impressive whitetail buck. I remember the day vividly. The meat was given to the families of the Royal House servants for wintertide. Something I could never see Andrej X doing.

A small clock on one of the buffet tables that lines the room chimes brightly. Before it stops, a deeper yet faraway sound from the effulgency temple joins in. The sounds overlap like lovers embracing.

It's eightbell.

The sound of many footsteps comes my way.

Simultaneously, three of the room's doors open. The fourth, which leads to the balcony, remains closed, though its windows reveal dusk advancing upon the square below. Dozens of gloved servants spill in, carrying covered dishes. A musician has his violin perched upon his shoulder, and he begins playing the moment he steps into the room. The servants set their dishes down and then stand still against the gold-leaf walls. Finally, the king enters, wearing blue robes that match the carpet.

I stop admiring the memory of his father and bow.

He lets out an enormous sigh. "Do you know how glad I am that it's just the two of us?" he says, approaching the table. "I am so sick of dealing with people."

I stay in a bowed position, since he has not told me to rise.

"Your majesty, it is an honor to dine privately with you tonight," I say, to the orange fish at my feet, feeling sorry for them. We all seem to be trapped in the king's nets.

"Stand up straight, Dem. Come, let's eat."

The king sits at the head of the table. My assigned seat is next to his. A servant holds the heavy chair for me, and I settle into it.

"I heard what happened with that slut wife of yours."

For a moment, I am too shocked to speak.

"It is saddening and humiliating, Your Majesty," I answer. There is no other way to handle this situation than with guarded honesty. If the king wants to discuss my heartache, then I must discuss it. But I do not have to embellish.

I look left toward Andrej, sitting at the head of the table. He is so young—in his late twenties. He is soft, clean skinned, and overweight, and his hair is parted perfectly, almost to the point of oddity.

A mischievous smile creeps across his face. "I saw the head effulgent in the gardens. He said you were scouring Xi Bay Road for her. Based on your demeanor, I assume you came up empty."

I close my eyes in frustration as he laughs. He grabs his empty wine glass and taps the table with it a few times. A servant comes running over and pours us both red-currant wine, starting with the king.

"Why the two of you don't get along, I will never understand," he says, referring to the effulgent and me. "You're very similar, you know."

"I fail to see how."

"Well, for one, you both exist to do my bidding." He follows up the statement with a large gulp of wine, and I have to refrain from wincing. This vintage is probably one of the best in the Northern Kingdom, and he's not even savoring it.

"You are correct, Your Majesty, but I fail to see how the effulgency does your bidding, unless you actually believe in the so-called power of their prayers."

The day's events have caused the offensive slip of the tongue, and I grip my crystal glass tightly. But shockingly, he continues, as if I had not overstepped any bounds.

"Of course I don't believe in that pig shit. We had thirty effulgents from across the kingdom praying over my father when he fell, and it didn't help."

He downs the rest of his glass like a fool, and yet there is something about him that is still impressive. That's when I place it.

*He's a master of perception.*

In public, Andrej presents himself as the holiest of acolytes. He defends the faith and recognizes the head effulgent's supposed authority, yet here in private, all of that falls away. His public persona is like the dark dining room table, polished to perfection, a reflection that everyone wants to see. But what lies underneath the sheen? What other guarded truths is this man built of?

"You know what the head effulgent brings me?" he asks.

"No, Your Majesty."

"The people. He brings me the people."

Servants silently set down plates of food in front of us, our first course. Aromas of seafood, lemon, and bitter arugula engulf me. I'm surprised to see baby squid. They come from the Xi Bay, which is practically ground zero in the war with the Southern Kingdom. I've not had it in years.

"You see, I need the people on my side."

"I see."

"And of course, I also need them to behave."

"Behave?"

He sticks a baby squid into his mouth and continues to speak while chewing.

"I don't have the resources to patrol this kingdom for petty criminals. Not when there is a war going on."

"But you are the king," I say. "Obedience should be implicit."

"My blood right is not enough," he barks. "The memory of my father is not enough. The fact that my people don't starve to death in winter is not enough. That's why I need the effulgency. They instill morals into the people. If the effulgents tell the people to pray for me, the people will follow my orders as well. The effulgents are my donkeys, and on their backs they carry the masses."

Young Andrej's perspective is certainly unique and interesting, but it's darkly elaborate, and it might be more complex than how the world actually works. A small part of me thinks he might be brilliant. But the lion's share thinks he's just lazy and perverted.

*If you want to be a good king, then be a good king. Rule your kingdom justly and through hard work, and your people will love you back. It's that simple.*

"Then what am I, Your Majesty?" I ask without thinking.

My question takes him off guard, and he looks at me with a confused expression. Since I've already passed the point of no return, I give him a softened explanation.

"You said the head effulgent is your donkey, and you also said that he and I are very much the same. So I am wondering if I am your donkey too."

His eyes narrow, just slightly. Others don't usually ask him such pointed questions.

"No, Dem. You are my warhorse."

I break eye contact with him and face downward, stabbing my food with my fork. My reaction is borderline offensive, but it's better than a snide reply.

The king refers to his exploitation of the voiders.

It's hard to believe that for four years, ever since the war started, all my students who've graduated have been recruited for his new purpose. This isn't the way it used to be. Voiders always provided a service to the people. I used to assign each student a destination when they graduated—from the Second Ring here in the citadel to the furthest reaches of the Northern Kingdom. Their duties were to assimilate, aid their appointed village with their struggles, help cure their sick, educate the unenlightened, and in general, make life better for the scores of people born into commonality.

The new king found a darker use for them.

"I need more voiders, Dem."

I look back up at the young ruler as I swallow.

"My commanders say that your students provide significant help to the cause. They're a weapon that we're lucky to have. The Southerners have them too, mark my words. But the Xian are not as organized or well trained."

"I'm glad to hear that, Your Majesty."

"Which is why I need to ask you for more," he says pointedly.

I hesitate before responding. "More?"

"With more voiders we can end this war," he says, as though I am daft.

"Your majesty, I do not have the power to create voiders out of commoners. One has to have the gift."

He waves me off while tapping his glass again.

"We already test every child in the citadel," I say. "We do routine visits to the countryside, catching those we may have missed."

"Obviously, we must double those efforts," he says. "There are likely voiders out there we have not yet identified."

"But the issue of the stones remains."

He grunts and leans back, his excitement deflated by the truth of my words.

"There are only so many voidstones in existence, Your Majesty. We confiscate the stones of all voiders who die. They're handed down to new recruits. I have a handful locked up in my lab. But there has always been a stasis. An odd balance. We've always had all that we have ever needed."

"Well, now we need more," he says.

"Have your commanders been successful in capturing enemy voiders?"

"Why do you ask?"

"It is the best way to gain more stones. If we confiscate a Xian stone, we weaken their force and strengthen ours."

He purses his lips. "That is a good thought, but the Southerners protect their voiders as we do ours. Always behind enemy lines and hidden in their ranks. We need to think of other means."

I shrug. "We continue to excavate them, now and then. Farmers uncover them in their fields every generation."

"Ah, but those are rare," the king insists. "And their sizes are getting gradually smaller. The largest ones have already been found, I'm told."

"That is true."

For a brief moment, there is silence between us. The only sound is the violin.

"What if we found a stone larger than you can imagine?" he asks. "More powerful than any stone in our possession. What would you say then?"

I look at him, confused by the question. His cheeks are flushed. He seems already drunk—he probably had a bottle of wine before coming into this dining room, and he's almost had another, here with me. "If we had larger voidstones," I answer levelly, "you wouldn't need more voiders. The ones you already have would be significantly more powerful."

"They'd be like gods, wouldn't they?"

The king is not looking at me anymore. He's staring at a candelabra, the flames reflecting in his eyes. The violinist, who has been playing softly all this time, ends his song, and the room is suddenly filled with an eerie stillness.

"They need to graduate faster," he eventually adds.

I set my fork down on the plate with an audible *clink*. "If you rush my students, they will not be ready."

"I will be the judge of that."

"Your majesty, the risk of voideath would be significant. Especially confronted with the horrors of war, they may not know when to disengage—"

He pounds his fist on the table and the plates jump in place. "I told you I will be the judge of that!"

In the corner of the room, the violinist appears to be thinking twice about playing again. His arm that holds the bow upright is quivering.

"Your majesty, it is my responsibility to always tell you the truth, even when it is in neither of our best interests. If the voiders are a special weapon in the war, you risk rendering this weapon unstable by producing it too quickly."

I can sense that he's not fully listening—he's staring into the candlelight again.

He turns to me, and King Andrej X's face is made of stone. "I'm beginning to wonder if I need to find myself another master voider."

His reply has caught me in midsip, which buys me a precious moment to think upon an answer. The only sound in the room now is the ticking clock on the buffet.

I do not have a choice. The king is right about one thing—I exist to do his bidding. If I refuse his demands, he will have me hanged and then replaced by a voider who will be a puppet and quickly ruin the university. If it were his father sitting before me tonight, I could talk him out of it. But then again, we wouldn't even be having this conversation. This is Andrej X's war, not his father's.

*How quickly things have changed.*

"When do you need them ready, Your Majesty?"

"Wintertide," he answers immediately. It's apparent that he has already thought long and hard about this.

*That's six months from now.*

What must be done will be done. Studies will be doubled. Holidays and retreats will be canceled. I will move my few teachers and their families into the Royal House to cut down on their travel time. We will need to be preparing these young men and women around the clock for this to work.

*But the deal! I need to ensure it is still intact.*

"Your majesty, we will celebrate another graduation in wintertide. All I ask in return is that you continue to honor your commitment to the one-student exception."

His stone face returns. He was probably not expecting a negotiation. Any bystander might even mistake his expression with confusion, but I can tell that he understands what I am talking about.

The one-student exception is very clear: in every graduating class, one student of mine is spared from enlistment. This student is sent out into the countryside—the way things used to be. And I get to pick who the student is, and where they go.

The clock ticks. The servants shuffle. I lean back as my plate is taken away and notice a dark smile upon the king's face when I turn back to him. He chuckles silently.

"My father was so right about you."

I wait for him to clarify.

"He loved you dearly, but he said you had your weaknesses too. Most people do, I imagine."

"Your father was a brilliant leader and mentor," I answer truthfully. "I will take any criticism he offers to heart."

"He said that you were idealistic, Dem. A perfectionist. You don't bend, you break. I think those were his words. But you are also honest. My father said that it was very difficult to get an honest opinion in this court, and I find it just the same. Everyone around me wants to tell me only what I want to hear. They all suck my cock with their pleasant answers. You don't, and I admire that."

His harsh language takes me by surprise. "Thank you, Your Majesty."

"But there's another side to that coin. You of all people should know that. Look at that young, hot wife of yours. That little nymph. She's slipped away."

The memory of what Marine did stabs me once more, but there is nothing I can say in reply. He downs another glass of wine, and I can easily see now that he's drunk. "There are some things I can never tell you," he continues. "I'd like to, but I know you'd disagree, and you'd be too proud to fall in line. I don't want to break you, Dem. So I keep you safe, instead. My trustful warhorse."

I wonder what he could be referring to, but based on his current temperament, I know better than to ask.

Soon, we're on to dessert, and finally anise liqueur and water pipe. The conversation keeps returning to Marine, but I don't go into any details about her unfaithfulness or the veiled figure. Nor do I tell him about the black pitch. I don't even tell him that I spent the four fullbells leading up to dinner madly scouring the riverbank for missing ships only to come up empty-handed. I'm barely sober enough to keep my intuition focused on the reflection in the dining table.

I don't trust what's underneath that sheen.

By tenbell, the table is cleared and all the servants have left the room. They're replaced by his harem, five women barely clothed in transparent silk. The king insists I take one of them back with me tonight. I initially refuse, but he proclaims that it is not my place to deny his overflowing generosity.

"It's our secret, Dem," he says, slurring his words. "Don't tell the donkey."

A few of the women resemble Marine. Their blonde hair and blue eyes are a painful reminder. But one audaciously steps forward. An olive-skinned woman with thick black hair in bangs, wider hips, and far-set eyes—clearly from the archipelago. Again I refuse, but neither she nor the king will take no for an answer. Thus is the pattern of the night.

I tell her to retrieve her cloak, and then we both stumble out into the darkness.

# A WALK IN THE MOONLIGHT

The girl from the archipelago snakes her arm into mine as we leave the king's residence and walk down the long, circular drive to the public street beyond.

"You look like a gentleman," she says, her face upturned cautiously in the moonlight.

"That's because I am one," I answer, taken aback by the odd statement, which almost sounded like a question. "What is your name?"

"Chimeline, Your Grace," she answers.

"You're from Scorpiontail," I say.

She nods. "How did you know?"

"I'm familiar with the features of archipelagian women. I've been there many times. Your dark hair and almond-shaped eyes are a dead giveaway."

"And our beauty too?" she asks playfully, but I am in no mood for games. I simply nod, and she smiles, tightening her grip on my arm.

"It's unfortunate that the chain of islands looks like a poisonous tail on a map," I continue. "I never liked the name of your homeland. The people there, by my account, were always welcoming."

"Thank you, Your Grace."

"What does it mean? Your name."

Suddenly she is quiet, not answering me until we approach the street. It's brighter here—the evergreens and hedgerows of the king's front gardens falling away and glass-covered lamplights taking their place. They've all been lit, and the full moon reflects off the damp street. A handful of workers are watering down the cobblestones to get rid of the stench of horse shit. They all look at us, and I am thankful that Chimeline is wearing a black robe to hide her nakedness underneath. Everyone here knows who I am, and I don't need additional rumors. Master Voider Democryos walking a female companion home—that is nothing too out of the ordinary.

"A father's pride," she says, flatly.

As we walk together, arm in arm, I look sideways at her. Her bangs cover her eyebrows. Her robe is parted slightly in a V, revealing her delicate neckline and soft curves, which hint at what's below. She must have applied some sort of makeup before we left, as her full lips reflect the same wet moonlight as the street. She is beautiful, and part of me wants to take advantage of the king's offer, but I cannot. It makes me just like him. The veiled man.

Besides, I am a little drunk, and exhausted after my grueling search in the sun. Even if it weren't morally reprehensible, I am not sure I would be willing to share my bed with this woman tonight. I am in no mood. I only want to remove these formal clothes and fall into my downy bed, to get a good night's rest before a fresh day of searching tomorrow. There are a handful of harbors I have not checked.

*Marine, I have not given up on you yet.*

But then the king's hideous words come back to me. With a rough slap on my back, he uttered them as we left, moments ago. "Go and fuck the memory of Marine right out of you, Dem. I need you to concentrate on the war."

*What a complete ass of a ruler.*

I stop in place, exhaling into the night.

*What am I doing with this woman?*

Chimeline has intuition. She senses my welling hatred and reluctance, and steps in front of me. She gently pulls upon the belt of her robe and it parts subtly in the night breeze, just enough to reveal her pristine body to me in the moonlight. I look over her shoulder at the workers down the street, but they are not paying attention. Her movements are purposely subtle. She knows there is a line here that cannot be crossed.

She looks up at me with dark-brown eyes. The scents of oranges and sugar waft over me.

"Take me to your bedchamber, Your Grace."

"Chimeline," I say. I am about to say more, but then she subtly weaves one of her small hands underneath my flaxen cloak, and any words that were on my tongue escape me.

"I can help you forget her," she whispers.

"No, you can't," I answer, even as my body is saying something else. I gently push her away. "I will walk you home," I add.

The look on Chimeline's face is one of disappointment and concern. She has only simple goals. She was given a job to do: to take away my pain. And I can tell that she wants to do it with all her heart.

"If you don't take me home with you, I will be disgraced."

That's when an odd understanding comes over me. This woman and I have more in common than I originally thought. We are both vilified by parts of society. And we are both being used.

Chimeline's power is her sexuality. She was born with the gift of beauty. It cannot be earned with money, hard work, or birthright.

My power depends on my ability to use a voidstone. Like all voiders, I was born with the gift. It, too, cannot be earned. While it has been proven that the sons and daughters of voiders show an inclination for the gift, it's not guaranteed. Voiders have been found in every part of society—from daughters of wealthy landowners to sons of wainwrights.

We are who we are. We didn't ask for this.

*And the king is using us both.*

"Come on," I say. "I'm not going to disgrace you."

I wrap her back up in her black robe and tie the belt securely. Then I put my arm around her and we slowly stumble down the recently washed road, toward the Royal House where I reside. It is hidden around the bend in the near distance. I am not about to send this girl home in tatters. Let the king think his puppet strings are all intact.

We stand at the topmost part of the citadel, where everything is tightly packed upon a single hilltop. Streets follow curves as dramatic as those of Chimeline's body, and we take many steps down, leaning against stone walls to regain our balance. Even sober, this is no easy stroll.

Soon, the Royal House towers above us, behind slender pear trees. But Chimeline instead admires the view across the narrow street.

Past the stone wall, which is only as high as my waist, a sheer cliff covered in flowering vines and rough brush drops away. A hundred king's feet below, the road snakes past us again, and then a third time after that. But that's not what Chimeline is looking at.

Out in the midnight-blue distance lies the Northern Kingdom, bathed in moonlight.

Block upon block, house upon house, the clay rooftops of the citadel fade to mist. Orange lamplight glows from tiny windows amidst the cobwebbed streets. Slim smokestacks reach for the clouds, but nothing comes out of them on this warm night. I can just barely see the spire of the effulgency temple against the imposing First Ring, and then the patches of dark countryside beyond.

"You can do anything you want to me, Your Grace," she says. "All I ask is that you are a gentleman. Be gentle with me."

Now her prior comment makes sense. Chimeline has apparently been through some rough experiences as one of the king's harem.

She cautiously puts a hand underneath my flaxen cloak again. This time, she lightly traces her fingertips across my chest.

Now I fear that her path in life wasn't chosen by her after all. As we look out upon this pristine civilization built of stone, clay, and iron, darker undercurrents cross my mind. How she got here is a mystery, and suddenly I want to speak to her about it. She could have been sold into slavery as a child. Or perhaps her parents are aging and poor, back in the archipelago, and moving north to sell her body was the only way she could provide for them.

"Have other men hurt you?" I ask. "If so, I will tell the king myself."

Her eyes open wide. "Please do not, Your Grace. I would be chastised for even bringing my lowly concerns to your attention."

"Tell *me* then," I say. "I won't tell the king."

She turns her face back to the moon and whispers, "It was only one man. A voider, like you."

*A voider, like you.*

I grasp her shoulders and gently turn her to face me. Her hand drops away from my chest. "A voider hurt you?" I ask.

She pauses, as if suddenly regretting bringing it up in the first place. Eventually, she nods once.

"Who was it?" I see fear in her eyes, and I quickly add, "No harm will come to you. I am in charge of the university, and will punish the student accordingly without risking your safety."

She shakes her head. Her bangs part, revealing a furrowed brow. "I do not know his name, Your Grace."

"You have my word," I reassure her.

"He never told me, Your Grace," she insists. "I would tell you if I knew."

"How could you not know who he was?" I ask in disbelief. "What did he look like?"

Her body trembles in my hands. "I know you will not believe me, Your Grace."

"Try me."

"His face was always covered in a haze. It made me feel dizzy just looking at him."

Anna's words fill my mind.

"He would do things to me, Your Grace. Use his powers to make me feel things. Some of it was . . . painful."

*A cloud always hung about his face. It made him blurry.*

My hands have been grasping her too tightly, so I remove them and grasp the stone wall in front of me instead. My vision spins anew, but this time I know that it's not the red-currant wine at work.

"Can you take me to him?" I say.

She tilts her head, leaning in next to me. "I do not know where he lives, Your Grace."

"But where did you—"

"He always took me to his laboratory."

I shake my head. "That's impossible. The university laboratory is under my control. Only I have the key, and it is scryed with voidance. I would know if someone broke in."

Chimeline looks confused. "He had his own key, Your Grace," she whispers.

"Well, it's just down the road," I answer. "On the university campus. We can go there now and you can show me—"

I stop talking once I realize what I am doing. I am back on the hunt, this time by moonlight.

Looking sideways at her, I anticipate her reaction to be one of disappointment or annoyance. I am observant enough to understand that my needs are completely different from what she expected. But she seems as confused as ever—the reaction I was least expecting.

"Your grace, his laboratory is not nearby," she says.

"What do you mean?"

"It's well past the First Ring, off Xi Bay Road. There's a barn there, near the river. It's quite hidden."

I grasp the wall even tighter to prevent myself from falling down.

*Off Xi Bay Road, past the First Ring.*

That's where Marine went. And it's practically where I was this morning. I was so close. There must be a rogue laboratory that a student of mine set up. Maybe a ship docked there.

"Do you remember the way?" I ask her.

She nods, but her face is now covered in fear.

Letting go of the wall, I close my eyes and take a few deep breaths. I ask myself if I am in the correct frame of mind to do this. Am I sober enough? Am I detached from all emotion? The world is no longer spinning. But this seems like madness. I could turn around, take Chimeline into my home, and the two of us could go on this journey tomorrow.

But how will I be able to sleep? How will I be able to do anything until this place is found?

The problem is, it will take all night to even reach this rogue lab.

*Unless I improvise.*

I open my eyes and look directly downward, past the low wall and sheer cliff. Far below, the street crew is working on rinsing away the manure. Their two horses pull a cartful of water. It's easily a fall to the death for an ordinary person.

But I am no ordinary person.

I slowly climb onto the thick ledge made of stone and reach out my hand to Chimeline.

"Trust me," I tell her.

Her dark-brown eyes are wide, reflecting the moonlight. I am not sure what she's more afraid of—what I am proposing now or going back to the place where she was hurt.

"Not all voiders are evil," I tell her. "I am not going to let anything happen to you. I promise."

Her hesitancy is palpable, so I search for more-convincing words.

"Chimeline, you said that you can help me forget her. But that's not what I need from you. I need your help *finding* her."

The young woman looks back and forth between the moon and me. But then she nods firmly.

"Thank you."

She climbs up and we stand carefully, together. She tries not to look down at the dizzying heights.

"Grab on to me tightly," I tell her, as I wrap my left arm around her narrow waist, pulling her into me. In my right hand, I grasp the voidstone. My head fills with a cacophony of voices as I bring my power to bear, and the moonlit world disappears.

We jump off the ledge.

# THE LABORATORY

We fell at least a hundred feet before I slowed our descent by packing the air below us. Chimeline kept asking how I did it and I used the analogy of stuffing a pillow with too many goose feathers.

The street washers wouldn't take my gold for the horses. They had seen what I had done and were not used to the public display of voidance. It was probably the first time they had ever witnessed such a thing. One of them even sank to his knees, making an effulgency gesture. I promised to return their horses by sunup, and I plan on following through with that promise.

A slender path winds through the darkness, just beyond the grove of pines where I fell asleep earlier. If I had walked a few hundred feet more during my frantic midday search, I might have seen it: a horse trail exiting off the graveled Xi Bay Road. Trampled weeds lead into the thin forest. On the trunk of one pine, four deep gouges exude dried white sap, looking like a bear's claw. This was the marker that Chimeline was looking for.

"How much farther?" I call out to her. She is riding before me. The path is too narrow for us to ride side by side.

Our horses go slowly. Old and confused, they are used to pulling wagons full of water, not carrying people through a forest in the middle of the night. But still, we've arrived at the marker much sooner than we both expected.

"A long way, Your Grace. A halfbell's trot, but these horses seem incapable of that speed."

I utter a groan of impatience before forcing myself to relax. I am in no position to be disappointed—my introduction to Chimeline and her revelation is a boon. I am incredibly lucky to even be traveling on this path right now, no matter the speed.

Above us, the moon sheds light that the trees diffuse—making this forest brighter somehow than the citadel with all its streetlamps shining. The pines whisper in the wind.

The trees eventually thin out, and the pathway opens to an endless field with grasses tall enough to brush my feet. The seeded tips undulate in the breeze like the turquoise waters of Xi Bay, and even their sound reminds me of the gentle lapping of waves upon the beach. I can almost imagine that my horse is swimming in night waters instead of walking over solid ground.

It reminds me of a much happier time.

Marine and I honeymooned at Xi Bay. My submaster, Mander, was stationed there and had agreed to represent me at the citadel in my absence. His private house on the bluff overlooked the waters. The air smelled of lemons and salt. He left the house staff, pinnace, and rowmen at our disposal. This was right before the war. It was another world, a time when things had not yet fallen apart on so many levels.

"Do you still love her, Your Grace?" Chimeline asks me softly.

I did not even notice that she had pulled her horse in next to mine. Her black robe has fallen open, revealing her legs. For once, the look is not by design—she is obviously not clothed for this journey.

A mix of emotions courses through me at her question, like the complex winds that blow through the tall grass.

On one hand, her question shows impudence. I cannot imagine Elrich or Anna asking such a thing. It is not their place. And if they did ask me, I would tear into them well deservedly.

Somehow, the question is not insolent coming from Chimeline. Perhaps it's because her profession lies within the crosshairs of love, or what many men confuse as love. Asking me for my intimate thoughts on my wife must feel as natural to her as an effulgent questioning if someone is on the way of unwanting.

I exhale, feeling bitter relief.

Unconsciously, I have wanted to talk about this with someone. Keeping such hopes and fears bottled up is not wise. Emotions are the enemy of a voider. Such things cause a certain pressure, which needs to be released. Even smoking hilma would be a better alternative than harboring this weight.

The head effulgent had offered guidance and counseling. I know he is exactly the sort of person I should want to talk to at this moment. Dealing with such problems is his specialty, but I don't want his self-righteous help. When we passed through the Southern Gate at elevenbell, his temple hummed with the sounds of revelry. I saw his large silhouette holding up a glass of wine. He shouted a toast behind his curtained windows while a pianist played an upbeat song. I mouthed his slogan back to him, full of irony: *Be nothing*.

No. I'd rather talk to a woman from the king's harem, who wouldn't be so quick to judge.

"Have you heard of the indivisible?"

"No, Your Grace."

"It is a voider term. It's what everything is made of."

She nods politely.

"I used to tell Marine that the two of us were the very nature of love. That true love was something that could not be broken. It was perfect and whole and forever, just like an indivisible."

Chimeline studies me, waiting for me to continue.

"I was wrong," I say, biting my lip and trying to keep my emotions from spilling over. A slow, controlled trickle is better. Taking a deep breath, I try to simplify such complicated internal thoughts for this non-voider, though I would struggle to explain them even to myself.

"When using a voidstone, the power is temporary. The world always goes back to the way it was. Now, I believe it's the same with love."

"What do you mean, Your Grace?"

"The nature of the world is chaos. It is made up of more void than indivisibles. The moment love is born, it immediately dies. It unravels into chaos. And you can never get it back, so the only thing you can do is make new love."

A white cloud passes over the moon and the shadows disappear.

"But I never answered your question," I add. "You asked if I still love her. I think the answer to that is yes. I think that I will always love her, despite what she did to me, but it is a different sort of love now."

"So you *do* love her," Chimeline says, not seeming surprised. "That's why you are going after her, isn't it?"

I know I should shake my head, but I don't seem to have the energy. It just hangs there upon my neck like some foreign weight. Instead, I stare out into the night and finally summon the courage to vocalize the words that I have been thinking for quite some time.

"She's gone to me, Chimeline. I still need to find her, but it's to gain answers, not to win her back. There is no such thing as restoration in this life."

I look back to her, and I am shocked to see that her eyes are wet in the veiled moonlight.

"Where I come from," she says quietly, "we have eleven different words for love. Eleven kinds of love." She smiles to herself. She must be remembering her homeland.

"One for each kind of sand."

I don't say anything.

Her nose wrinkles in a charming way as she struggles with the explanation. "It does not translate into the Northern tongue, Your Grace. There is white sand and black, volcanic sand. There is pink, orange, and coral too. There is sand so fine it is as soft as silk, and then there is course sand, which can clean off any grime. There is sand that is made into delicate glass art, and there is sand that is made into cast-stone, to build kingdoms with."

She looks at me, to make sure I am following her. "It is the same with love."

The cloud passes, and I see something shimmering in the distance, through an approaching patch of trees.

"Is that the River Xi?" I ask.

She nods and points straight ahead. "Do you see it? The laboratory is stained dark green, so it nearly blends in with the trees. The roof is easier to make out."

I am at a loss for words.

I'm not sure what I was expecting. Most likely some sort of shed. An amateurish, ramshackle structure created by someone with limited time, money, and resources.

But what lies far in front of me, secretively within this forest, is easily twice as big as the university laboratory, and it looks just as immaculate.

*It was no student who built this place.*

Once we're near, I dismount and hitch our horses to a branch of a willow tree next to the riverbank, and they both start drinking immediately. This stretch of the river is at least a hundred feet wide as it passes the citadel, but I cannot see anything in the darkness. Besides, the willows droop into the water at the river's edge, blocking our view.

The ground is muddy and well trodden—it looks as though someone tethered horses here before. Because Chimeline is barefoot, I carry her to the immense front door of the barn. On the way, I notice three shallow graves. They're at the side of the barn, away from the river, and they're unmarked. Not a stone or bouquet decorates them—only the mounds of dirt give them away.

"Do you know who's buried there?" I ask Chimeline as I set her down.

"Three of my sisters who came before me," she answers. "They were not as lucky."

"What do you mean?"

She looks straight ahead at the door. She's purposely not staring at the graves, or me.

After it's evident that she's not going to answer, I switch my attention to the door. Chimeline was right—a padlock secures it, but it's just standard smithware, probably meant to keep out any local hunters or fishermen who happen to come across this place.

Using my voidstone, I easily dismantle it by twisting the wooden beam it's mounted against.

Once that's done, I slide the door open—it glides easily on an oiled rail up above—and we both cautiously step inside the pitch blackness.

Within a few steps, she screams and puts her arms around me.

It's just small forest birds, taking flight.

I frown in the darkness, wondering why birds would be in here. But then I see that a section of roof is entirely missing. The moonlight shines through the large square, casting angular blueish light on the walls and floor. The silhouette of a cat runs across a ceiling beam and jumps out.

Chimeline looks around fearfully, but soon it's obvious that we're the only ones here besides the creatures of the forest, and they will do us no harm. She finds a large oil lamp hanging on the inside wall, lights it, and hands it to me.

When I raise it over my head, I inhale sharply.

*This can't be.*

A fully functioning laboratory lies before me, and it rivals the university's in every way.

The barn seems to be sectioned into dozens of open-walled rooms, each devoted to a unique experiment in mid-design.

The one immediately to our left is empty except for chains and cuffs that dangle from the tall ceiling and a drain in the floor underneath them, which must go outside. A raven perches upon one of the open cuffs, silently eying us. The other cuff moves in the darkness—a second bird must have recently taken flight, causing it to sway and rattle in place.

To our right is a mattress made of straw. A large stain decorates the middle of it, black in the lamplight. Somehow I know that it's dried blood. Chimeline looks at it and then turns away into my shoulder.

The next sections are stranger.

In one, I find an immense box, larger than a man, seemingly made of lead with no doors or windows. I touch my voidstone to be sure—it's true. I cannot see into it, with or without my voidstone. There are no seams.

I try to move it, but it's immovable and impenetrable. I look at the worn floorboards and notice that they transition to stone underneath the box, which makes sense. There is no way standard floor joists could support such weight.

"Do you know what this is?" I ask, turning to Chimeline. She just shakes her head.

Across the center aisle, stations are set up with glassware, scales, a large mortar and pestle, a trough plumbed from the outside, and an oven at least twice as large as the one we have at the university. A cylindrical mechanical device rests on a metal tripod. Glinting in the lamplight, it resembles a spyglass—the kind a ship captain might use—although it's nearly ten times the size.

Next to this is a room that looks as if it belongs in the king's armory. Swords, javelins, breastplates, helmets. Hanging from the wall, they glimmer in the lamplight.

"You did not know about this place, Your Grace?"

I reach out to touch the breastplate and notice that it's warm.

*How is that even possible?*

"Your grace?"

"No," I answer distantly.

"But do you know what all of this is for?"

I keep walking in disbelief, and she follows me.

The next section contains maps of the Southern Kingdom and Xi Bay. And books, some which I have been looking for in my library for quite some time. I figured they had been misplaced. Students always leave them around instead of putting them back where they belong. Others I have never seen before.

*Xian Islands and their Native Fauna*

*Poisons of the Archipelago*

*Conditional Ruptures and Voideath*

*Blackscar*

*A History of the Effulgency*

"Your grace—"

"Yes," I snap, cutting her off as my anger gets the better of me. "I know what this place is for. It's for death and suffering."

Soon, I am standing underneath the hole in the ceiling, through which I see the moon and cottony clouds. When I entered this place, I assumed some sort of accident had occurred here. Perhaps a bolt of lightning struck a nearby willow tree causing it to fall on this section of roof.

But no. This roof was designed to open this way.

Hinged panels account for the gap. Two large sections of the roof hang downward, tied up against metal hooks. Whoever did this did it on purpose. And did it hastily.

The floor here is completely empty, but something used to stand here. Something large. This room is at least twenty feet square. Footprints litter the dust, and some black paint covers the thick floorboards as well.

I turn to Chimeline and raise the lantern between us.

"Tell me everything you know about this place."

She looks tired and scared. "Your grace, I never came this far back. He would only take me to that first room." She turns, but I know which one she's referring to.

"His face was behind a veil?" I ask, using my free hand to indicate my face.

She nods. "That is a good way to say it."

"Was there anyone else here when you visited?"

"No."

"Did the man say anything of the work he was doing here? Anything at all?"

"Never, Your Grace."

"Well, he must have said something!" I shout, my voice echoing off the high ceiling.

She backs away, and despite the dim light I see the fear in her dark eyes. Fear that I am just like *him*.

"I'm sorry," I quickly add.

She takes a tentative step closer. "He seldom spoke," she says. "He mostly watched. He always wanted me to talk to him."

I tilt my head in confusion.

"He wanted me to tell him what I was feeling. When he—"

"When he *what*?" I frown.

"When he performed his experiments on me."

I swallow, feeling more anger rise in me.

"What kind of experiments?"

Chimeline closes her eyes tightly, and at first I think she's trying to remember. But when she opens them, they're full of tears. Even though her robe is wrapped around her, she adjusts it while shuddering, pulling the belt tighter.

"He would speak to me in my head."

"In your head?"

She shivers. "I don't know how else to explain it."

"Never mind," I say, turning with the raised oil lamp and making a mental note to ask her again once she's far away from this dark place.

"Did he say if the king knew of this laboratory?"

She shakes her head. "It never came up, Your Grace."

*It doesn't matter. Of course the king knew. How could he not?*

*This place was built for his war.*

I quickly walk up to the last three rooms, which are equal in size to the one with the open roof above it. In fact, each of the three seems to be identical in purpose to the lit-up fourth. Large black sections of fabric hang like wall-to-wall curtains, except they don't reach the floor. Instead, they fold over themselves only to rise again to the ceiling, where they're secured on the next hook over.

In each of these three rooms also rests an oversized wicker basket, large enough to fit a few people.

I turn to Chimeline, about to hand her the lantern, but then realize that it's too heavy for her to hold indefinitely. So I turn in place and look for a hook to rest it on. Something high up, to provide as much light as possible.

Directly on the thick wooden post in front of me is a black metal rod, so I reach up and set the lantern's handle over it.

Except the metal rod isn't fixed to the post. It's a lever.

I push it down.

Chimeline screams as the roof far above us opens. Its two large panels swing down and bang against the rafters. Dust falls over us like black snow, and I set the lantern down on the wooden floor planks. The young woman's mouth is open in shock, and mine must be as well.

With the added moonlight, all is suddenly clear.

"Your grace, what is it?" She approaches, resting her hands on the edge of the immense wicker basket.

"It's my invention," I answer slowly, almost in a trance.

*It's right here, in front of me. In fact, there are three of them here—one in each room.*

"I don't understand."

"It's my flying machine. An airship."

My body frees itself from its initial paralysis, and I rush over. I inspect how the basket is secured and notice the fabric is royal silk that has been covered in some sort of black paint. A ladder leans against the wall nearby, and I use it to start unhooking the looped bundles of fabric from the wall.

"What does it do?"

"This was an idea I proposed to the king years ago," I say while working. "At the start of the war. As a way to safely spy upon enemy-troop movement from the air. He said it was a stupid idea. He already had spies for that."

She shakes her head in confusion.

"Have you ever noticed that in summer it is always hotter on the upper floors of a home? And always cooler on the first floor or in the cellar?"

She nods.

I continue to move the ladder, carefully letting down more of the fabric. There's so much of it. This airship has to be immense when it's full.

"Hot air rises. That's how my airship works. At least in theory. If one could trap air in a large sphere of fabric, and heat that air, the entire sphere and anything attached to it would rise."

"You mean fly."

I am panting with exertion and take a deep breath to calm myself. "Yes!"

I've let all the fabric down, so I throw the ladder out of the room and return to Chimeline's side near the basket.

"How can you fill all of this with hot air?"

I smile, seemingly for the first time today. "That," I answer, "is where voidance comes in."

"Your power."

I nod. "There is only one problem—the seams."

"The seams?"

"I never solved it in my prototype. The airship needs to be large enough to carry the weight of a few people. This takes a tremendous amount of silk, which means a lot of sewn seams. Via these seams, hot air can leak out, just like water can leak into a ship's hull."

I pause, my mouth open.

"Your grace, are you feeling alright? Your hands are shaking."

I lift one of them and touch my voidstone.

The entire airship is covered in honeycombs.

I let go.

*It's the black pitch from this morning.*

"This is it," I say quietly. "This is how Marine got away."

"I thought you said she took a ship."

"Yes, but I was wrong. She's not sailing, Chimeline. She's flying."

She looks at me as if I am crazy, so I rifle through my cloak pockets and throw the swatch of fabric on the floor between us.

"I found that in Marine's room today. It's covered in the same black pitch as this airship."

She picks it up and studies it while I grasp my voidstone.

*This is going to drain the life out of me.*

I start moving the air, creating a current from the open roof to the bottom of the fabric attached to the basket.

At first, nothing happens, but then I feel Chimeline against me. Her long, thick hair falls across my face, and I breathe in the scent of oranges. The fabric of honeycombs moves and expands, rustling in the night, like some sea creature rising from the depths.

Black upon black.

It takes some time to fill the fabric with the cool night air, and then more to command the indivisibles to move at ever greater speeds. Heating them, over and over again. Faster and faster. The screams of the voidstone urge me on. Or maybe they tell me to stop.

When I finish, I let go of the stone. I am sweating profusely underneath my black flaxen cloak and leaning my chest on the basket's railing. I slump to the ground. My fingertips are numb, and I let out a meager cry of fear. I haven't come this close to voideath since I was young. It is beyond careless.

My cries of fear turn to screams of accomplishment.

The base of the airship is before me, but that is all that can be seen. Above us, the black fabric rises into the roof's opening and then disappears from view. It's a towering presence. It is so beautiful.

There are groans under me.

Each corner of the basket is secured to iron rings with rope. These are in turn mounted to the wide floorboards. The ropes and rings hold, but the old floorboards buckle under the pressure. While I study all this, one of them cracks free, and the basket lurches to the side.

"Your grace!"

It will be only a fleeting moment until the rest of the boards snap free, but there is one more thing that I must do.

"Get in!" I yell to her.

Her eyes open wide, again looking at me as if I am mad, but I reach out my hand and scream, "If you stay here, you'll die!"

"Why?"

"Trust me!" I tell her, as I push her toward the basket. Grabbing the oil lamp off the ground, I add, "I'll be right back!"

I stumble down the length of the dark barn to the open door we came through. About halfway there, I look over my shoulder and see that Chimeline is inside the basket, looking at me with both hands clutching the railing.

Once I'm near the exit, I toss the lit lamp through the air in a clear arc. My aim is true—it hits the straw mattress, and the glass shatters to pieces.

Flames instantly engulf the bed and start rising.

*That's not enough.*

Touching my voidstone, I create another channel of wind, this one violent and coming from the open door, right through the flames. I fan the lit oil with my hatred as it splays across the room and through the center aisle, splattering everything with light. I am a painter, and my brushstrokes are built of fire and rage.

There is screaming everywhere, inside me and in the world outside. The swirling sounds of the voidstone pain me now, as if a million souls are pleading for me to let go. And when I do, a different sort of screaming takes its place.

It's the horses outside.

Staggering toward the exit, I see that they are both caught within their tethers, eyes white and legs thrashing.

I cannot even feel my fingers anymore, but I touch my voidstone one last time, cutting both of their reins. Immediately, they run off down the willow-lined riverbank.

I'm barely able to walk back to the airship—I cannot feel my feet anymore either. The basket is already over my head. I find the ladder that I used to unhook the fabric and lean it precariously against the edge. After taking four or five hesitant steps upward, I grasp Chimeline's tiny hands, and somehow she pulls me in as the ladder falls.

The two of us collapse onto the floor of the basket, my body landing on top of hers as the last remaining floorboard snaps free.

The feeling of acceleration is half-ecstasy, half stomach-churning. The world pulls us down, but we rise up, defying it. I roll my body off hers, and we both lie on our backs, side by side, staring up at the pure black of the fabric sphere. My eyes find the section of sky between the painted fabric and the sides of the wicker basket. Treetops quickly pass us and disappear, leaving blue moonlight and spun clouds in their wake.

Chimeline finds my hand with hers.

"We are flying, Your Grace!" she whispers excitedly. The night whistles around us, and her lips touch my ear.

"Yes, we are," I answer, my voice mixed with a laughter that I thought was lost for good. "Yes, we are."

# PART TWO

# THE EFFULGENT

# THE RISE AND FALL OF MASTER VOIDER DEMOCRYOS

I wake up and orient myself.

I'm still lying on the floor of the basket, and with the absolute blackness of the airship above me. I look to the blueish space between the bottom of the sphere and the top of the basket and see that it's still night.

Chimeline is kneeling next to me, her eyes closed. Her palms press against her temples. Her body trembles.

"Chimeline," I say, my voice hoarse.

She doesn't seem to hear me. She's shaking her head, mumbling something. As I watch her, the sounds crystallize into words.

"No," she says. "I'll do it tonight."

I sit up.

"Chimeline!" I repeat, my voice louder. I give her a good shake at the shoulders. This time, she opens her eyes, blinking rapidly.

I look deep into them and wait.

"Your grace," she says. Another few blinks, and she swallows. "Your Grace. I don't know . . . what . . ."

"Who were you talking to?"

She looks away. "Nobody . . . it was nobody. I . . . I was having a bad dream."

I frown. "You didn't look asleep to me. You were on your knees, like you are now."

"Was I?"

I press the muscles at the back of my neck, sore already from the angle at which I slept.

"I fell asleep too," I say, letting go of her as I struggle to stand.

I grasp the wicker railing with both hands. Flexing my fingers and toes, I can barely feel them. They're better than before, but only marginally. I've used the voidstone far too much.

After I help Chimeline up, I inhale and admire the view of nighttime beauty.

We're slowly and silently floating over rolling farmland, somewhere away from all civilization. I cannot see a single person. There are no houses or villages here, only empty dirt roads. A single campfire burns far away, its slender column of white smoke curling in the direction we're moving.

"Are we slowly falling?" Chimeline asks, standing next to me.

It takes me a moment to sense that her instincts are right. "Yes," I answer.

The terrain is hilly, but it's been carved into shallow, curving terraces. These sections are engorged with standing water—almost like tiny crescent-shaped pools. They reflect the moonlight in different ways. Some are bright, some are darker, and all are full of vegetation. Given our high perspective, the first thing that comes to mind is a stained-glass window in one of the effulgency temples. It looks as if thousands of curved pieces of glass cover the entire world in blues and greens.

"Rice paddies," I mumble.

"I thought that's what they were too," Chimeline says. "Except they look so different from up here, Your Grace."

"You don't need to call me that anymore. Dem is fine."

Out of the corner of my eye, I can tell that she's looking at me with an open mouth.

"When you say *Your Grace*," I clarify, "it implies that I am in the good graces of the king. Which I am not, now."

She's quiet for a moment before answering. "Because you stole his airship?"

I laugh bitterly. "No. Because I disappeared without permission. He will not forgive that. Over dinner, he specifically asked me to get the next class ready for graduation. For his idiotic war. The fact that I am gone now . . ." I exhale. "It's treason, plain and simple."

She puts her hand on mine as I search the skies for O'Eridani, the End of the River. I quickly find it behind me—the star is brighter than the rest, and quite easy to spot on a mostly clear night.

"We're traveling south," I say.

"Can you see the citadel?"

"No." I point to O'Eridani, explaining that it's always true north, and she nods.

"And the rice paddies," she adds. "Rice doesn't grow near the citadel. It's too far north for that."

I nod, impressed. "That is a keen observation." Turning to her, I ask, "How long was I asleep?"

She shrugs. "I don't know. I fell asleep too, your gr—"

I smile as she quickly covers her mouth with a slender hand. "That's going to be a tough habit to break," I say, turning to the east.

"There's no hint of sunrise, which means that it's probably only threebell," I say. "Maybe fourbell." Then I swivel to the west and point at the campfire's pillar of smoke, which is now behind us. "We're moving quite fast. The way that smoke quickly dispersed—it's already so far away."

I purse my lips, deep in thought. "I think we're a day's hard ride south of the citadel. Two days' without killing the horses. From my recollection, that's about where the rice paddies begin."

She nods, yawning wide.

As I involuntarily mimic her yawn, I look around. I can see more details below. The branches of trees. The stacked stones lining the road. Farm equipment, left for another working day in the sun. A scavenging dog.

The airship falls so gradually that we cannot feel it, yet in the time we've been talking, we've dropped significantly. When we shot out of the burning barn, we must have climbed incredibly high. Because I never witnessed our initial height, the sense of change has been lost on me.

At this rate, within a halfbell, we're going to hit the ground.

I flex my fingers on the railing. They're still somewhat numb, and the thought of touching my voidstone again fills me with dread. But I need to do it if I want to keep traveling. And I need to keep traveling if I am ever going to find Marine. It's only been one day since she left, so the weather patterns should be similar enough.

*But how far?*

The problem is, the two of them could travel a very long distance, assisting each other. I can imagine it now. One of them sleeps while the other manages the airship, ensuring that the air remains heated. When one of them becomes weak or near voideath, they switch places. Marine isn't a powerful voider, but she'd be able to sustain flight.

The idea of the two of them, in a confined space, under the moon and stars . . .

I push it out of my mind.

"Are you tired?" I ask.

One glance at Chimeline tells me it was a stupid question. She's visibly exhausted, but she nods anyway. "What about you?"

I shake my head. "We're going to take turns. While you're sleeping, I'm going to heat the air in this sphere, so we fly higher. For a fullbell. When I'm done, my body will be depleted and I'll need to rest."

"Alright."

She's already slinking into the corner and covering her face with her black hood.

"I'll wake you in a fullbell. You'll need to stay awake and warn me if we're getting too close to the ground."

She mumbles something as she shifts in place to get comfortable.

"What's that?"

"How far are we going to fly, Your Grace?" she says, already forgetting to call me by my name.

I look out at the hills rolling by. "Until the end of the world, if that's what it takes," I say.

But she's already asleep.

Looking down at her, I am envious of her peace. But I remind myself that I will soon be in her coveted position.

Taking a deep breath and holding on tightly to the railing with one hand, I ready myself for the storm to come.

My body shakes as I touch my voidstone, the chorus of wind sudden and deafening. I picture a cave in my mind, the analogy my teacher used when I was a child. But this chorus is far more than he ever imagined, so the analogy morphs and becomes something new.

The wind forms dark swirls that whip around me in a cyclone. Sometimes I think I see faces mixed within the black currents, looking at me in outrage. Dark eyes, wide. Dark mouths, screaming. *How dare you! You are hurting us, and you are killing yourself too! You fool!*

It's only my imagination.

Looking up, I push the voices away and concentrate on heating the trapped air. It takes a long time but eventually I see the indivisibles moving faster, bouncing off their confined walls, like slaves searching for elusive freedom.

We're leveling off.

My feet eventually become numb, and I can no longer stand. I slink down into the corner of the basket next to Chimeline, but I continue to hold on. Just a little bit longer. For the memory of Marine, and the revenge that is yet to come.

*The man behind the veil. I am coming for you.*

When I feel us rising, I let go. The world seems hesitant to come back, as if it's unsure whether I still belong in it. Collapsing next to Chimeline, I try to wake her. Only her chest moves. I watch it rise and fall. I open my mouth to say something but cannot speak. I try to peel back her hood to reveal her face, but my fingers are incapable. My mind as well. Everything is silent and still and I can no longer think upon anything except the rise and fall.

*The rise and fall of Master Voider Democryos.*

# VOIDREAMING

It is late afternoon on the last day of the first week's sessions. And so, predictably, all the students have fled the campus—their tiny minds so overfilled with this new world that they need a brief respite. Except for Marine. She waits for me after class underneath an arched walkway. Leaning against a stone column twice as wide as her, she wears an elegant black dress and sandals that would look completely out of place in Giriya. Just beyond the shelter of the portico, dark storm clouds loom and heavy rain starts to fall.

"Master Voider," she says, coming near and handing me the book I lent her weeks ago: *Asima's Complete Writings of Xiland, Volume 1*. "I believe this is yours."

"Did you enjoy it?" I ask, placing it in my satchel.

"Very much so."

A sharp crack of thunder fills the courtyard, but Marine seems oblivious to it.

"I was wondering if you had time to discuss it," she says.

"Now?"

She grasps her ponytail, fanning it out behind her. "Whenever is most convenient for you."

I look out into the thunderstorm and then back to her. She stands in front of me, one leg crossed over the other, her head down but her eyes looking upward.

It's been only a few weeks since the submaster brought her to the citadel, but already she seems a different person. I remember the first time she charged into my room, a brazen young woman covered in the sharp edges of her lake-town upbringing. A big fish in a small pond, as they say. But now all these edges have been smoothed over, leaving an appealing self-assurance.

And she has done this all on her own, in an amazingly short amount of time.

"Walk with me," I say.

I briefly touch my voidstone as I step beyond the shelter of the stone portico's ceiling. I create a sphere of pressurized air that encircles me and keeps me dry from the elements.

It's wasteful voidance. But I cannot help myself.

She runs to my side within the tight sphere and grabs my arm, and the two of us begin walking through the courtyard. The heavy raindrops above us sound like distant taps upon glass.

"Is this part of the air-manipulation lesson?" she asks excitedly.

"Yes," I answer. "You will learn this later in the year. The hardest thing to do—as I am doing right now—is to keep the manipulation dynamic."

"Dynamic?"

"Centered around me, while I walk. You'll notice I am not touching the voidstone now, but this sphere of pressure still exists."

"Ah."

"This is called dynamic voidance. While initially manipulating the indivisibles, you must program them to be relative to a source. In this case, the source is me."

I look briefly at her, to see if she is paying attention. She is rapt.

"Although, like most actions within the void, dynamic voidance lasts only temporarily."

"There is great disorder in the natural world, and the power of a voidstone holds no permanent sway," she replies, reciting from memory.

I nod. "Very good, Marine." I clear my throat and look down and sideways at her. "So, tell me what you learned about Xi Bay."

She takes a deep breath, obviously bottled up with much excitement and opinion. "It is a wealth of beauty and mystery," she says. "The indigenous species of fish, alone, could fill a voider's life with purpose."

"Are you interested in the study of underwater organisms?"

"Very much so."

"Well, then you should speak to Submaster Mander. The study of living organisms is his specialty. In fact, he has made several travels to Xi Bay to collect specimens and bring them back to the citadel. Last year, he brought back a species of seahorse with a membrane that makes it invisible to the human eye. We are studying its indivisibles for reapplication purposes."

"The pygmy seahorse?"

"Yes." I chuckle to myself as I recollect a past conversation.

"What is it?"

"I find it humorous that Mander likes to embark on his trips to Xi Bay only when the citadel is covered in a layer of snow and ice. How convenient for him, to escape winter."

We have left the courtyard of the master wing and are now walking down the length of the university grounds, toward the Royal House. A few upperclassmen amble around—their spheres of air surround them as they move from building to building, stacks of books in hand. As long as the books stay dry, I tell myself, it is valid use of voidance.

Despite the dour weather, a smile crosses my face—it gives me great pleasure to look upon all of this and realize the great work we are doing here.

We are the instruments of great change in the world.

"Does he use air manipulation as well?"

"Hmm?" I shift my attention back to Marine. Her eyes seem to be the only source of blue in the gray world right now.

"When your submaster dives below the waters of Xi Bay to do his research. To collect specimens, and such. Does he create spheres like this one?"

"Oh, yes. It's very much the same thing, except it's far more effort."

She looks at me in confusion.

"It's the pressure." I extend one of my hands above us. "To create this sphere of air does not take much effort, since all that exists above it is more air. And the raindrops, which are negligible. But when you go underwater, the weight of the water presses down on you. This creates a challenge."

I grab the gold setting of my voidstone to illustrate.

"When a voider needs to breathe underwater, they must remain in the void much longer, and must maintain the sphere of air against the weight of the water. And the deeper one goes, the more the risk increases. Exponentially. That is why we have never explored—"

"Blackscar!" she exclaims.

I nod. "Much of Xi Bay has been explored, but a trench rips through the middle of it, where the turquoise waters drop off into the blackest and iciest depths you can imagine."

"Have we ever been able to explore the depths of it?"

"No," I say. "It is beyond our capabilities. Some have tried."

"You mean they—"

"Died."

"By voideath?"

I hunch my shoulders. "They never came back. Whether they succumbed to voideath or drowning, it does not matter. They died."

"Is that how they came to name it?"

I turn to her and purse my lips. "Blackscar? I imagine so."

Soon, we are walking down the sinuous black-brick road leading to the Royal House. Past the short stone wall at our side, the entire Northern Kingdom is on display, thousands upon thousands of clay rooftops, glistening with rain. The low, dark clouds extend to the horizon.

We walk up the stone steps of the Royal House then stop. I turn to her before entering my home. Rolling thunder echoes in the distance as the rain picks up.

A few drops leak through the sphere that I have created, and we both look up to the gray skies.

"You see?" I say. "Nothing lasts forever."

She smiles, wiping some raindrops from her fair cheeks.

"I should return to the dormitory," she says, glancing back across the courtyard. "This will be a good test."

I look at her in confusion. "What test?"

She twists the ring on her small finger—the ring every student wears. It contains the tiniest of voidstone fragments.

"Air pressure," she mumbles, studying my crumbling dome around us.

"Oh no, no no no." I shake my head, suddenly understanding her intent. I put my hand on hers. "You are not even close to being ready for that."

She looks genuinely surprised at my protest. "I can do it."

"No, you can't."

"The other students were doing it in the courtyard!"

"They were upperclassmen."

She pulls her hand away from mine and gives me a look of stubborn acquiescence.

It's coming down harder than ever.

"Listen," I say, the words coming out of my mouth despite my knowing that what I am about to do is dangerous and wrong. "Why don't you come in for a bit, at least until this storm passes."

She rises onto the tips of her feet. "I do have more questions. About Xi Bay. About the pygmy seahorse."

"I'm sure you do."

I laugh as I try to push my moral restraints away. They warn me that this might be the first step on a path that I should not take. But I don't want to think about the consequences. I don't want to see the destination.

Suddenly, my sphere dissolves and the fullness of the rain hits us. Marine lets out a playful scream. I grab her arm and pull her with me into the shelter of the Royal House.

*Careful, Dem.*

# CAGES

Three things shepherd me awake: singing birds, a crying woman, and blinding sunlight.

My lips and eyelids crack in dryness, and for a long time I simply lie where I am, motionless and with my eyes closed. The light is too harsh, so I just listen to the strange, layered sounds of my new surroundings, wondering if this is a voidream.

But this is no voidream. And I am not on the airship either.

Except that I don't remember landing, safely or otherwise. The last thing I recall was heating the trapped air for a second time, before falling asleep. I tried waking Chimeline. Was I successful? It's so hard to remember. The black folds of her cloak. The winds full of screaming faces. The rise and fall . . .

A new sound joins the strange symphony. It's close. Clucking chickens. And then the crying starts up again, further away, a woman's soft whimpering. The faraway bird sings in reply, as if trying to soothe her with a love song.

My body is sore, but nowhere specific. I'm lying on my back on something hard.

I move my fingers and toes—there is some feeling in them. I take this as both a good and a bad sign. It's good because it means my body has healed from being so close to voideath. It's bad because it means time has passed. Probably a lot of it.

*My voidstone.*

Immediately, I bring my hands to my chest, where my necklace usually rests. But my fingers find only useless fabric.

Opening my eyes and squinting against the harsh light, I check every pocket in my cloak. And then I check them again.

The voidstone isn't there.

I look desperately on both sides of me, checking to see if it fell off while I was sleeping, but there is only dirt.

I blink rapidly. My vision is still a little blurry.

Inhaling deeply and urgently, I smell life. Fertile ground. Flowering vegetation. Grilled food, somewhere, which causes my mouth to water.

*Water.*

I raise my head off the ground and move it back down as I reel in pain. I silently ponder the cause. It's either a result of my prior closeness to voideath, dehydration, or a crash that I cannot recall. Most likely it's the combination of all three.

I need to get up. I know that it's going to be painful, but my thirst and my desire to locate my voidstone win.

I sit up, gritting my teeth at the pain. I look around patiently. It takes a while, but my vision mostly returns.

I'm in a jail cell, empty except for me.

The enclosure is small and ramshackle, made of vertical bamboo sticks that extend into the ground. The floor is simply dirt, but it's dry and clean. The roof over my head extends at least ten feet—too high to touch if I stood or jumped—and it's made of layered palms, thick enough to be completely opaque. It's dark and cool in here, but just outside, the sun oversaturates everything. It's still too hard to make out any details.

The bars on my cell cast short shadows. It must be midday.

The clucking chickens I heard earlier are feeding on dropped seeds just on the other side of the bars.

A small closed door marks the only exit. It's built of the same bamboo and locked with some sort of contraption made of rope. A terracotta bowl of clear water is just inside, and I crawl over to it. Raising it, I take a careful sip. Brief dizziness comes over me as the warm water goes down my parched throat. I choke.

"Your grace!"

I turn my head and see Chimeline. She sits in a matching cell far enough away to allow a few people to walk side by side between them. In fact, it seems that many people have done exactly that, wearing a dirt trail between our cages.

She runs over to her bars, approaching me. They are wide enough apart that I can see her face, but not enough for her to stick her head entirely through. She clutches them while looking at me wide-eyed. Her dark bangs are matted to her sweaty forehead, and her face is dirty and moist with tears.

I approach the bars of my cell—the ones that are closest to her—and use them to stand up with a groan.

"What happened?" I ask her.

She shakes her head. "I don't know, Your Grace. I think we crashed."

"My voidstone—did you see it?"

"Your grace?"

"My voidstone!" I yell, and she leans away from the bars slightly. "It's missing," I add, a little more softly.

She only shakes her head.

My vision has acclimated. Before, the outside was a white light that I could not focus on—it made my head spin in agony. But now, details are emerging.

We're in the middle of a small farming town.

About a hundred feet in the distance is a circular well surrounded by a bench, both built out of stone. A girl bends there, tanned by the unforgiving sun, collecting water. It's hard to tell her age from this distance. Perhaps twelve or thirteen.

She fills a terracotta pot twice the size of her head while looking at me with piercing eyes. I call out to her, but she ignores me.

She finishes and places the pot on her head with a grunt, somehow balancing it, and then walks off down a curved dirt path lined with reeds.

There's not a single other person I can see, so I look at the surrounding buildings.

The well and bench are the only things made of stone, besides an effulgency temple in the distance. It's fairly small—not even a quarter the size of the temple in the citadel—but somehow it seems regal with the wooden steeple that easily makes it the tallest structure around.

A dozen round huts dot the landscape, each with a thatched palm-frond roof similar to ours, though their walls are solid. Homes, most likely.

While I ponder this, an ox slowly meanders through the town, the bell around its neck clanging out.

*Where in Temberlain's Ashes are we?*

"Dem?"

Much less disoriented, I can now see that Chimeline is clothed in a white-lace dress that starts with a high neckline and goes down to her bare feet. She also wears a necklace of ivory effulgency beads. Her black cloak is gone, and she's supporting one hand in the other.

"I just remembered to call you Dem," she says, sniffling.

"Has anyone spoken to you?"

"No."

"Then who gave you that dress?"

"I don't know. I woke up in it."

She winces in pain.

"What's wrong?"

"My hand hurts, your—" She sniffles again. "It really hurts, Dem. I think I injured it in the crash."

"Can you move it?"

She shakes her head.

"Let me get a better look."

Very carefully, she weaves her right hand through the space between two sticks of bamboo and lifts it up on the other side. She eventually weaves her left hand through as well, and uses it to support the right.

I can see a large red swelling above her right wrist.

"You have a broken bone," I say. I unconsciously reach for my necklace then remember it's gone.

I exhale. "I could heal you, if I only had my voidstone."

She nods. "Maybe whoever locked us up will give it back."

I nod, but as I look at the effulgency temple in the distance, doubt fills me.

I walk over to the door and inspect the locking mechanism. It's an elaborate device that uses some sort of counterweight, which is only accessible from the outside. Again, if I had my voidstone, I could cut the rope in the blink of an eye, springing it. I could sever every bar of bamboo and turn these cells upside down.

If I only had my voidstone.

Chimeline whimpers again, and I look back at her. She slinks down onto the ground, her back to the bars and to me.

A strange combination of guilt and gratitude fills me. Fullbells ago, this girl was safe and pampered in the king's residence with the others in the harem—her sisters, as she referred to them. I took her from that place, made her cross the citadel barefoot and on horseback to a hidden laboratory. I forced her to climb into an airship to escape a burning room. And now, because we've crashed due to my negligence, she's maimed, in pain, and imprisoned. All because of me.

But then I think about how lucky we are. We survived the apparent crash largely intact and have traveled far south of the citadel—undoubtedly closer to Marine and the veiled man.

My mind wanders to one of Chimeline's prior comments. *Three of my sisters who came before me. They were not as lucky.*

I walk back to the bars closest to her and press my face to them.

"The three graves," I say. "By the laboratory. Were others from the harem buried there?"

Her head turns slightly in my direction.

"The king gave you and your sisters to the veiled man," I surmise. "His majesty knew full well that the bastard performed experiments on you. He allowed it to happen."

I watch her closely. She remains motionless for a while, but then she nods subtly in the shadows of her cell. "Yes, that is true," she says quietly, sniffling and wiping her face with her good hand. "The king knew."

I decide to push further. She didn't answer me in the macabre barn. But now, with her back to me and her body caged, perhaps she will let some of her dark secrets free.

"What did he do to you?"

She casts her head downward. I hear her fidget with the ivory beads of her necklace.

"He made me sit on the bed and face him. He also sat down, but in a chair, facing me. He held his voidstone. His face was behind shimmering air, but I knew he was looking at me the entire time. He kept asking me, 'What do you feel now?' Over and over. If I stopped talking, he would get very angry."

"And what did you feel?"

"All sorts of things."

"I don't know what that means," I mumble.

"It means all sorts of things!"

I'm taken aback by her uncharacteristic outburst but also encouraged by it. If anger is part of her letting go, then so be it.

I wait for her to continue.

"Excruciating pain in my head, like what my wrist feels like now, but worse. After a while, I could hear his voice in my head."

"What do you mean?"

"Just like you're talking to me now. Except in my head."

I don't think that she's lying or misinterpreting things. The veiled man was obviously using his voider powers in a perverted way. He was doing something unthinkable—manipulating the indivisibles that make up her mind.

Manipulating the indivisibles of the body is only allowed under special circumstances, which always involve healing. Healing Chimeline's broken wrist would be a prime example. To manipulate them to interrogate someone, to make them feel pain, to communicate remotely . . . It is an aberration of the highest order.

She said that her sisters were not as lucky.

The veiled man must have learned from them. By accidentally killing them with his voidance, he learned which lines were never to be crossed. By the time he got to his fourth test subject, death was avoidable, but apparently not pain.

It's hard to believe that this monster was once a student of mine.

He must have asked the king for test subjects, and the king had given his harem. Why not? They have no family. Soldiers are too valuable with the war. And it would be too risky to reveal that hidden place to lowlife criminals. Hilma addicts? Too unpredictable—their minds are already half gone. He needed reliable people nobody would go looking for when they went missing.

My knuckles are white, clutching the bamboo.

"Chimeline," I say.

Her head turns to the side, but her back is still facing me.

"I don't know who did this to you—this veiled man. But he had to have been a student of mine. And I want you to know that I would never condone such a thing. To use voidance on the mind of another is strictly forbidden. It is punishable by exile from the university."

As soon as the words leave my mouth, I realize how futile they sound. Like leaving bouquets on the three unmarked graves of her sisters to wither and decay under the shade of weeping willows.

No. What those three young women need is what Chimeline needs. And if I'm being honest with myself, it's what I need as well.

*Justice.*

"I'm going to find him, Chimeline. This man who tortured you."

"Thank you."

"And I'm going to kill him."

# INTRODUCTIONS

At threebell, villagers begin shuffling in from the fields.

I know the time because the effulgency temple's steeple has a bell in it. It must be small, to match the scale of the building, because the sound is tinny. While it probably does not carry far into the rice fields beyond, here in the center, it commands attention.

*Which means someone is in there, pulling upon the rope, fullbell after fullbell.*

Meanwhile, Chimeline and I have been stuck inside these cursed cages.

Only women are walking into town. I see them easily from my darkened spot underneath the palm fronds and behind the bamboo bars. They trudge in the hot sun, their sunburned shoulders rounded and their gaits dreamlike. A few carry infants nestled in slings across their chests. Children old enough to walk travel with them. They stop to look at me, to the admonishment of their mothers. The women threaten to spank their behinds if they don't keep moving.

Soon, smoke from cooking fires emanates from the centers of the thatched huts.

The men and older children come at fivebell, some walking oxen burdened with large burlap bags. Remembering the moonlit fields I recently flew over, I wager that the bags are full of rice.

*When exactly was that? Last night? The night before?*

*How long were we unconscious?*

As a possible indication, my hunger has reached the point where it has begun to weaken me.

I call out to the villagers, asking for food. For Chimeline and me. I feel hollow inside. To think that my last meal was a feast with the king . . .

I'm sure that everyone can hear me, but most don't even glance in our direction. The few who do have looks of fear in their eyes. They've probably been warned by the local effulgent. I can imagine his words now: *Brothers and sisters, guard yourself against his corrupting influence!*

By sixbell, my throat is painfully hoarse, and I've already exhausted the bowl of warm water that was left for me this morning.

The doors to the effulgency temple open.

The temple stands proudly on the opposite side of the small village, past the many rounded huts, the stone well, and even more homes on the other side. But as it's on a hill, shining white-orange in the evening sun, I clearly see a young Xian man exit and then descend the front steps, looking in our direction. His dark skin reflects the sun in a metallic way.

He's carrying what looks to be two terracotta bowls of food.

Both Chimeline and I stand and walk to the front of our cages, grasping the bars in silence as the man approaches. He is almost as tall as I am, but much skinnier. His brisk walk and face free of wrinkles suggest that he's in his teens.

It's soon obvious that he's not an effulgent but a graycloak—the child of an effulgent. The familial practices of these supposed holy people confound me, but I know enough. They consider long-term sexual relationships to be evil—a sign of ownership over others. Effulgents do procreate—always with a non-effulgent—but the act itself is done out of necessity and always within the trappings of a holy service. Outside of this, celibacy endures. There is no marriage.

One day, this graycloak approaching me will become an effulgent, and the entire process will begin anew.

Once he passes the stone well in the center of town, I can see more than just his rough, drab cloak and dark sandals. A necklace of ivory beads hangs around his gaunt neck. He's bald, of course, and his skin is completely hairless, like an effulgent's.

All of them are hairless from birth. King Andrej IX once told me about a birthing celebration he attended years ago. When the graycloak infant was sleeping, it looked like a statue carved from alabaster or obsidian. Only movement and crying revealed it to be a living thing.

*Something in their heredity, I suppose.*

"Be nothing," the graycloak says in a bright voice, coming within arm's reach of our bars.

I inhale in surprise.

This is no man standing before me. She's a woman.

The lack of hair on a woman is still strange to me. I've met female effulgents in other cities before, but they were far older than this girl. Thus, their gender was more obvious. Wide hips, the presence of breasts. You could just tell.

This graycloak is younger than twenty, thin and waiflike.

"Be nothing," says Chimeline, and the woman smiles kindly with a nod.

The graycloak is waiting for my reply, and even though it pains me to utter their stupid phrase, my hunger pushes my pride aside.

"Be nothing," I mumble.

The graycloak carefully slides a large bowl and dining sticks into Chimeline's cage through the space underneath the door. Chimeline immediately begins eating, using the fingers of her good hand instead of the provided dining sticks.

I shut my eyes momentarily, telling myself that I will not allow myself to lose so much composure as to eat with my bare hands, like some animal would. Even though my body urges me to do what Chimeline is doing, I must restrain myself and act with the dignity of a master voider. I feel regret now for how I acted earlier: begging for food, like some homeless hilma addict. Even though my voidstone has been taken away from me, who I am has not changed or been diminished.

When the graycloak slides the bowl of food underneath my door, I sit on the dirt floor, legs crossed, and accept it calmly with both hands. My mouth watering, I use the dining sticks to gather a small bite carefully and put it in my mouth. It tastes bland. White rice with pieces of chicken so small I silently and comically consider them indivisibles. And broccoli, in a clear broth. No salt or seasoning whatsoever.

It's euphoric.

Before I realize it, the woman has swiveled and is walking away.

"Wait," I say, and she stops suddenly, turning back in my direction as a small cloud of dirt blows away.

"May I speak to your father?"

She cocks her head. "*Your father* implies ownership. Ownership is evil. I do not own a father."

"But you have one. The man who raised you."

She shakes her head. "I have nothing. I was raised by the Unnamed."

I resist rolling my eyes and try a different strategy. "May I speak with the effulgent?"

She nods. "Yes. His Effulgency wishes to speak to you as well. He has been praying for you ever since you fell from the sky. He will be with you at sunset."

With a smile, she walks on.


"Where is my voidstone?" are the first words out of my mouth as the effulgent nears my cell. I don't return his greeting, since he offers me nothing besides open arms.

Even with the sun just below the horizon, the man's skin gleams with smoothness. But unlike the head effulgent at the citadel, this man is very thin underneath his white robe, just like the graycloak.

Now that I think about it, I am not too sure that he is even her father. The girl, with her dark skin, is obviously of Xian descent, while this man is clearly a Northerner, pale as snow.

There is not one strand of hair on his body. Below where his eyebrows should be, his eyes are dark and cavernous.

"May I enter?" he asks me pleasantly, ignoring my question.

I suppress bitter laughter. It's just like an effulgent to act in this way. He has imprisoned me here in this cage—all day—yet the way he speaks to me now makes it seem as if he's a neighbor stopping by for a friendly visit on a summer's eve. So typically hypocritical.

"Yes, by all means, make yourself at home."

*I too can play this game.*

The man unlocks the door. I try to study his movements, but his hands are blocked from view by the bamboo.

He steps inside, leaving the door ajar behind him.

*He's testing me.*

But there's nothing to prove. I need my voidstone before I need my freedom. Can I overpower this man with my bare hands? Possibly. I am no trained fighter, but most likely neither is he. Will the other men in the village come to his defense? Perhaps. Am I capable of beating this man within an inch of his life, just to take back what is rightfully mine?

I fear the answer to that question.

In the end, I decide that the open door means nothing to me. I need to convince this effulgent—a man who loathes possessions—to return the greatest of mine.

I am already sitting cross-legged on the dirt, and he mimics me, a few feet away. A small groan escapes his mouth as he bends, but it carries with it a tint of contentment. As if the pain in his legs is a blessing.

He's probably the same age as I am.

"How was your dinner?" he asks me as he settles into an upright cross-legged position, resting his hands gently on his thighs.

I decide to continue my new strategy. The man ignored my initial outburst, so I will match his courtesy, but I also need to be careful with my answer. If I say it was delicious or it was bland, he will chide me for my preoccupation with my sense of taste.

"Filling," I eventually say. "Thank you for feeding us."

"The Unnamed is the one who feeds you, Master Voider. Not I."

Ignoring his platitude, I raise my head at the sound of my name. "You know who I am?"

He nods.

"How?"

"I am under the authority of the head effulgent at your citadel, and I travel there once a year. You and I have met before."

I don't remember him.

He looks to the cell next door. Chimeline is lying on her back. Her eyes are partially open and her head rests on her good arm. Some of her bangs are swept aside, and underneath them, the wrinkles of her furrowed brow are visible. She's listening, although she's not being obvious about it.

"That's my assistant, Chimeline," I say, hoping that she is listening attentively. The need may arise for her to continue this lie.

"Assistant." He shakes his head. "Another word that implies ownership."

"She has a fractured wrist and is in need of attention," I say.

"Fear not. Despite your being so far off the way of unwanting, I have prayed for you both."

*She needs voidance, not your useless prayers!*

I close my eyes, summoning patience.

"At the very least, there is no need to keep her locked up," I add. "She is innocent."

"We are all innocent, Master Voider. And we are all guilty. The sun both rises and sets."

"What I mean is that she's not a voider. You have no reason to fear her."

He tilts his head. "Is that why you think I am keeping you locked up? Because I fear you?"

I let out a bitter laugh. "I don't presume to understand what you think."

"You're in these cages for your protection."

"My protection?" I ask, hearing the derision in my voice.

He nods. "The villagers wanted to kill you when you fell from the sky. They still do."

*Fell from the sky.*

"My airship," I say. "Where is it?"

"Is that what you call it?" he says. "It's destroyed, I'm afraid."

"Perhaps I can repair it."

He shakes his head. "Do you see what wanting does? You so casually dismiss the fact that some in this village seek your death. Instead, you fixate on your possessions."

"Nevertheless, where is it?"

"It's been reduced to ashes."

"What do you mean?" I ask, feeling even more ire than before. Without the airship, how are we going to continue south?

"I can see that you're frustrated," the effulgent says, almost with a smile of amusement. "This attachment complex you have will one day be your downfall. Nothing is permanent. Ownership is an illusion. Do not let the loss of a thing affect who you are."

My teeth grind together. "What happened to it?"

He shrugs indifferently. "The farmer whose field you crashed in was going to stick a pitchfork in both of your bellies, but his wife convinced him otherwise. She came to me. I had to transport the two of you into the village on a donkey's back. By the time I returned, the farmer had set fire to the airship. I heard that it was consumed immediately."

I cannot help but groan. "That was the property of the king, you fool," I say.

"Property." The effulgent shakes his head once again. "Always, your perspective leads down the dark path of ownership."

"I said *king*. Didn't you hear me?"

He nods. "Being part of the Northern Kingdom, I must respect the king. But the airship was unmarked. There was no heraldry."

My breathing returns to normal as I realize that I cannot blame this man. He is telling the truth. Misplaced beliefs aside, effulgents don't lie. Besides, the farmer's reaction makes sense. Few in the world have ever seen an airship before. People flying across the sky? Even an educated man would be confused. Frightened, even. An illiterate man whose only responsibility is to protect his family and land? People have been killed over smaller misunderstandings.

"Well, I suppose that I owe you my thanks," I eventually say. "You've saved our lives."

He spreads his hands, palms facing me. "You credit me with powers that I do not possess."

"It is true. I will speak highly of you to the head effulgent and to the king when I return to the citadel." I pause then decide to get to the heart of the matter. "If you'll be so kind as to hand over our belongings, we'll be on our way."

He smiles wryly, his dark eyes becoming slits. "There is no such thing as belongings, Master Voider. We belong to the Unnamed, not each other. And we certainly do not own anything as evil as that dark stone you carried."

"Where is it?" I ask, my teeth clenched.

He must sense my mounting anger because he answers quickly. "It is in a safe place."

"Do you intend to return it to me?"

I can see him swallow in the waning light. He also shifts in place and interweaves his fingers to crack them before placing them back on his thighs.

"I'm afraid not."

I feel my entire chest enlarge as if it's a sail catching the wind, but I keep my voice as level as glass. "Listen to me, effulgent. I am Master Voider Democryos. I report directly to King Andrej X of the Northern Kingdom. Do you not respect the office that I inhabit? Do you not fear what will happen to your temple and this entire village if you do not return what is rightfully mine?"

"The temple does not belong to me, nor does this village. Everything belongs to the Unnamed."

"You're avoiding my question."

He takes a slow breath and looks at me. "How can I trust that you will not strike me or the graycloak down, should I return the black stone?"

I shake my head. "I am a man of my word. I would never harm you. I have never harmed a single soul using voidance."

He winces. "You harm countless souls every time you work your black arcana. The souls trapped inside the fragments. You just do not realize it."

My instinct is to argue, but something he said has sparked my curiosity.

"Fragments?"

He looks at me in confusion.

"You said *fragments*."

"Did I?"

I wave him away. "It doesn't matter. The idea of ghosts living in voidstones is nothing more than a haunt story that we tell to children on Husks Eve."

"It is not a story. It is the way of unwanting."

"Can you prove it?" After a span of silence, I grunt. "So your lack of trust in me is rooted in blind faith."

He looks away, momentarily deep in thought.

"Not entirely, Master Voider."

I wait for him to explain.

"I have personally experienced the evil nature of voidance with one such as yourself. The black power corrupts. You seem like a man of your word, but so did he. It did not turn out well, and I promised myself never to make the same mistake again."

"Another voider?"

He nods.

I lean forward. "Did this man hide his face from you?"

He tilts his head in confusion.

"The voider! Did he cloud himself behind a veil?"

"No," he answers, shaking his head. "I do not know what you mean."

I lean back in disappointment and stare at the well in the distance. Movement there catches my eye.

"Why do you ask?"

I ignore him for a moment while I look at the stone well. The same girl from this morning is there, with her large bowl. But she's not filling it. She's sitting on the stone bench, staring at us.

"I am looking for another voider," I say. "I thought that he might have been through here in the past few days."

"No. I'm afraid not."

"So this supposedly evil voider that you met. What was his name?"

He looks back at his temple in the distance, which is now purple with the dusk. The girl by the well notices him looking in her direction, collects her bowl, and walks away.

"I do not wish to speak on the matter," he says, his voice almost a whisper.

He seems distracted now, and his words are mumbled. I cannot tell if he is talking to me or to himself. " . . . tying it to a pigeon yesterday, hoping that I could send it back to the head effulgent. Unfortunately, it was too heavy. She could not fly."

"What are you talking about?"

He turns back and meets my gaze, blinking a few times. "I cannot give the stone back to you, but I cannot steal it from you either. So I am intent on sending it back to the citadel, where you can reclaim it. The graycloak will ride out in the morning. That is the only option on the way of unwanting."

I shake my head.

"I will free you a day after she leaves, and you can—"

"No!" I yell. "I'm not going back north," I add, softer this time. "I must head south."

"South? The war is to the south."

"I'm looking for a veiled man," I say. "He's a murderer and a thief."

He groans. "Well, if it is justice you seek, I wish you the best of luck. Perhaps when you find this man, you will also learn to accept the truth. That all power corrupts."

The bell rings eight times, and the effulgent looks back to his temple again.

"I need my voidstone for my journey south."

He purses his lips. "I am not sure what to do. I will pray upon it tonight."

"That makes me feel so much better," I mumble.

Ignoring my comment, he slowly stands and looks at the empty bowl just inside the door. "I will send the graycloak with more water for the two of you."

I stand as well but do not approach the door.

"Tell me. How far south are we?" I ask.

He turns back to me. "Halfway."

"Halfway?"

"Four days' ride from the citadel. Four days' ride from the Southern border."

Stepping outside, he locks the door to my cage, and I get as close as I can to him. "What is the name of this village?"

He sniffles in disapproval. "Naming people or places does not serve any purpose. It implies ownership. The land, the soil, the plants. We own none of these things. These are gifts from the Unnamed."

"But what do people call this village? If one looked upon a map, what would they see?"

He sets his hands down upon the bamboo, and it groans as he leans in.

"Fiscarlo," he whispers, as if it's a secret.

Then with a tired nod, he stands up straight. "May the peace of the Unnamed be upon you this evening."

He begins walking back to his temple in the darkness. The moon must be low in the sky, since I don't see it, nor any shadows it creates.

"Fiscarlo," I slowly repeat to myself, watching him pass the round huts.

When the effulgent is about halfway home, by the circular well, the word finally hits me. In my mind, I picture the oversized map of the Northern Kingdom on my bedchamber wall. Red pins stick everywhere on it, along with small sheets of paper with names and years written on them.

My students.

Since the war started, I have placed only four red pins upon the map. One student for each year. The brightest student. The one most likely to instill change in this impoverished world.

*A place just like this.*

I can see it now. Southeast of the citadel, yet still far from the edge of the map or Xi Bay, is one red pin. The name *Anaxarchis* is written on it.

It's placed squarely on the remote farming town of Fiscarlo.

"Wait!" I yell out into the night, grasping the bars of the cage tightly and wedging my face between them. The effulgent turns around, waiting for me to continue.

"I remember this place! I sent one of my students here!"

He continues to stare at me from the well. I cannot see his expression in the darkness.

"His name was Anaxarchis," I add, lowering my voice. Here in the countryside, the only sound is the locusts in the trees, and my voice carries easily.

The effulgent looks down at the ground for so long that I wonder if he's praying.

"Did you hear me?" I ask him.

He looks up. "Yes. I heard you."

"My student's name is Anaxarchis."

"I know," he answers.

"Well, you can speak to him, then!" I say, feeling my heart rate rise. "Surely you trust him by now. And if you trust him, you can trust me. He was my student—"

"He's dead, Master Voider."

I'm not quite sure if I heard him correctly. But then, after a moment of silence he adds, "I'm sorry."

Before I can reply—before I can even think—the effulgent turns and walks back to his temple.

The locusts continue to sing.

# YERLA

Last night, before returning to his temple, the effulgent wished me the peace of the Unnamed.

*Whatever in Temberlain's Ashes that is, I didn't receive it.*

How could I sleep? I kept thinking of Anaxarchis. Now, with approaching sunrise and the slow awakening of the village, people and animals alike, I am still thinking of him.

He was a gifted student—and a young one at that. Dedicated, smart, insightful. Kind.

It's hard to believe that he's dead.

There's so much running through my mind. The effulgent spoke of a voider who became corrupted by the power of the voidstone. It's why the effulgent is so reluctant to return mine.

*You seem like a man of your word, but so did he.*

He must be referring to Anaxarchis. If so, what happened? While the effulgents and voiders have always been at odds when it comes to beliefs, our quarrels have never devolved into violence or death. There is common ground, if you look for it. Certainly, many of my students at the university are arrogant and quick to judge—young men and women I could see causing this sort of tragedy—but not Anaxarchis. He was Marine's gentle cousin from Giriya. His opinions were like his physique: small of stature.

This is why I choose only the best students for these stations. It is precisely the quality of their character that is most important—because they are out here on their own.

Outside of my supervision, they are left to their own devices. I need to trust them to carry on the voider name with honor.

But apparently, it all fell apart here in Fiscarlo.

*What is happening?*

I feel as though my entire life is a castle I've built upon sand, and now, high tide has arrived.

Chimeline inhales between her teeth.

She could not sleep either. Her grimacing betrays a great deal of pain, and I am full of empathy for her. She is now caught up in this journey of mine. She didn't ask for this, yet she has not uttered one word of complaint.

"Chimeline," I say. Though she lies on the ground, I know that she's awake.

"Yes?"

"I'm going to do everything I can to get my voidstone back, and the first thing I'm going to do is heal you."

"Thank you," she says, but I hear doubt in her voice. She heard my conversation with the effulgent last night. She knows it could be days until I get it back.

There's a stretch of silence, save a rooster crowing far off.

"We're going to get out of here."

She doesn't answer.

"After I heal your wrist, I'll make sure that they take good care of you. After I leave, that is. The only reason that you're locked up is because they're afraid you'll let me out."

She opens her eyes and sits up.

"I assumed I was going with you."

"I don't think that's a good idea. It will be dangerous. My trail still goes south, possibly into war-torn territory."

"I cannot stay here," she says.

"Why not?"

"I'm not going back to that life. Wherever you are headed, it is better than what I left behind."

"You're referring to being in the king's harem. Back in the citadel."

"Yes."

"But that sort of life is already left behind. The king's men will not find you here."

She doesn't immediately answer, and for a long time, I hear only her soft breaths. Then she speaks up.

"I know that it's important for you to find the veiled man. But you mustn't underestimate him."

I wait for her to continue.

"There is no limit to what he's capable of."

I shake my head in disagreement. "Every voider has limits. It's called voideath. I nearly reached mine flying here with you."

Her good hand plays with her bangs.

"That's not what I meant. I meant limits to what you are *willing* to do with your power. There is a goodness in you, and in him there is not. Even if your powers are the same, you are not equal."

"Goodness is never a weakness," I say. "Even the effulgency agrees with that."

She lies down, as if unconvinced by my answer.

Movement in the corner of my eye draws my attention to the outside rear corner of my cell.

The tanned girl from the well is standing there, watching me silently from behind a nearby hut. She wears what resembles a dirty sheet. Taking a hesitant step toward me, she looks back at the temple. She's still many feet away, in the shadows, but within earshot.

"They say you are the master voider," she whispers forcefully.

I nod. "That is true."

"Can you heal someone with it?"

I know what she means by *it* and take a step forward. "Is someone sick?"

"Can you heal someone with it?" she repeats, much louder this time. She almost spits out her words while risking another nervous glance at the temple.

"It depends on the sickness," I reply. "Why do you ask?"

But she never gets a chance to answer.

We both turn toward a sound—it's the doors to the temple opening.

Both the pale effulgent and the dark graycloak exit, alone. They are carrying what I presume is breakfast and bowls of fresh water.

When I turn back to the bronzed girl, she's gone.

When the pair arrive, I give them space. They slide the bowl of water underneath the door. Breakfast consists of eggs and rice wrapped in corn husks, hot enough to elicit steam in the already warm morning air.

"So what did your prayers tell you?" I ask, breaking the silence. I sit in the center of the cell, calmly drinking my water and getting ready to eat the food in my lap.

The effulgent looks down at me solemnly through a space between the bamboo.

"You said that you are headed south."

I nod.

"There is a village one day's ride southeast of here. For you, I will use its name. Gales."

"I've heard of it. It's a windmill town."

He nods and points to the graycloak. "She will ride there now with the stone."

I exhale, set my food aside, and slowly stand, readying the script in my head. Throughout the night I thought about what I was going to say to this effulgent. My words of convincing. But now, I realize that I underestimated the amount of time I would have with him. The graycloak is wearing long gray pants, worn boots, and a matching tunic with a burlap purse cinched about her waist. She's already dressed for the journey, my voidstone undoubtedly already in her possession.

My words come out hasty and whiny, as if I had given no thought to them at all.

"You don't have to do this. I've given you my word. Whatever happened between you and Anaxarchis is unfortunate, but it is forgiven. In no way is it a presentiment of the future—"

"Master Voider, please. I have made this decision with guidance from the Unnamed. It is not up for debate."

He places his hand on the graycloak's slender shoulder and quietly speaks to her. "Tell the master voider where you will leave it."

The graycloak clears her throat and looks at me. She no longer has the innocent smile from yesterday. Instead, her face shows only seriousness. Maybe it's because she is journeying south alone. Or maybe it's because she's carrying what she believes is an evil relic. Whatever the reason, her voice is rushed and shaking.

"All the windmills have numbers on them. Your voidstone will be inside number thirteen. There is a worktable inside of it, next to the runner stones. I will leave the pouch on it."

"What if someone takes it before I arrive?"

"I will speak to the miller," she says. "He is a righteous—"

The effulgent screams in pain.

I had been looking at the graycloak, so I have no idea what is happening. All I can see is the pale, bald man dropping to his knees and reaching behind him, as if he's trying to touch his arched back. He becomes silent, as if he is holding his breath. The graycloak sees something that I cannot, and she screams too. Her voice is horrific, a high-pitched sound that makes my skin crawl.

To the left, out of the corner of my eye, I see Chimeline scramble backward in her dark cell. Meanwhile, I rush forward to the edge of mine, as close as I can get to the effulgent.

He falls toward me, grasping the bamboo bars, and I lower myself toward the dirt with him, our hands overlapping. That's when I see it.

His pure-white cloak is turning red.

The small tanned girl from the well stands behind him, her arms hanging at her sides like a ghost. Her face is soiled and as serene as death. She's looking at the effulgent, and then I see the glimmer in the morning light.

Her right hand grasps a bloody knife.

"Good Unnamed! What did you do?" cries the graycloak. She screams hysterically. Kneeling by the effulgent's side, she gently touches the wound in his back, as if she doesn't believe it's real. Then, leaving the morbidity behind, she caresses his head in her hands.

The effulgent tries to turn himself over onto his back, and his face twists in agony. His wide dark eyes fix on me through the bars. Near the effulgent's body, the graycloak's tears fall, darkening the dirt like the first drops of an approaching thunderstorm.

As I silently watch all of this, the girl from the well springs into action once again.

Quickly leaning over the other two, she tugs the cinched rope around the graycloak and slices it with the bloody blade. The burlap purse falls free, dropping to the ground.

Without hesitation, the girl kicks it with her bare foot.

Judging by her aim, she's intending for it to skid across the powdery dirt and land inside my cage.

But she sacrifices accuracy for speed, and the graycloak is prepared.

With a cry, the graycloak extends an arm and connects with the purse in midair using her open palm.

Instead of landing inside my cell, the bag ricochets off the edge of her hand and falls upon the dirt path directly between Chimeline's cage and mine. The smallest of dust clouds rises in the calm morning air as it slides to a stop.

For an unmeasurable moment, everything is silent and still.

I push away from the bars and dive to the left to grasp the side wall. I pull my body forward, reaching as far as I can through the bars and onto the dirt path, until my shoulder and neck stretch in pain.

I shout out. The purse is at least a foot away from me. I can't reach it.

Chimeline is in the shadows behind her bars, her arm reaching through, just opposite mine. The purse landed closer to her cage than it did to mine, but her hand is not as long.

I watch, powerless, as she does the same as I did—stretches her body against the bars to gain a few precious inches. She screams in pain. I cannot see her broken hand, but she must be putting weight on it to stretch this far.

Her slender fingers grasp the dirt an inch away from the burlap bag, but she cannot reach it either.

Shouts bring my attention back to the front of our cells.

The graycloak stands over the body of her father, simultaneously protecting him and blocking the girl from coming down the path in our direction. The woman's hands are out, and she's yelling at the young girl to drop her knife. The girl is crying, her lips quivering in either regret or anger. It's evident that even though the young girl is armed and the graycloak is not, the latter has the upper hand.

I look back to Chimeline and my breath catches in my throat.

She's taken off her effulgency necklace of ivory beads and is grasping the loop in her outstretched hand, beyond the bars. She's using it as a net, casting it into the dirt to lasso the purse just out of her reach.

On her second cast, she surrounds it as I hold my breath.

Carefully, she drags the purse toward her across the dirt path. It passes between the bars and into the darkness of her cell.

A moment later, it reappears, sailing through the sunlit air between our cages, and I grasp it.

Rolling away into the center darkness of my own cell, I open the purse and pour its contents onto the ground.

It's my gold necklace. My voidstone.

Once the graycloak sees me with it, she backs away frantically. She utters more screams of terror, pulling the effulgent's body from my cell by his ankles. Next to her, the girl mindlessly drops the knife at her side, and the blade sticks into the ground.

*Enough of this.*

I drape the necklace over my head and touch the black stone. The world disappears and the winds come. It's been days since I last heard them, but it takes only a moment to acclimate to the world of black upon black.

I cut through the bamboo.

It takes no time at all. As I step out, the palm-frond roof collapses behind me. I cut Chimeline's cage open as well, and her bamboo bars splinter apart with a loud *crack*. Letting go of the voidstone, I rush to the effulgent's body. The graycloak screams again, but this time she directs her words at me.

"Don't touch him!"

I pry her bloody hands from the man's ankles and push her forcefully. She loses her balance and falls backward to the dirt.

When she looks up at me, I see wrath in her eyes, but she does not attack me. There is no fight in her. Violence seems as foreign to her as using a voidstone. Instead, she gets up on her knees, closes her eyes, and begins praying.

*Just don't interrupt me.*

Kneeling next to the effulgent, I analyze the wound. There is a small rip where the blade went through, so I take my fingers and place them there, tearing the cloak apart.

"Let me be!" He grimaces, his face sideways against the ground, the veins on his forehead pronounced. "Do not use your black arcana on me!"

Ignoring him, I clutch my voidstone again and study his body.

The indivisibles of his skin. His veins and muscles and the tighter-packed forms of his ribcage. Moving between them all, I see where the blade entered. It left a black valley between colorless mountains, where a lake is deep and cold.

The lake goes straight into the bottom of his right lung.

*This is not going to be easy.*

# VOIDREAMING

Marine rips off her backpack, fur coat, hat, and mittens and tosses these snow-damp belongings on my bed before warming her hands by my fire.

"Good Unnamed, it's freezing out there," she says, cupping her hands around her mouth and blowing into them.

I walk over to my terrace. It has been glassed in for the winter, but I close the damask curtains nonetheless. The bluish light of the midwinter afternoon is replaced by the flickering glow of my meager fire, and I have the sudden urge to pour myself a glass of red-currant wine.

Which I do.

"Do you realize this fireplace is larger than the one we have in the dormitory commons?"

I let out a quick laugh despite my heavy heart. "You should see the one in the king's dining room. It could swallow you whole."

Drink in hand, I walk back across the room but suddenly stop in my tracks. The silhouette of Marine's shapely body against the fire is so perfect that it momentarily eclipses all thoughts.

But then they return, with one concern leading the way: It is becoming more and more difficult to think of her as a mere student.

*What in Temberlain's Ashes are you doing, Dem?*

Her passion for voidance and eagerness to learn is attractive in itself, but if that weren't enough, she is simply the most stunning woman in the citadel.

Because her back is to me, she's oblivious to my gaze, but if she saw my face, she would see a man full of longing and dread.

*This cannot continue.*

I hate that it's cold out. I wish that I had ended this weeks ago, when the leaves were still falling from the trees and the air was crisp and sunlit with limitless possibilities. I wouldn't feel as guilty. Now, it feels as if I am kicking her out into the snow-filled gutter to freeze to death, alone.

"I think it could use another log," she says, rubbing her palms together and then extending them toward the fire.

Without thinking, I touch my voidstone and make the flames roar back to life, and she jumps back in surprise.

"That's against the rules!" she says, before settling into a cunning smile.

My mind races as I study her face. It's as if she knows I am trying to impress her and enjoys having me wrapped around her finger.

"Not for me."

"But why can't we do that at the dormitory?"

"Can you imagine a hundred students trying to play with fire? The dormitory is made of wood, and it's been burned down three times. My rules are to prevent a fourth."

Two bloodred leather armchairs flank the fireplace, facing it at forty-five-degree angles. I tap the one on the right and say, "Take a seat, Marine."

"But my notes are in my—"

"No notes today," I say, as I walk over to the left chair and collapse into it.

"What's wrong?" she asks softly. She must sense that something is different. Maybe it's my curt tone, or the drink in my hand.

"We can't keep meeting like this," I say.

For a long time, silence fills the room and the bitter wind howls outside it. I hear it through the heavy curtains and the glass enclosure. I even hear it echo down the chimney between us. It sounds almost as it does in the void.

"Is it because I am not good enough—"

"No," I say loudly. "It has nothing to do with your gift. You are an excellent student, Marine. I am honored to have you at the university."

"Why, then?"

I shake my head. "You are the only student that I privately tutor in my bedchamber. It's just not appropriate. As master voider, I have a reputation to uphold."

"Oh?" she says playfully, but I see through her. She is trying to brush off this important conversation with her charm. And on any other day, it just might work. But not today—I look away in order to steel myself.

"Just think about how people perceive what is occurring here."

"But nothing is happening."

"That doesn't matter. Perception can make or break a person—especially a man in my station."

"But you are the master voider."

"Exactly. All the more reason for me to manage perceptions."

I look back at her, and her smile is gone.

"A few of the submasters have approached me." I down my glass of wine, stand, and walk back to my dresser to pour myself another before continuing. "Let me put it bluntly: I have to choose. I don't want to, but I have to. And the university—it's everything that I stand for."

Marine speaks softly behind me.

"You want me to go?"

I look back at her, nestled in her armchair. She's wearing brown leggings and a cream sweater that covers almost her entire body. She has kicked off her boots, and she curls her bare feet beneath her. The leather armchair looks massive with her on it.

"Of course I don't," I say.

I down half of the glass of wine and refill it before walking back to my chair.

"But there's a difference between what I want and what is right," I say weakly, falling into it again.

"And what is it that you want?"

I turn to look at her and become paralyzed by her expression. The way she looks at me, with the firelight dancing on her face, is so bold I am at a loss for words.

"Dem?"

I must look surprised. Nobody has ever called me that except for my closest friends. Certainly no student.

But then again, Marine isn't just any student.

*This is wrong.*

Before I can say anything, she gets out of her chair, walks over, and gently sits on my lap.

I swallow and put my wine glass down. I can hardly think with her so close to me, but I try to focus on her last question.

What is it that I want?

*This is wrong.*

Despite all logic and reason, I know what it is. Or, more accurately, who it is. My feelings for Marine have slowly grown to the point where they now threaten everything.

I am the head of the university, which is, quite possibly, the most important institution in the Northern Kingdom. My responsibilities are unmatched, save for the king's. Every day of every week is full of meetings with submasters, dignitaries, foreign ambassadors, philosophers, effulgents, and the like. My mind is bursting with the theoretical applications of voidance. My submasters execute my strategy. My students travel the lands in my name.

But all of this pales in comparison to the rare, intimate time I spend with this untamed woman, talking about nothing at all. Because this is what makes me feel alive.

*Marine has become my indivisible.*

Leaning forward, my body acts on its own. Softly cradling her pale face in my hands, I forget that I am the master voider. I forget that she is my student.

I kiss her on the lips.

And I feel her return the kiss.

Without breaking contact, she moves her body, straddling me on my chair. We embrace even tighter, and our bodies become one until the fullbell rings out in the distance and the fire next to us dies.

*Where do we go from here?*

She gets off me and walks to the opposite end of the room as if none of the past fullbell ever happened. She begins to organize her notes and books that lay strewn on the bed. I get up and tidy my desk by candlelight.

I feel as though I have been washed up on the beach by a towering wave, sand in my pockets and saltwater in my mouth. I see another wave coming. It's not here yet, but it's unstoppable.

I don't know if I want to keep standing on this beach.

"Where do we go from here?" I ask, breaking the silence.

"Hmmm?" she says, not looking up.

I both love and hate how she has not thought this through. On one hand, it's maddening how blind she is to the judgmental wrath coming our way. On the other hand, her free spirit and confidence are her most attractive qualities.

"We can't keep meeting like this," I say again.

"What do you mean?"

"It looks bad. I have a reputation to uphold."

Marine shrugs indifferently as she continues to shuffle through notes.

"I'm serious, Marine. This is a problem."

"I don't see it that way."

I shake my head. Her stubbornness tries my patience.

"It doesn't look that great for you, either," I add.

She stops what she is doing and looks at me. "What is that supposed to mean?"

I sigh. "Never mind."

"No, Dem, tell me," she snaps. "We make love, and now you want to toss me aside?" She releases the papers from her hand to emphasize her point.

I approach her. "No. I'm not suggesting that we stop seeing each other. I just . . . I just don't want to risk my reputation. The other nobles, here in the citadel, they'll—"

"Well, what are you suggesting?"

Now that I am in front of her, I tenderly touch her cheek and rake my fingers through her golden hair. My heart and my mind tell me two different things.

I don't want to lose her. It is now clear to me that in the past few days I have fallen deeply for her. It isn't only her beauty. I am captivated by her spirit—her passion for learning, her ambition.

But what will the court think? The master voider, dallying with a student . . .

"We have to be more discreet, that's all," I say.

She raises an eyebrow.

"We can meet somewhere else," I continue. "Somewhere private. Where servants and submasters will not see us."

She rolls her eyes and shakes her head and begins to throw her books inside of her backpack. She forcefully ties the drawstrings.

"I see. So, we'll sneak around, behind everyone's back," she says, with a tone that leaves no question as to her feelings on the matter. "That way you can keep your reputation but still sleep with me."

"That's not what I—"

"I understand completely," she says, grabbing her backpack and turning toward the door.

"Marine, wait." I grab her arm.

She stops but doesn't look at me. She's looking at the floor.

"What do you want from me?" I ask quietly. "If you want my heart, you've got it. If you want my body, you've got it. If you want my soul . . . you've got that too."

Her expression softens. She looks up at me with an ever-so-slight smile. Touching the button on my shirt, she idly adjusts it. "What if you allowed me to graduate early? Before everyone else."

I frown. "Graduate?"

She nods. "That way, I wouldn't be your student. I could move in with you, and you could continue to teach me privately."

I shake my head, unsure which point to address first. "To graduate, you would need to pass the final tests. And that would require using a real voidstone."

"I can do it. I have memorized all the voidance structures—"

"None of that matters if you can't control yourself in the void. There is both a mental and a physical aspect to voidance."

"I can control myself just fine."

I fish my voidstone out from underneath my flaxen cloak, and lift the entire necklace over my head.

"Hold out your hand."

She does as I say.

"Palm up."

I lower the gold chain into her outstretched palm. It puddles there, and I make sure the voidstone is facing upwards as it lands, centered within its gold setting and not touching her skin. It is as large as the pit of a peach, and it looks absolutely enormous in her hand. As it drops, I can't help but notice her long fingernails, which are painted bright pink but chipped on the edges. It's a perfect symbol of where she is in this world. Half ready for anything, half vulnerable to everything.

She inhales sharply.

"Do you feel it? How heavy it is?"

She nods, eyes wide.

"Alright. Now, touch it. With one finger, and only for a moment."

Her eyes open even wider as she takes her other hand and places her index finger upon the matte black surface.

Immediately, she lets out a sigh of ecstasy, and her eyes roll into the back of her head. Then her head swivels in all directions and she falls into me. I take the voidstone and grab her shoulders.

"You see?"

She opens her eyes and blinks rapidly before focusing on me with eyes the color of the winter-afternoon sky. "It's so loud." She exhales.

I smile. "The wind?"

She nods. "And the indivisibles. I saw everything. Not just what's in front of me. I saw you. I saw the walls, the floors. The dust in the air. The entire—"

There's a knock at the door. Marine goes silent.

"Yes?" I call out in annoyance.

"It's Elrich, Your Grace."

"Shit," I mumble under my breath, as I gently guide Marine into one of my bloodred leather chairs, my hands still on her shoulders. "Sit here for a moment. You're still disoriented."

After hastily setting my dangling voidstone upon the desk, I walk to the front door and unlock it.

When I open it, the red-faced young man looks past me to Marine sitting on the chair, but I clear my throat and his eyes dart back to me.

"What?" I say.

"Your grace, you have a dinner tonight with Submaster Herrophilus and the hospital staff. I am here to assist with your preparations."

I don't like the way he keeps looking at Marine, so I step into the hall and close the door behind me, leaving the two of us in shadows.

"That's at sevenbell," I say.

He nods nervously. "It's currently sixbell, Your Grace."

"What?" I say, into the dark hallway. "I must have lost track of time with my studies."

I detect the faintest of smirks in the dimness. "I am sorry to interrupt your studies, Your Grace."

Normally I would tear into this boy for his veiled impudence, but my mind is too preoccupied. All I can think about is what I should do concerning the dinner.

It's impossible to dislodge from my mind what has just transpired in the warm candlelight, just beyond my closed door. The heat and feminine sweetness of the room. And I realize that I don't want this to end. I understand the importance of the new hospital, but mingling with these people over drinks and dinner is the last thing I want to do.

Instead, I want to stand on the beach as the next wave crashes into me, sending me into oblivion.

Elrich must sense my apprehension. "Your grace, I can come back in a halfbell or fullbell. I am sure the others will not mind if you are late." He clears his throat. "I will not mention your present company."

I nod. "Come back in a halfbell," I say. He bows and turns away.

"Make it a fullbell," I call out, as the echoes of his footsteps diminish into the distance.

When I am finally alone in the dark hallway, I pause, my hand on the doorknob.

*This is a crossroads if ever there was one.*

I can enter my room and tell Marine to leave. I can tell her that she is only a student, and what we did was wrong. It was emotion taking over reason, and reason must prevail. Duty over dreams. I can ring the bell and re-summon Elrich, and still be on time for my obligations.

Or I can enter my room and embrace her, and feel my age, responsibilities, and loneliness wash away into a void more beautiful and powerful than the real thing.

Closing my eyes, I take a deep breath in preparation.

And smell smoke.

"Marine?" I call out hesitantly, as I open the door and enter my room.

For a moment, all I can do is stand within the doorframe and try to comprehend what is happening.

Marine stands at my desk, my voidstone in her hands. Her blue eyes are entirely white, and her body shakes violently.

Next to her, my candelabrum roars. Flames erupt from the white candles as they melt too quickly. Their sticks shorten in front of my eyes. The flames consume the damask drapes and curl upwards. Black tendrils of smoke snake across the ceiling toward me.

*Temberlain's Ashes.*

I run over to her, rip the voidstone from her hands, and immediately douse the fire with it before the entire Royal House is consumed.

When I return from the void, I find my body in the throes of a coughing spasm. The tendrils have dissipated, but a thick cloud of smoke now fills the entire room. I cannot see more than a foot in front of me. The remains of my curtain panels are full of red sparks that flicker.

Someone is knocking on my door, loudly this time.

I stumble over to the balcony. I tear open the remains of the curtain panels and open the glass enclosure, letting the winter wind whip into the room to clear the smoke. The cold air hits my lungs like a salve.

After a few deep breaths, I turn around. Through the thinning smoke, I see both Elrich and Anna standing in the open doorway, their mouths wide.

Then I notice Marine crumpled on the floor by my desk.

I run over and stoop, grasping her slender shoulders.

"Can you hear me?"

For a moment I see only the whites of her eyes, and then she blinks and shuts them as shivers course throughout her body. Feeling her fingers, I notice that they are ice cold, and I know it has nothing to do with the balcony's open door.

"No," I mumble.

I pick her up and carry her over to my bed.

"Go," I tell the statuesque Elrich and Anna. "Draw a bath!" After I set her down on the bed, I turn back again and see that they have not moved. "Go now!" I scream.

"But Your Grace, I have not tended the fire since morning. There is no hot water—"

"Bring cold water!"

They both flee.

Drawing back my bedsheets, I cover her with my thick goose-feather blanket.

"Can you hear me?" I ask her again.

Her eyes are still closed, but she nods and mumbles something.

I bend down to put my ear next to her face.

"I'm sorry," she whispers.

"I know," I answer. I press the blanket tightly around her, trying to make a cocoon while trying to shut out the obvious.

I am moved to tears as I realize what she's done. What she's continuing to do. Her cursed ambition has brought her to the brink of death. And I have come face-to-face with the realization that I cannot lose her. I will risk my life to save hers.

Whether she is using me to gain more power with a voidstone or to gain influence in citadelian society as my future wife, it doesn't matter. I am hopelessly in love with her. If I am but a milestone in her road of ambition, I am powerless to do anything to stop her.

She opens her mouth as if to speak, but her teeth start clattering as a fresh wave of shivers overtakes her.

"Dem, I'm scared," she finally says.

"I'm not going to let anything happen to you." I try to keep my voice level and optimistic for her. "Elrich and Anna are fetching some water. I'm going to give you a hot bath, and then you'll be fine. Everything is going to be fine."

Elrich storms into the room carrying a large wooden bucket that is obviously heavy with water. As he rounds the corner, some of it spills onto the marble floor, but he keeps running into the bathroom, his leather-soled shoes squeaking in the puddle.

Anna comes in after him, with far more grace.

"Is there another bucket that I can use?" I ask her, and she nods.

I leave Marine's side to help fetch water from the kitchen down the hall. There is a stone channel from the aqueduct that comes through the wall. I lift the lever, and chilled water from outside gushes forth with chunks of ice and snow, filling my wooden bucket in no time.

After running as fast as I can back to my room, I pour the frigid contents into the copper clawfoot bath. The ice chunks hit the copper like strikes from a hammer.

I do all of this over again.

And again.

As I reenter my bedroom the fifth time, I notice that Marine's body is starting to convulse on the bed. She's not just shivering but fighting something that cannot be seen.

She's in voideath.

Pouring my last load of water into the bathtub, I toss the bucket aside and run back to my desk to fetch my voidstone. The room is clear of smoke now, but it's freezing cold, so I shut the balcony door.

Back in the bathroom, I sit down on the white-and-black marble floor next to the clawfoot tub, draping my arms over its curved edge. The water level has finally crept up significantly. At this depth, it will cover her body, which is the crucial detail.

The only thing left to do is heat it up, which is not going to be easy.

Just as I am about to enter the void, Anna and Elrich storm in again carrying their buckets. After emptying them, they look at me sitting on the floor and hesitate.

"That's deep enough," I tell them.

"Shall I fetch the submasters?" asks Anna, wiping sweat from her forehead.

Past the bathroom door, Marine's body is writhing uncontrollably, and her whimpers are nonsensical. Her movements have pushed my goose-feather comforter away from her, and I can see her hands are balled into fists.

"No," I say quickly. "They are too far away. Go, and close the door behind you."

"Your grace, are you sure—"

"By the time they arrive, she'll be dead. Go!"

I don't even wait for them to leave before I touch my voidstone and enter the void, preparing myself for a task that may kill me.

Heating up water indivisibles is not the most complicated undertaking. It just takes patience and time. At the university, we systematically timed how long it took to heat controlled volumes of water using both voidance and non-voidance approaches. They were the same.

Which means safely heating this bathtub of near-freezing water is going to take a fullbell.

Marine doesn't have that long.

My only option is to heat it much faster, ironically risking voideath myself.

I let my guard down. All the walls of my common sense and education come crashing down. I let the wind encircle me, rip into me, into every indivisible that composes me. Faster and faster the indivisibles move below me, as the wind pulls me apart, faster and faster. An indivisible for an indivisible. They want to take me with them, back to where they have always been.

Just before it's too late—before they grab me by every indivisible of my body and pull me irreparably into the void—I release my grip on the stone. It falls onto the marble tiles below. There's the hard sound of stone upon stone. The light of the world returns.

Glorious steam rises in front of me.

I cannot feel my fingers, so when I dip my hand into the bathtub, I don't know how warm it is. I extend my entire arm in. It is hot. It is lifesaving hot.

I try standing, but I lose my balance and fall. Crawling over the black-and-white marble tiles, I reach the bedroom beyond. Marine is not moving anymore. My heart drops.

*How long was I in the void?*

Finding her grayish-blue arm, I'm barely able to pull her down off the bed. She lets out a thin cry.

She's still alive.

Snaking my arms underneath her armpits, I try to lock them together across her chest. It works well enough. Our bodies entwined, I use my legs of clay to kick the two of us backward, toward the bathtub and rising steam.

My last wave of energy picks up her body. I slip it into the steaming water of the copper tub. The bottoms of her feet touch the end, leaving only her head above water.

The coldness is coming on, radiating up my arms and legs and grasping my heart and lungs with fists of ice. The void wants me, but it's not going to win.

I try holding Marine's hand, but I slip and fall back onto the marble floor.

# THE LESSON

I open my eyes to dusty shafts of colored light.

"Where . . ." My voice cracks in dryness.

I hear the familiar soft echo of a heavy book being shut. A moment later, a smooth hand brushes my forehead. Fingers gently comb my hair.

Chimeline smiles and looks down at me, and I slowly sit up with a groan.

We're alone in the effulgency temple, sitting next to each other on the rearmost wooden pew. A large white tomb rests on the other side of Chimeline.

This place looks as small from the inside as it did from the outside—capable of containing a hundred people, at most. But it's impressive in its own right. Diffused light from the painted glass pours down like rays of wisdom from the Unnamed. At least that is what the effulgent would say if he were here.

"The effulgent is sleeping in the back room," Chimeline says, pointing to a closed door past the altar. "The graycloak is watching over him." Her hushed voice echoes off the dark wooden ceiling.

My hand goes to the gold setting of my necklace, and I exhale in contentment. The time in the cell without my voidstone now seems like some bad dream. A dark moment when I was reduced to nothing.

I move it so it sits between my cloak and undershirt. There's no need to have it on display.

"She didn't take it away," I say quietly.

"Your voidstone?"

I nod. "The graycloak could have taken it after I passed out."

"Maybe she forgot. She had her father to worry about."

I grunt. "Or maybe she's finally been enlightened."

Outside, I hear the clanging of a bell tied to an ox. It makes me wonder what time of day it is, and how long I've been voidreaming.

She places her hand on mine. "Thank you for healing me."

A memory surfaces. The moment I was done with the effulgent. The weightless feeling of success, of having saved a person's life. The man's breathing had normalized, and the bleeding had stopped. Even though my fingers were numb, I was full of a brazen self-confidence, so I healed Chimeline's wrist right then and there. It was far easier—just a simple bone-mending. It was the last thing I did before passing out.

"I gave you my word, Chimeline."

She kisses me on the cheek. "I think it was also very kind of you to save the effulgent. You had every right not to."

"Whatever people may think of us voiders, we're not murderers."

She pauses. "It took you a long time. It must have been very hard work."

I nod. "I am no specialist in the area of human anatomy. This is my submaster Herrophilus' area. He could have healed him within a halfbell."

"It took you nearly four fullbells."

*Four fullbells. Too much time.*

I look around the stagnant surroundings again, my eyes finally settling back on Chimeline.

"We should leave."

"This temple?"

I shake my head. "This village."

"But the graycloak said that the effulgent wanted to speak to you. When both of you woke up."

I exhale. "I have nothing left to say to him."

"But Dem, he may want to thank you."

I'm filled with an intense urge to stand up, take Chimeline, and quietly walk out of here, heading south.

But that would be foolish.

We need supplies for our journey. Food and water. Chimeline is still barefoot. We also need horses if we ever hope to catch up to Marine and the veiled man.

And there is something else that I need, something that contradicts my recent headstrong words to Chimeline—information on the fate of Anaxarchis. Only the effulgent can give me this, and I can't leave here without it.

I reluctantly nod. "Alright, we'll wait."

She seems happy with the decision and lets out a deep breath while smoothing her borrowed dress.

"Tell me what happened while I was out."

She bites her lip.

"It was scary, Dem."

"How so?"

"The villagers wanted to kill you. When you were in the void."

I furrow my brow.

"You were just sitting there over his body while touching the stone. For four fullbells! There was confusion. The two cages were destroyed. Many of the men thought you attacked the effulgent—that you were *causing* his bloody wound instead of healing it."

I could see how the poor farmers could easily interpret such a thing.

"But the two of us were able to calm the storm."

"You and the graycloak?"

She nods.

I take a deep breath. "Thank you, Chimeline. I had no idea of the danger, being in the void."

"Everything worked out in the end. The graycloak seems like a decent woman."

I nod in agreement. "Whatever happened to the young girl?"

"The one who stabbed the effulgent?"

"Yes."

"She ran off."

I utter a groan.

"What is it?"

"I still don't know why she did what she did. She had approached me in the cage previously and asked if I could heal someone with voidance."

"I heard that."

I shake my head in confusion. "I think that she was referring to the effulgent. She planned on stabbing him. She wanted to set me free."

"Why?"

"I don't know." I turn to her. "Did the graycloak say anything about her? I'm surprised she let her get away."

"No. We had bigger things to worry about."

"The villagers."

Chimeline nods, her hands tracing the lace patterns of the dress. "Apparently, this dress is hers, but she will not admit it. It seems very expensive. The weaves on it are Xian in design."

She's right. From a distance, it would seem like any Northerner's white dress. But close up, the unique diagonal patterns in the lace are pronounced.

"Don't you think it's odd?" I ask.

Her nose wrinkles in a mix of confusion and offense. "My dress?"

"No. The dress suits you. I was speaking about the graycloak."

"What about her?"

"I just think it's strange that she was so concerned about him, yet she can't even admit that he's her father. Some sign of ownership or something."

She nods, squinting up into the rays of color. "She's more like me than I care to admit. I would give anything to have a father who loved me for who I am, not because of the role that I was destined for since the time I was born."

"What role is that? Surely you cannot mean joining the king's harem."

She shakes her head but doesn't answer me.

I watch her, lost in her memories. In the soft light from above, the white dress contrasts her olive skin. She must have washed up a bit, since her face is clean, the lines from her earlier tears carefully rinsed away. Her hair, too, has been brushed, the dark tendrils wound behind her ears.

A contradictory sort of beauty surrounds her. Something more complex than what her former occupation in the harem would imply. It is difficult to define. It's a graceful resourcefulness. As if, had I not known any better, she could be a wealthy merchant from the citadel. Or a member of the king's council.

Yet, despite this grace, her eyes betray knowledge earned at a cost.

*The role that I was destined for since the time I was born.*

I keep studying her while she's lost in thought, speculating on what this destiny could possibly be. Perhaps a past that involved tricks like the one she pulled today. But in this past, she must have had no effulgency necklace. I imagine that she had no tools whatsoever, except her instincts, which she used to lasso treasures of a different kind.

We both snap out of our thoughts as a sweeping sound echoes throughout the temple.

Up ahead, past the altar, the door to the back room opens and the effulgent exits, followed by the graycloak, who is carrying a glass box in her arms.

I stand, and Chimeline follows suit. The old wooden pew moans in complaint.

I don't know what to expect. I healed the effulgent with the voidstone, even though he did not want me to. He pleaded with me to let him die. Will he be grateful? Remorseful? Vengeful? A combination of the three?

*Am I a fool to still be here?*

The effulgent walks slowly across the altar and then leans upon the stone table, facing us with his head downcast. We're all the way in the back, with a dozen or so empty pews between us, but the temple is small enough for me to make out most of the details. He wears a new cloak without any traces of blood. The graycloak's riding gear has been replaced with the same simple gray cloak that I first saw her in. A white linen runner graces the center of the altar, and the graycloak carefully sets the glass box down upon it. It's about one foot cubed, and it contains something that catches the diffused sun.

"You may approach," the effulgent says, lifting his head.

"Come on," I say under my breath, as I take Chimeline's hand.

We walk down the center aisle and up the stone steps, until we're standing at the edge of the altar, directly opposite the effulgent and his daughter, with the glass box between us.

"Do you know what this is, Master Voider?"

Peering inside the glass box, I lean in to get a better view.

It's a twisted piece of blue metal.

The sides of the glass cube shimmer subtly, as if we're underwater. Likely a trick of the light caused by the sun's rays pouring through the stained glass far above.

The piece is only the size of my hand and has a few symbols painted on the side in bright red. I do not recognize any of them.

"No," I answer softly.

"This is a relic. A piece of a ship long since lost. We are exceedingly blessed to be in the presence of it here." After a moment of silence, he adds, "Not many outside the effulgency have ever witnessed such a thing."

I nod, not quite sure how to answer. It seems as if he is bestowing some sort of honor on me by letting me view this, but I have no idea what it is. "I've never heard of an effulgency ship."

He nods to his daughter, and she picks up the glass case carefully then slowly returns it to the back room.

"Nor should you have. Even your historians have no record of it."

It seems as though he has more to say, so I wait.

"I must be careful," he says, "for much of our history has been handed down from generation to generation, and only within the privacy of the effulgency. But I will say this: it is very old, and it is how the effulgency first sailed across the sea from the land beyond."

"How old?"

He shakes his head. "As I said, it's been passed down for generations."

"Why show it to me?"

He smiles knowingly and looks at me from across the altar. "Because I believe that you are the answer to my prayers, Master Voider." He glances at Chimeline, by my side. "Perhaps both of you are."

I shake my head. "I healed you because it was the right thing to do. It wasn't because the Unnamed told me to do it, nor was it because of your prayers. I was not going to let a man die—"

He shakes his head forcefully, cutting me off. "That is not what I meant. This goes far beyond what happened today. This is about what is yet to come. The Unnamed has much in store for you."

I exhale, feeling somewhat let down. I have the sudden urge to walk back down the altar steps and leave this place. I am tired and hungry, and have no patience to discuss matters of elusive faith with a man who told me to let him die.

"Did you say the same thing to Anaxarchis?" I ask him angrily, my voice echoing. "Did he die helping you as part of some sort of vague prayer?"

The effulgent looks down, his pale skin becoming paler.

"You never told me what happened to him," I say, my fury barely contained.

"I know. And I suppose this is as good a time as any."

I wait, my eyes narrowing.

"The death of your student was my fault."

"What did you do?"

He shakes his head. "It was a tragic misunderstanding. We had an altercation," he says, running a hand across his bald head. "He fell to his death."

"What misunderstanding?" I say, between clenched teeth. My hands grip the edge of the stone altar but relax when Chimeline lays her own hand over them.

"I was convinced that your student was trying to subvert the villagers. To turn them against me."

"Why would you think that?"

"It doesn't matter now. All that matters is that I overreacted, and things got out of hand. I am sorry."

The effulgent looks back up at me, meeting my gaze with his dark eyes. "This is what I meant by my prayers. The Unnamed never answers them in the way one thinks. I had asked for a quick resolution to your arrival, to avoid the act of stealing and false imprisonment. To avoid repeating what happened with your student. But what I received was a near death sentence, and an act of compassion from the most unlikely person. It was a lesson from the Unnamed. And I believe he is not done with this lesson."

"What lesson?"

"You were sent here to help us."

I laugh bitterly.

I know I am being rude, answering this man's naked concerns with such frivolity, but I cannot help myself. *The man killed Anaxarchis, and he thinks I will help him?*

"I really didn't know what to expect from you," I say. "I saved your life when you asked me not to. I used my voidstone on you when you declared it as evil."

"It *is* evil," he interjects. "But that is part of the lesson."

"Listen," I say. "I have my own lessons that I am still reeling from. My wife left me for another man. Another voider—one who is truly evil. A man who has committed horrible crimes in the name of my institution. For years, my service to the king has been twisted for his stupid war. My gifted student Anaxarchis is dead. And you think that my coming here is a sign that I should help *you*? I have my own problems to solve."

He slowly shakes his head. "*My* wife. *My* institution. *My* service. *My* student. *My* problems."

For a long time, I am speechless. I stare him down with eyes that must look like hot coals.

"You're welcome for saving your life," I finally answer. "But it's time that I go because there's another thing that's mine. *My* path. I have *my own* path to follow."

Chimeline grabs my hand before I can turn away, and when our eyes meet, she tilts her head to the side, as if saying, "Are you sure?"

I pull her toward me. "We're done here."

We walk down the steps, but before we are halfway down the aisle, the front doors to the temple break open, and a man enters with a child. The sunshine makes them appear as silhouettes, but I can see rope around her neck. The man pulls her forward as he would an animal. He yanks the rope forcefully and she falls upon the floor, crying out in pain as her knees strike the stone.

"We found her, Your Effulgency," bellows the man. "The one who stabbed you."

# ONE DOES NOT OWN THE DARK

"Why?" the young girl screams at me from the temple's stone floor. "Why didn't you help me?"

The thick rope tightens about her neck, forcing it to crane upwards sharply. She creates slack by lifting her upper body with two outstretched arms, palms on the floor.

"You were supposed to come with me. Not help him."

"Quiet, you little bitch," says the man standing next to her. He yanks the rope, and she falls forward again, caught off guard. Her face bangs against the stone tiles and she lets out a scream, blood pouring from her nose onto the gray tiles like wine from an upturned glass.

Instead of answering her, I touch my voidstone and sever the thick, coarse rope around her neck. Before anyone can react, I create a wall of pressure to force the older villager back. He flies a few feet through the air, crashes into the half-open doors of the temple, and falls onto the steps outside, unconscious.

"Enough of this!" shouts the effulgent at my back, coming near with his daughter.

The girl from the well cups her hands close to her face to collect the dripping blood. She then looks up at me with a haunted expression. "You weren't supposed to save him." Her clenched teeth are more red than white. "You were supposed to come with me."

I lean back in surprise. This young girl has committed a heinous crime and is now caught. Her sentence may be death, but incredibly, she doesn't seem to be scared.

Instead, she is full of wrath—the sign of someone who has nothing left to lose.

I stoop. "I am grateful that you freed me, but what you did was wrong, child. Surely you know this."

She looks up at the towering, gleaming effulgent at my side and uses one of her bloody hands to point at him. "My sister is dying." She raises her voice and addresses the effulgent directly. "Did you hear what I said? *My* sister is *dying*! And you don't care!"

"Do not speak to His Effulgency in that way," admonishes the graycloak.

But the man silences both of them with an outstretched hand.

"It is alright," he says calmly. "She is still learning the way of unwanting." He turns to his daughter. "Get a bucket of water and rags for this mess. The grout may stain."

She nods and shuffles away without a word.

The bronzed girl starts to cry, her anger perhaps washed away by sadness, and the effulgent sits down on a clean section of the stone aisle, crossing his legs underneath his white cloak and placing his hands gently upon his thighs. Just as he did in my jail cell.

"Look up at the windows, child." He rifles through his cloak and takes out a spotless white handkerchief, which he hands to her. "The blood flow will stop quicker this way. Here."

She looks at him suspiciously but finally snatches the cloth out of his hand and raises it to her face.

She looks up.

"What do you see?"

The young girl lets out a confused groan.

"The pictures in the windows," he clarifies. "What do you see?"

The rag muffles her childlike voice, but I can still understand her. "Thou shall not own the living. Thou shall not own the dead."

The man nods. "That is correct. Anger is due to our emotions, which are rooted in ownership. You say *your sister*, but she is not your slave. You do not own her. You also say that she is dying, but her life is not her own. It is a gift from the Unnamed, and when that gift is destined to be returned, we have no reason for anger. We should be celebrating a gift richly lived. It was never ours to begin with."

The girl continues to look up at the stained-glass windows, her forehead creasing in skepticism. It seems that she's heard these words before and that this additional explanation will not convince her.

"What else do you see?" says the effulgent, his voice calm and silky.

"The light. The dark."

"Thou shall not own the light. Thou shall not own the dark. Do you know what that means?"

The girl moans again, turning the rag to a clean section.

"The light is our dreams," says the effulgent. "Our aspirations. We need to give them up to the Unnamed. We should pursue only what the Unnamed wants of us. If our personal wishes get in the way of that, that is a problem, and we must give them up. You wish for your sister to live—if that is what the Unnamed wants, it will come true. If that is *not* what the Unnamed wants, then you are trying to own the light. One cannot own the light."

Chimeline has sat upon the ground and is listening raptly, but I straighten from my stooped position, arching my back and stretching my arms out at my side. I've heard this drivel before, and I am not interested in hearing it again. I am only interested in the girl and her dying sister. I am biding my time, waiting for her nosebleed to stop.

The least I can do is repay her for freeing me before I go on my way.

The young girl has quieted down. Amazingly, this man seems to have extinguished her hatred with his calm words. Like some back-alley hypnotist from the citadel.

"Similarly, one does not own the dark," he continues. "The dark is what we want to hide. Our past transgressions. And the transgressions of others we refuse to forgive." He takes a deep breath and looks upwards momentarily to the specific stained-glass piece he is referring to. "What you did to me this morning is forgiven. I do not own any hatred toward you. I do not own the dark."

She nods awkwardly while keeping her head tilted back.

"Do you own hatred toward me?" he asks.

She shrugs.

"What about yourself? Do you forgive yourself for what you have done?"

She flashes him a confused expression.

"So many people think that hatred is always directed outward, but I tell you, more people have hatred for themselves than for others. They cling to their darkness as if it is their prized possession."

"That is true," says Chimeline.

"You must give it up," he answers, swiveling to meet both of their gazes. "Give up all the darkness in you."

"Yes, Your Effulgency," they both say in unison.

I shake my head and start pacing, suppressing a bitter laugh. This effulgent belongs in the Grand Bazaar at the citadel. He could sell a worthless rug full of mites for a thousand gold.

The graycloak comes back with a bucket of water and some rags that match the color of her cloak. The group of three stands and disperses to let her in, and the girl removes the bloody rag from her nose hesitantly.

"I believe that it has stopped," says the effulgent.

The girl hands the now-sodden handkerchief back to him, but he directs her to give it to the graycloak.

"Your sister," I say, turning to the bronzed girl. "Can you take me to her?"

She blinks a few times, as if in a trance. She looks up at the effulgent and then back to me, as if unsure how to answer.

I step in front of the effulgent and place my hands on the girl's shoulders. She jumps slightly, and I don't blame her. My black flaxen cloak eclipses the shining whiteness behind me.

"*Your* sister," I say, emphasizing my words. "The one you say is dying. Take me to her before it is too late."

This time, my words seem to take root. She nods, sniffling and wiping her hand upon her nose to check for blood. There isn't any there.

"Wait," says the effulgent, and I spin around to face him.

"Don't mistake my not owning the dark for an endorsement of more dark."

I don't understand his statement, and my expression must reflect that.

"I forgave you for using the black arcana to heal me," he explains. "That doesn't change the fact that it is evil."

"You forgave me for healing you," I repeat slowly, emphasizing the absurdity of his words.

"Of course," he says, with no shame at all in his tone. "It was the will of the Unnamed."

"But you just told me that the Unnamed sent me here for a reason."

"Yes, for a lesson."

"Did it ever cross your mind that maybe me using my voidstone *is* your confounded lesson?"

He shuts his eyes tightly and keeps them closed, taking a deep breath. It's as if reason is the light, and he's trying to shut it out. Or maybe, for the first time in his life, he's contemplating the wisdom of a voider.

I spin again to face the child.

"Let's go," I say.

She scampers barefoot out of the temple's front doors and down the length of the curved dirt path. With her white sheet of a dress, she resembles a ghost raising clouds of brown-red dust.

I follow her.

# THE THIRD SHAPE IN YISLA

I follow a dirt trail as slender and sinuous as the girl I pursue. She moves far quicker than I do, but she pauses every few hundred feet until I catch up. Each time I see her around a bend in the foliage, she skirts off, a white flash against the greenery.

Through a forest of bamboo trees, I finally stumble upon a sun-drenched, dirt-covered clearing. The girl waits for me within the shade of her dilapidated home.

From the edge of the trees, I can pick up certain details.

There are no solid walls to her house—only thick wooden posts at the corners and midsections. The structure sits within the center of a barren field that used to be fenced, but even the fence has decayed to gray and fallen in places. I step over its splintered remains.

A few chickens meander, searching madly for scattered seeds in the dusty ground. Their coop is only slightly smaller than the house.

I pass an outdoor firepit full of white ash and walk into the shade of the home, right through where an exterior wall should have been.

The girl taps her bare foot impatiently. But I am short of breath from my brisk walk here, so I lean against a post.

The inside of the house is sparse. It's been divided into two rooms: a kitchen that contains nothing more than a wooden table and a cleaning trough, and a bedroom, which peeks out from beyond a thin bamboo wall. Through the vertical spaces between the stalks, I see sunlight and white sheets but no movement.

"Is your sister sleeping?" I ask between breaths, motioning to the other room.

She nods.

"Where is everyone else?"

She looks at me strangely.

"Is your family working in the fields? Your mother and father?"

Her confused expression dissolves into a strange mix of sadness and disappointment as she shakes her head. "It's just me and Yisla now."

"Your parents are dead."

"Yes."

I scratch my head, looking back at the coop.

"You raise chickens?"

"We sell the eggs."

"Is it enough to live by—"

The young girl stamps the ground. A small dust cloud blooms at her feet.

"Are you here to ask me questions like the effulgent or are you here to save my sister?" she nearly yells.

I can't help but smile at her perseverance and irreverence. She's right, of course.

Standing upright, I motion forwards with my outstretched hand. "Take me to her."

We round the bamboo wall, and I'm met with a fragile girl even smaller than her sister. Sunlight shines through the vertical spaces in the wall, highlighting her unnatural pallor. She lies on the bed covered in sweat, her skin like wet gauze stretched over bone. I imagine that this tiny girl is full of spaces too, gaps where the sunlight filters in. She's almost not of this world.

She must be only ten years old.

I softly sit down upon the edge of the bed. I don't know why I had assumed she would be older. Perhaps it's just that the bronzed girl seems so helpless and incapable of running a household on her own. She is a child. But that is exactly what has happened here.

Tragedy never affects one single thing. It is a web that reaches outward, ever expanding with time.

"Her name is Yisla?" I say quietly.

She nods.

"What is yours?"

After a pause, she says, "We're not supposed to say our names."

I shake my head at the absurdity of such a rule.

"Well, you can say your name to me. I'm Democryos."

"I'm Yerla."

*Yerla and Yisla.*

Pursing my lips, I think of the dead parents who gave these siblings similar names, perhaps hoping that the girls' lives would be linked together in happiness.

"How long has Yisla been like this?" I ask.

Yerla stands on the opposite side of the bed. She raises her gaze to the roof before meeting my eyes. "At least ten days."

"Are you sure?"

She nods. "Every ten days we go to the temple for sacrifice. She missed the last one."

"How did she feel?"

Yerla kicks the ground again. "I don't know. She can't eat anything. Sicks it up. Even water. It's gotten worse." After a moment of silence and another kick at the ground, Yerla adds behind tears, "She's been sleeping since yesterday. I couldn't wake her up this morning."

I nod and settle in close to Yisla's body.

"This will take me some time," I say. "Do not interrupt me."

Looking up at the older sister, I make sure she understands. She nods nervously.

I touch my voidstone.

I move close, inside Yisla's skin, delicately, not touching a precious indivisible. Her thin veins are now wide rivers and I move along them, as if I am carried by an invisible raft. But the black water around me is not normal blood. It is overcome with an invading army, soldiers coiled, taking her over. A rush of black snakes slithering upon themselves.

It's revolting.

Submaster Herrophilus' teachings come back to me in the darkness and choral wind: *There are three kinds of shapes to our invaders. The first is spherical, resembling a seed or berry. The second is rod shaped, like a staff. The third is spiral. A snake. And like the poisonous snakes of the archipelago, this shape is by far the deadliest.*

This girl is being overcome by the third shape.

I fight the urge to let go, away from these grotesque spirals, and instead focus on one of them floating by me. I slice it down the middle, as if cutting through its skin. Instantly, it's destroyed. Pus pours out, and it loses its spiral shape, fading into the abyss.

*The only way to fight these invaders is to cut their skin. As in an army, each soldier must be cut individually. But also, as in an army, once you cut through enough of them, the rest will fall back, for each soldier knows that success is a numbers game.*

In the beginning, it is painstakingly precise work. I focus on each coil surrounding me, I cut it open, and I watch it drown.

It gets easier with time. I am able to focus on entire fields of soldiers, since they all look and move the same. I time my slices just so. They all float above the black blood every so often and that is when I strike, a cut across the horizon.

I sever hundreds of thousands of them.

Eventually the black waters become smooth. I ride the rivers of her body and the soldiers become fewer and fewer. Some I see far off on the horizon, and they sink under the weight of their own fear. They must see me coming. As Herrophilus said, a soldier knows when to flee the battlefield.

When all is done, I let go. The chorus goes silent, and one kind of darkness replaces another.

In the midst of my exhaustion, I understand.

It is night.

I hear the crackle of a campfire. I smell cooked meat. The moon is out, just above the trees. It's cut into slivers through the bamboo wall, shadows cutting across the girl's body and white sheets.

Yisla's wide eyes stare directly at me.

"Who are you?"

I collapse to the floor.

# VOIDREAMING

The front doorbell echoes throughout the Royal House's main hall.

"Excuse me, Your Grace," says Elrich. He sets the silver tray of nuts and cheeses down on one of the walnut buffet tables lining the wall.

As he leaves the room, I look past all the guests in formal attire to the far side. The massive clock says it's a quarter past elevenbell.

"I hope that's your odd submaster," booms Bartholu, the master voider of Xiland. He takes a sip of tawnywine and gently slaps me on the back. "For his sake, not yours."

I smile. I, too, hope it is him, on this eve of my wedding. But if it is not, worry will not fill me. I am full of drink and high hopes, eager for a different life. I have not been this unburdened since before I became master voider. Possibly even before I was a student.

I raise the drink in my hand. "Come, let's see."

Among the hundreds of invitees is my tidy group of four. A party within the party. My submaster, Herrophilus, and the Xian master voider, Bartholu, are both large men—the former is mostly overweight while the latter is built solidly of muscle. To round out this group is a petite and elderly woman named Aphelime, the master voider from the archipelago. A brilliant woman, she is known for discovering medicines derived from the essence of moonspit—an incredibly toxic poison indigenous to the area.

Through an elaborate wooden archway, we all look on as Elrich opens the front door.

The air sings in a high-pitched wail. And even though we're in the next room, the icy wind cuts through and hits us.

In the darkness, Mander appears.

He looks ridiculous bundled up in hooded furs, looking twice his size, and the four of us cannot help laughing. We are all drunk, so our inhibitions have long since eroded. His wild, curly hair looks as if it is part of the brown fringe beneath his hood. His round glasses immediately become clouded with the moisture of the hall. He pushes them up his nose, looking around blindly, as he steps in from the ice and snow.

"Democryos?" he asks, turning his hooded head in all directions.

I turn to my laughing friends. "Pardon me. I should greet him after his long travels."

Walking into the entrance hall, I hand a passing servant my glass and then embrace Mander.

"You made it."

"Barely," he answers. "It's, um, amazing how much the temperature, um, changes across six hundred king miles."

I laugh. "You mean that it's not snowing down in Winter's Baiou?"

He pushes his glasses up the bridge of his nose again and begins to slowly remove his hood, patting and scratching his curly hair. "No. Certainly not."

Elrich closes the door, shutting out the winter winds. "I have your room all made up, Submaster. I can have Anna draw you a hot bath. The hearth is still going strong this late at night."

"Yes," he says, straightening his shoulders. "Yes, soon. Very soon. I will have a drink here with my, um, the master voider first. And then I will retire. I am exhausted from the road."

Elrich nods and takes off his coat as I wave my three friends near. I begin making introductions.

"Oh, I know Mander," Bartholu booms. "He's stationed in Winter's Baiou. He's always out to sea, searching for the Unnamed knows what."

"Ah, the, um, Master Voider from Xiland. Somehow you beat me here. A Southerner besting a Northerner at his, um, own game."

A sudden thought comes to me. Something the king mentioned in our last private meeting. So, even though it's the eve of my wedding, I cannot help speaking briefly about work.

I put one hand on Mander's shoulder and one on Bartholu's. The men stand on either side of me. "That reminds me. His Majesty and the Xian emperor have just agreed to build a new hospital together." I nod toward Herrophilus. "Herro here has built three of them already, to the north. We're thinking Winter's Baiou is the perfect place for our next build. The city is right on the border."

"Excellent!" Bartholu booms. "I know this is very important to the emperor. I will ensure that my voiders are at your disposal."

I take my hands off their shoulders. "Herro, when I am back from honeymoon, I'd like you to travel south with Mander and begin scouting out a location." I turn to Mander. "This will be your top priority. The king will instruct you in my absence."

Mander presses his eyebrows with his thumb and forefinger. "A hospital, Dem. Very unexpected."

Elrich hands him a glass of tawnywine, and he takes it, delicately bringing it to his lips.

"Did I miss His Majesty tonight?" he asks.

I nod.

Aphelime steps forward. "King Andrej IX and his lovely queen made a showing," she says, and then looks at me, winking. "I thought it was a very gracious visit. It shows how much your king respects the master voider." As it always does, her voice trembles, as if she's running out of air. I used to think it was because she was scared but have since discovered otherwise.

"Nonsense," I say, waving the compliment away.

"So, did you find the confounded thing?" Bartholu asks Mander.

We all turn to Mander.

"Find what, um, Bartholu?"

"Your little pygmy seahorse." He laughs as he spits out the words.

"Ah, um, yes. We have brought back a few specimens, but they have all, um, died, and the indivisibles of their skin decay. Losing the, um, fantastical properties. So I must continue to search and somehow, um, capture them alive."

"I hear from my men that you're following along Blackscar into our waters. You should know that they all think you're crazy." Even though the words are harsh, Bartholu clearly means them in jest. His chest rises and falls in soft laughter.

I point to my submaster with my glass. "Mander says that the mysterious creature is invisible to voidance."

He clears his throat. "Yes, um, very nearly correct, Dem. It is my belief that a substance on their skin reflects voidance, much like a mirror reflects light."

"You mean scales," Herro says.

"No. Seahorses are unlike other fish, as they, um, don't have scales. They have a thin skin."

I turn back to the other three. "Mander wrote an impressive thesis on the subject. A membrane that reflects voidance. Cancels it out, in a way. The implications are profound."

"Absolutely," Aphelime says.

I turn back to Mander. "Sorry to be a wet blanket, my friend, but the hospital will have to take precedence. You'll have to assist Herro and work your dives in when you can."

Mander fingers his bushy eyebrows. "Yes, um, certainly, Dem. The seahorses can wait."

He lifts his glass, and I clink it with mine.

"Who knows," I say. "Maybe Marine or I will catch one."

"That's right," Bartholu says, inhaling sharply. "You're going to Xi Bay tomorrow."

I nod.

"So exciting," Aphelime says. "A respite from this horrible weather."

"Is she here?" Mander asks, looking around. His glasses catch the candlelight. "Your lovely, um, Lady Marine?"

"No. She didn't want me to see her the night before the wedding."

"Very wise," Aphelime says, as she places a hand on my arm. "That reminds me. I have a gift for you two."

"A gift?"

She finds the redheaded Elrich standing nearby. "Elrich. Please be a dear and fetch my handbag."

Herro, Mander, and Bartholu are already speaking about the hospital, so the master voider from the archipelago and I step aside to relative privacy. Elrich retrieves her handbag, and she rifles through it for a moment before finding something.

"Here it is," she says, taking out a sealed glass vase about the size of a pear, along with a small book. She hands the bag and her empty tawnywine glass back to Elrich.

She raises the vase up to the candlelight tenderly and then gives it to me.

"What is this, Aphelime?"

She smiles knowingly. Her expressions are magnified, probably because she is a little drunk. Her eyes become glassy, and the smile fades a bit, as if her emotions are getting the better of her.

"We've known each other a long time, Dem. Haven't we?"

"Yes, of course."

"And you know that I care for you deeply, my dear."

I nod. "The feeling is mutual." I hold the vase up in front of me, more curious now than ever.

It seems to be full of granules. Different layers, each a finger's width thick and a different color and coarseness. Black, white, pink, coral, beige.

"My gift to you is the eleven kinds of love. One for each kind of sand from my homeland."

"Eleven kinds of love? I've never heard of such a thing."

"I wrote all about it in here." She hands me the small book. "Don't read it now. Read it when you have time. It goes into detail about where each sand is from, its uses, and what it symbolizes in terms of love."

I flip through the pages with my thumb. Her handwriting is beautiful and precise.

"This must have taken days to scribe," I say, looking up at her.

She waves her hand at me. "The older I get, the more I need to write. A sharp quill makes for a sharp mind."

I smile. "Well, tell me about one of the eleven then. I'm intrigued."

She purses her lips in thought, blinking rapidly, and then nods hesitantly. "Alright, dear. I'll tell you about the black one."

I point to the bottom layer.

"Yes. That. We call it tephra, the love of destruction."

I raise my eyebrow. "Destruction?"

"It comes from volcanic eruptions."

"Ah, that makes sense."

"It is also the most immature sand. It has not been weathered by time. So while it is youthful, beautiful, and exotic, it is not strong. It is the product of burning passions that have spread out of control before suddenly flaming out."

Within the span of a breath, my smile fades.

Aphelime is very much like the name of her homeland—Scorpiontail. A small and subtle woman, she can also strike hard when she wants to. Brutal honesty layered with a salve of charm. A combination that usually only the elderly get away with.

"We usually say that someone is consumed by tephra—by the love of destruction—when they are enraptured in new love. They are overcome with emotions so powerful they're like lava cracking through the crust of their world. Their emotions tear them apart."

Nearby laughter erupts.

I jump in place as the three men behind me guffaw, heartily consumed in their conversation. They are oblivious to ours.

Leaning in, I bite my lip, concerned. "Aphelime, I . . ." I clear my throat. "Do you not approve of this marriage?" I whisper, looking around.

She shakes her head, still smiling. "No, my dear. Of course I approve. I would not be here celebrating with you if I did not."

I straighten up, feeling slightly better, but then she continues with a finger pointed at my chest.

"But you should have known better."

I tilt my head as my heart tightens. She means my past with Marine. How we grew close.

This was the last thing I'd thought I'd be discussing tonight. And from any other person, it would be met with my anger or dismissal. But neither of those feelings are within me. Aphelime is perhaps the mother I never had. There is love behind her sting.

"We've all heard the story of her near voideath. Dem, she was your student. You should have known better. That was tephra acting within you."

At first I don't answer her. I only shake my head and look at the bottommost layer of sand in the vase. "We both decided that she should be expelled. To avoid any confusion. So that we could have a proper relationship."

"Well, you had to! She nearly burned down the Royal House!"

I nod.

"She nearly destroyed you too, Dem. And you nearly destroyed her. You could have been removed as master voider, and she could have died from voideath."

"I know."

She withdraws her finger and takes a deep breath, still careful to keep her voice down. "Look at this room."

I subtly raise my head and look around.

"These people. If you were not surrounded by powerful men who protected you, you would not be standing here today. It is a good thing you are so well-liked. Something like this, it could have been an excuse to get rid of you."

She grasps my wrist. Her hand is shaking slightly, but I know this is only due to her age. She's not afraid of anything.

"I don't wish to dwell on this, Dem. That was not my intent."

"Then what was it?"

"Tephra is not bad, when it is mixed with the other ten kinds of love. A little destruction is good for us all. Just make sure that the Lady Marine is more to you than black sand. And the same goes for her."

"What do you mean?"

"Are you sure she loves you because of *you*? Or just the black flaxen robe that fits you so well?"

"She loves me, Aphelime," I proclaim with all my heart. "And I love her."

But her eyes pierce through me as she continues to squeeze my wrist.

Her hand shakes, but her gaze does not.

# SOMETHING IN THE WATER

It's still night when I awake, but it must be many fullbells later. The moon, once near the horizon and filtered through the bamboo wall, is now high in the sky. There's a small hole in the thatched roof directly above where I lie, and I can see it clearly.

I take a deep breath.

It must have been the mix of aromas that caused me to regain consciousness. The orange scent of Chimeline and the bittersweet smell of cooked meat hang in the air.

A few bright voices echo out in the night. The campfire is on the other side of the house. I can't see it directly, but orange light laps against the sides of everything. The sound of laughter is like a trickle of fresh water over stones. It's this laughter, more than the empty deathbed across from me, that tells me I was successful in saving Yisla's life.

Chimeline stands in the shadows near the edge of the room, looking out into the moonlit clearing. She seems lost in thought and must think that I'm asleep, but as soon as I slowly sit up in the straw bed and swing my legs over the side, she turns and approaches me.

Sitting down on the bed to the right of me, she curls her feet under her.

"You healed her," she says. I detect a hint of surprise in her voice.

I only nod, looking back at the empty deathbed.

"Yisla's sitting by the campfire with her sister," she adds. "Her appetite has returned."

Chimeline softly scratches my back with the fingers of her left hand. "What about you? Are you hungry? Yerla killed one of her chickens for you."

"Yes," I say immediately. "I'm famished."

"Are you well enough to walk? I remember last time you had trouble."

I move my fingers and toes. There is only a trace of numbness.

It's interesting. I worked on Yisla for the entire afternoon. Time does not pass in the void the same way it does in the real world. Yet I am not even close to voideath. A small action repeated slowly over time is much more manageable than, say, heating all the indivisibles inside an airship, simultaneously. Or water in a tub.

It's like the rain. Each raindrop weighs practically nothing. But lifting a lake is impossible.

I look sideways at her. She's still wearing the same white-lace dress and ivory effulgent beads, but she's clutching something in her right hand.

"I thought you stayed at the temple."

"I did, for a time. But then it started getting dark out, and I was worried about you. The effulgent said it was a good idea to check on you."

"Well, if the effulgent said so, it must have been the right thing to do."

She nods, oblivious to my sarcasm.

"What do you have there?" I ask.

"Oh this?" she says, bringing a small book out of the shadows and into the moonlight. "The graycloak gave it to me. It's the Book of Unwanting."

She opens the bleached-leather cover and riffles through the few hundred pages of handwritten text. "The graycloak says that there are many other books, but they are private and only meant for the effulgents and graycloaks. This here is their public writings meant for us commoners. The writings are handed down over centuries." She takes her hand off my back and gently caresses the white cover.

"Do you even know how to read?" I ask her.

She flashes me a disapproving look. "Is that what you think? That just because I am a harem girl, I'm illiterate as well?"

I hunch my shoulders. "I don't mean any offense. It just strikes me as improbable. A blacksmith wouldn't know either."

"Sometimes people are not always what they seem," she snaps. But then I see her body relax, and her voice softens as well. "My father taught me. He said that his greatest treasure was his ability to read, and he passed this treasure on to me before I left him."

I murmur an utterance of surprise, sensing the frailness of her words. "Well, he was a good man, then," I say.

"Sometimes," she replies distantly, as she continues to caress the small book in her hands. "I've never owned a book before. They are far too costly. It's beautiful, isn't it?"

I can't help but let out a short laugh. "It sounds to me like that little white book of yours is a corrupting possession. Don't you think that's ironic?"

She narrows her dark eyebrows in confusion.

"Wanting the Book of Unwanting?"

Slowly, her expression turns to outright anger.

"You know, the effulgent is a decent man," she rebukes sharply. "You should listen to what he has to say."

I let out another laugh, this one louder. "Alright."

"I'm serious. Maybe you should read this book. We could discuss it."

I turn to her as I point to the empty bed in front of us. "You do realize that Yisla would be dead if it weren't for voidance. What the effulgent wanted to do—what is probably written in that stupid book of yours—is let her die, if she was meant to. Which is complete bullshit."

I stand up, but she grabs my hand, preventing me from walking away.

"But what if we never came here?"

"What?"

She stands as well, coming close to me in the darkness. "I mean—what if we died when the airship crashed? You would have never been here, in this village."

"Then Yisla would have died."

Chimeline tilts her head up to gaze at the moonlight coming through the hole in the roof. "Don't you think that's important?" she asks, in a high pitch. "That maybe you and I are here for a reason?"

"No."

"Well, I think you misunderstand him. The effulgent never wanted Yisla to die. He just wished to let whatever was supposed to happen, happen. And maybe I'm part of this too, somehow. Maybe the Unnamed has been speaking to me. Telling me not to do things when I was instructed otherwise. He knows what we should do, and he knows that we are all part of something greater."

"Something greater?"

She nods.

"Like what?"

She shrugs. "Maybe he will let me know what he wants. In time."

I shake my head. "What do *you* want? What is your *something greater*?"

She clutches the book close. "I don't know yet. But I think that I will find it, traveling with you."

I glance at the book, which she holds lovingly. "Do me one favor. Just don't trade one master for another."

She wrinkles her nose curiously.

I push her bangs aside and gently touch her forehead with my finger.

"*This* is your master now, Chimeline."

She opens her mouth, about to say something, but joyful shouts break the silence.

It's the two sisters—they see us standing just inside the shelter.

Their eyes glow blue, orange, and red in the light of the fire, and they both stand and run over as if I am Father Wintertide himself, bearing an armful of honey candies.

Yisla drops to her knees in front of me, but I immediately pull her up, and they both wrap me in a tight hug that almost knocks me off my feet. When they pull their faces from my waist, I see tears in their eyes, and they excitedly talk over each other for my attention.

I silence both of them with my outstretched hands.

"I hear that you have made an excellent dinner. Is there any left for a tired, old man?"

They both erupt in invitation, leading me back to the fire.

I motion for Chimeline to come as well, but she shakes her head, continuing to stand where she is.

Yerla hands me the rest of the charred bird, wrapped in large clean leaves, and the three of us sit down on the stumps of old trees.

"I wish I could offer you more," Yerla tells me. "This was my best hen. She laid two eggs most days. I don't have anything else to give you."

"You don't owe me anything," I say, trying to keep my voice both kind and instructional. They both nod stoically, but then Yerla speaks up, her chin raised defiantly in the firelight.

"Can I ask you a question?"

"Of course."

"Why did you save him?"

"The effulgent?" I ask, after a pause. "Because, despite our differences, he deserves a chance at life. Just like your sister."

She tilts her head, and I stop eating for a moment.

"Listen to me, Yerla. I am glad that you freed me. I truly am. But please understand that what you did— stabbing another person—is never right. I know that you were scared for your sister, but you must always try to do what is right. And killing and hurting is almost never the right thing to do."

"But he locked you up."

I nod. "And that's only the start of our disagreements. But that doesn't mean we should resort to stabbing people in the back. Death comes for us all." I look at Yisla and then back to Yerla. "Unfortunately, both of you girls know this all too well, given the suffering you've been through. Don't you think the world gives us enough death on its own?"

Eventually, they nod and lean back into the shadows. Out of the corner of my eye, I notice that Chimeline is watching us from the house.

For a long time, everything is quiet. I return to tearing into both wings and a leg. The only sounds are my hasty eating, the crackle of the fire, and a flurry of bats flying overhead. Then, the sisters start up a private conversation, arms wrapped over each other's shoulders, all hushed giggles and whispered talking.

When I have finished the bird, I clear my throat and lick my fingers clean. "There is one other important thing to discuss," I say.

Yisla and Yerla break away from their huddle and look at me across the fire.

"Yisla, your body was invaded. I destroyed the invaders inside of you, but it's important that we understand the cause of them, or else you might be at risk of becoming sick again. Or your sister could get sick next time."

They look at each other fearfully and then back to me.

I finger the gold setting of my voidstone. "I wish Submaster Herrophilus was here. He would know exactly what to do. Exactly what questions to ask. But hopefully I can get to the bottom of this."

When I look back at the sisters, I realize that they have no idea what I am talking about.

"It usually comes from food or water," I say. "Improperly cooked food or contaminated water."

Both girls tilt their heads in confusion as a worried thought comes over me.

*The bird.*

I touch the voidstone and analyze the remains of the bones on the ground between my feet. I am looking for any sign of the coiled snakes that invaded Yisla's veins. But there is nothing.

Sighing, I let go.

"I had worried that perhaps your chickens are the cause. That the meat had turned."

"We never kill the chickens," they say in unison, and despite the gravity of my thoughts, I cannot help but smile at what remains of their innocence. "Tonight is special," adds Yerla.

"Yes, it is," I answer. "Thank you for that. It was an excellent dinner." Then I turn to the coop, which is a few feet away. "What about the eggs?"

Yerla speaks up again. "We always sell them fresh. Most of the time we don't even eat them—we get more money from selling them in the village and then buying maize."

I stand and walk to the coop. I open the rotting door and take a step inside, both sisters following me. The birds start to cluck, perhaps noticing a stranger in their midst.

"Do you need me to light a torch?" asks one of the girls. "We used to have a lantern, but we sold it."

"No," I say, waving her off with a hand.

Touching the voidstone again, I spend some time inspecting the entire room. Inside of the birds' bodies, inside of their eggs, inside of the droppings on the floor. Nothing resembles the grotesque spirals that had taken over Yisla.

I close the flimsy door. "It wasn't the chickens," I say.

Scratching my head, I meander back past the firepit and reenter the open-walled house. The kitchen table is full of feathers. Yerla must have prepared the bird there. The large clay urn I saw Yerla use at the well numerous times rests on it too.

I peer inside the urn.

"Are you thirsty?" Yerla says, at my side. She hands me a small, malformed clay cup from the nearby counter, next to the trough.

"Thank you," I say, taking it from her. I *am* thirsty, but before I dip the mug into the half-filled pot, I touch my voidstone again and analyze the water, checking it for the spirals.

It's clean as well.

After dipping my cup into the urn, I take a cautious sip. It tastes pure.

"I boiled it," adds Yerla.

"I don't understand," I eventually say, downing the rest of my cup and setting it on the table forcefully.

Both sisters are quiet, but Chimeline, who had been standing under the shade of the house the entire time, takes a step nearer. "What don't you understand?"

"Why Yisla became sick and Yerla didn't." I point to the coop. "The chickens are all fine. Eggs are all fine. This water came from the well in the center of town that everyone drinks from, and it has been boiled too. It's fine. I'm trying to think of what would have caused the invaders."

"Maybe there is no reason, other than the Unnamed wanted it to be so."

I glare at Chimeline, annoyed by her unexpected and irrational statement, but I don't say anything. I only silently reflect on how the effulgent and the graycloak have been busy proselytizing rubbish while I have been saving lives.

I turn back to the two girls. "Is there anything that you're not telling me? Anything that is different between you two?"

They look at each other in confusion.

"Think back to before you became sick," I say calmly to Yisla. "Was there something you did that Yerla did not do?"

Yerla replies for her. "I am older. I do most of the work. She only fetches the water in the morning while I build up the fire. Everything else we do together."

"From the well in the center of town," I add uselessly as I exhale, tapping the table with my empty mug.

I gaze out into the moonlit clearing—the dying fire, the swooping bats overhead, the faraway stars. How did all of this happen? Days ago, I was on my way south, flying through the skies in my airship to find Marine. Now I am in this ruin of a house trying to solve the mystery of a dying peasant. A girl who, if she died, would be mourned only by her equally doomed sister.

*Look how far I have steered off course.*

But my journey was destined for failure from the start, even before my airship crashed and burned in some farmer's field. The glittering prize had already been won by someone else.

*The man behind the veil.*

I am not so disillusioned to expect that my life will ever be the same. I will never get Marine back. I will never get my old station back, fleeing the citadel without permission as I did. But I *will* get my revenge for all that has happened—not only to me, but to every poor soul hurt with his voidance.

*Which must be why I am still here.*

A road laid with bricks of gold stretches between redemption and me. And each brick matters. Fiscarlo is one of them.

"Master Voider," says Yerla.

Tearing my gaze from the night sky, I look back down at the sisters.

"Tell him," she whispers to her younger sister, poking her in the arm.

Yisla looks up at me before dropping her gaze to the ground as she talks.

"I did not get the water from town," Yisla says.

I frown. "You didn't?"

"No."

"From a nearby stream, then?"

She shakes her head, her lips pressed tightly together.

"Tell the master voider," whispers Yerla again.

"There is another well," offers Yisla. "It is much closer than the one in the center of the village. I went to it because it is easier for me to carry water from there."

I look back to Yerla. "Then why did I see you at the village well when I was locked up in my cage?"

"I was curious about you. And I am stronger and can carry the water easier than Yisla. So I don't mind going into the village. The other well is far closer, but it is boarded up. After the voider left town, the effulgent told us not to use it. So what Yisla was doing was disobeying—"

"What?" I stoop to be at an even height with Yerla. "What about the voider?"

"There was another voider here. He left some time ago."

"I thought he fell . . ."

My mouth hangs open. The effulgent admitted that my student fell to his death, here in Fiscarlo. What Yerla had heard about him leaving town was probably a lie to cover up what really happened.

I gently grab Yerla by her shoulders. "What has he to do with this other well?"

"The voider was building it. He had built his own house just down the road, further from the village. A very nice house. He was digging his own well there, too. Not with his hands or tools but with black arcana. Just like you can do. It is just down the path a ways."

I let go of Yerla and turn back to Yisla. "You were taking water from this well?"

She nods. "One of the boards is loose."

Running my hand over my short hair, I turn to the older sister. "But you drank from this water too, did you not?"

She nods. "And the chickens too."

"Did you boil it?"

She nods.

"Yisla," I say, "did you drink directly from the well? Before bringing it back here to boil?"

She stares at the ground for a moment, drawing a line in the dirt with her bare foot.

"Yisla?" I ask gently. "This is very important, and I won't be angry with you if the answer is yes. Did you drink the water directly from the well?"

After a moment, she nods.

I stand back up. "That's it," I say quietly, turning to Chimeline. "That's the reason. She drank directly from a tainted well."

Chimeline has no reply. She only looks down at the white book in her hands, but she seems to be clutching it tighter than necessary.

"There's something in the water," I say. "And I have an idea of what it is."

# ANAXARCHIS' CAMP

It's the middle of the night, but that doesn't matter to anyone. The sisters can't sleep. After being so close to death, Yisla clings to the exuberance of waking life, and Yerla is content to be with her. As for Chimeline and me, after languishing in our cells for days, a night walk through a bamboo forest is a most welcome change. Besides, pink flecks the edge of the horizon. Sunrise is not too far away.

We are heading toward Anaxarchis' camp.

I never noticed it before, but the slender trail that I took here from the village cuts through the girls' dirt clearing and continues. It's this path that we follow.

We climb over a gentle hill and cross a creek. The bridge is nothing more than three downed trunks laid together and bound with rope. Yerla leads the four of us across it barefoot, a lit torch in her hand.

We reach another clearing, and immediately I understand why Yisla preferred this place. It's at least half the distance, compared to the village well.

"It's over there," Yerla says, gesturing to the right with her torch.

"Where's his house?" I ask.

She points to what looks like a dirt hill on the left. In the predawn light, it's impossible to discern what it is.

"I don't understand."

"He burned it to the ground."

"Who—the effulgent?"

"Yes."

"Why in Temberlain's Ashes did he do that?" I yell angrily.

"You should not swear, nor should you jump to conclusions," answers the effulgent.

The pale, bald man walks out of the forest clothed in white that reflects the moonlight.

I hear the children and Chimeline inhale in surprise.

"You were waiting for us?" Chimeline asks.

The effulgent nods, slowly walking into the clearing. "I always wake before sunrise, and I heard you at the sisters' camp," he says calmly. "So I knew that you would be coming here." He clears his throat and extends his hands at his sides in invitation, palms upward. "In many ways, the moment I heard of your crash, I knew that you would be coming here."

Instead of replying, I ignore the man and walk up to the ruins of the house.

The mound is not made of dirt, as I had previously thought, but ash. I also find some charred logs and iron hardware—the latter presumably for the doors and windows.

I turn and address the effulgent. "If you didn't burn it down, who did?"

He doesn't answer.

"It appears as if it was a perfectly good structure," I continue. "Made of timber and iron. Certainly more sound than any of the huts in your village."

The effulgent remains silent.

Stooping, I pick up a handful of white ash and let it fall through my fingers. "Who would have something to gain by burning down a voider's house?" I ask.

"I assure you, it wasn't me," the effulgent says. "I do not own the dark."

"You're lying," I answer, flicking the remaining ash to the ground as I stand. "Anaxarchis' work was a threat to you, wasn't it?"

"A lie is just another form of ownership," he says, without moving from his place.

Chimeline turns to me. "Dem, I don't think—"

"You don't understand how far back this goes," I say, cutting her off. I quickly walk past all of them, heading toward the well, which is situated more in the forest than the clearing. If Anaxarchis cut a path through these woods while he was still alive, it's overgrown now. In the faint pink light, I navigate around weeds, saplings, and downed twigs that snap.

"You don't want to talk about who burned down Anaxarchis' home? Fine. Let's talk about his death."

I reach the well.

It is far smaller than the one in the village, and simpler too. Anaxarchis used no stone, relying instead on a wooden canopy to house the rope and crank. It's fairly new—the wood has not even grayed with age. Someone shuttered the circular entrance with flat boards, just as the girls said.

I turn back to the others. The effulgent looks at me, his furrowed gaze a mixture of defiance and sadness.

I tap the boards with my palm. "What I want to know is, how did my trusted student end up at the bottom of this well?"

"What?" Chimeline says, though the word comes out as more of a gasp.

The effulgent says nothing, responding instead with an infuriating silence that only confirms my suspicions.

Turning back around, I touch my voidstone and shatter the boards to pieces.

And immediately, I have to back away due to the stench.

A horrendous rotting smell wafts over all of us.

Yisla says mutedly from behind a hand, "It was not like this before."

"There is something dead in there," Yerla adds.

I turn to the sisters. "Go now and wake the graycloak, and bring her back here."

They look back and forth between the effulgent and me with wide eyes.

"You are worried that she will be angry at you for waking her," I surmise. "Don't be. Tell her that I sent you. Tell her that I am at the voider's well with her father, and that we're about to discover his little secret together."

"Master Voider, you don't have to do this," the effulgent utters.

"Oh, I think I do. This is part of the lesson."

The children nod and scamper away, carrying the torch with them.

"Tell her to bring a shovel from the smithy," I call out.

They shout confirmations and continue. I watch the ring of flickering orange disappear into the shadows of the forest.

"I freely admit it," the effulgent finally says, his voice louder and containing more emotion than I have heard thus far. "As I have admitted to you in the past. There is no reason to bring up the dead. That is why I shuttered the well. To protect everyone."

"You mean to protect yourself."

He shakes his head. "There is no crime here, despite what you think. I did not murder him. He fell in accidentally."

"Of course," I say, my voice spilling over with sarcasm. "How clumsy of him."

"I do not lie, Master Voider! Lies are just another form of ownership. But, then again, I hardly expect someone lost within black arcana to understand such things!"

The hypocrisy of this man is more than I can handle.

I lunge toward him, grab a fistful of his white silken robes, and pull him back with me to the edge of the well. In our twisted embrace, we lean precariously over what remains of the low, shattered boards. They groan as I force him to stare into the blackness with me.

And see what he has done.

I had envisioned my student's body lying upright, staring back at us with a final look of betrayal. But all I see is a darkened body crumpled on its side, barely recognizable. It bisects the moon's reflection in the water.

"Tell me," I say, through clenched teeth, his head by my side. "How exactly did this *accident* happen?"

He swallows nervously. "We were having a quarrel. It became heated. He lost his reason and lunged at me—much like you are doing now—and we grappled. He slipped and fell in this hole. I give you my word. I shuttered it only to prevent others—"

"That is what was killing Yisla!" I shout, pulling both of us up to safety. "She was drinking from this well because she didn't know any better. She's just a child! She was drinking corpse water!"

His wide eyes dart to Chimeline and then back to me. "But I never meant—"

"These people trusted you," I say, cutting him off while pushing him away. "Instead, your secrets are killing the very people you claim to protect. And all you have to say for yourself is that your Unnamed wills it."

"The Unnamed has willed all—"

"That's horseshit!" I shout. "You're nothing more than a common peddler. You should be ashamed of yourself."

The effulgent closes his eyes and takes a deep breath, and then begins coughing uncontrollably, likely a result of the stench.

I can see my words sink in, so I walk back to the ash hill, regaining some much-needed composure and fresh air. The effulgent rushes toward the opposite side of the clearing, puts his hands on his knees, and retches into the dirt.

"It was the house, wasn't it?" I ask after a while, staring into the ruins. "That is what the fight was all about."

My voice comes out in little more than a whisper. The rage has drained everything else out of me, much the same way this fire has left only ashes behind. The predawn forest is so calm that I know he can hear me.

"It was because Anaxarchis could easily build solid structures for every man, woman, and child in this village," I add. "That was a threat to you. Homes that could be considered luxurious. Structures so well-built they would be points of pride. Possessions, even. And if they started feeling good about their *homes*, who knows what else they'd feel good about. They might even feel good enough to not need you anymore."

The shrill crow of a rooster reaches us from the girls' camp nearby.

"You are very observant, Master Voider," he eventually says, still looking down at the ground as his retching stops. "The Unnamed has obviously chosen you, whether you curse him or not."

I ignore his twisted compliment.

"But it was not I who burned down his house," he adds.

"Well then, who did?"

"I don't know!" he answers, his voice loud. He calms himself. "The truth is, it could've been any of the villagers. The black arcana is frowned upon here, and—"

"It's frowned upon because of you!"

"The truth is persuasive."

Before I can respond, he quickly adds, "Your student thought it was me, but it wasn't. I would never do such a thing. I do not own the dark."

The effulgent spits one last time. Then, standing up straight, he stares sadly at me and wipes his mouth with his gleaming sleeve. And for the first time, I think I believe him.

But even so, covering up Anaxarchis' death is unacceptable.

"When the girls get back," I say to him, "you are going to admit to your daughter what you have done. And then, you will dig Anaxarchis' grave."

He nods.

Silently, I stumble back to the well. I have nothing left to say, only things left to do.

Grabbing my voidstone, I begin to raise the dead.

# LEAVING FISCARLO

As I break from the colorless, windswept world of the void, the harsh morning light hits me. I have to close my eyes and sit down against the flimsy wood of the well. Phantom trails dance in my vision.

While my eyesight adjusts, I hear the sound of shoveling punctuated by deep breaths and wonder who is more exhausted—the effulgent or I?

During my brief time in the void, the girls returned with the graycloak. The three of them huddle around Chimeline in the distance. They all sit cross-legged upon a rare patch of grass in the sunlight, while the towering bamboo trees surrounding the clearing whisper in the breeze.

They are roughly the same age, but the women look profoundly different from each other. Chimeline has caramel-colored skin and glossy black hair, while the skin of the dark and bald graycloak reflects the sun like oiled metal.

Chimeline reads from her copy of the Book of Unwanting. She points to something on the page and then looks sideways to the graycloak for approval. The graycloak nods and says something in reply.

Meanwhile, much closer to me, the effulgent has dug an impressive grave. He stands in it now, and all I can see of him is his soiled face and upper chest.

"That's deep enough," I say.

He startles and stops working, wiping his brow with his cloak.

"I didn't realize that you had finished," he says.

I nod. "I also purified the well. You don't need to keep it shuttered anymore."

He tosses the shovel out. "At least Yisla will be pleased," he says. I detect a trace of annoyance in his voice, as if using voidance to do a good deed invalidates the deed.

He looks around while he wipes his hands on his chest. "Can you help me out?"

I slowly stand and approach the grave, feeling a little light-headed as I pass the recently raised body of Anaxarchis.

It no longer resembles my student. It doesn't even look human. The body is gray and bloated, like some deep-sea creature my submaster discovered in Blackscar. Even the tatters of his cloak resemble strands of seaweed. I would doubt that the body was his if not for the voidstone still hung around his swollen neck.

Subtly, I rip the necklace off the body and stuff it in my pocket before walking over to the grave.

With my higher vantage point, I can see that the effulgent is entirely covered in dirt and sweat—it's pasted on his skin and clothes. He did not remove his formal white cloak before getting to work. It almost seems to me that this was done on purpose—an outer sign of his inner turmoil.

Kneeling in the dirt, I grasp his wrist and pull him up. He gives me an utterance of thanks.

Then, without speaking, we both grab a gray arm and carefully pull the decaying body of my student into the hole. I am worried that the body has decomposed to the point that the arms might rip off in place, but they hold.

The corpse makes a wet sound as it falls.

For a moment, the two of us stand there at the edge of the grave, looking down upon the twisted remains. The effulgent walks around it, picks up the only shovel, and begins filling the hole, using the mound of dirt he recently created.

I sit down in the shade and watch him, feeling vindicated. My fury has burned itself out.

Halfway through the task, the effulgent stumbles. He regains his footing, preventing himself from falling into the grave. But this convinces him to take a break. He leans his head and arms on the shovel's upright handle, his chest heaving.

The daughter sees all of this from the sunlit clearing, stands, and quickly walks over.

"Your Effulgency," she says formally, "I have asked you—repeatedly—if I can help, and I am now asking again. Will you relent?"

"No," he snaps, uncharacteristically. "I committed the offense here, and therefore the sentence is mine to bear."

"But you are clearly spent."

He nods in the direction of the others and softens his tone. "I see you teaching the others the way of unwanting. That is the place for you. Not here. Not with me."

She puts her hand on the shovel. "My place is always with you."

He wipes his hairless brow with his arm and then shakes his head. "You do not realize it yet, but the time has come for you to enter the fullness of the effulgency."

This seems to take her off guard. "I don't understand."

"The Unnamed has plans for me," he says, giving me an ever-so-brief glance. "It appears that he is leading me away from Fiscarlo."

She lets go of the shovel and stands straighter. "But my place is by your side."

"No," he responds. "Your place is where you already are—with the ones who will listen to the teachings. You make me proud. You are ready."

For a moment, all the daughter does is stare at her father. A strong breeze rips through the camp. The tall bamboo trees sway.

"You're leaving," she says, incredulously. It is not a question.

Instead of replying, the effulgent picks up the shovel and begins filling the grave again.

"You're *leaving* me?" the graycloak repeats, but this time her voice is much louder.

"It is the will of the Unnamed."

She hesitates only a moment, a rapid conflict of emotions crossing her pale face. Then she takes a step toward him and says, "But you can't leave!"

The effulgent slams the edge of the shovel into the dirt and looks up at her.

And then something very strange happens.

They begin conversing in another tongue.

I see their mouths moving, but I hear whispered sounds, almost like the wind. I look up to the treetops, momentarily confused, thinking that another strong breeze has made its way through the clearing, but the bamboo is motionless.

No. It's coming from the two people in front of me.

*I've heard this language before, but I can't remember where.*

Then, suddenly, they both turn to me and go silent, as if they know that I've witnessed something private.

"We will talk about this later," says the effulgent, in the Northern tongue. "After I am done here."

The daughter's lips quiver as she wipes a tear from her eye. She keeps further tears at bay, breathing in and out a few times before testing out a smile to no one. Only then does she walk back to the children and Chimeline, though I see her hands are balled into fists.

The effulgent puts his hand on the upright shovel, but he's clearly overcome, both physically and emotionally. As he stares at the ground, an unexpected feeling stirs in me.

My feeling of vindication is gone. It's been buried with Anaxarchis' body. Now, I feel guilt, as I sit idly by while the effulgent toils. If I am honest with myself, I am just as much to blame for Anaxarchis' death as he is. I sent him here, alone. A student, unprepared.

I get up, silently take the shovel from the effulgent, and begin to fill the remainder of the grave.

As the layers of soil grow, I hope that we are burying more than just a body. I hope that this dirt covers our fears and prejudices, too. That every shovelful marks a small step toward reconciliation, creates a common ground between faith and reason.

I've heard the effulgency talk about miracles, acts performed by their supposed Unnamed.

It just might take one of them for this to come true.


Anaxarchis' grave is filled by midday.

The effulgent is adamant that we return to the temple before departing. So after we say our goodbyes to Yisla and Yerla, Chimeline and I reluctantly do so.

I remind him that I need horses. At least one large one for Chimeline and me. Preferably two, to carry each of us individually. And some gold. It was stupid of me not to bring any, but I never planned for this journey. I offer to sign a promissory note, which he could take to the citadel for repayment.

He will have none of it. He says that beasts of burden are creatures of the dirt. And like the dirt, they are not to be bought and sold. He therefore freely gives me as many horses and as much gold as I need for my journey, which I graciously accept.

He also says there is one more thing I need to take with me. He won't tell me what it is, only that he needs to retrieve it from the temple.

And so, we wait.

Chimeline and I sit on a decorative iron bench within the temple's shaded, stone-walled garden. Fragrant flowering vines in shades of blue and lavender crawl up the walls. Birds chirp from a gnarled tree above.

It's so beautiful here, so full of cavalier life, that I can almost forget that my student is dead.

Chimeline is preoccupied with the pond. She dips her feet in the clear water and laughs as goldfish nibble at her toes. But when she looks at me, her smile dissipates, like the ripples below.

"What's wrong?" she asks.

I hunch my shoulders and feel a different sort of guilt—the last thing I want to do is unnecessarily drag her into the mire of my thoughts. "It's nothing."

She bites her lip. "No, something is wrong. Tell me."

After a pause, I give a hesitant nod. "I was just thinking about Anaxarchis. That's all."

"It was not your fault."

"Actually, it was. Partially, at least."

She kicks her feet out repeatedly, letting the water droplets fly away, but her face is all seriousness. "Why do you say that?"

"He was an excellent student. But he wasn't made for war. That's why I picked him to come here, to save him from the king's idiotic draft. To save him from harm." I shake my head. "Anaxarchis was five feet tall. One hundred and thirty pounds. He was so timid, but he had the biggest of hearts."

She puts her hand on mine.

"Sometimes all you can do is point people in the right direction."

Her kind words make me smile, but they don't help.

"He gave me a gift when he graduated. It's in my office, hanging upon the wall."

"A painting?"

I shake my head. "Anaxarchis came from a family of wainwrights. So he carved for me a wheel made of millionescent wood."

She wrinkles her nose. "A wheel?"

"It's meant to be displayed, not used. There are four inscriptions on it. Not done with voidance but with a chisel. *Happiness*, *Loss*, *Suffering*, and *Hope*. Those are what he called life's four stages."

With my free hand, I gesture in midair, drawing a circle in front of us. "Just as a wheel continually turns, our lives continually change. If we find ourselves caught up in love or overwhelming happiness, it will not last. Just as nothing done with voidance lasts. The world moves on."

I move my finger a quarter of the way down the wheel.

"Love eventually leaves, happiness wanes."

"That's horrible, Dem."

I nod. "I know. But from my experience, it's true."

I move my finger to the bottom of the wheel. "Then, when we think it's as bad as it can get, it gets worse. We suffer. Sometimes greatly."

I keep moving my finger through the air until it's on the other side, almost near the top. "But we are strong, and we rise out of our suffering wrapped in hope. Elusive happiness is out there, to be found again. The wheel continues to turn."

I withdraw my hand and wipe my eyes with it.

Chimeline squeezes the other. "It sounds like a beautiful gift from a student who cherished their teacher."

I nod. "Yes, it was." I take a large breath to help push away the thought. "So, anyway, that is what I was thinking about. I was thinking about Anaxarchis' wheel. I was wondering if it was still turning."

Shortly past twelvebell, the effulgent finally steps out of the temple and into the small garden. He's cleaned himself up and wears a striking change of clothes. Gone is the white effulgency cloak. Instead of this, he's dressed as a graycloak—with a putty-colored burlap cloak over his gray shirt, a braided belt, and a slightly darker pair of pants. He also wears dark-brown boots made for riding.

As I look upon him in shock, he raises his cloak's thick hood around his bald head, hiding most of his face in shadow.

"Are you ready?" he asks me.

I nod and look back at Chimeline. She's standing now, strapping her new sandals on and grabbing the Book of Unwanting from a nearby stone pedestal.

As recently as this morning, I would have wagered that Chimeline would stay here in Fiscarlo. She is obviously taken with the ways of the effulgency. And regardless of the reason, I would have been fine with her decision to stay. She is a resourceful, graceful woman, but my path forward is not going to be easy. I warned her of this before—danger lies ahead. Far more danger than drinking from the wrong well.

But here she is, seemingly as eager as I am to leave.

"The horses are waiting outside," the effulgent adds.

He leads us through a side door of the temple, into the soft, colored light of the main room, and then back outside, via the wide front doors. There, at the bottom of the steps, a wrinkled villager holds the reins of three horses. I immediately recognize him as the one who brought Yerla to the temple on a leash. He glares at me.

The graycloak stands there too, but she looks remarkably different. She wears a blindingly white cloak that contrasts her dark skin. It goes all the way to the dirt. She takes a few steps to meet us, and as she moves, the ripples in the fabric reflect the sun so effectively that I have to look away.

When I turn back, I see her hug her father tightly, tears falling down her smooth face.

Sensing that the father and daughter need privacy, I turn to Chimeline and motion to the waiting horses. We walk over together, and I pick out the smaller, tan one for her. She pats the side of its muzzle in greeting, and the horse seems to study her with its massive eyes. I'm about to help Chimeline up when she gathers her white-lace dress around her hips and climbs into the saddle with surprising ease.

With far less elegance, I mount my black-and-white-spotted horse. It shakes its head, braying, as I gather the reins from the villager. I have already settled into the saddle when the effulgent pulls away from his daughter. He climbs atop the third horse, a black mare that flicks its tail as if in impatience.

"I wager it's pointless to ask you to stay," I say.

He nods. "I have made my decision."

"Even though the lesson has ended and your village needs you more than I do."

He turns his face, shadowed under the hood, to me. "You are wrong. The lesson is not yet finished."

I shake my head in annoyance. I had been looking forward to leaving this impoverished village behind me. I had been looking forward to a brisk afternoon ride southward with Chimeline. Whatever awaits us on this journey cannot be stranger than what has transpired here. But this effulgent tagging along—he's going to be a constant reminder of it. Wherever we go, a small piece of Fiscarlo will be with me as well.

My horse whinnies, dragging me from my thoughts.

I let out a small sardonic laugh. "That's the final thing, isn't it?"

He looks at me from beneath his gray hood.

"You said that I needed to take one more thing with me on my journey. Something that you needed to retrieve. You meant yourself."

"Ah. No," he says, as he pats his thigh pockets. "I have something for Chimeline."

I am surprised that he used her name. Perhaps he is acclimating to reason.

He guides his horse over to ours and extends his upturned palm to Chimeline. On it rests a clear glass vial containing a grayish liquid. "This was on the black robe you were wearing when you crashed. It seemed important."

"What is that?" I ask.

Chimeline ignores me, takes the vial carefully between her thumb and forefinger, and places it in a small compartment in her saddlebag. Only then does she flash a smile and thank the effulgent.

"What is that?" I repeat.

"The extract of jasmine leaves," she says quickly. "From the archipelago. It's something of a good luck charm."

She does not look at me as she talks, but I see the effulgent studying her intently from within the darkness of his hood.

Part of me is intrigued by this peculiar interaction, but the overwhelming part of me that wishes to flee this village wins out.

"Alright then," I say impatiently, alternating my gaze between them. "Let's go."

I squeeze my legs and gently direct my horse down the path, away from the temple and through a row of at least a hundred slender palms. The high sun shines between the trunks, but it's already started to fall into the west. It's situated to the right of me, which means that I am headed in the correct direction.

South, and away from this cursed place.

But before we've passed a dozen trees, the graycloak yells out behind us, and I stop, cursing while I turn my horse a bit.

She's running down the road, her dress causing rays of reflected sun to flicker in the half-shade. But before she approaches us, she stops suddenly in place, at least twenty feet away, as if she's afraid to come any closer.

The effulgent pulls back his hood but stays perched upon his horse.

"It was me," she yells out to her father, and then she meets my gaze briefly, before turning back to him. "I was the one who burned down the voider's house."

She stands straighter, steeling herself for her father's reaction. Her gown shimmers in the wind.

The effulgent does not say a word.

"I wanted you to know, so that I would no longer own this secret. I do not own the dark."

Everyone looks at the effulgent now, waiting for his reaction. He doesn't nod, nor does he shake his head. He doesn't even look at his daughter, who begins to tear up. He simply pulls up his hood once again, slaps the reins, and continues south, down the dirt road.

"Don't you have anything to say?" she calls out to his back.

"Be nothing," he finally says, almost flippantly. His voice is weak, and he barely turns his head.

"Be nothing? I did it for you!" she yells. And then much softer, she says, almost to herself, "I did it for you, Father."

*Father.*

I turn again, and for a long time, I watch the man on horseback head down the road. I keep wondering if he will turn back to glance at his daughter one last time. Offer some parting gesture of intimacy. Offer some final words besides the common salutation.

But he doesn't turn back. His body seems lifeless. As the beast moves, its burden sways side to side, as if it is governed only by the forces of the external world and nothing else. A heavy sack of grain. Not once does the effulgent adjust his position on the saddle. He remains motionless, with his head cast slightly downward, even after he has become only a gray shape in the distance.

*He was telling the truth the entire time.*

"I should go and talk to her," Chimeline says.

I turn to her and nod. "Perhaps you should stay here in Fiscarlo. It will certainly be the safer option."

"I want to go with you."

"If you're coming with me, we leave now."

Chimeline looks empathetically at the woman, obviously conflicted. The graycloak has dropped to her knees, and both of her hands cover her face.

I surprise myself by studying Chimeline as a different sort of conflict arises within me.

I want her to come with me more than I care to admit.

"Alright."

I feel a tremble of relief.

"She is a strong woman," Chimeline adds. "She'll get over it. Just like I did."

I open my mouth to ask her what she means, but I sense that this is not the right time or place.

So we turn our horses south and follow the effulgent, who is now but a dot on the hilltop. As we catch up, the shouts and laughter of two distant children are carried on the breeze. They're running full speed through the tall grasses, but they cannot match the pace of our horses.

It's Yisla and Yerla, waving goodbye.

# PART THREE

# THE SKULLMAN

# THE WINDS OF GALES

During the first day and night, the three of us barely speak to one another.

The effulgent is even more distant than usual. Despite the sunshine, he keeps his gray hood pulled up around his head, as if he wants to shut out the entire world. The only thing the two of us speak about is navigation.

Fiscarlo is a remote town. It's an entire day's journey on horseback to Xi Bay Road, which is one of the thoroughfares that cuts through the Northern Kingdom. Running parallel to the River Xi, the road extends all the way to Xi Bay. We agree that we'll make better progress on a well-maintained, level road than on uneven paths full of boulders, rain-washed gullies, and dead ends.

Chimeline spends most of the day lost in thought. As the sun begins to fall, she asks us to stop so that she can find her blanket in the saddlebag. As she tugs the blanket free, her glass vial of jasmine extract falls upon the rocky ground, and she breathes in quickly. I turn at the sound, but luckily, it doesn't shatter, and she stuffs it back inside the bag without a word.

It seems I am the only content one on our journey, knowing that I am on my way south again toward Marine and the veiled man.

But I keep even this optimism guarded.

I desperately need a sign. Some evidence that I am on the right path. Yes, I am headed south, but I still have no idea where the two are headed. The airship could've taken them anywhere by now, although it's a safe bet they didn't cross into the Southern Kingdom. We're at war. Any airship flying south of the border would be shot down by Xian flamebowmen or voiders. Which means that their destination is probably somewhere between Xi Bay and me.

*Destination.*

I keep wondering if they were being pushed or pulled. Four nights ago, when they left in a rush, were they fleeing the king's wrath or some other danger? What if the veiled man was a Xian spy, his cover blown? Is it possible that they have no destination at all and are simply trying to run away as far and as fast as they can?

I doubt it. There must be something drawing them south.

The rogue lab that Chimeline and I stumbled across never strays far from my thoughts. It was filled with sick military applications of voidance. The harem women were sent there for tests, with three shallow graves their only repayment. And Chimeline said that the king knew.

Something dark and secret happened there, and I fear that it's still happening now, somewhere south of us. Something the king would not tell me, since he knew I would not approve of it.

His slurred words from our last dinner together come to mind. He'd had too much to drink and had let his guard down.

*There are some things I can never tell you. I'd like to, but I know you'd disagree, and you'd be too proud to fall in line. I don't want to break you, Dem. So I keep you safe, instead.*

Slowly, my suspicions harden into stone blocks in my mind, building a foundation of hatred. I will make this sad joke of a king eat his words. Whatever he's doing with the help of the veiled man, I'm going to find out. And I'm going to stop him.

And Marine? What is her involvement in all of this? Is she a lover or an accomplice? And which is worse than the other?

I have too many questions and too few answers.

All of this is pure conjecture. My fortress of hatred is built upon a shaky foundation. What I need is proof, something beyond a missing airship and a black-pitch stain.

Desperate for information, I approach everyone I meet on the broken-down road. A few farmers with their rusty plows. Two mothers cradling babies, exchanging milk for maize. A royal surveyor from the tax authority. I am really hoping this last one might have heard something, but all I receive is a shake of his head as he drives a painted spike into the ground.

I must have patience.

Nobody is invisible. Everyone leaves some trace of their passing. Especially a voider masked in a blur, traveling with the most beautiful woman in the Northern Kingdom.

The next morning, as we ride through Gales, a wicked thought comes to me.

"This is where you were going to send your daughter with my voidstone," I say, giving my spotted horse a nudge so it rides to the right of the effulgent's dark one. I purposely use the words *your daughter*, like an alley thief stabbing someone in the back with a dagger. But it's not his gold I want. It's his reaction.

Still, the effulgent remains predictably silent.

"You know, she called you father," I add, thrusting again with the knife. "Back in Fiscarlo. You were already a ways off, so you probably didn't hear her."

More silence, so I look in all directions as we pass through Gales.

There must be two dozen windmills dotting the golden fields, but none of them are moving. I look for villagers, wanting to ask them if they saw an airship, but nobody is around. The stillness—both within us and outside us—is disconcerting.

He draws back his hood and looks at me with cavernous eyes. "The events of the last few days have been too much for her to bear. I will pray upon it."

Chimeline utters a short laugh behind us.

Surprised, I turn and look at her. Despite the pleasant weather, she still has the colored patchwork blanket wrapped around her, hiding most of her white-lace dress. She shakes her head as she surveys the calm landscape.

"You have an opinion, Chimeline?" I ask her, eager to have some dialogue after almost an entire day and night of introspection.

For a moment, she seems to weigh her desire to share her opinion against her caution to not offend anyone. Eventually, her desire wins out, and she nudges her tan horse to the right of mine, so that I am between the effulgent and her.

"If you're going to pray, perhaps you should be praying for forgiveness."

"Are you referring to the new effulgent, who took my place?"

"Yes! I'm referring to your daughter!" Chimeline replies, with surprising forwardness.

He winces. Then he alternates his gaze between the two of us with what looks like summoned patience. "That term is not on the way of unwanting. One does not own the living." His stare settles upon her. "But to address your comment, I imagine that I will never see her again, unless the Unnamed wills it."

"But she loves you—she *needs* you," Chimeline replies. "Can't you see that?"

He takes a deep breath. "You say 'love,' but you do not mean it. True love does not mean clutching to the transient things of this world. It is the absolute giving of one's self. She knows this. She knows that she gives all of herself to the Unnamed and so do I. Becoming an effulgent has been her calling ever since birth." He looks down at her, riding by his side. "Did you not read this in the Book of Unwanting?"

Chimeline nods weakly, mumbling something.

"Can you speak up, child?"

"I'm not sure that I agree."

I look to the effulgent to gauge his reaction. Surprisingly, it's not one of annoyance or disapproval. Instead, he only nods and says, "The way of unwanting is no easy path. There are very few who choose to walk it. Many who attempt to eventually leave."

"The way that you said goodbye to her wasn't right. It was cruel." She gathers up the blanket around herself tighter. "When you said 'be nothing,' you might as well have said 'you are nothing.'"

He narrows his eyes in confusion. "Those two phrases mean completely different things."

"Ugh!" She lifts her hands underneath her blanket. "You have no idea."

He tilts his head.

"How much you're hurting her," she finishes.

"I don't see how saying 'be nothing' has any—"

"It hurts!" she yells, her boldness waxing. "Alright? It hurts, more than anything you can imagine. I don't care if she's a graycloak or not. Sure, half of her comes from your bloodline. But the other half of her is normal. She had a Xian mother, didn't she?"

"That implies ownership—"

"Did she, or did she not?"

His expression is one of tolerance. "I suppose you could say that."

"Well, do you think she was born without needs? Like your hairless skin? Or do you think she's just a scared girl who never knew her mother or Xian heritage and all she had in this world was a distant father, and now she doesn't even have that?"

As she uses her blanket to wipe her eyes, a sad smile crosses my face. I admire her courage. She's baring her emotions to two ill-tempered men—an effulgent and a master voider. When she was in the harem, emotions were probably one thing that she was never asked to share. In the short time that I have known her I have never seen her this way, but it feels right. I only wish that these emotions were not rooted in pain.

I lean to the right, closer to her. "Are you okay?" I ask.

"I'm fine," she snaps. She doesn't seem done speaking to the effulgent. Looking past me to him, she says, "You remind me of my father when I was young. It took me years to realize it, but he didn't love me for who I am. He loved me for the role for which I was destined. And you . . . you are the same way with your daughter. It sickens me."

"One does not own the darkness," warns the effulgent.

"My father is not dead."

"But your memories can be darkness. You must give them up. Forget them. Allow your mind to be filled with the Unnamed—"

"Are you seriously telling her not to remember her past?" I ask.

"As I said, memories can be darkness."

"But we learn from that darkness," I say. "The entire university is built upon such philosophy—the method of systematically repeating your failures until you succeed. Burying your head in the sand accomplishes nothing. It is the absence of reason."

The effulgent doesn't respond.

Chimeline turns to him, a pointed finger exiting the folds of her blanket. "What you have done to your daughter is wrong. She's no different from any child. All she wants is to be loved by you. If only you would listen to her without judgment and let her live the life she wants to live instead of the one which you thrust upon her."

I can tell the effulgent desperately wants to say something, but by now Chimeline has started to tear up, and he seems to have the wisdom to favor silence over proclamation.

"That is why I don't agree with what is in that book. If holding back all of those words and feelings is part of the way of unwanting, then that is a road which I do not wish to travel."

I let out a deep exhale.

We're quickly approaching a line of thick trees. The way ahead goes into a shaded tunnel made of arching leaves and branches.

"We should reach Xi Bay Road by nightfall," says the effulgent, perhaps changing the subject on purpose. "It is on the other side of this forest."

He gently kicks the side of his horse and the animal trots ahead.

Chimeline remains at my side. Her patchwork blanket whips around her as a breeze comes in from across the fields.

"We must be careful," the effulgent adds over his shoulder. "Past this forest is plantation country. There are hilma fields."

I let out a sharp laugh. "Are you worried that we'll have the sudden urge to smoke it?"

"It is not the drug that I am worried about, Master Voider. It is the hideous men who cultivate it."

I wave him off. "If we stay on Xi Bay Road, we'll be fine. Any hilma plantations will be the king's."

He shakes his head. "I do not share your confidence. There is a war going on to the south that has sapped the king's resources. The countryside has suffered. Lawlessness is prevalent. The way of unwanting is not taken. There could be skullmen."

"Skullmen," I murmur.

"I have seen these hilma growers with my own eyes. They must know the evil that they do, since they disguise themselves from the world."

Chimeline looks at me, motioning to her face. "They paint skulls on their face?"

"Sometimes," I say, trying to sound reassuring.

"Fear not," the effulgent calls out from up ahead. "The Unnamed will protect us."

Shaking my head in frustration, I exhale and stop my horse, just to put some space between us. The irony is too much. It's inconceivable that this man chides me for my confidence in the things of this world while blindly trusting in ghosts.

I turn around to catch a final glimpse of the sunlit clearing before entering the cool shade.

As we were arguing, we passed through the entire sleepy town of Gales without seeing a single soul.

But something is different. The breeze has picked up.

The windmills are spinning.

# RED PETALS

The second day on Xi Bay Road, the first red petals blow in on the wind.

The dense forest we passed through has thinned out, and the terrain has become rocky, almost barren and desertlike, even though plenty of grasses still poke out from the ground. Trees dot the landscape, but the oaks, pines, and willows of the north have diminished considerably. I count a few palms, but here, millionescent trees reign supreme. Entire towering lines of them hug the road and mark the boundaries of neighboring plots of land. Their glimmering leaves flicker on their branches like sequins. Gold leaves that will never fall.

The dusty breeze carries a maroon petal up from the gravelly surface of the road, past my horse's feet, and I catch it in my hands, studying it.

"May I see that?" Chimeline asks. She's riding to the right of me.

I hand the flower to her and watch as she brings it to her nose and breathes in deeply.

"Hilma," she says, as she lets go, letting it join the hundreds of others. "I recognize the smell."

On the other side of her, the effulgent nods. "I have seen these flowers. Red, like the blood upon the hands of everyone who partakes in this evil."

"These don't look like hilma fields," I say, looking out at the plantations that flank the road, past the millionescent trees. I don't see any color there—just row upon row of waist-high, brown-green plants baking in the sun.

"They aren't," says the effulgent. "The fields on this side of the forest are mostly cotton and tobacco."

"Then where are these petals coming from?" I ask.

"We will find out soon enough," he answers, motioning to the crest in the road up ahead.

The effulgent is correct. We've been on a gradual incline for most of the morning, and within a halfbell we reach a meager summit. The ground levels off, the horizon drops slightly, and we can see into the distance.

We stop our horses and take in the view.

Patches of green, gray, brown, and tan are everywhere, all dissected with lines of gold from the millionescents. But about a half-king-mile away is a brilliant patch of red, a fresh wound upon the land. Speckles of crimson extend to the road, as if it has been touched by some artist's half-dry brush.

"There," the effulgent says, pointing. "We should stay clear of it. There will be skullmen."

"I don't want to deviate from the road," I answer. "We're making good time. Besides, I'm sure that's a royal plantation."

"How do you know?" asks Chimeline.

"It's not hidden. No rogue plantation would be situated directly off Xi Bay Road like that. It's too obvious."

I hold a hand over my eyes and try to make out any details. It looks as if there are people working in the fields, shapes moving within the huge parallelogram of red. A few observation towers sit above the field—small wooden houses perched upon thick beams with narrow ladders.

The effulgent looks at me and lowers his hood. Again, I'm drawn into his strangeness. Every time he does this, the utter smoothness of his face takes me by surprise. No eyebrows or facial hair whatsoever. A pristine mask. If it weren't for the sharp lines of his jaw, I would almost think that he wasn't a man at all.

"There was a side road a mile or so back," he says. "We might be able to take it west and head south a different way."

"We're not going out of our way," I say.

"Why seek out danger?" he asks, almost in a whisper, even though there are no others about. "Skullmen only know violence. They are beyond the way of unwanting."

"I'm not seeking out danger. I'm seeking out information. Somebody there may know something."

He huffs.

"Trust me," I add, as I nudge my horse forward. My body shifts upon the saddle as I feel the shallow decline of the road ahead. A moment later, the soft sound of horses' hooves on the gravel tells me that the two are following close behind.

"Do people smoke the petals?" asks Chimeline. I turn back and see that she's riding next to the effulgent and addressing him.

"No," he answers. "The flower is harmless. It's the sap that is turned into the evil drug."

"It's not entirely harmful," I say, loud enough for them to hear. "We have studied it at the university for generations, and there are many fields in the Northern Kingdom where it is grown safely. I am sure that the one ahead of us is this kind. Hilma, when used judiciously, can be very beneficial."

"How can you say that?" he asks.

"It is a painkiller," I answer. "Watered-down doses are given to our hospitals' sickest patients, to aid in their recovery. We've recently sent shipments south for the war."

"Such a waste," he replies.

I'm not sure if he's referring to the war itself or our wartime use of hilma, but I don't bother asking him to clarify.

"Imagine the pain that a soldier goes through after losing a limb," I say. "Our voiders can save a life, but they cannot take away pain. Pain is in the mind—it is off-limits to our power. That is why hilma can be useful."

"When pain is bestowed on us, it is a gift from the Unnamed," the effulgent says. "It is bestowed on us for a reason."

I feel a spark of anger in me and hold up my horse until the two catch up. "What if your Unnamed bestowed the hilma plant for a reason as well? Did you ever think about that?"

"Nothing evil can come from the Unnamed," he says dismissively. "It is humankind that turns it evil."

I shake my head at his readied remarks, and for a while we travel in silence. But then the effulgent continues.

"The plant goes through two main stages of development. The first stage is the blooming stage. These are the red flowers."

I turn to him. "And they are worthless?"

"Nothing from the Unnamed is worthless."

"You know what I mean," I snap. "I'm speaking about the petals being used as a drug."

He nods. "You are correct."

"They are beautiful, though," Chimeline adds.

"The second stage is the wilting stage," he says. "This is usually signaled by the petals falling off." He points to the hundreds of them that we're trampling over. "As you can see, the plantation we're approaching is just entering this second stage."

"And what happens then?"

"Each stem has a bulb on its tip—just underneath where the petals fell off. By now these bulbs have grown to the size of an egg, and they are engorged with sap."

"I've seen samples of that substance," I say.

"There is a special tool. A scorer, like a sharp fork. The workers use this to cut the sides of each bulb during the day. Overnight, the sap oozes out, and the next day it is hand-collected, bulb by bulb." He takes a deep breath in the dusty afternoon air. "I imagine that it's a tireless process enabled by forced labor."

"The workers of our royal plantations are treated very well," I interject.

"But what about the workers on the rogue ones?" he asks. "The ones run by skullmen? You think that these evil men care about the poor people working in the fields?"

"I've never seen a rogue plantation, so I really cannot say."

After a moment of silence, he replies. "That is the problem with you, isn't it?"

I look at him. His dark, inset eyes are filled with judgment.

"What in Temberlain's Ashes are you talking about?"

He nods, as if he has just convinced himself of a newfound belief. "You sit in the citadel, surrounded by luxury. Surrounded by the things that you perceive you own. You study black arcana and you work through odd experiments, but everything you see is distorted. Like a person talking into a seashell, you hear voices but they are your own. You are in a prison of your own comfort."

I give a bitter laugh. "I've seen more of the world than you."

"Maybe," he answers. "But I wager only the perfect places, which are really instances of the same thing. When you travel these roads to foreign lands, you are probably in a carriage, are you not? Surrounded by guards and servants, your windows covered with silk curtains."

I don't answer since I don't want to admit that he's mostly right.

"Have you ever seen an addict? Someone whose life has been destroyed by the very drug you proclaim is lifesaving?"

I purse my lips, knowing where he is headed. "One doesn't need to physically experience something in order to mentally comprehend it. I fully understand the risks of misuse. Risks exist with nearly everything—"

"It's not the same thing. Thinking something and feeling something are entirely different."

"Maybe for you." I sharply turn to him as my passions rise within me. Not hatred for this man. Rather, pride in my students. Great young men like the late Anaxarchis.

"You speak to me as if I were a child," I continue, "unaware of the poverty and injustice in this world. Don't you realize that this is why I have insisted on sending my brightest students into the countryside? To places like your cursed Fiscarlo? I don't have to do it. I could just submit to the king's demands and have them go to war with the rest of their class. But I care enough to fight for what's right. To give them up to the world. My best for the worst."

"But do you ever visit them?" Chimeline says, before the effulgent can reply.

I take a deep breath. "My students? No. My schedule does not allow it. But we have discoursed via letters, on occasion."

"And do they share with you their progress?"

I find myself vaguely nodding because the truth is harder to explain.

I recall when the last letters arrived from my most recent students. The ones I sent out after the war began. It was last wintertide. A half a year ago. One of the letters was from Anaxarchis. He asked me to send him a shipment of coffee and ink. And the others? Cleanthes? His responses were curt. He shared few details of his experiences, which I attributed to his busyness. Same with the others. They were mostly curious about citadelian developments up north. When I wrote back to them, it was mostly local news that I shared, along with words of affirmation and encouragement.

But now I wonder if I should be concerned. The reason I had not heard from Anaxarchis was because he was rotting in the bottom of a well. What does that mean for Cleanthes? The others before him? They have not returned my letters either.

"Dem?" she asks, pulling me out of my paranoid thoughts, and I clear my throat.

"Times are tough, Chimeline. My students may not have access to paper or parchment, and not many letter carriers go through the remote towns anymore. And the ones who do can become easily lost along the way."

"So you have no idea," the effulgent says.

"That's not what I said."

"I know, but that's what I heard. I do not doubt your noble efforts. Despite your black arcana and our war-hungry king, you are trying to make a positive difference. There is something to be said about that, but you are stumbling in the wilderness of your own making."

"Even your compliments are insulting."

"I only say the truth, Master Voider. You are not on the way of unwanting, and therefore you scatter your seeds on rocky ground." He looks down. "Anaxarchis. He was one of them, and only tragedy sprouted."

"Because you killed him!"

"One does not own the dark" is all he says. It's a maddening reply, and I have the urge to do him harm. But I simply close my eyes and focus on my breathing.

"I only hope that your other seeds have not suffered the same fate," he adds quietly.

"That will depend on if they run into any other clumsy effulgents."

"Look!" Chimeline shouts. I open my eyes and see that she is pointing ahead of us.

Movement against the blue sky captures my attention. It's coming from one of the wooden observation towers perched over the field of red.

Someone inside of it waves a black flag.

"What does that mean?" she asks.

"I don't know. Maybe they see us."

"It is not too late," warns the effulgent.

"I said we're not turning back."

"Unlike you, I've been to the imperfect places. And this is one of them. This is a rogue plantation."

"It can't be. I told you, we're right off Xi Bay Road. A rogue one would be well hidden from the royal guard. It's one of the king's."

"Then why are there no flags waving besides a black one? Why isn't the king's sigil being flown?"

I look back to the field and notice that he has a point. There are no royal accoutrements at all.

"Dem?" Chimeline asks me, concern obvious in her voice.

"Everything is going to be fine."

But nobody relaxes. We continue to ride in silence until we reach the corner of the incredibly large hilma field. The effulgent pulls his large hood back over his head.

The sweetness blows in on the wind, making me light-headed in the midday sun. Chimeline wrinkles her nose in a charming way, while the effulgent covers his mouth and nose with a cloth.

The sound of our horses' hooves upon the gravel goes silent, and I look down. The road underneath us has become an unbroken red carpet of soft dead flowers.

To the right, hundreds of workers stand hunchback in the field, spaced out across the narrow rows between the chest-high flowers. Both men and women, young and old. They are almost hidden within the wildness. But their headdresses give them away—white towels coiled high, probably meant to ward off the sun.

Chimeline cries out in surprise as a large muscular man exits the field to our right in wide strides. None of us saw him in the field since he's not wearing a white towel on his head. In fact, he is dressed entirely in black and has dark skin as well—a Xian man. He wears baggy black pants and a tight sleeveless shirt. A patch covers his right eye.

The only thing that *isn't* black is his face. A chalky-white skull is painted there.

"I told you," the effulgent mumbles.

# IL-COLU

Chimeline, the effulgent, and I pull our horses to a stop as the Xian man enters the red-carpeted road only a few feet in front of us.

He smiles, his white teeth perfectly matching his painted skull. His black eye patch is partially painted over.

He pulls a machete from his side and brandishes it at me. "Black cloak. You're a voider?"

"I am Master Voider Democryos," I answer loudly.

He grunts. "Lots of interesting things coming by here lately. At least you're on the ground, where we can reach you."

He twirls the machete in his hand.

Chimeline inhales sharply, and I see that three other skullmen wait at the edge of the field, kneeling within the shade of the hilma rows. They hold reeds to their mouths, probably ready to poison us with their darts.

"What did you say?" I ask the Xian man reflexively, even though I heard him perfectly fine.

"*Lots* of interesting things."

"Did you happen to—"

"Shut up. No sudden moves, voider. I'm going to take that stone of yours. Redskull's orders. You'll get it back once you're on your way."

Reflexively, I remove a hand from the reins and raise it to my voidstone, which is resting over my cloak and hanging from its gold necklace.

"Hey! I said no sudden moves!"

The Xian man takes a large step toward me, raising his machete over his shoulder, as if he is going to throw it.

Movement to my right makes me glance in that direction. All three skullmen in the shadows are now pointing their reeds at me.

"You touch it, you die."

"There is no reason to resort to—"

"Put it down!"

My hand hovers in midair, halfway between the reins and the stone, as I briefly ponder my options. I could grab hold of my voidstone and cut this Xian's throat, or simply sever the hand that is holding the knife. My eyes dart to the right—the shadows in the hilma rows. I could create a membrane of air that pushes their reeds through the backs of their necks. I could probably do all of this before they could blink, but I don't know if there are more of them out there, out of my range.

Besides, the Xian man's words haunt me. *Lots of interesting things coming by here lately.* He can't share information if he's dead.

I drop my hand.

"Did an airship pass by here?"

The Xian man wastes no time. He strides up next to my horse, reaches up with his free hand, and pulls my voidstone off. I wince as the gold chain snaps free from my neck, but I remind myself that I still have Anaxarchis' stone in my pants pocket.

"The redskull will be eager to meet you," he says, backing up.

Perhaps trying to remind me who's in charge, he bounces my voidstone in his palm a few times. The chain makes a crystalline sound in the golden midafternoon air.

I glance at Chimeline and see fear in her eyes while the effulgent sighs next to me, a different form of *I told you.*

I don't share their fear. Instead, I am full of a guarded excitement I have not felt since stumbling upon the rogue lab in the moonlight.

"An airship," I repeat, pointing to the sky. "A black sphere. Did you see one?"

He nods. "We tried shooting it down, but it was out of range."

"Did you see who was in it?"

"Two people."

"How many days—"

His head snaps up. "You can ask the redskull all these questions. Until then, shut your fucking mouth."

*They passed by here.*

The Xian man whistles, and the three other skullmen drop their reeds and come running onto the red road. They're all Northerners, tanned by the sun but not nearly as dark as the one with the eye patch.

"Get off your horses," he says gruffly, waving his machete in illustration.

"It's alright," I tell Chimeline and the effulgent as we dismount, but their petrified expressions do not change.

As we stand on solid ground, the other skullmen come near. Two of them silently grab the reins of my horse and the effulgent's, while the third Northerner slowly walks around our group, making no attempt to hide his interest.

He approaches the effulgent. "What's this? A graycloak?" he asks, peering into the shadows of the effulgent's putty-colored hood before roughly lowering it.

His eyes narrow suspiciously. "What sort of unholy business would put a voider and graycloak in the same party?"

Nobody answers. The Northerner's gaze passes right over me and lands on Chimeline. The whites of his eyes are not white at all but a saffron yellow, and when he flashes a crooked smile at her, his teeth are grayish green.

He looks at her from head to toe in gratuitous objectification.

"Got ourselves a little Scorpiontail," he says, as he reaches out and grabs the patchwork blanket off Chimeline's shoulders, revealing her white-lace dress. He lets the blanket slip through his hands onto the red petals at his feet.

"Jie, just take her fucking horse to the stables," says the Xian man.

"Shut it, il-Colu," he snaps, but he doesn't break eye contact with Chimeline. Instead, he slowly reaches back out to her, grabs one of her dress straps, and pulls it down over her shoulder to reveal her bare skin. She shivers, and I doubt that it has anything to do with the wind.

"Let go of her," I tell him.

He spins.

"You have no power here, voider. You ain't pig shit without your fucking stone." He briefly looks at me with an oily smile before turning back to Chimeline, eying her hungrily. "I'll let her go when I'm done with her."

My anger rises rapidly, and I find myself touching the gold chain of Anaxarchis' voidstone in my pocket. It's right there, at the ready, but I hesitate.

I have no way of knowing what danger lies ahead. If I use it now, I will lose any element of surprise with the redskull.

He pulls down her other dress strap, and I grind my teeth in frustration.

I will not let this depraved man reproduce the horrors of old.

Leaving the chain in my pocket, I lunge toward the yellow-eyed man, shoving him as hard as I can.

He stumbles but doesn't fall—he seems more surprised than anything. Recovering quickly, he turns toward me and approaches. My eyes go to the knife at his belt for only a moment, but that is all it takes for him to punch me squarely in the face.

I go down, hitting the back of my head against the road. Red petals float around me. Black spots dance in my vision. A swirl of black and red.

And then the glint of silver.

Legs straddling my body, he looms over me, brandishing his knife.

He lunges down and forward. But the Xian man reacts first.

A dark blur, he swings his machete, knocking the smaller blade out of the skullman's hand with an audible clang.

"Enough!" the Xian shouts deeply, looking at the two of us with his one eye. "Orders are to take all voiders alive!"

"He fucking touched me."

"I don't care. Take the horses and go."

Yellow Eyes flashes me a sick smile before standing upright.

"Not so quick," he says, rubbing his hand while backing up against Chimeline's tan horse. "Not until I have a go at this Scorpiontail. Ain't no orders about not killing no tail."

Slowly, I roll onto my side and spit out a mouthful of blood. The other two skullmen have taken out their knives. Both have crescent shapes.

"No one needs to know about her," one says to the Xian. "We'll bury her in the ditch."

"She's no voider," the third adds.

"Now, now," the effulgent suddenly proclaims. "There is no reason to resort to violence. We must be nothing. One does not own—"

"Shut up," the Xian man and Yellow Eyes say in unison.

For a moment, everyone is still, until the Xian speaks up. "We will all go to the redskull. Now. We have no idea who she is, or if he wants her."

"Then don't take a turn, old man. Probably can't fuck at your age anyway."

Another pause. "Don't do anything you're going to regret," the Xian says.

Yellow Eyes looks at him and spits. "If you say anything to the redskull about this, you gonna be the one to regret it. You fucking Xian. You ain't no helmsman here. You're just a one-eyed old man who won't see death coming before it's too late. You ain't nothing."

The Xian man alternates his gaze between the three Northerners, his one eye wide. I can tell now that he is different from them. The other three all have yellow eyes. Those of the one who hit me are the worst, but the other two have eyes nearly as yellow. The Xian's eye is clear. And he carries himself straight, his hands loose at his sides.

I find it odd that Yellow Eyes keeps calling the Xian an old man. He's probably around the same age as I am. And while the other skullman may be half our age, they don't look it. Their drug use has aged them prematurely.

The Xian is in impeccable shape, and the other three look emaciated and wrinkled. The Xian's hair is cut short, while the Northerners' hair is longer and tangled.

Yellow Eyes turns Chimeline around on her horse, which is now whining and stamping its feet in either excitement or agitation. Then he grabs both straps of her dress and rips it apart, tearing the lace down the middle.

Chimeline screams.

"You son of a bitch." I try to get up.

Quickly spinning, Yellow Eyes kicks me in the gut three times.

My breath is knocked out of me. The black spots return.

Someone tries to help me up, but my hands slip on the flowers and I go back down. It is the effulgent. I hear the other two skullmen laughing now, cheering on Yellow Eyes. Chimeline screams again. Her horse lets out a loud neigh and tramples off, which elicits more crackles of laughter. The Xian's deep-sounding objections are like rolling thunder to their lightning. Red petals flutter around me. Bloody snow.

When I raise my head, Chimeline is lying on the ground in tatters, looking at me from underneath her bangs with an expression that breaks my heart. It's the look of disbelief that I would betray my promise and let this brutality happen to her.

The three skullmen stand above her, undoing the ties around their pants.

I shove my hand deep into my pocket and pull out Anaxarchis' voidstone by the chain.

Once it's free, I grab it in my hand.

Anaxarchis' stone is smaller than mine, so it takes me a moment to adjust. The sound of the wind is not as loud, the imaginary voices in the cave not as persistent. The blackness not as black. But I can still see the indivisibles in front of me. The legs of the three skullmen are clear enough. Skin, hair, muscle, sinew, bone.

*Butter.*

Feeling as though I'm jumping into a sea of ice, I briefly open myself up to the wind and cut through them all, while the wind cuts into me. It takes no time at all.

I let go.

Chimeline screams again, but this time her screams are different. Staccato, repetitive, one form of disbelief replaced by another.

The world of sunlight, gold, and red returns. But there is more red than before.

Two of the three skullmen have already fallen to the ground, their legs severed at midcalf. Yellow Eyes still stands. Somehow his body's weight is perfectly balanced upon the stumps of his feet.

None of the skullmen have screamed yet—their minds have not caught up with the present. But Chimeline's has. She kicks her legs out, to get herself away from the carnage, and this causes Yellow Eyes to topple like a marionette cut from its strings.

And then, finally, the full fury of their pain comes forth.

Blood is spraying in arcs, reminding me of the fountains in the Royal House, but it's mostly lost on the carpeted road.

The effulgent scrambles around it all, over to Chimeline.

Holding the gold chain of the voidstone, I slowly stand.

I ignore the writhing and screaming bodies. I even ignore Chimeline and the effulgent, who are now huddled together in the middle of the road. Everything is muted and distant. The world is soft, layered with petals.

My eyes find the Xian skullman.

He glances down at the voidstone in his hand and then at the one clutched in mine.

"You have another one."

I nod.

He exhales, looking out at the hilma field and then up into the blue sky. His entire body seems to slacken, as if he's giving up, wanting to be carried away by the sickeningly sweet wind. "Well, if you're going to kill me with that thing, do it quickly. Cut my neck. Not my legs."

*Kill me with that thing.*

I glance back at the writhing skullmen. Yellow Eyes is holding his severed foot in his hands, turning it around as if it's a missing piece to a puzzle.

I look back to him. "I'm not going to kill you."

He purses his lips, probably wondering why.

I ask myself the same question.

The first reason is this man's protest of his fellow skullmens' earlier behavior. That's worth something.

The second is what he saw in the sky. I'm not done questioning him. He's seen Marine and the veiled man, and that alone is enough to spare his life.

But the final reason is probably the most important.

I simply can't do it.

*Good Unnamed. I've never killed anyone before. Ending the lives of three people.*

*And I did it with voidance.*

Holding out my hand, I try to keep it steady. And my voice as well.

"I'll take that back now."

# THE GOODWIN MASSACRE

The Xian man named il-Colu drags the bodies of his three fellow skullmen past my grazing horse and to the roadside. Gone are their screams and the pressurized fountains of blood. Everything has become slow and silent, the coagulation of blackened sap. Only Yellow Eyes moans softly.

"I should end their pain," il-Colu says, putting his hand on the hilt of his machete. I nod distantly and walk toward Chimeline.

She's sitting cross-legged upon the flower-covered road, wrapping herself back up within her patchwork blanket as the effulgent gallops away to search for her runaway horse.

I sit down, touching the soft ground with my right hand to check my balance. In my left, I hold my recently returned voidstone, dangling from its severed gold chain. Anaxarchis' smaller stone is back in my pocket, where it belongs.

"Are you alright?" I ask her, my voice as soft as the dead flowers.

She pulls the blanket tighter around her and looks at the remains of the skullmen in the gully. il-Colu is efficient, making three clean hacks upon their necks, as if clearing a path through the wilderness.

A few crows take flight, and I follow them against the blue sky to the horizon.

When Chimeline turns back to me, our eyes never meet. She avoids them, instead fixated on the voidstone that dangles from my fist.

Eventually, she gives me an almost nonexistent nod.

*She is not alright.*

"I can mend your dress with my voidstone," I say.

"No," she answers quickly, cutting me off with a surprising amount of energy. "I am fine," she adds, quieter this time.

A gust of wind comes by. Petals dance between us.

"Please just leave me alone," she whispers.

I open my mouth, about to tell her that we should talk about what just happened, but then think better of it.

She's in distress, which is natural. So am I, in a way. However, she seems fearful of me now. It's understandable.

*I am fearful of myself.*

I look down the road. The effulgent trots toward us in the hazy distance, leading Chimeline's tan horse by its reins.

I stand and approach il-Colu.

Before reaching the roadside, I touch my voidstone and quickly mend the gold chain. I then drape it over my head again, letting it rest upon my chest in plain sight.

"Tell me everything you know about the airship," I say.

He wipes the blood off his machete using Yellow Eyes' black pants and then sheathes it.

"There is not much to say."

"How long ago did they pass by?"

"Two days."

I purse my lips and then frown in concern. At the rate at which they're traveling, they could be anywhere by now.

"There was a . . ." He makes a phantom box with his empty hands.

"A basket?"

He nods. "Yes. A large basket underneath the black sphere with two people in it."

I take another step toward him. "Could you make out any details?"

He tilts his head. "A man and a woman. They were very high. Higher than the millionescents. But I saw enough to tell that they were Northerners."

"What do you mean?"

"Blonde hair. Long. Fair skin."

"The woman or the man?"

"The woman."

"And what about the man?"

His forehead furrows. "He was strange looking. He was fair and bald, but . . ."

I take another step closer. "What is it?"

"Something was off about his face."

"Blurry?"

He shakes his head. With a scowl, he points to the effulgent, who's moving in our direction.

"He almost looked like *him*. Not as pale, but just as strange."

"An effulgent?" I ask, hearing the shock in my voice.

He looks at me and nods. "Yes," he answers. "He looked like an effulgent."

"That's impossible."

"Why?"

I look at il-Colu, with his eye patch and rough countenance, reminding myself that I can't trust this man. Despite his sliver of honor, he could still turn on me at any moment, and I may be forced to kill him. But ultimately, any information that I share might be a seed that yields a harvest of new information.

I decide to be truthful.

"The man I am pursuing—that man in the airship—was a voider," I answer. "And effulgents cannot use voidance."

After a moment of silence, he grunts. "I figured."

"What?" I ask.

"There is no other explanation for an immense black sphere flying through the air than voidance."

I purse my lips, agreeing with the logic of his statement.

"I'm sure they're headed south to kill more Xians in the war," he adds. "The redskull thought the same thing, and he would know."

"How would he know?"

"He's a voider too," he says.

My mouth opens and my heart skips a beat.

He taps his chest. "He has one, just like yours. Except I've never seen him use it. At least, not like how you did here."

"What's his name?"

He hunches his shoulders. "Redskull."

"No. Not that stupid title. His *name*."

il-Colu shakes his head. "He doesn't go by any name."

"What does he look like?"

"Northerner. Younger than us. Slightly reddish hair. Thin, average height. He's gotten thinner since I first met him."

I look at him questioningly, and he puts two fingers to his pursed lips. "Partakes in the pipe."

I run my hand over my short hair as I watch the effulgent approach on horseback with Chimeline's horse in tow, his back straight and proud.

"What towns are near here?" I ask il-Colu.

"Towns? There are a few, a half-day in either direction. Prainise is the farthest, but also the largest. There's a hilma field there run by another faction. Very dangerous place."

"What else?"

"Chartise to the west, Joscaio to the east. But they're very small, almost nothing to them. Ghost towns."

"Master Voider, are you ready to continue south?" the effulgent shouts. "Or do you need to kill anyone else before we go?"

I ignore him.

"Joscaio," I say, behind closed teeth, and then I find myself making fists at my sides.

*Cleanthes.*

There must be some logical explanation to all of this. My former student Cleanthes—the one I sent to Joscaio a few years ago—would never have turned into a depraved redskull. Simply not possible. A hilma addict, even less so.

The lanky redhead I knew was as straight as they come.

There must be some other explanation.

"Master Voider," the effulgent says, "are we going—"

"No," I say. "We're going to see the redskull first."

Both Chimeline and the effulgent look at me in surprise.

The effulgent gets off his horse and storms over, still holding both reins.

"Would you care to explain why?"

I point at il-Colu. "Based on what this skullman said, the redskull is a voider."

He takes a breath as he mentally digests the information. "The one you're looking for, to bring to justice?"

"No."

He shakes his smooth head, looking into the blue sky. "Then I do not see how it's relevant."

"This one was a student of mine. Like Anaxarchis."

He breathes in and out. "What are you going to do with him?"

"What do you mean?"

"Let's say that the Xian man is telling the truth, and your student has transgressed. What are you going to do?" He points to the three bodies in the ditch. "More of this? More killing?"

"I killed them to protect Chimeline. And you know that."

"Only after putting her in danger."

"She was never in any real danger," I say, but I wonder if that's entirely true.

I walk back to my black-and-white-spotted horse and climb into the saddle.

"You have a fairly twisted view of danger, Master Voider," the effulgent answers, loud enough for all to hear.

"Which I find quite ironic, given that you're only accustomed to the perfect places of the world."

"Go back to Fiscarlo then," I snap at him. "Go back to the daughter you left behind. It's safer there for you, and safer for her too," I add, nodding toward Chimeline. Part of me doesn't mean it, but part of me does. Perhaps pushing them away is the only thing that will keep them safe. "As for me, I'm going to visit my student and give him one last lesson before I head south."

Neither of them answer, so I guide my horse over to the skullman. "Let's go," I tell him.

He glances down at the three bodies before looking up at me. "Shouldn't we bury them first?"

I shake my head. "Do it later, when you know how big a grave to dig."

The mansion is up ahead. It's smaller than the Royal House but much larger than any normal home. Three stories, symmetrical, chimneys on each side. I count twenty-four windows on the facade, from this distance. It looms over the field, a mile or so away, its white siding and slate roof gleaming in the afternoon sun with a false purity that makes me livid.

The air is heavy with sweetness.

We make slow progress down a dry dirt path half-covered in trampled, decayed petals. It's similar to all the other endless hilma rows, except this one is wider. Drooping flowers line both sides of the path, but they're far enough away that we don't brush them as we pass.

I can see the black sap seep from the claw-shaped marks, where the bulbs were scored. The effulgent's recollection of the harvesting process was disturbingly accurate. But it's not the oozing sap I see. It's the blood of ruined lives.

As the Xian man is the only one walking, he dictates our pace. He walks at my side, while Chimeline and the effulgent reluctantly follow far behind.

"il-Colu," I say, breaking the silence.

He looks up at me with an odd expression, perhaps surprised that I addressed him by his name. "You can just call me Colu. The prefix was meant to be honorary."

"You are a helmsman?" I ask, remembering Yellow Eyes' taunt.

He gives me a bitter laugh. "I *was* a helmsman in the Xian navy, a long time ago."

"Before the war?"

He shakes his head. "No. For a brief time, I defended our homeland against the Northern aggressors, until this happened." He points to his eye patch.

There are many things that I want to ask him. How he became blind in one eye. How a helmsman in the Xian navy wound up becoming a skullman in a rogue hilma plantation in the Northern Kingdom. What it was like fighting for the other side. But I assume that none of these questions have simple answers, nor would he likely share them with a stranger, so I focus instead on the unexpected term he used.

"'Northern aggressors'?" I say. "Seems a bit overstated, don't you think?"

"And what would you call what your people have done?"

I clear my throat. "I am a voider, not a commander or politician, so I do not speak from any seat of authority. But I believe the trouble started when the south started taxing our ships going through Xi Bay."

He blows air through his dry lips. "That's a lie."

"How could it be, when there were multiple accounts of our ships being boarded and cargo being taken?"

"All lies," he repeats.

I pause. "If these stories were fabricated, then what happened?"

He forms a fist and repeatedly hits his chest with it. "I was stationed there, during the times before the Goodwin

Offensive. There were no armed boardings of any ships coming from the north."

"Perhaps they happened without your knowledge."

He just shakes his head.

"Well, from our perspective, that's what was happening, and it was getting worse over time. We had to defend ourselves."

"Defend yourselves?"

"Xi Bay is a critical piece of geography. All our ships travel down the River Xi to the bay, and from there they go to the different lands. To Xiland. The archipelago. The lands across. Our economy was being strangled—"

"We didn't tax your ships!"

My brow furrows. "Then how do you explain the Goodwin Massacre?"

"You mean the Goodwin *Offensive*."

I study him as he continues, his motioning arms in front of him. "It was a brilliant tactic. That much I will admit to you. Sending a trading ship supposedly full of oil—"

"It *was* a trading ship full of oil. Which your people set fire to."

He stops in place and turns to me, so I hold my horse up as well.

"I was *on* that ship. I boarded the *Goodwin* on that fateful night," he says, through clenched teeth. "And I'm telling you, it was a trap."

"You said that you never boarded our ships."

He looks back as Chimeline and the effulgent come near, and then back up to me. "That was in the beginning. By the time of the Goodwin Offensive, tensions were high. Our ships were already amassed in the bay. We were expecting your army or fleet, but then word came of a sudden truce. We needed oil, and your young king agreed to send a shipment to us. A token of goodwill."

I stay silent, waiting for him to continue.

"We let the *Goodwin* through our barricade after a brief inspection. I was one of the people who went aboard during that inspection. The upper and lower decks were full of barrels, stacked together so tightly it was hard to even walk through them. We checked the first few, prying their covers off. It was oil, all right. The crescent moon was reflected on the surface. I even dipped my finger in and tasted it upon my tongue."

He looks back at Chimeline and the effulgent and pauses, realizing that he now has a bigger audience.

"We disembarked and let the *Goodwin* sail on. A halfbell later, when it entered the south side of the bay near our Imperial Docks, the attack started. It was a trap. A masterful trap."

"How so?"

"Your barrels were full of bowmen."

My horse stamps his feet and raises his mane, eager to travel on, but I don't move, nor do I say a word.

"A bell rang out. All of them rose out of their barrels, arrows at the ready. I'm still not sure how they did it. False bottoms? Air vents? Reeds? Custom bows short enough to fit but long enough to carry an arrow the needed distance? Regardless, they lit their flaming arrows and fired at our ships, which were still docked. Within no time at all, one-quarter of our fleet was consumed in flames."

"And then what?"

"We retaliated, of course. We didn't have flamebowmen, but a few of us took smaller fishing boats, which they didn't see in the darkness. Once we got close enough, all we had to do was throw some lit bottles of sugarcanex on the deck, and the *Goodwin* was consumed immediately. But by then the damage to our fleet was already done."

"And that is how wars begin," adds the effulgent solemnly.

Colu nods and then looks up at me, his face a painted snarl. "You are the master voider. You probably knew of this plan well before it was executed."

I shake my head. "If what you say is true, I had no part in it."

He doesn't seem to believe me, the way his eye narrows.

"I should have killed you when I had the chance," he says. "We could have hit you with the darts before you even touched that stone of yours. Now, you're going to head south to the front, just like the voiders in the airship, so you can murder more of my people."

"I have no interest in the war," I say. "In fact, I hate it. It has stripped my university of students. Voiders are not meant for bloodshed."

He lets out a bitter laugh. "You sure about that?"

I hear the effulgent mumble a groan of agreement behind me.

"You of all people shouldn't judge," I tell Colu, glancing back at Chimeline as my anger flares. "You stood by while your companions were going to rape and kill her."

"So? I was outnumbered," he mumbles.

I try to calm my horse and my rising anger. "Are you telling me a helmsman in the Xian navy cannot take on three hilma addicts?"

He puts his hand on his machete, takes a step back, and raises his head and voice. "I told you, that man is dead. I'm a different person now." His chest rises and falls several times before he looks at Chimeline. "If you had met me a long time ago, you would have run into a man of honor. But I am no longer that man."

I look at Chimeline again to gauge her reaction. She just wraps herself tighter in her blanket and gazes fearfully at the white house in the distance.

"I give you my word," I tell Colu, turning back to him. "My presence here has nothing to do with this stupid war. I am on my way south for personal matters."

"Personal matters," he mimics slowly, and then spits into the dirt. "So what is it? Revenge or a woman?"

I don't say a word, and he flashes his skull teeth mischievously.

"That's what I thought."

"You don't know as much as you think," I tell him.

He grunts. "I know enough. I know that there are only two things in this world that can drive a man crazy. That look in your eyes—you're hunting something, no matter the cost. To the point where you will risk your own life and the lives of those around you."

Colu's one-eyed gaze falls upon Chimeline and the effulgent.

# AN AUDIENCE WITH
# THE REDSKULL

Leaving the wildness of the hilma row, our horses cross onto a sandy circular road. A three-tiered bronze fountain sits in the middle of it, within the shade of the immense white house beyond.

A bathing crow watches us, and I hear the sound of a woman's laughter far away.

Colu sighs by my side. "I was just getting to like this place," he mumbles under his breath. "Easy work for the money, and a comfortable bed too."

I look at him in confusion. "You speak as if I am going to burn this mansion down."

"I wouldn't put it past you. But that's not what I'm getting at."

After I don't turn away, he points to the white building as if I'm dense. "You're going to walk in there with your voidstone. Which means the redskull is going to kill me as soon as you leave. No doubt about it. I fucked up. Let you in with your stone. I'll need to flee this place before he has the chance."

"Don't worry about him. He and I are going to have a long talk."

He blows a sharp breath through his lips. "I'm not sure you know what you're walking into."

I look past him to the mansion. "I've got a pretty good idea."

He shakes his head slowly. "I hope so."

As we near the fountain, I dismount and signal to Chimeline and the effulgent to do the same.

"There is a delicate balance here," Colu continues, his voice quieter now. "And you are riding in like a storm. Whatever good you think you're doing, have you considered that you might unleash something worse?"

I turn to him. "Worse than the demise of a rogue hilma plantation?"

For a moment, he just presses his lips together, but then his emotions seem to get the better of him. He shakes his head again. "You're like a child playing in the sand."

I narrow my eyes.

A metallic sound echoes across the fountain—the sound of a door being unlocked.

The double-wide front doors open and four men exit clothed in black-and-white formal uniforms, not unlike the servants at the Royal House.

I'm surprised that no skull paint decorates their faces.

Two palehounds exit behind them. The dogs are lanky and about one hundred pounds, and their heads almost reach the hips of the servants. They easily tread away from the four men, coming near and sniffing us in curiosity. My horse jumps nervously, and one of the palehounds retreats, flashing his red fangs behind fine, bone-colored fur.

I want to speak to Colu more about this subject, but the timing is not right. He kicks the sandy ground once as we walk our horses around the fountain and into the shade of the mansion. The sudden coolness feels pleasant. Over the course of the afternoon, the sun's heat has grown strong. A testament to how far south we have already traveled.

We hand our reins over. I glance quickly at all four of them, looking for the telling signs of hilma addiction: yellow eyes, green teeth, and protruding veins. I see none.

One of them is older and stands straighter with his hands behind his back. He looks to my voidstone and then back to Colu, tilting his head subtly, but not subtly enough. I can almost read his thoughts.

*A voider bearing a voidstone? Are you insane?*

"It's fine," Colu says. "We're here to see him."

The head footman reluctantly nods and then whistles. The two palehounds perk up their bone-white heads and run inside.

The other three footmen lead our horses to a small white stable in the distance while the rest of us climb the brick stairs of the redskull's mansion.

I grab the gold setting of my necklace in anticipation, as the effulgent's voice rings in my head.

*Why seek out danger?*

Up until now, he has been wrong. His fears have been unwarranted. They were the dark to a privileged child, starvation to a farmer during a bountiful harvest. Even when things got out of control with Yellow Eyes, I was able to course-correct.

*But now?*

Despite the calmness of this courtyard and the comfort of the shade, we are in danger.

I feel it.

Cleanthes isn't just a voider. He was one of my brightest students. Until I understand what has happened here, I must treat him as a threat. A significant threat—far more dangerous than a mere skullman.

Or a hundred of them.

I feel eyes on me and turn sideways. Chimeline and the hooded effulgent both look at me in concern.

"Whatever happens, stay behind me," I tell them. "Make sure that I am between you and the redskull at all times."

Chimeline nods with seriousness while the effulgent shakes his head in disbelief.

As soon as we're through the front doors, I briefly touch my voidstone.

I create a membrane of dynamic voidance.

It's barely discernible to the naked eye, but shockingly, even with one eye, Colu sees it. Maybe he felt the momentary breeze. He looks back at me with a deeply furrowed brow, but I don't say anything and he doesn't either.

The air directly in front of us shimmers in subtle distortion, as if above a bed of hot coals. It is tethered to me, so as I move, the membrane moves. Any voider on the other side will be unable to see the indivisibles beyond without first breaking through the membrane itself. But if that happens, it will be noticeable, and I will have time to react.

With that taken care of, I finally look around.

Inside the grand foyer, an elaborate wooden staircase borders all four walls, climbing three stories. A few clusters of young women clothed in colorful silk nightgowns gather on the second- and third-floor landings, looking down at us like songbirds in a rainforest. The roof, far above, is made of paned glass stained turquoise.

For a moment, fear fills me. Cleanthes might be *above* me, somewhere on the second- or third-floor landing. I am prepared to create another membrane that covers us all, but then the footman looks back at us through the faint haze.

"The redskull is in the library," he says to me, his voice echoing. "He has been expecting you."

I turn to Colu with a confused expression. "How is he expecting us?" I whisper.

"I waved a black flag when I saw you on Xi Bay Road," he replies. "They sent word back here."

"Black for voider?"

He nods.

We walk through the dim foyer, past towering palms in elaborate, hand-painted blue-and-white pots large enough for a man to sit in.

"These are from the archipelago," Chimeline whispers, her fingers grazing the tops of the pots without her having to bend down.

We pass a large standing mirror, and I pause when I see my reflection. My face is bloodied and swollen.

"Can you heal yourself like you did my wrist?" Chimeline whispers.

I nod. "Not now, though. There is no time."

The palehounds slowly walk past us, and their claws tap on the floor like fingernails on glass. I leave the mirror behind.

When we reach the opposite side of the foyer, the head footman turns to us.

"One moment, please," he says, and he slides the massive pocket doors open slightly before disappearing into the room beyond. He closes them behind him, but not all the way—a sliver of orange sunlight crosses the floor at my feet.

I turn to Chimeline and the effulgent. "Both of you, stay here."

"Dem?" whispers Chimeline.

I shake my head. "Right now, it's safer if you're away from me. But if any skullmen come for you, run inside and find me."

The effulgent puts a hand on her shoulder. "It is alright. I will stand here and pray with you."

Turning back to the pocket doors, I push them open wide. Then I enter.

It takes me a moment for my eyes to adjust to the bright sunlight and bizarre surroundings.

The immense library stands two stories tall. The high ceiling is coffered and wooden. Three of the four walls—including the one I just passed through—are entirely covered in bookshelves and hanging ladders.

A mix of sweet hilma and musty old tomes hangs in the air.

Natural light streams through the glass wall opposite me. The glass windows and doors lead out onto a brick patio with a formal rectangular pool. It's full of clear water, and the sunlight reflects off it blindingly. At least five skullmen stand guard outside among the potted palms, and a few women tan themselves on wicker lounges. One exits the pool, squeezing the water from her chestnut hair.

I turn my gaze back to the library. The waning afternoon sun casts sharp shadows within the room. Bright orange on dark-brown wood. Long shadows from the dozen or so skullmen standing guard against the four walls.

The head footman in the center of the room looks back at me, surprise and annoyance upon his face, before turning back to where he was headed: a lifeless fireplace, fifty feet in the distance. The redskull rests upon a leather chaise there.

It's him. Cleanthes. Even though his face is covered in paint and the air between us is not entirely still, I am certain of it.

As I peer at him, I realize that his skull is not red, as his title would indicate—it's actually pale orange, the same color as his hair. The color of a once-fine metal, rusting away.

He's not wearing the black flaxen cloak of voiders. Instead, he's covered in a red cloak made of thin silk that hints at the hollowness of his body.

But his voidstone is draped around his neck.

I hear the heavy footsteps of Colu as he enters behind me, and then the nail-upon-glass sound of claws. The palehounds stride past me, heading toward their master.

I quickly assess the skullmen surrounding me. They're all standing against the walls, about ten feet apart from one another, arms at their sides, like statues. The one closest to me is near enough that I am able to pick out certain details—he has yellow eyes.

Another glance behind me. Some of these skullmen are positioned there, flanking the doors that I came through.

I count fifteen, but they are not my concern.

Turning back to Cleanthes, I see him get up off his chaise longue, his lanky form and hunched shoulders evident underneath his crimson robe. He stands on a black bearskin rug. Facing me, the dead beast's jaws are opened wide as if it is still alive and roaring.

I realize then that there is a woman on the chaise longue as well, lying on her stomach. Her dark Xian skin blends in with the bear fur. She looks to be asleep, an open book at her side. The palehounds walk in small circles before settling down beside her with groans of pleasure.

Through the barely discernible shimmering air, I watch my former student closely, wondering if he is going to reach for his necklace. The moment he does, I will be ready.

But he doesn't attempt to grasp it. For a long time, Cleanthes simply stands there with his hands down and palms together, as we regard one another in silence. Outside, the women are talking and laughing in the sun, oblivious to what is occurring just on the other side of the thin glass.

The head footman must sense that his responsibility has ended—or that bloodshed is soon to follow. He wisely bows and leaves the room, passing through my dynamic membrane without even realizing it.

"You didn't follow my orders," Cleanthes says to Colu, his voice deeper than I remember.

"He had two stones, Redskull," Colu answers. "One was hidden."

Cleanthes raises an eyebrow.

"Voidstones are a lot like eyes," I say, breaking the silence between us. "One is fine, but two are better."

Cleanthes smirks. "Still, it looks like my skullmen did a job on you."

"Your skullmen are dead."

My words wipe the smirk off his face and cause a stirring around the perimeter of the room.

He looks to Colu and in my peripheral vision, I see him nod.

"I never took you for a violent man, Democryos."

I say my next words loudly. "I could say the same for you, Cleanthes."

For a moment, the redskull is a statue. In the still room, no one makes a sound. Outside, one of the women screams playfully and jumps into the pool.

Eventually, he smiles wide without showing his teeth.

"I was wondering if you remembered me," he says.

"Remember you?" I ask, shocked. "How could I forget? You were one of my best students."

"Whom you sent into the wilderness to be forgotten."

"It was either that or send you off to war. And you were not forgotten. You were *entrusted*."

"Entrusted with what?"

The volume of my voice rises with my anger. "Your gift! The people of Joscaio!"

A few of the skullmen turn to me. Apparently, people do not raise their voice to the redskull.

"Trust." He says the word slowly, like a hissing snake. He brings his hands up to his mouth, palms still together, as if praying to the Unnamed. His fingers are very close to his voidstone. "Once it's lost, it's lost for good. Isn't that right, Democryos? That's why you come into my home maintaining a dynamic membrane."

In a bitter way, I am impressed that he can notice the disturbance in the air from so far away. "No friend of mine is a redskull. And no redskull can be a voider."

"But it's because of you that I am here. You made me who I am today."

I shake my head in disappointment. Of course he would blame his addiction on me. That's what addicts do—they blame others.

"While at the university, should I have educated you on the negative properties of the hilma plant?"

He shakes his head. "You have no idea, do you? What happened to Joscaio."

I know he is goading me so I stay silent.

"We exchanged how many letters in the past few years?"

"At least two."

He takes a step forward.

"It was *exactly* two. And neither inquired about my well-being. They were full of preaching commentary, as if I were still a student listening to one of your lectures."

"I was trying to help you."

"No you weren't. You were trying to stroke your ego. Which is why I never brought up what was happening. I knew you wouldn't care. You were too busy with your endeavors for the king to bother with one of your *best students*. If you had really cared, you would have asked me. Or visited me, in person."

"Well, I'm here now."

"It's too late. The damage is already done."

He stretches his neck, rotating his head in a circle. "You sent me into a wasp's nest, Master Voider. You saved me from one war, yet you placed me squarely in another."

He grabs his stone.

Instantly, I enter the world of the void and move my dynamic membrane forward with urgency. I change the tether, centering it on Cleanthes rather than me. I enlarge it so that it reaches across the entire room, from the wall of books to the panes of glass and all the way up to the coffered ceiling, two stories above me.

It is exhausting and painful work, but I have no other choice. There are too many other things he could do without proper restraint. He could create a rift in the floor or the ceiling. He could cause the windows to shatter and cut us to pieces. And at least a dozen other things I have not thought about.

As I release the stone, I immediately feel numbness in my fingers and almost fall.

The light of the world returns and the sound of the dark wind dies, replaced by the crystalline sound of wind chimes.

I look to the light.

Most of the panes of glass have shattered outward and are still in the process of falling from their iron frames.

It was probably my action that caused this. A dynamic membrane extending the full width of the room could easily cause a buildup of pressure if moved quickly enough.

Or perhaps it was some offense that Cleanthes was attempting, until my use of the voidstone collided with his.

Regardless, everyone in the room is doubly as confused as me.

The skullmen have all stepped away from the walls brandishing shortswords, but they're awaiting orders from their leader before attacking. Colu stands next to me, his machete in his hand. The sunbathers outside have risen and are wrapping white towels about their midsections. The palehounds have risen as well, showing red teeth. But the Xian woman is still passed out on the bearskin rug.

Cleanthes begins to laugh. He releases his voidstone and claps slowly, like a madman.

"Oh, this is more fun than I've had in years. Two great voiders, testing their powers against each other. I see what you did there, Democryos. Very bold. You risked voideath in order to defend yourself from my attack."

My legs are weak. I am struggling to stand.

"Did I overcome you?" he asks, as he stops clapping.

"I warn you," I say, ignoring his taunt while I kneel upon the wooden floor. I make sure that Colu is not directly behind me. I don't trust him—he could sever my head with that machete before I have a chance to stop him. "I still have enough voidance in me to kill every skullman in this room. And when I am done killing them, I will kill you."

He looks insulted. "Democryos, you are my guest of honor, not my prisoner. And certainly not my victim."

He begins to walk slowly toward me.

"Master Voider, do you know what you're doing?" Colu asks me under his breath.

"Yes."

The brilliance of my prior move is that the dynamic membrane moves with Cleanthes without my having to touch my voidstone again. He looks to both sides and up toward the ceiling, noticing this, and opens his mouth with a look of wonderment.

"Very nice work."

Once he crosses the room, he suddenly stops in place. It is a calculated move. He is standing only a few feet away from me, the membrane mere inches from my face. It hums with a life of its own.

I clutch the gold sides of my stone in readiness, for if my membrane is penetrated, I will be exposed once again to his power. I'll be forced to kill him before he kills me.

What is the quickest way? A shot through the heart? No. Too slow. Decapitation? Too slow as well. It needs to be instantaneous. Holes at each end of his skull and enough pressure to blow his brain matter through, creating a clap of thunder in the room.

*Such an act would surely take me into voideath.*

But he doesn't take another step toward me.

Instead, he sits cross-legged on the ground, eye level with me, and unclasps his necklace, holding it by the chain.

His hand shakes.

"You were my teacher once," he says. Past the humming of the membrane, I barely hear him.

Gone is his bravado. Now, his words are the quietest of whispers, the brushing of hilma bulbs in the wind. "Are you willing to be my teacher again?"

Clearly, he doesn't want anyone else in the room hearing these words.

He's so close to me now that I finally understand his miserable condition. His eyes are yellow, the skin of his hands almost transparent, riddled with sinuous veins. His collarbone protrudes. His teeth are grayish green.

Feelings course through me. Sympathy, rage, but mostly suspicion. I narrow my eyes, fearing a trap. "What do you wish to learn from me?"

"I want you to teach me to remember," he says, his voice softly breaking.

"Remember what?"

"How to use voidance."

When his lips begin to quiver and his yellow eyes become glassy with tears, I know that there is no trap. Madness, perhaps. Tragedy, for certain.

I open my mouth but no words come out.

Impossibly, Cleanthes has lost the ability to use a voidstone.

I've never heard of this happening. The gift is constant, from birth to death. But there is no way the man in front of me is lying. He's been lying to everyone else, but not to me. Not here. Not now.

I suddenly understand. Everything in this room has been a show, but I was not the audience. The audience was the other skullmen in the room—the soldiers he commands with a phantom fist. And the show has just ended.

He extends his shaking hand through the dynamic membrane and drops his voidstone into my lap. Then he grasps my hand in his.

"Please, Master Voider. Teach me to remember."

# GRAVESTONES AND MOONSPIT

"I would give anything to feel what you're feeling now."

I don't open my eyes to respond to his ludicrous statement. He's been carrying on this way for a while now, and I'm too tired from being in the void—to create the dynamic membrane as well as heal myself in front of the foyer mirror.

I cannot believe that I exerted myself so unnecessarily. All this time, he was as powerless as a child.

"The coldness," Cleanthes continues next to me. "The numbness in the fingertips. Is that what you feel?"

"Yes," I mumble, as I take a deep breath and slink further into the teak bench.

We're outside in the garden. There are many benches like the one we're sitting on. Most are in the shade of lemon trees, but I purposely picked this one. It's been in the sun the entire day, and the heated wood radiates into my body.

"When you take hilma, you get warmer, not colder. That's why I guess I miss the cold. You would think that wouldn't be something a voider would miss. But I miss it. Crazy, right?"

The way Cleanthes carries on about trivial things makes me wonder if he is nervous. He knows that serious matters lie ahead. Like the disappearance of his gift, and his addiction.

More laughter from the nearby pool erupts, and I squint. Past a hedgerow of yews being trimmed by an old man in a straw hat, Chimeline is on the patio, talking to the other women with a smile upon her face. I can't hear their conversation, but it's obvious that they're joking about something.

Many of the women still have white towels wrapped around their tan torsos, and Chimeline has followed suit. A maidservant in formal attire inspects Chimeline's ripped, lace dress in her hands. She nods and then walks away with it.

"Tell me what happened in Joscaio," I say, closing my eyes again.

This shuts him up for a moment.

"It was a disaster from the very beginning," he eventually says. "Joscaio is only a half-day's walk from here. When I arrived there, people were being taken almost every night by the skullmen at this plantation. They lived in fear, and looked to me as their savior."

I sit up straighter and reopen my eyes.

"There was already a rogue plantation here?" I say, pointing at the ground. "When you arrived at Joscaio?"

He nods and I shake my head in confusion.

"Cleanthes, this plantation is off Xi Bay Road. It's impossible to miss."

He flashes a green smile. "Good for business."

"That's the thing. This place surely was a royal plantation at one time. It was His Majesty's property."

He motions to the mansion. "You're correct. There are old records signed by the king's delegate. Production numbers. Transactions with some of the hospitals the university set up. Very thorough bookkeeping."

"So what happened? How did it get into rogue hands?"

He purses his lips. "I don't know. Maybe the kingdom abandoned it due to the war effort?"

I don't answer.

"Soldiers pass by weekly. They never give me any trouble. They're some of my best customers, actually."

I clear both my throat and my mind. "So, they were taking people when you arrived?"

"Yeah. The skullmen scouted the village during the day, then came back at night. They knew the exact people they were looking for. The exact huts. They only took the healthy adults. Both women and men. They left the older ones and the children behind."

I shake my head.

"The skullmen put them to work." He points to the fields in the distance, past the pool. "Well, most of them, that is."

"Most of them?"

"He kept some of the women here. You see those women by the pool?"

I stay silent.

"The strong men became skullmen. The others, they worked the fields."

"And none tried to escape?"

He cracks his knuckles. "Most people had family back in Joscaio. A son or daughter. Father or mother. Brother or sister."

"You mean they threatened them."

He nods as he continues to fidget, nervously tapping his hand against his knee. "When I arrived, this is what I had to deal with. This is the mess you threw me into."

"I had no idea."

"The citadel is far from here. How could you?"

I sigh, wondering if he's being truthful or providing me veiled sarcasm.

I turn my body on the bench to face him, wanting to read his body language. But the moment I do, I forget my intent and instead am overcome with pity.

In the harsh light of day, he looks worse than before. Beneath his red-orange paint, which is dry and flaking, his cheeks sink inward. I have the feeling that even if a skull weren't painted on his face, he would still look like a skeleton. His yellow eyes fixate on nothing in the distance, and he whispers something to himself, his body softly rocking back and forth.

"You asked me to help you," I say.

With these words, his whispers cease and his bony hand claws at my arm. "Will you? Will you teach me, as you once did?"

I take a deep breath as I struggle to formulate a strategy. This is Cleanthes, one of my best students. I remember when he came to the university as a young, lanky teen. A bright spark of idealism and talent. I honed him into the best of voiders. I nurtured his gift, challenged him with tests to the point of tears, made him grow from a boy into a man.

And then I sent him to Joscaio.

I cannot help but feel somewhat responsible for his predicament. He's right, at least in this regard. I threw him to the wolves.

But on the other hand, I cannot endorse the operation of this illegal plantation. Nor leave a voider in charge of it.

"Before I help you, I need to understand what you are doing here."

"Ask me anything."

"Let's start with how you became the new redskull."

His body goes completely still for a brief moment, before the fidgeting returns.

"It was easy." He shrugs. "I dyed my hair black and pretended to be a man on their list."

"What do you mean?"

"This guy in Joscaio. They came for him one night, but he was passed out drunk in the middle of the road, so they missed him the first time around. The next night, he and I switched places. I slept in his hut until they came for him. When they took me, I waited until I was brought to the redskull, then I used my voidstone."

I raise my eyebrow. "You killed him?"

"I had to protect my people."

I nod.

"It didn't end with him. I had to dispose of some of the skullmen too. Nobody from Joscaio, of course. When they realized how much power I had, they quickly fell in line. Before I knew it, I'd gone from intruder to leader."

I clear my throat. "I see."

"All of these people"—he waves his hand toward the pool—"they are my family. And despite what you may think, I have given them a much better life here than they had before."

My eyes narrow, wondering if this is perception or reality. Based on his body language, he obviously believes it. The question is, do the rest of his people believe it?

"Can you expound on that?"

He leans forward on the bench. "Are you strong enough to walk?"

I ponder his question and then nod. My strength is returning.

"Then come," he says, extending a shaking hand covered in sweat, which I take. "I will show you."

I follow him down a narrow sandy path, through a garden full of low lemon trees and arborvitae. In the distance is the white barn I saw when we arrived, where I presume our horses are being kept.

The path curves around the corner of the mansion and goes through tall grasses and blue flowers. There are more older men here, silently pruning trees and bushes. Butterflies dance in the late-afternoon air, and we pass through a stone archway into the perfect shade of the millionescents. It's a formal design—dozens of them planted in a perfect sequence. They form a square about fifty yards in size, four walls of glittering gold higher than the First Ring of the citadel.

It feels as though I am entering a massive room with a ceiling painted to look like the sky.

I take my attention off the dizzying heights and surrounding wall of trees and instead look at what's enclosed within this private place.

*Headstones.*

We're walking through a graveyard.

In a far corner, the effulgent is kneeling upon the mossy ground. A hooded gray form that, had I not known any better, I would have assumed was a statue.

"These unmarked ones predate me," Cleanthes says quietly. "The former redskull never bothered to mark them. I'm actually surprised that he even buried these people at all. He was an evil man."

We slowly walk past two rows of dirt mounds, five mounds on each side of the center path. Twenty bodies altogether. And all the while, I am focused on his comment: *He was an evil man.*

Doesn't Cleanthes realize that he is the new redskull? Somehow, he has compartmentalized what has happened. Justified to himself that he can take an evil man's place without himself turning evil.

At the third row of mounds, the headstones begin.

"There's a pile of fieldstone stacked in the barn," Cleanthes says. He continues to walk slowly ahead of me down the center path. "I used to work on the headstones myself, back when I could see the void."

I look at the mounds of moss-covered dirt next to me, names on each one of their markers, in perfect lettering.

One of them simply says *Redskull.*

"You buried these people? And marked their graves?"

"Yes."

"That was decent of you," I say.

He ignores my compliment and points with a shaking hand. "This group right here, these were the skullmen I told you about," he says quietly. "The ones I had to kill."

I see the effulgent lower his hood.

"I don't judge you for that," I say. "I was forced to defend myself against three of your skullmen. On the road, just before coming here. They were going to harm my companion."

He looks up at me with a surprising lack of emotion. "The ones with Colu?" he asks.

I nod.

"None of them were from Joscaio. They were probably traitors."

"Traitors?"

He ignores me again. We pass another ten or so graves and reach a new section, which is very close to where the effulgent is kneeling. These are more recent. The stones are a different shade of bluish gray.

"Here are my people. Most of these came from Joscaio."

I count the mounds in front of us. Three rows, five mounds on each side of the center path. A total of thirty.

"There's a lot of dead here, Cleanthes," I utter.

He nods once. "I know. It's more than I anticipated."

I look sideways at him as he exhales and shakes both of his arms loosely at his sides, looking up into the square patch of sky far above. And for the first time, I seriously wonder if he is entirely sane.

"Many are skullmen," he says.

"Why did they die?"

"Prainise," he says, as he looks back down, his gray-green teeth gritted.

"Colu mentioned that place. He said it was dangerous."

"There's another field there. They mostly stay away, but I know that a few traitors remain within my family. Weeds that I have not yet pulled. I can never let my guard down."

"You keep mentioning traitors."

He walks to the foot of one grave and looks solemnly down to a headstone that simply reads *Terstine*.

"Not all of them are men," he says quietly. "They sent an assassin from Scorpiontail to poison me. It didn't work."

He looks at me with eyes that are almost the color of the millionescent trees beyond. "So, you see, it's not my fault."

I point to the next row, where the effulgent is praying. "Were these natural deaths?"

He slowly rolls his head in a circle. "Those were thieves."

"Thieves," I repeat levelly.

"Some of the workers in my fields try to partake in the pipe. Smuggle bulbs in their clothing and cook it on their own. I have to put a stop to it."

He stops talking suddenly and then looks up into the square of blue sky again. "I'm not an evil person."

"I never said that you were," I say.

"You don't have to, Master Voider. I see the way you look at me with your white eyes. So white they're purer than new-fallen snow. The way you're looking at all of my dead, as if I killed them."

*But you did kill them.*

He flexes his fists at his sides.

"They broke the rules!" he shouts. "And the rules are meant to protect the student body. Isn't that always what you said?"

I blink, struggling to understand why Cleanthes is bringing up my teaching methods. Even the effulgent raises his head. There is confusion upon his shadowed face.

"Yes, but I never killed my students if they broke the rules," I say after a pause. "I only expelled them."

"To a voider, there's no difference. Many days, I think I'd rather be dead."

He eventually takes another few steps, moving very slowly, turning his head in each direction as if he's reading the names on the stone markers. I see his lips moving.

That's when I realize that the writing on the stones progressively get worse in quality.

The second row's headstones are similar to the first row's. Clean cuts, perfect letters, straight lines, and graceful curves.

But then, grave by grave, the inscriptions begin to become unreadable. Almost like a child's handwriting.

At the third row, the headstones cease.

Cleanthes must see me staring at them, my brow furrowed and head shaking.

"I had lost the gift completely by then," he says quietly to me. "And I don't have a stonemason. No other way to carve letters into rock out here. We tried painting on wood but it rotted away."

"It's the hilma," I tell him. "It has taken away your gift of voidance."

"No," he says, shaking his head. "That can't be it."

I wave my hand to the headstones behind us. "This didn't happen all at once. You lost the gift gradually, as your addiction took hold of you. Can't you see? It's practically written on these stones."

He shakes his head again. "I know there is another way," he says. "If there's anyone in this world who can help me, it's you."

I pause, disappointed by his stubbornness but not surprised.

Cleanthes' back is still turned to me, so he doesn't see my forlorn expression.

There is only one way forward. Not just to restore his gift of voidance, but to restore his very life. He must leave hilma behind and never look back.

It will be the hardest test of all for him to take. A test that I don't have the heart to tell him about yet. I must break the news gently.

He sucks in air through his teeth, as he scratches his mangy red hair. "There is something else I want to show you," he says.

Without waiting for my answer, he suddenly walks off, to the edge of the graveyard. I have no choice but to follow him through another archway. But before I leave, I turn and look back into the shade. The effulgent has raised his hood once again, a statue among the dead.

Briefly closing my eyes, I step into the sunlight.

We're closer to the barn now, and for the first time, I see another white structure in the distance, long and narrow.

He points to it.

"I had that built."

"Another barn? For what?"

He smiles. "It's not a barn. They're row houses. My family lives there. There was not enough room in the mansion for everyone."

"Your family?"

"I brought everyone who was left in Joscaio. The children and elderly. Even the cats and dogs. Nobody was left behind."

"You put them to work in your fields?"

He narrows his eyes and briefly glances at me. "No. They just live here. I knew that I could never kill innocents if my workers ran away. But if I brought everyone here, there would be no reason for anyone to leave me. We would be a loving family."

I'm not quite sure what to say as I no longer believe Cleanthes is in his right mind. On one hand, he murdered his own people—tore entire families apart—for petty theft. On the other, he proclaims he is trying to keep them together. It is hard to tell what is the truth and what is a lie because in Cleanthes' world, everything is distorted.

Over the whispering brush and toward the white row houses, I hear the sound of children playing.

"There's over three hundred of them. Between the ones that live in the mansion and the row houses. My people are better off here than in Joscaio. We have enough money for anything."

"Blood money," I mumble.

He ignores me. "We might even build a school for my children."

*My children.* I am not sure if he is being literal or figurative, and then I realize that it doesn't matter. It's disturbing in either case.

"Sometimes I think that I even passed your test. You sent me to Joscaio to make their world a better place, and in my own way I think I've done it. Without voidance."

I sigh, deep and heavy. The road in front of him is going to be very difficult.

"There is only one test, Cleanthes," I softly answer. "And it's still in front of you. If you come out of it alive, you'll get your gift back."

He looks at me excitedly, but his expression drops as my meaning becomes clear.

The sound of running children gets louder, and then I see two boys trample up a hill on a slender trail in the grass and enter our path. They are around seven years old. One had been chasing the other, but when they see us, they immediately go silent, their faces turning white.

The taller boy taps the shoulder of the other, and they run back in the direction that they came from. My eyes follow them until I realize that they had been running from two older men, who now approach us from the very same hill, with wide strides.

One of them is the footman who led my horse away. The other is a skullman.

The latter carries a folded white towel in his outstretched hands. He flashes me a distrusting look before addressing Cleanthes.

"Redskull, we found something."

Cleanthes tosses his hair back with his hand, looking annoyed with the sudden interruption.

"What is it?" he asks curtly, his tone markedly different.

The skullman glances at me again.

"Out with it," Cleanthes adds. "This is my former teacher, whom I trust."

The skullman carefully unfolds the white towel and reveals a glass vial resting in the center.

I lean in, getting a better look.

"We found this in the girl's saddlebag."

It's Chimeline's vial.

"Oh," I explain. "The woman I am traveling with is from the archipelago. I believe that is the extract of jasmine leaves."

Cleanthes picks up the clear vial full of grayish liquid and twists off the rubber stopper. Placing it directly underneath his nose, he breathes in deeply and then carefully replaces the stopper.

"This is not jasmine," he says, placing Chimeline's vial back on the white towel. "It is moonspit."

I look at him in confusion.

"From the skin of the moonfrog."

I take a deep breath and shake my head. "Cleanthes, I don't think Chimeline would lie to me."

His red-orange face turns to me, for once not shaking.

"She is an assassin."

# A CHANCE AT LIFE AND VOIDANCE

Cleanthes takes a step closer to me and begins whispering. His entire body reeks of hilma.

"This is how Prainise tried to do it. They sent a woman into my bed. If it weren't for my instincts, and a little bit of luck, I would be dead." His yellow eyes shift left and right quickly. "Somebody sent her to kill me."

I put an arm over his crimson cloak, ushering him away, out of earshot of his two men. "Not everyone is out to kill you."

He turns to me. "Maybe she was sent to kill *you*."

"That's your hilma talking."

He puts his face close to mine. "Do you have any enemies?"

"I have disagreements with many, but none that would resort to murder."

"You think that I am paranoid. That my mind is dulled. But it's sharp. And I'm telling you, she's an assassin." His eyes keep flickering left and right. "She's probably another gift from Prainise."

"She's from the citadel. And she had no idea that we'd be coming here."

From far away comes the sound of a woman's laughter, and he spins in that direction, as if he can see her beyond the tall grass. His crimson robes flare out at his sides as he looks back at me.

"You should kill her with your voidstone," he whispers. "Or I could have one of my skullmen do it, if you prefer."

"That won't be necessary."

"It can be painless, if you want," he insists.

"Stop it!" I yell, wiping my dry face with my hands. "You need to stop this madness," I add, quieter this time and through clenched teeth.

I shake my head and take a deep breath, briefly wondering if I should tell this crazed man the truth. But the complexity of any lie is more than I can bear right now.

"She's one of the king's harem," I say.

"Harem?" he shouts in disbelief.

"I'm not going to get into details, but I had dinner with the king the night we left the citadel. His Majesty practically pushed her on me."

"The king," he whispers, his eyes like gold coins. "Why would the king send an assassin with you?"

My mind goes back to the blue dining room, to King Andrej X's face and words made of stone. *I'm beginning to wonder if I need to find myself another master voider.*

"Have you been sharing your bed with her?" he whispers.

"No!"

*But I would have, had I given into her advances.*

I recall the moonlit street after my argument with the king. Her dark-brown eyes and the scents of oranges and sugar. *Take me to your bedchamber, Your Grace.*

Is it possible that the dinner was some sort of test to gauge my reaction to sending more voiders to his cursed war? Is it possible that I had failed that test, and Chimeline was the price of that failure?

No.

"We took an airship," I say, vocalizing my thoughts. "I had passed out from being in the void. If she had wanted to kill me, she could have easily done it then."

"That's not their way," he says, with an upraised finger.

"What does that mean?"

"To an assassin, the manner of the murder is as important as the murder itself."

"Let me guess. Poison."

He nods.

"Cleanthes, I've heard such talk. They are all spurious claims. Superstitions passed down within ratty bars by older men to a younger generation."

He grabs onto my robe with a fist. "It nearly happened to me, Master Voider. Had I not heard these spurious claims and been prepared, *I* would be the one buried in that cemetery and not Terstine."

I give him an icy stare.

"Moonspit comes from the moonfrog," he continues, "which is native to Scorpiontail. It's a very slippery, oily substance, and is extremely deadly. If it gets into your bloodstream, it will stop your heart within a halfbell. Moonspit is much deadlier than your common blade-coating poison. Or the sap my skullmen dip their darts into. With moonspit, you don't even have to break the skin."

I look at him skeptically. "That's what I heard. It just needs to be rubbed in."

His yellow eyes smile. "The assassin applies it to her body. Inside of her." He clears his throat as he brings his hand to his groin in hideous illustration. "You understand my meaning?"

I turn away to take a deep breath.

"By the time the man is engaged, it has already begun to work. The moonspit has entered his bloodstream with friction and his heart begins to race. In the throes of passion, it begins to beat faster than it should. Then suddenly"—he snaps his fingers—"it stops."

"If these stories were true, it would kill the woman as well."

His eyebrows rise. "This is where the seed of the rumor comes from. They say the women of Scorpiontail are as dangerous as they are beautiful."

I give a begrudging nod.

"The women of Scorpiontail—a rare few, that is—are slowly introduced to the poison when they are young. A drop at a time. And they build up a tolerance over the years. It does not kill them, but it's not painless either. I saw this firsthand."

"How?"

He claws at my hand again, tighter this time. "When Terstine lay naked in my room, her body was already covered in sweat, and we had not even begun. Her hair was matted to her face. The sheets were soaked through. So I knew something was wrong. Had I not been playing piano, I would have been dead."

"Playing piano?"

"Let me back up," he says. "We both undressed. Things were progressing. She then said that she needed to go to the bathroom. Alright, I thought. Killed the mood a bit, but no big deal."

He hunches his shoulders.

"She was taking a while, so I started to work on my etude to pass the time. When she emerged from the bathroom, she was eager to make love. Very eager. But by then, I was in the middle of the etude."

I just shake my head.

"A beautiful piece in C minor from Northinglight. A female composer by the name of Friedchappe. Have you heard—"

"So you were intent on finishing the song before you and this Terstine . . ."

He nods. "This is the critical piece. It took a tenthbell to finish the etude. Meanwhile she started to get very upset with me. She began breaking out in a sweat and then had to rest on the bed. The sweat was practically pouring out of her."

"What did you do?"

"Well, I was naturally suspicious. So I went into the bathroom and that's when I found the empty vial. A vial that looked remarkably similar to the one in your companion's possession."

I look down at the sandy ground, wondering if Chimeline could be more than she seems or if I am simply getting caught up in the delusions of an addict.

"It all makes sense," he whispers. "Your companion is quite beautiful. A look worthy of her weapon of choice."

*This is enough.*

I leave Cleanthes' side and walk back down the sandy road in the direction we came from, toward the skullmen. One of them is still bearing the white towel with the vial resting upon it.

I point to it.

"Take this back to the stables. Return it to her saddlebag exactly like you found it. And make no mention of this to anyone."

The skullman looks to Cleanthes, who has followed me. "Redskull?"

Cleanthes nods anxiously and brings his praying hands up in front of him. "Yes!" he says, his voice a loud whisper. It's as if he wants to be quiet, but like a child, he cannot control his enthusiasm. "The master voider's tactic is brilliant. Let the assassin believe she is winning at her own game. Fight deception with deception."

He looks at me, perhaps for approval, and I give a single nod, even though his assumptions are not even remotely correct.

Let Cleanthes think we're playing some sort of master game. As long as he doesn't harm Chimeline, I'm fine with it. I have serious doubts about his moonspit theory— whatever Chimeline is doing, I will talk to her about it myself. It's Cleanthes who needs to be dealt with right now.

The two men bow and walk back down the gentle slope toward the stables.

As soon as they are out of earshot, I turn to Cleanthes and say, "Don't say a word of this to anyone. I want to handle this in my own way."

"Of course."

A moment passes, and my body slowly relaxes. I look around at our bleached gold and white surroundings: the barn, row houses, tall grasses, towers of millionescents, all of it.

And I shift my thoughts to Cleanthes.

I was never going to kill him—if I were, I would have done it in the library when we were first reacquainted.

Which means that there are only two paths forward.

I could simply move on from this place. Leave him to his own devices. He will be dead in no time, either due to the drug or his own men—once they realize that he is a charlatan. He's already lost the gift. He is no more of a threat than any other skullman.

Or I could rehabilitate him. Wean him off the drug and retrain his mind toward voidance. But that would require taking him with me. Taking him back under my wing.

I'm not sure what drives my decision more: the remains of his moral compass or the remains of mine.

"Let's head back," I say.

We slowly make our way toward the pool and back patio—not through the graveyard but instead continuing down the circular path through the tall grasses. Along the way, we pass a sizable vegetable garden tended to by at least a dozen people.

Eventually, I see the pool. Chimeline is wearing her white-lace dress again. It looks as though it's been repaired.

As she sees us walking on the path, I wave to her, and she shyly waves back. She then spreads out the hem of her dress. There is a hesitancy in her movements and in the look upon her face, most likely caused by the recent violence on the road. But I think I can see a hint of a smile there too, a hopeful indication that her dress was not the only thing that was salvaged.

"Assassin," Cleanthes mumbles under his breath.

"Sit down," I tell him.

We're back at the same bench as before, but now the sun is lower. The lemon tree on the opposite side of the path shades the entire area.

He sits down, and I join him.

"I will help you restore your gift."

He exhales, leaning forward to place his elbows on his knees, his fingers interwoven.

"I knew you would."

He begins rocking his body back and forth in glee.

"But you need to leave hilma behind."

And just as quickly, Cleanthes goes still.

"There is no other way," I add quietly.

"That's impossible. I can't."

"Yes, you can," I answer, my voice optimistic.

I purse my lips, watching him closely as he wrings his hands, his emotions taking hold of him. "I understand that addiction is hard to overcome. But the drug is what's preventing your voidance from working."

Suddenly, he turns to me and clutches my black robe. "You don't understand. You don't know the power of this stupid fucking little flower."

I have the urge to push his hands off of me but let him be.

"What do you want?" I ask him. "Hilma or the void? You can't have both."

It takes longer for him to answer than I expected.

"The void," he finally says.

"Are you sure?"

He mumbles something that I can't hear, so I grab his shoulders and give him a violent shake. He's so frail underneath the crimson cloak.

"Are you sure?" I repeat, louder this time.

He nods.

"Are you sure?" I shout.

"Yes!"

I push him away from me.

"Then you have a chance to survive. As long as you want something more than this hideous drug, you have a chance at life and voidance. It will be the hardest test you have ever taken in your life. Harder than anything you did at the university. But I will help you."

He shakes uncontrollably now, and I put my arm around him, letting his face fall back into my shoulder. A few women from the patio crane their necks past the yews. They hear the shouting but do not understand what is happening.

"You can stay here," he says. "And the assassin and graycloak, too. As long as you need. Anything you need. My guests of honor, forever."

I press my lips together, wondering if now is the right time to deliver more harsh news. I decide that it is.

"Actually, it's not just hilma you need to leave behind. It's this place altogether."

He lifts his face from my shoulder and looks at me in confusion. His orange-red paint is smeared, revealing some of his freckles.

"I'm on my way south," I say. "I want you to come with me."

He squints further. "Where are you going?"

I pause then decide to be truthful with him. "Do you remember the Lady Marine?"

"Your wife?"

I nod. "She left me."

His lips make shapes as he tries to formulate a question.

"She left the citadel days ago with another voider. They took an airship and passed through these parts. I am intent on finding them."

His face goes through a complex mix of emotions. The smeared paint on his face makes them almost impossible to read. He smiles bitterly and then looks down.

"What is it?"

He doesn't respond.

"Did you see the airship?"

He nods.

"Do you know where it went?"

"Xi Bay," he says, to the sand beneath his feet. "Colu mapped it out."

I lean forward. "Where is this map?"

"My bedroom."

"Will you show it to me?"

He looks up at me, and then I finally interpret the emotion upon his face. It's disappointment.

"You didn't come here to visit me," he says quietly.

"What?"

He motions with a shaking finger to Xi Bay Road, beyond. "I thought that after all this time, you were journeying here to visit me. But you weren't. You were going south to find the woman who left you."

I pause, a sliver of guilt stinging me.

"You didn't even plan on running into me, did you? It was an accident."

After a moment, I nod.

He looks down, forcing a laugh.

"Does it matter?" I ask. "Regardless of the circumstances, we are reunited. Much good can come of this."

It's impossible to read his reaction. He puts his elbows back on his knees and looks down at the sand.

"We should leave tonight," I add.

He wipes his face with the back of his hand. It comes away with more paint. He nods at the ground. A clock from inside the mansion rings out. It is fivebell.

"I'll appoint Colu as the new redskull," he says. "Inside, he is a good man. Outside, the people fear him."

I don't reply, since I don't care. In a matter of fullbells, all of this will be behind us.

# CLEANTHES' TEST

The freestanding clock against the dining room wall begins playing a tinny and discordant nursery rhyme.

It is a halfbell past seven.

"I will see what is keeping the redskull," says the head waiter. "I heard him playing piano earlier."

Colu flashes me a concerned look from across the flames of a candelabra.

"Do not enter his bedchamber," Colu replies in his deep voice. "Knock only, and politely remind him that we await his presence for dinner."

"Yes, sir," the head waiter says, backing up into the shadows, as I silently look about the candlelit room.

Thirteen people sit around the table. Half of them know what is happening, and half of them do not.

Chimeline, the effulgent, and Colu are present. Colu has reapplied his skull paint—it's bright white for probably the last time in his life, and perfectly drawn.

Four other skullmen sit at the table, along with five women who were outside by the pool. The men wear black shirts and vests. Not exactly formal dinner wear, but they don't look completely disheveled either. It's too dark to see if their eyes are yellow. Once Cleanthes shows up and we begin eating, I'll be able to study their hands to see if they are shaking.

One of the skullmen is clearly sober. He has a scar that cuts upward from the bridge of his nose all the way into his hairline. He keeps playing with his steak knife, twirling it with deft fingers.

The women all wear silk gowns in deep, colorful hues. A fur wrap or two. One of them looks like a child, she's so petite.

If fact, they all look like children, in a strange way. As if they are pretending to be a real family, with true prosperity and learned demure. It wasn't just Cleanthes putting on a charade. They are all in this together.

Colu takes out a cigar from his black vest. "Fuck all this waiting. I'm going outside for a smoke."

He stands and walks around the table, exiting the dining room.

I push my chair back and follow, feeling everyone's gaze.

We pass through the dark library and then head outdoors, onto the brick patio. There is nobody here, and the only sound is the trickle of a fountain at the edge of the empty pool. The moonlight is reflected in it.

Colu lights his cigar off a lantern, mumbles something, puffs upon the cigar, and then takes it from his mouth.

"You're dead set on leaving tonight?" he asks.

"I'm afraid so," I say.

He nods. "I'll make sure your horses and the redskull's mare are packed and ready to go."

"I appreciate that."

He looks at the cigar in his hand and grunts a laugh. "I'll throw in some sugarcanex. You're going to need it."

"Sugarcanex?" I give Colu a dark look.

"If you plan on weaning the redskull from hilma, you better have something else for him to lean on."

"That's a good idea."

Colu takes another puff of his cigar and looks up to a candlelit window. "I don't know what the fuck is taking him so long."

"He said he had some things to prepare before he left for good. A letter to his family or something."

"Must be writing a fucking memoir," Colu says.

A breeze comes by, bringing with it a chill, so I raise the collar of my flaxen cloak.

"You seem to have come out of this on top," I say.

He forces a deep laugh. "You presume that I want to be the redskull."

I nod.

"Well, I don't."

"Why not?"

"The power is appealing, of course, but it comes with a price," he says, turning to face Cleanthes' candlelit window again.

"But you are Xian military," I say. "I would think that this sort of promotion would suit you."

"Ex-military," he corrects me. "And no, it does not suit me."

"Then why did you agree to it?"

"You gave me very little choice," he says.

"You always have a choice."

"Do I?" He looks at the tip of his cigar. "I've been searching for a new life ever since I left my home. I am a helmsman no more, and while I have no desire to live out the rest of my life as a redskull in Northern lands, perhaps this is my destiny."

I purse my lips in the darkness.

"You don't use hilma, do you?"

"Fuck no."

I nod. "Your humility is probably a good thing for this cursed place. I hope you are the ruler these people deserve."

"This place needs more than humility."

He takes a puff, the tip lighting up like a red-hot coal.

"What do you mean?"

"It's only a matter of time before we're attacked."

I pause in surprise. "By whom?"

"Prainise." He flicks the ashen tip of his cigar away. "They're brutal fuckers over there. When they realize that we have no voider . . ."

As he trails off, I frown in confusion. "But Cleanthes has lost voidance. Even if he stayed, it would do no good."

"Nobody knows that," Colu says, then spits. "Not here, and not in Prainise. The mere threat of his power has been the only thing keeping them in check. Once they sense an opportunity, they will come tearing through here."

"Come through here?"

He illustrates by waving the cigar between the mansion and himself. "They'll kill all of these people."

His one eye looks at me, and I suddenly realize why he's telling me all of this. "I'm not changing my mind, Colu. I can't stay any longer."

The wisdom of his age shows in his graceful yet disapproving nod.

"Prainise will eventually learn of what has happened, but if we're lucky I'll be ready by then. I'll need to step up our defenses. Fortify our field towers. Lower our production as I train more fieldmen into skullmen for a season or two. Shift more of my men from daytime to nighttime watch."

He blows out smoke and then spits again. "We've gotten lazy, Master Voider. We've replaced might with make-believe. We've forgotten who we are."

I look at him, trying to read his expression.

"And who are you?" I ask.

"Something tells me that we're going to find out."

After these words, the two of us stand in silence until it is broken by a woman's scream.

Colu looks up to the orange-lit window. Someone there opens the glass doors of the small balcony, banging them against the outside siding.

A man leans over the railing, a lantern in his hands. He looks downward and sees us on the patio.

"Come quickly!" he shouts.

Colu tosses his cigar on the bricks and stamps it out.

"Fuck," he mumbles.

By the time Colu, Chimeline, the effulgent, and I reach the third story, the dark hallway has become congested with people—young women in gowns, maids and footmen, and even skullmen. Nobody is speaking. I see a few of the women crying, so I know something serious has happened.

"Move it," Colu booms, and everyone hugs the walls to let us through.

As soon as I enter the doorway into the bedroom, my heart drops.

Cleanthes' body leans over the keys of his black grand piano.

The room is bright. At least four candelabras glow, along with the lantern, which is still being carried by the head footman. The room is filled with hilma smoke. It curls beside me like the swirls in a tide pool, thickly sweet and ghostly gray.

The room is similar to the library. Dozens of bookshelves, along with a few circular tables covered with papers and maps. A bed in the corner.

I head straight toward Cleanthes.

His body sits upon the black tufted-leather bench. His hands, head, and chest rest upon the keys, almost as if he is softly playing the final, delicate notes of a song. An etude in a minor key.

His crimson robe is off, discarded on the floor next to the pedals. He wears only a thin undershirt and underpants, the attire of a man planning for a long night's sleep.

Leaning over him, I gently pick his face up. A few of the touched piano keys hit the taut hidden strings, causing a discordant tone to fill the room.

His face, free of paint and already gray, is unblemished, save for his youthful freckles.

*He was practically a boy.*

A slender white trail of smoke comes from a pipe in a glass ashtray resting on the piano.

I gently set his face back down upon the keys, so slowly that not a note sounds.

"Is he dead?" asks the head footman, raising his bright lantern.

I nod, covering my face with an outstretched hand to ward off the light.

Suddenly, I feel dizzy and my body breaks out in sweat underneath my clothes. It's probably the hilma smoke, which is a fog within the room. But it might be more than this.

I head to the alcove and push on the same set of glass doors that the head footman opened moments ago. There is a small balcony, and I step onto it, looking down onto the brick patio where Colu and I recently stood. Where we discussed plans that are now irrefutably broken.

I take a deep breath, letting the pure night air fill my lungs.

But it doesn't help as much as I was hoping for.

*It's my fault he's dead.*

First, I sent Anaxarchis to his death, and then I sent Cleanthes to his. And all this time, I did nothing. I navigated between perfect places, forgetting the people who needed me most.

The same is true with Marine. I lost her too, and it's probably my fault somehow. Maybe I neglected her the way I neglected my graduates. Night after night, I left her alone while I studied, coming home at dawn. I put my university first, and my wife second. I put the void before everything else, and all these great men and women—all the people in the world who matter to me—are now gone.

*Indivisibles divided.*

I jump, startled by Chimeline. She puts a hand on my shoulder as she settles in beside me against the iron railing. I feel her hip next to mine.

I hadn't even known she was here.

"You're crying," she says, looking sideways at me.

I quickly wipe away a tear with my hand. "It's probably the smoke."

She puts her slender hands on top of mine.

"I am sorry," she says. "I know that he was your student, just like the man in Fiscarlo. You wanted to help him."

For a while I don't say anything. I'm keenly aware of more and more people coming into the room. It's filling with vultures. Colu speaks to them, but I can't hear him from the balcony. And I don't care.

All I can think about is how everything I have built has crumbled, and I just want the night to take me. I want the breeze to pick me up away from this place, to be among the stars. Freezing and alone. The world doesn't need me. It has plans of its own.

"It was too much for him," I eventually say. "Everything has fallen apart. Colu was right. I'm a child playing in the sand."

She squeezes my hands.

"Sand is the strongest thing in the world," she replies.

I look at her, blinking away tears.

"Not every rocky mineral is equally built to last," she adds. "Over time, the weather takes its toll. The world takes everything back to the sea, and only the strongest is left. Only the sand remains."

She leans in, kisses me on the cheek, and then whispers in my ear, "You are strong, Democryos. You will endure, like the sand."

I pull her into me, embracing her tightly, almost as if the railing has fallen away. I clutch her for fear of falling.

In a way, she could be anyone. I could be grasping Colu or the effulgent, or even a stranger, here on this window ledge. Some living person offering me hope and encouragement, an anchor that tethers me to this world. Because right now I feel that it's the world or nothing. It's the indivisible or the void.

As I breathe in Chimeline's scent and feel the curves of her body against mine, this universal feeling of companionship evolves into something more. This is not just kinship. This is not just hope. The fit is far too perfect.

I have forgotten the feeling of a woman's caress. A man's need and a woman's need. How the two, so different from one another, are such perfect complements.

I used to tell Marine that our love was indivisible.

When I close my eyes, her memory swirls in the darkness, but for the first time, she fades slightly from view. It is as if she is standing on the opposite end of Cleanthes' bedroom, a cloud of hilma smoke between us. The thin hair against my face—it's Chimeline's dark tendrils instead of Marine's bleached ones. Deep brown eyes instead of the blue tones of Xi Bay. Caramel skin instead of milky white.

*A heart full of love instead of a head full of schemes.*

At the time, Marine was the strongest of tethers, but if I focus on letting go, I can feel a similar pull now.

Is it possible that the feeling can be found again?

*Things fall apart, Dem. I've fallen in love with someone else, and we are indivisible no more.*

Marine's last written words mix with the Cleanthes' paranoia. The stain of black pitch. Was the moonspit meant for me? Are these tethers meant for safety or treachery? Am I embracing the very woman tasked with murdering me? The desperate flailing of a drowning, lonely man?

Colu calls out to me.

"We should go inside," I say, pulling away from her and reentering the bright, smoke-filled room.

I'm dizzy.

Colu speaks urgently to everyone, telling them that Cleanthes was going to leave with me tonight, and that he had silently transferred power. He raises a parchment with Cleanthes' handwriting on it.

He looks at me with his one eye. "Tell them," he says gruffly.

I nod. "It is true," I tell the packed room. "Colu is your new redskull. It was Cleanthes' decision, and I supported it."

Murmurs cascade through the crowd as I slowly work my way back to the center of the room, toward a round table with a map on it. Flat-bottomed iron finials have been used to keep the rolls from closing in upon themselves.

One of the skullmen—the one with the scar—steps forward.

"Why would he transfer power to Colu?"

A few of the others in the room repeat his question and the momentum builds.

"He had lost his gift," I say loudly, quieting down the crowd as I hold my voidstone by its gold setting. "This cursed drug you grow here consumed his mind and he lost the power of voidance."

I look at Cleanthes' dead body, still huddled upon the piano. "I had promised to take him with me, to help him regain his gift, but it was too much for him. He wanted the drug more."

The one with the scar looks from him to Colu and then to me.

"Then why aren't you the new redskull?" he says to me. "We need a voider."

A few others mumble in agreement. "We need a voider!"

I shake my head. "I cannot stay here. I have responsibilities elsewhere."

The complaints cascade almost immediately.

Colu steps forward, a look of annoyance on his face. "We don't need a voider," he says. "We never have. What we need is power, strategy, and leadership, all of which I possess."

"But you're Xian!" someone says, hidden in the crowd.

"How can we trust someone we're at war with?" says another.

With that, the room erupts in argument again.

I push the noise to the back of my mind. It is like the thick fog that has filled the room, only bitter instead of sweet.

I stand over the map—watercolor over black ink. It's a beautiful work that rivals anything we have at the university.

It doesn't show the entire Northern Kingdom, and shows almost none of Xiland. In one corner is the measurement *100x100 King Miles*. At one edge is Xi Bay, its tones faded blue amidst a subtle pattern of waves. There are dozens of towns there, up and down the shoreline that runs hundreds of linear miles around the immense curved gulf. Each of them is marked with dots and named.

In the center of the map is a red dot near *Prainise*, *Chartise*, and *Joscaio*.

But there are newer markings besides these.

An inkwell, gold coin, and wooden ruler rest in the center of the map, and I push them aside.

My action reveals three circles, freshly drawn, looking as if they were traced with the gold coin. Lines connect them to each other.

One of these circles is directly over the red dot—obviously the location of this hilma plantation. The other two are about ten miles in either direction.

I look up, hoping I can get Colu over to explain, but he is in fervid conversation with the crowd, so I turn my attention back to the map.

This was what Cleanthes was saying before he died. Colu mapped this out. He saw the airship from the watchtower and must have transposed its location and course on this map based on geographical details.

Putting a finger to the parchment, I run it along the length of the line going southward, until it ends abruptly at the shoreline of Xi Bay, where the green meets the blue.

There's a town there, its name written in tiny flowing letters: *Winter's Baiou*.

I bring a hand to my temple.

*It can't be.*

Suddenly, I wish that I were out on the balcony again, breathing in the clear night air. The hilma smoke makes the room spin, and I need to place both palms on the table, leaning over in delirium.

*Winter's Baiou.*

Finally, I know where Marine is headed.

She's in the place where our marriage began.

And where it will soon end.

# THE SPY FROM PRAINISE

Chimeline's face hovers over mine as I blink against the light.

"What is it?" I ask, my voice hoarse.

"Colu said to wake you," she answers, her voice silken, her small hand on my bare chest. "He wants to show you something."

I look around at the luxurious bedroom, realizing I don't know where I am. I see green ivy wallpaper and the morning sun shining through threadbare pink drapes. This is a woman's bedroom. I've never been here before.

I peel back the covers and notice that I'm wearing only my undergarments.

I exhale.

"You passed out by the map table," Chimeline explains, her voice pleasant.

I sit up in bed. "The map. Where is it?"

"It's over there." She points to an ornate white dresser near the closed bedroom door.

Chimeline walks over to the fireplace and fetches my clothes and boots then sits back down on the edge of the bed as I swing my feet over the side. But not before looking to the other half of the bed, at the tossed bedsheets and pillows there.

"I had them carry you here after you passed out," she explains, standing up and straightening the sheets. "Colu was too busy to look after you, so I insisted on it myself."

"You did?"

"I was worried about you," she says offhandedly, focused on making the bed and smoothing the sheets.

I stand up, getting out of her way, and begin pulling on my clothes. "Thank you."

She glances at me. "I just kept thinking about what happened last night. What you said on the balcony. I don't know—you have a lot on your shoulders right now. I just wanted to make sure you're alright."

I hesitate in the midst of buttoning my shirt. Her kindness isn't completely unexpected, but her understanding my myriad feelings makes me wonder if we are more alike than I thought.

*Or maybe she is just getting close enough to kill me.*

"I appreciate that very much."

She stops working on the bed. "Do you feel better?"

"A bit."

But the truth is, the dark thoughts of Cleanthes' death still consume me. No amount of sleep will dilute them.

*Two students. Dead.*

I push all these morbid thoughts aside and flash her a smile. "Yes, I am better. And for good reason."

She returns the smile, warmly, genuinely, without knowledge of my weight. "And what reason is that?"

I finish buttoning my shirt and nod toward the rolled-up map in the corner, its image permanently imprinted upon my mind. "I know where she went."

"Lady Marine?"

I nod. "Winter's Baiou," I say. "Have you been there?"

She shakes her head and stays silent the entire time I lace my boots. When I'm done, I turn back to her and see a distant look in her eyes. Her previous sunny demeanor is suddenly overcome with shade, and I'm not sure why.

"Do you want to stay here?" I ask.

She doesn't answer.

"This is a rogue hilma plantation. Misery will descend upon this place. It's not a question of *if*. It's a question of *when*."

"I know. I just wish it didn't have to be so soon. It feels so good to be in a house again. To sleep in a bed again."

I nod. "Once we get to Winter's Baiou, you'll get that. And it will be safe. I'm not leaving you here at the mercy of the skullmen."

She looks down and nods.

I furrow my brow. "What time is it, anyway?"

"Almost twelvebell."

I mumble a curse—already half the day is done.

She fetches my cloak from a hook on the door and holds it as I snake my arms through, much like Elrich used to do at the Royal House. But unlike Elrich, Chimeline continues to stand close in front of me, spreading my cloak out against my chest with her palms, her head tilted up toward me.

"You said Colu wants to speak to me?"

"Yes."

"Where is he?"

She wrinkles her nose. "In the stables, I think."

I nod.

"So are we leaving soon?" she asks. "For Winter's Baiou?"

I gently shake my head. "There is something I need to do first."

"What's that?"

"Bury Cleanthes."


I walk through the large open door of the white barn and my eyes take a moment to transition from the harsh midday sun to the cool shadow. Colu leans over a bale of hay in the darkness, his back to me. But then he stands straight, backing away slightly, and I see what has been left behind.

A young boy, surrounded by a buzzing cloud of flies.

His throat has been cut deeply, the wound gaping wide in shades of pink and white. Blood covers his entire body and the surrounding pile of hay.

I momentarily look away, having not expected such a macabre sight.

"This was a spy's doing," Colu eventually says, teeth clenched. "From Prainise."

He points to the stalls in the darkness. "The redskull's mare is missing."

It takes me a moment to comprehend what has happened. "Were you onto him or something?"

"What?"

"Did you know who the spy was? Is that why this happened?"

"No," he says, glancing at me. "*He* was onto *us*."

"I'm not sure what you mean," I say. I take a step forward to peer at the body, and the cloud of flies momentarily disperses. The blood on the boy's shirt is dry and the material stiff. "This happened fullbells ago."

"Exactly," he replies. "I'm guessing last night, right after your speech in the redskull's bedroom."

I put a hand to my head as I try to remember the moments leading up to my passing out. "I'm not following."

"He left to tell Prainise the news. That the redskull is dead. That we are defenseless."

He brushes past me, exiting the stables into the sunlight.

"Where are you going?"

"Time for roll call."

"What?"

"I need to find out who the spy was. Find out what others may have told them over the past day."

"Does it matter? The spy is already gone. The damage is already done."

"Damage?" Colu asks, as he continues to march forward. "You haven't seen damage yet. This whole place will burn."

"How can you be so sure?"

He stops and turns to me. "They're coming, Master Voider. Your arrival here"—he gestures to the mansion— "the redskull's death has started a chain of events that may be our ruin. We spoke about this last night, but things are happening far quicker than I had planned."

"And you're blaming me for all of this?" I ask in disbelief.

"No," he says, shaking his head while looking at the sandy ground. "I don't have time for blame. All I need to know right now is if you are planning to stay or not."

I look to the front door of the mansion. It's open, and Chimeline leans against its frame, a cup of tea cradled in her hands.

"I'll stay to bury my friend, but I'm not about to help you fight this cursed drug war with voidance."

He takes a deep breath, his chest rising and falling as he glares at me with his one eye.

"Then get the fuck out of my way," he says, and then marches off.


The effulgent helps me carry Cleanthes' body out of the mansion and into the millionescent-enclosed graveyard. We do the same with the stablehand boy, who is apparently an orphan. No one else comes to look at his body. Nobody is here to mourn either of them. I use my voidstone to bury the two, but not before taking Cleanthes' necklace from his gray neck and putting it in my cloak pocket.

I now have three voidstones. Given the circumstances, I do not wish to possess the extra two treasures.

I remember that Cleanthes mentioned stacks of fieldstone in the barn, so I go back there and search for them. True to his word, I find them all the way in the corner, behind leaning rakes and shovels and tangled in strands of cobwebs.

I pick out two large, beautiful slabs and haul them over to the fresh graves.

Then I spend a fullbell inscribing them using my voidstone, as Cleanthes had once done.

One reads *Jacyon, Stablehand.*

The other, *Cleanthes, Citadelian Voider.*

I'll be Temberlain himself if people remember my student as a redskull.

He was so much more than that.

It is late afternoon by the time Chimeline, the effulgent, and I leave the hilma plantation.

Colu must still be angry—he doesn't see us off.

But as our horses meander past the center fountain, down the sandy path, and onto Xi Bay Road, I have the instinctive urge to turn around. When I do, I see him standing there, watching us from within the shadow of the white house.

I hate to admit it, but I'm going to miss the Xian man. There is an honesty honed in him that few other men possess. It's a shame that he has chosen to waste it on this forsaken place.

Once the field of sagging bulbs, pregnant with black sap, hides the mansion from view, I feel a weight lift from my shoulders. I am back on the road southbound, and this time I have a specific destination.

Of all the towns where that line could end, it had to be Winter's Baiou.

We ride briskly for two bells, and when we slow, the sun lingers low on the horizon, turning everything into shades of deep gold and purple. We notice a campsite up ahead, just off the road in a trampled grass clearing. A slender trail of white smoke rises there.

Chimeline and the effulgent both look at me in concern, but I can see a royal banner waving in the gentle breeze.

"It's Northern military," I say, surprised, my brow furrowing.

"Is that a good thing?" Chimeline asks me.

After a moment of thought, I nod. "It's better than the alternative."

"And what would that be?" the effulgent asks.

"Xian scouts."

As we approach the camp, the reason for its chosen location becomes obvious. It's at the intersection of Xi Bay Road and a wide stream. The tributary to the River Xi cuts underneath a wide-planked bridge in the road up ahead. Four dressed horses stand tethered there, drinking fresh water on the sandy shore.

Closer to us, four soldiers in full armor eat around a small firepit in the center of a clearing. All of them are young—in their twenties, most likely. Full heads of hair without a hint of gray. One of them has a red cloak draped across his back that matches the banner stuck into the sandy ground. He stands up, places his food down upon his tin plate, and wipes his hand on a nearby rag. Then he meets us at the roadside, his hand resting on the hilt of his sword.

"Greetings," I say, dismounting. "I am Master Voider Democryos."

His eyes widen and then narrow. "Do you have the king's signet?"

I show him my ring.

Once he sees the gold seal of Andrej X, he takes his hand off of his hilt and bows. "This is an honor, Your Grace. I apologize for the formalities. I only ask because we are far from the citadel."

I nod, extending a hand to the other two. "This is Chimeline and a graycloak. My travel companions."

He subtly raises his eyebrows, but he's too educated to make a fool of himself by asking me about them. Instead, he shows proper respect by signaling the other three soldiers to stop eating and stand at attention.

"Please, as you were," I say.

"Won't you join us at our fire?" he replies.

For a moment I vacillate, but night is quickly approaching, and this is a fine camping ground. It's near fresh water and the road. And there is already a fire burning and news from the south to be had. It would be foolish to keep going just for another few fullbells of darkened travel.

So I thank him. We tether our horses alongside the soldiers' and join them for dinner, sharing some of our dried fruits and nuts while they give us the remains of their turkey.

The conversation is pleasant but cautionary. Despite my station, they are guarded. All the soldier says regarding their reason for travel is that the four of them are headed north with urgent news for the king—information that is too risky to be carried by pigeon.

That's when I have an idea.

Excusing myself, I walk into the approaching darkness, find my horse by the bridge, and search in the saddlebag for something that was meant for Cleanthes.

As I rifle through our supplies, I hear a shuffle in the grasses. A few of the horses flap their lips in distress.

Swiveling in place, I look out onto the darkened grasses. One hand is on the gold setting of my voidstone while the other is still searching in the saddlebag.

After another meager shuffle in the purple distance, a bird takes flight.

Meanwhile, my hand comes across something smooth and hard in the saddlebag. It's what I was looking for.

The bottle of sugarcanex.

I quickly grab it and return to the campfire, looking over my shoulder as I go. When I enter the ring of light, I open the cork, and three soldiers erupt in claps and cheers.

"Is that what I think it is?" one asks.

"The finest sugarcanex for the finest soldiers."

"We must be on our way soon," warns the commander. "We are riding through the night and only stopped here for a brief rest for us and our horses." But he sees the excitement in his three men, so he nods reluctantly. "A little will do no harm."

"To the king!" I say. I take a swig from the bottle and grimace. It's the words that make me grimace, not the strong, sweet taste of the liquor.

"To the king!" they all reply, as I pass the bottle to the soldier next to me.

"Let's just say that the war is won," the commander says, finishing the bottle and tossing it into the fire, where it shatters. "Well, practically speaking. The details are what I'm bringing to the king."

"I see."

He shakes his head distantly. "I cannot wait to see my wife. I have a son, I've been told."

"Congratulations," I say. "May he grow to be as strong as his father."

The other soldiers offer their congratulations in their own, slurred, ways.

"So the war is won, you say. How is that possible so fast?" I ask.

He raises his eyebrows as he stares into the fire. "That's for the king's ears only."

"I understand, soldier. I admire your virtue."

He picks up a stick resting on the ground and starts to draw in the dirt between his feet. "I guess it's alright to share, you being the master voider and all. Besides, you're headed south. You'll find out eventually."

I nod, trying to hide my excitement.

"We pushed them back to their own lands," he says, smiling wide. "Out of Xi Bay."

I purse my lips. "Completely?"

He nods. "Their navy is decimated. Whatever few ships they have left, they've retreated with them."

"Will we pursue them on land? Move south into Xiland?"

He snaps the twig. "No. We're holding the front lines. We already burned their imperial ports on the southern side of the bay. There is no way they are climbing out of this hole."

"But you have them on the run," I reply. "I would imagine that the commanders would want to keep the momentum going and attack them on land. Keep pushing them southward."

He shakes his head while looking at the ground. "No. We've achieved our objective. Established control of the bay."

I lean forward in the firelight, closer to him. "The bay?"

"The bay was always the objective," he says. "It was never about invading the south. It was always about taking control of Xi Bay."

I frown in confusion. The king never mentioned anything about the bay being a specific objective. In fact, he hardly ever brought it up at all.

"Why is the bay so vital?" I ask.

"Gold," one of the soldiers barks out. Another silences him with a shove.

The commander scowls as he breaks the stick and throws the pieces of it into the fire. "Ignore him, Master Voider. He's a young fool spreading nonsense."

"I'm just saying what I heard, is all. There's gold underwater."

"And pearls," says another.

"And a massive voidstone," says the fourth.

The lead soldier chuckles to himself as he stands. "It's our ability to trade, you fools. Getting our exports out of the north and taking in the imports. I know that's not as interesting as gold, pearls, and voidstones, but it's the boring truth. Isn't that right, Master Voider?"

I am half-lost in thought, staring at the soldier who mentioned a voidstone, but I am aware enough to understand that the one in the lead addressed me. So I nod and clear my throat. "That is right. The more boring the story is, the greater chance of it being true."

"Pack it up, men," the commander barks, rising to his feet.

"What, you're leaving?" I ask in surprise.

"As mentioned, we never intended to stay the night," he says. "We are under orders to report our news to the king immediately. It cannot wait."

"No, it certainly cannot," I answer.

He extends a hand. "Master Voider, it has been a pleasure."

"Mine as well."

With that, the four soldiers pack up camp in remarkable time, given their lack of sobriety. They guide their impressive horses onto the road and immediately spur them into a canter and disappear into the north. For the longest time, all I hear is the diminishing sound of hooves upon the sandy road.

"That was interesting," I say.

"Seems like good news to me," Chimeline says.

I shake my head but don't answer her.

"Isn't the end of any war good news?" she adds.

"Yes," I say. "It's just that the king never mentioned anything to me about Xi Bay. And apparently, it's what this whole war was about."

"Foolishness," the effulgent scoffs. "One cannot own a bay. Xi Bay will be here long after all of us are gone, and it certainly doesn't recognize this absurd war."

Before I can respond, I hear another rustle of grass.

It comes from the darkness on the eastern side of camp, just on the other side of the fire.

"Do you hear that?" the effulgent whispers at my side.

I nod and then touch my voidstone.

Within the void, I fly ahead. After taking a piece of fire, I move my created sphere into the night air, all the way to the rear of the camp, near the eastern edge of the tall grasses. I do this so quickly that the man hiding there, spreading the grasses wide, has no chance to react.

For a brief moment I see his indivisibles.

When I let go and reenter the world, his recognizable face is near the ground and between stalks of grass. My ball of fire hovers ten feet above him, and he looks at it in fear before lowering his gaze back to me.

He's one of the skullman from our dinner table last night at the mansion. The one with the scar across his forehead.

He's the one. The one who murdered Jacyon and took Cleanthes' mare.

Chimeline, who is sitting on the south side of the fire, screams and runs toward the effulgent and me while the man with the scar disappears.

"Good Unnamed, that was a skullman!" she cries, grabbing onto me. "He's here to kill us."

I break free of Chimeline's hold and grab my voidstone again. I watch his glistening indivisibles retreat through the field, getting smaller and hazier as he runs. He was about twenty-five yards away from me when he was hiding. Now he's at least fifty. Too far to use voidance on him now. I would risk voideath simply by trying.

"No," I answer as I let go. "He's running back to Prainise to deliver the news."

"You mean what the soldier was saying? That the war has ended?"

"No," I say, shaking my head and looking at the ground. "That a war is about to begin."

# AN ORANGE LINE

"Blythe," I say absently, looking across the campfire at the effulgent. His hairless face glows red against the moonlit blue darkness. It seems like the first word spoken among the three of us since the soldiers and spy departed nearly a fullbell ago.

Admittedly, I am torn between apprehension and hope, and with this single word, I consciously choose the latter.

"Are you speaking to me?" the effulgent asks, looking up.

I gesture to the horses tethered out of sight, near the bridge. "Blythe. The word is branded into your saddle."

"Oh," he says. "The man who rode the horse before me must have done it."

I look at him slyly, eager to break the heavy silence with some much-needed lightness. "You mean the former *owner* of *your* horse *named* him Blythe."

He clears his throat, looking away. "You are just goading me now. It will not work."

"Perhaps," I admit. "I know you don't believe in ownership or names. But sometimes names are necessary. And as we were riding here, I saw the word on your saddle and thought it might be offensive to you."

"Giving a name to a horse is not offensive, Master Voider," he responds. "It only proves my point. Whoever *owned* the animal felt it necessary to *name* it. So when I say names imply ownership, you now know what I mean."

I grunt. "Yes, it's all perfectly clear to me now."

He nods as if unaware of my facetiousness. "I am happy to have helped. It is part of my duties to educate the ignorant."

I grunt a laugh. "I could say the same."

He looks as though he's sucking on a lemon. "The effulgency may be many things, but ignorant we are not."

"You don't think it might be even a little shortsighted to go through life ignoring the names of everyone you meet?"

"Names imply ownership, and ownership—"

"I know," I interrupt. "I understand all that. My point is that names are convenient for everyone involved. Referring to you as *the effulgent*, while annoying, might work for a while. But what happens when we run into another effulgent? How do I differentiate you two without names?"

"I am a graycloak now."

"Exactly," I say. "First, you were an effulgent. Now, you're a graycloak. It's all very confusing."

"I am a graycloak forevermore because of what I've done."

"It's not just that," I say. "Titles may change, but your name should not. Your name is who you *are*."

He shakes his head in reply as a deeper thought comes to me. "By the way, what does not having a name do?" I ask. "It makes you unnamed—just like *the Unnamed*. Can't you admit that's a little sacrilegious?"

He looks at me as if I am daft. "It is never sacrilegious to esteem one's maker."

Chimeline sits next to me. She looks up from behind her blanket which wraps her face, tilting her head curiously. "Are you talking about giving the effulgent a name?"

"Yes!" I say. "Isn't it annoying to refer to someone by their title or occupation? I don't do that with you."

She looks down as I realize the awkward situation I've created. But she seems to shrug it off after a moment, looking back up to me. "For the longest time, I called you Your Grace."

"Yes, but I much prefer Dem."

I see the hint of a smile.

I look back to the effulgent. "So? What do you think about Blythe?"

"That's a girl's name," Chimeline says with a giggle.

"It doesn't have to be," I reply. "It fits the man perfectly. Carefree and indifferent to a fault."

He shakes his head slowly, a faraway look in his eyes, as he stands. "Good Unnamed, give me patience with these people."

"Blythe," I repeat to myself, laughing for what seems like the first time in days. "I'm going to start using that."

He walks in the direction of the horses.

"Where are you going, Blythe?" I call out.

After a moment of silence, he replies levelly from the darkness. "I'm getting the tents."

I nod and turn back to Chimeline, who is staring into the fire. "See how nicely that works?"

She nods and flashes a brief smile but seems troubled.

"What is it?" I ask her, leaning in.

"Do you think we'll be safe here tonight?"

"Of course," I say.

"But how can you be sure?" she asks, tightening the blanket around her. "If what Colu said is true, there could be trouble."

I put a hand on her shoulder, drawing her gaze to mine. "I'm not going to let anything happen to you."

Her features soften a bit as she nods once and turns her attention back to the fire. "I just don't like being out here."

"Colu packed two tents. You can share mine tonight, if it makes you feel safer. Or if you'd rather sleep alone, I can stay by the fire. We'll let Blythe have the other one."

She cracks a small smile at my use of the effulgent's new name.

"Master Voider," says Blythe loudly in the distance.

I look his way and see nothing but darkness.

"Stay here."

I walk briskly to the horses via a trampled path. As the firelight dims, I can see the effulgent's silhouette against the starlit horizon.

"What is it?"

I stand next to him. He's pointing far off, down the length of the tributary and past the rolling hills full of tall grasses. "Look."

"The spy?" Chimeline asks behind me, having ignored my warning.

There is a row of millionescent trees where Blythe is pointing. It runs parallel to Xi Bay Road, at least a mile away from us. The trees' towering silhouettes blot out the stars and indigo sky.

At their bases, and above the rolling grasses, is the slow movement of flickering orange light.

"Torches, I think. It's certainly a fire of some sort."

"A *lot* of torches," Blythe answers.

"You think it's Prainise skullmen?" Chimeline asks.

"Shh," the effulgent says in reply, putting a finger to his lips. "Listen."

Over the whisper of grasses and the wind, the sound of metal on metal rings out.

"Swords?" I ask.

"Armor."

"How many, do you think?"

He shakes his head. "At least a hundred. Look at how long the line of light stretches out."

"It looks like they're all on foot," I say.

Chimeline steps close to me—I can feel her fire-warmed body against mine. "Colu was right, then. Prainise is attacking. Tonight."

"It appears so."

"What are we going to do?" she asks.

I study the faint line of orange torchlight in the distance, feeling all the hope in me fade to guilt and regret. Why did the effulgent have to see this? If his hood had been gathered around him and his face buried in typical shadow, there would have been no chance of it.

We were back on our way southward. But now, the ghost of Cleanthes drags me back from across the fields.

"The master voider was right to leave," Blythe says. "This is bloodshed in the making, and black arcana will only make it worse."

"But what about all the people at the mansion?" Chimeline asks. "It's not just skullmen. There are women and children!"

"They are already doomed."

"That's ridiculous!"

"They strayed from the way of unwanting," Blythe explains. "They've embraced a life of selfishness built upon the destruction of mind and body. None of that is the master voider's fault."

I look sideways at him in shock.

"But Dem can help," continues Chimeline. "Despite the mistakes of these people, he can help."

"By doing what?" Blythe asks.

She looks to me in desperation and I shake my head. "I am not about to kill a hundred people with voidance."

"You don't have to kill them," she says. "You can instill fear in their hearts. Scare them so that they flee and never come back. Like what Colu said."

Chimeline reaches out and touches me gently on the arm.

"Dem, I met many of these women today. They are good people. Mothers. Sisters. Families. So many of them have already suffered. Lost loved ones to hilma—or the fighting over it. Don't let it happen again. Please."

*Families.*

I swallow, knowing what I want to do, and what I should do.

I want to continue south and let this sliver of light fade into the distance. Let the two villages destroy each other. Colu was right. I see it now. I only moved opportunity from one group to the other. Shifting sands in an unforgiving world.

*You are strong, Democryos. Like the sand.*

All selfish thoughts fade away the moment I look into Chimeline's wide eyes, full of moonlight and hope. I know what I am going to do.

I will cut sideways across this field and head the skullmen off. I will teach Prainise a lesson.

I'm not doing this for Colu.

I'm doing this for the memory of Cleanthes.

All the people back at the plantation were his family. Despite the cloud of hilma surrounding Cleanthes, there was selfless love there. He lost his gift for voidance but never his gift of innocence.

The same thing shines in Chimeline's eyes.

"Alright, let's go," I say to them both, as I walk around my horse and untie the reins. "Leave the fire to die on its own. And stay close to me."

At first, Chimeline stands there in disbelief. Then she rushes over and hugs me tightly.

"Good Unnamed, help us all," Blythe mumbles.

# ENTOMBED

We ride hard to the northeast for a quarterbell, running parallel and then passing up the line of golden light to ensure a buffer of darkness remains between them and us.

I want to head them off.

But as we near the line of trees, one small flame glows at the center of them. It is meager, unnoticeable until the last moment. Barely strong enough to cast a cobweb of wide, shadowy lines in all directions.

Someone is there, waiting.

This is not the approaching army—we're too far in front of them. But it could be a scout.

I approach cautiously.

The lowest branches of the millionescents hang high enough off the ground that I can bend down and grasp my horse's neck to pass through and underneath them.

Only then, under a towering ceiling of dimly glittering gold, do I finally see who it is.

The one-eyed Colu sits on horseback in the center of the road, a raised lantern in his hand. Covered in leather armor and a vest of chain mail, he looks at me, a surprised but tense look upon his red-painted face.

"You came back," he says gruffly.

I nod, peering down the length of the road in both directions.

The section of dirt path we're on has a gentle curve to it. It's about ten yards wide and nestled between two rows of tightly packed, alternating millionescents. They function as sheer walls, seemingly extending to the stars. It's almost like being inside of some grand effulgency temple. The branches begin about ten feet up. I can see past the thick trunks into the darkened countryside.

Chimeline and Blythe silently enter the road behind me.

The first signs of the approaching army appear in the distance: a faint yellow glow upon the trees up ahead, and the distant ring of metal.

Before I address Colu, I quickly turn to Chimeline and Blythe and point in the direction we came from. "Do you remember that cluster of pines we passed a moment ago?"

They both nod.

"Hide there until this is over."

"But, Dem—"

"Do it," I forcefully whisper, and then I softly add, "Please. I don't need complications."

"He is right," Blythe adds. "Only swords and black arcana will be used here. Words of peace and forgiveness will not."

Their horses flap their lips together in seeming agreement.

She nods hesitantly, and they both turn their horses around and head into the night.

"Dem?" Chimeline asks, turning her body as it disappears into shadow.

"Yes?"

"Be careful."

I nod and turn to Colu. "Are you alone?"

He shakes his head. "I have twenty skullmen flanking these trees," he says. "Ten on each side."

I look around in all directions. "I didn't see them."

"They're hidden. And it's a good thing they know who the three of you are. Else you'd be dead by now."

I nod again. "What's your plan?"

"I was going to stall them with conversation. At my signal, my men will take out as many as they can with darts."

"How many?"

"If they're able to take down two each, that's forty Prainise. Which should be about half of them."

I take a deep breath. "And then what?"

He hunches his shoulders. "That's the extent of my plan."

The first of the Prainise men approach from around the bend, fifty yards in the distance. I can already see in the torchlight that they're wearing full armor and carrying swords and maces.

One of them points in our direction, and the first few stop and spread out their arms, causing the entire column to come to a noisy halt.

The distant clanking turns into silence.

"Your plan is horrible," I say dryly.

He laughs. "I make do with the limited resources available to me."

He gets off his horse, walks it over to the closest trunk, and tethers it there. I do the same.

"I'm not here to commit any violence," I say quietly. "My goal is to intimidate. To get out of this without any bloodshed whatsoever."

He nods as we begin walking in the direction of the throng.

"Let me do the talking," he says. "I have an idea."

As we approach, some of the men murmur to each other. The words *voider*, *fake*, and *redskull* reach me.

Once we round the gentle bend in the road, we stop, about twenty yards from the beginning of their column.

Their torches go on and on into the distance.

There are easily a hundred armored men with painted black skulls upon their dull-gray breastplates, and I see a few semi-armored children mixed in the crowd as well. Boys wanting to become murderers like their fathers.

One of the lead men steps forward. A red skull surrounded in a circle of gold has been painted upon his breastplate. His face is entirely covered in metal. He holds a mace in one hand and an outstretched torch in the other.

"You have yourselves a voider," he says, his voice a muffled shout.

"Yes," Colu says. He briefly turns to me before staring straight ahead once again.

"Not just a voider," he says. "A *master* voider."

"I heard that your last redskull was a fake," the other redskull continues. "He had a stone but couldn't use it."

Colu stays silent.

"I also heard that the master voider already left town. He's headed south to the war. So I think that this man standing next to you is a fake too," the redskull says, his metal head briefly swiveling to me.

After a pause, he's seemingly made up his mind, as his armored head nods in the firelight. "Where are your skullmen? Hiding like cowards? Or have they all succumbed to hilma too?"

Again, more silence from Colu. He's too wise to let himself be lured with insults.

The redskull laughs behind his helmet. "You're weak," he says. But then his laughter turns to anger and his voice becomes a full shout. "You are built upon a lie! Tonight, you're finally going to taste the truth. The power of Prainise."

His men beat their sword hilts against their breastplates.

"If you think that this man is an impostor," Colu shouts, while pointing to me with his weapon, "then why don't you come over here and prove it?"

For the first time, I notice that his dirty machete has been replaced with a gleaming sword.

The armored redskull takes the bait.

He drops his torch to the dirt and swings his mace over his head while taking quick strides forward. All the men behind him stop pounding their breastplates. The *whooshing* sound of displaced air cuts through the silence of the night.

I enter the void.

In the cave, the imaginary voices in the storm speak to me as I direct my attention to the ground. It would be much easier to simply kill these people, but I am done murdering with voidance.

I'm going to teach them a lesson they will never forget.

Flying ahead of myself, I enter the indivisibles in the dirt between us. I see the thick, ancient roots of the millionescents, the thousands of insects and fragments of minerals and rocks and things long dead. I move between everything like a bird through branches, breaking all of it up along the way.

The indivisibles begin to collide, the larger pieces exploding into smaller ones. Vibration and homogenization.

First, I do this at the surface. It is easy here. But then I go deeper and deeper, into the hardened clay, where the indivisibles are more tightly packed and the wind whips around me faster.

*There it is.*

I reach hidden water and begin to raise it, to pull upon the black sea, long buried, so it sees the sky once again.

*Pull.*

At the first sign of pain, I remove my fingers from the stone and reenter the world of the living. I fear that I've taken too long already.

But my fears are unfounded.

The road between us has become a muddy oval pool.

The redskull from Prainise doesn't realize this. He walks into it and shouts out a muffled curse as his feet are submerged, but he continues to foolishly step toward me. It only takes him three steps to sink to his knees.

The sudden descent has taken him off-balance, and for a moment his mace falls motionless at his side with a soft thud. He grunts in annoyance, and then this grunt becomes a full-on, livid scream.

He stops trying to move and instead begins to swing his mace rapidly.

He's going to let it fly, so I grab the voidstone again and concentrate on the square foot where he is standing, warming it up further and deeper. I do it quickly, letting the wind rip into me, since I have no other choice.

When I let go, I see that he's buried up to his chest.

The redskull throws his mace, but it's too late. He has neither height nor leverage.

It flies toward me but slides across the ground and hits my feet.

The other skullmen from Prainise, clustered far behind their buried redskull, look to one another. Their soft metallic movements are the only sound. I wish that their faces weren't covered, so that I could see the fear present there.

The redskull must share this fear. I don't need to see his face—his shocked silence is proof enough.

He knows I am no impostor.

But the redskull is now trapped between his men and me. There is no way out.

"Attack the voider!" he screams desperately.

His men look at each other, unmistakably shaken by what they've seen.

*The time is now.*

Once more in the void, I repeat my tactic while I walk forward in blindness, through a colorless world full of screaming. Is it the screams of the wind or the screams of the men from Prainise? And does it matter?

*Yes, it matters. One is imaginary while the other is real.*

I let the wind rip into me again. I need to do this quickly. The wind hurts, but a sword or mace will kill.

Dampening the ground around me as I progress, I turn the entire road into quicksand.

This is an art, as if I am painting with a brush. I leave a snaking path of solid ground in the middle, where I can walk without getting stuck myself. Out of reach but not out of sight, I meander through the throng, working ahead of me until I reach the rear of their company.

A few of them escape and run off. Their forms are like glowing clusters of indivisibles, full of teeming life, the opposite of the decaying ground below. I let them go, since I cannot split my attention between two goals.

By the time I exit the void, I know I have gone too far. My fingers are numb and my body is so weak that I collapse against the trunk of a millionescent. I didn't even notice that it was there. I would have fallen upon the ground, but the thick, smooth-skinned tree appeared when I let go of the blackness.

Slumping to the ground with the tree to my back, I look down the length of the road. At my lesson to Prainise.

A hundred writhing necks and helmets stick out of the road like heads of lettuce growing in someone's macabre garden. Except these round stumps are silver instead of green.

The rest of their bodies are buried in the mud.

Most of them had held onto their torches while getting entombed, so it's much darker now with their flames extinguished. But a few had cast them aside. These torches now sit upon the surface of the mud, flames still raging.

One nearby skullman screams louder than the others, as his torch happens to be resting against his helmet. It's slowly cooking the skin off his face behind heated metal.

I let him scream.

Chimeline and Blythe come running in from the darkness of the tree line. A few of Colu's skullmen appear as well, blow darts at their sides and mouths open in shock. They stand on the opposite end of the quicksand, at least twenty-five yards away.

"Don't walk into the road!" I yell, but my voice comes out weak and hoarse. It's no match for the screams coming from the men in the ground, nor the distance my companions are from me.

"It's not stable," I uselessly add. It's a whisper.

"There are children in here!" Chimeline cries.

It's hard to make out details from my range and low vantage point, but I see enough. Blythe puts his arm across her chest, preventing her from moving closer. He then cautiously steps forward, testing the ground with his wide stance. Reaching out with his hand, he tries to pull someone up from the muddy ground with a scream of exertion. Colu comes near and lends a hand.

Together, they exhume a boy about ten years old from the road. He's covered in grime and shaking uncontrollably.

"Dem, you buried the children!" Chimeline screams at me from across the garden of heads.

I try standing, but I cannot seem to push myself up with my feet.

"There's another one!" says Blythe, pointing all the way to the back, near where I sit. I follow his gaze and see that he's right. A small boy's face is covered in mud up to his mouth, his small arm flailing.

"It's not safe!" I call out, but my words are drowned out by the drowned.

I hear Colu yell as well. "Circle around!" he shouts.

But Blythe doesn't hear him. Or he's too headstrong. He begins walking down the safe path that I made, which snakes through the center. His arms are out at his sides as if he is a traveling performer walking a tightrope. And he makes it most of the way there.

But then he slips.

Chimeline screams as Blythe's entire body falls into the road to his waist. He puts a hand on a nearby man's helmet, burying it completely in the mud and silencing the man's screams, but it doesn't offer the effulgent any leverage. Soon he's submerged to his chest, and the more he fights, the deeper he sinks.

"Stop!" I cry out to Chimeline and Colu, who are starting to walk down the same narrow path, as I try to crawl over to Blythe.

My legs are useless things. But every other moment, they hit something in the dirt and gain purchase. A shot of lighting courses up through me. It's barely enough for me to inch my way forward, using my limp arms as well.

He's close to the edge, where I ended the voidance, and because of this, I am able to reach him.

It looks as though he has found the solid edge too, but he's not leaving without the boy.

Lifting his chin to the night sky, he holds up one of his hands. It clutches the boy's hand.

"Give me your other hand!" I scream.

Out of the earth, it appears.

I grasp it by the wrist, but I don't have the physical energy to pull him. I cannot even feel my own fingers, but I can feel his fingers tightly wrapped around my wrist.

*There is only one way to do this.*

Using my other hand, I grasp the voidstone one last time and let the voices cut me even deeper. If it weren't for the screams in the wind, I would hear my own as I create a geyser of pressure underneath both Blythe and the boy.

As I am ripped apart, so is the world. It spits them out in dark bubbles and hisses.

They collapse on top of me as I let go of everything. The effulgent and the stone. Both life and death.

The boy is crying, Chimeline is crying, and Colu is still yelling at everyone to not move. Blythe writhes by my side, mud covering his face and body.

"I heard them!" he frantically says, wiping away mud to reveal wild eyes. He kicks himself backward, in disgust or fear of me, until he's almost at the opposite end of the road.

I lie on my side, unable to move. Darkness creeps into the edge of my vision, but I see enough. The effulgent points a shaking hand at me, a disbelieving look upon his face.

No, he's pointing at my voidstone.

"I heard my people! They are crying out for help!"

I want to reply. I want to ask him what he means, but I can't. As the darkness bleeds into the center of my vision, all that is left is his haunted face, and then his haunted words.

"They're entombed in your stone!"

# VOIDREAMING

"We should move here," Marine says, her arms around my neck. "Permanently."

"What?"

"Think of it, Dem—no more cold winters."

Her blue eyes are a window into our surroundings.

I let out a disbelieving laugh as I look around, thinking that the environment makes her request seem more absurd than it really is. But no. Even strolling through the winding walkways of the university commons wouldn't help.

We're entwined, underwater, bound within a sphere of air, courtesy of my voidance. And beyond us lies the flooded ruins of a Xian galleon—a wooden three-mast ship that sank years back, well before I was a child. We're in the captain's quarters, off the stern. Shattered paned windows surround us, a massive table is bolted to the floor, and small brightly colored fish swim past us in all directions. Outside, the endless turquoise waters of Xi Bay flow past us.

Our honeymoon destination.

"I feel at home here," she adds.

"Marine, our home is in the citadel, for better or for worse. That's where the university is."

"The university is like garden ivy. Its influence is far-reaching. It extends even here, to the border of the Northern Kingdom."

I nod once, slowly. "Yes, it does. But I am the master voider. I belong at its heart. Which is the citadel."

She rolls her eyes. "It's boring there."

"At times," I admit. "But that is where the important decisions are made. With the support of my submasters and in front of the king. With His Majesty's blessings."

"Ugh!" she exclaims. "I don't care about decisions in cold, stuffy rooms full of overweight, aging men. I care about this!" She briefly takes a hand off my neck and extends it to the sphere's edge. Rainbow luminescence that reminds me of a dragonfly's wings ripples out in concentric circles. "This is where voidance is meant to be. Exploring the edges of our world. Exploring the edges of our power."

I shake my head at her disregard of protocol and then realize that the sphere around us is slowly decreasing in size, due to the pressure. I briefly enter the void to maintain it.

At this depth, two patterns of voidance work in unison. The first is the sphere of air, allowing us to breathe. The second is the weight.

If all I manipulated were the pocket of air, this sphere would launch upwards at an impossible speed and spit us into the sky, as the world seeks equilibrium.

And so I must weigh the membrane down, keeping us at this depth indefinitely. One system of voidance fighting another.

She speaks to me as I reenter the world of blue.

"Did you ask His Majesty about the grant?"

"What grant?"

She looks at me dangerously. "The one we discussed last week."

I take a deep breath. "No."

"Why not?"

"Because he won't approve it."

"What do you mean 'he won't approve it'?"

"One of my submasters has already taken on that task."

She pouts. "I don't understand why that matters."

"It matters because the king isn't going to fund the oversight of sea research from the citadel, not when there's a voider stationed here who is already doing the same thing."

She folds her arms. "Well, that's exactly why we should move here. You can keep better tabs on him."

"You know that I need to be at the citadel. The king needs me."

"So do I."

Curiosity, guilt, and annoyance rise within me. "Are you seriously telling me you will not be happy in the citadel?"

She doesn't answer.

"Marine, when you agreed to marry me, you knew the life awaiting you."

"I know. I just feel that you're squandering an opportunity. Voidance is . . ." She looks around again in all directions. "So much more than burying our noses in books."

I follow her eyes past the membrane. A school of yellow fish darts around us, moving as one.

"What if we go on holiday?" I say, turning back. "Places like this. Xiland. The archipelago. Whenever I can get away."

She shrugs and looks away. "Which is what? Every few years? When the king gives you permission?"

I momentarily close my eyes, torn with conflict. I thought that all of this was behind us. The struggle of balancing the intensity of her love with the stability of my station. But it's found its way here, where no men dare tread.

*I cannot have her be unhappy.*

"We'll go as often as you need," I say.

She perks up. "Every year?"

"If that's what you need to be happy."

"Promise?"

I nod. "I would do anything for you. You know that."

"But what if the king needs you?"

"The king comes second."

She takes her hand from around my neck and gently places it on my bare chest, pulling the hairs there.

"I like the sound of that."

I kiss her. Gently at first, and then passionately deep, and she responds in kind.

"One moment," I say urgently, as I grasp my voidstone. "Let me give us more room."

I extend the membrane so it almost totally fills the captain's quarters, pushing out the water and multicolored fish through the dozens of shattered windows. It takes its toll. I feel the wind ripping into my being before the brief numbness sets into my fingers.

But her reaction is worth it.

Instead of floating, as before, we're now able to stand on our own.

Marine's eyes are wide at my display of power.

I pull the straps of her dress off her shoulders and let it fall to the floor. Then I pick her up and set her down on the angled table. The entire ship is lopsided on the seabed, causing the room, including the attached table, to slant abnormally in one direction. Briny seawater continues to drip off the table, hitting the floor, a small waterfall the only sound.

This seems like a fever dream. Outside the windows, the rays of light coming through the blue. The absolute silence and intimacy of this place, all pressure and sharp angles. The stunning beauty before me.

I enter her, bringing her body into mine and pressing the two of us up against the table. She brings me a rush of youth. Time and age are like the water and fish. The logic of the world says that they belong here, but they are absent.

She turns us around so that she is in control. Before, our bodies were dry because we were in the pocket of air—but now, due to the table, beads of saltwater curve and run down her body, dampening her blonde hair. The blue of the water reflects off her pale skin as she moves her hips.

Meanwhile, the sphere shrinks. Water rushes around us, coming up from the floorboards. It's the incredible pressure at this depth. The dynamic voidance is not holding.

I grasp my voidstone. The sound of the wind replaces Marine's ecstasy, helping me focus before the membrane collapses entirely. I feel pain and pleasure at the same time as I extend myself further.

When I let go, my eyes are not focused on her but past her, through the curvature of my membrane, beyond the shattered windowpanes and into the cerulean distance.

A mile or so away, a scar of darkness crosses the bottom of the ocean floor. A black stroke of a brush against the color of the reef and the sunlight from above. A sliver where everything is swallowed up.

*Blackscar.*

I close my eyes as my body tenses. There is a fringe of darkness here as well, in the back of my mind. Between the two of us, husband and wife.

An irrational fear.

Does she only love me because of my power?

Do I only love her because of her beauty?

All too soon we are done. The membrane collapses. Water floods into the room everywhere except the perfect, shrinking sphere surrounding us.

I grab her and we float across the slanted floor, following its decline, toward a jagged blue field. Part of the hull was breached years ago, and the wood is splintered away and rotten.

My fingers tingle as we float in the center of the room.

"Are you alright?" Marine asks me, as she covers herself.

"Perfectly," I lie.

She smiles, tracing the gold chain of my voidstone necklace before looking past me, eyes opening wide.

"Dem," she whispers.

"What?"

"Look," she adds. "But don't make any sudden moves."

I turn slowly and peer out through the jagged hole.

The seabed below is alive with pink coral and swaying plants. Filtered sunlight dances across the rocky surface.

"Do you see it?" she asks.

"See what?"

She slowly points past me. "A pygmy seahorse. By the coral."

"No."

"It's really small. Usually they are camouflaged, so they are impossible to see, but not this one. It must not feel threatened. A very rare sight."

Suddenly, a gray seahorse appears against the reef, floating between strands of seaweed.

"I see it."

She nods, her eyes fixed on the small creature. "We need to capture it. A specimen for Submaster Mander."

"Let me try something," I say, as I grasp my stone.

The silence of the depths is replaced by the wind. I see the indivisibles in front of me. The tightly packed sea. The currents teeming with invisible life.

I move past the dynamic membrane into the blue, which isn't blue at all. Only a colorless black here.

There it is, the seahorse, drifting in the currents around it. Hovering like we are. All I need to do is force the seawater surrounding it to be looser than the rest. Another dynamic membrane, but not made of air.

I start to create the membrane, but then the seahorse is gone.

It disappears in the void.

I let go of my stone in disbelief.

"What happened?" Marine says, turning to me.

"I . . ." My eyesight adjusting, I look in front of me and see that in the real world, the creature has also vanished. "I saw it right in front of me. I was moving in, about to trap it with a membrane, and then its indivisibles disappeared." I alternate my gaze between her shocked face and the reef. "What did you see?"

She points. "It suddenly turned pink."

"Turned pink?"

"Its camouflage. It looked exactly like the reef, and I saw it!" Her excitement deflates in front of me as she adds, "But only for a moment. Soon I lost it against the background."

Like the waves above us, another surge of excitement flows out of her. I feel her grasp me tighter, and she pulls us forward with her other hand, using the wooden exterior of the ship as leverage.

"We need to find it."

We float through the breach into the endless waters of Xi Bay.

Nearing the pink coral and the lime-green seaweed, we search for the creature. We move around, looking from different vantage points, but after a while we realize that it's hopeless. The seahorse is gone.

I sigh.

She shakes her head, and I turn toward her.

"Do you understand how incredible this is? When I was in the void, I couldn't see it. Not just here, in the real world, but in the void as well. Can you imagine the applications to voidance if we're able to understand what just happened?"

She smiles. "Let's come back here every day. We have to catch one alive before returning to the citadel."

I smile, infected by her excitement. "Absolutely."

Glancing up toward the rays of sun, I see the silhouettes of two small boats upon the surface—the pinnace that brought us out here from the shore, and another boat as well.

I point upwards. "We have company."

She glances to the surface and then back to me in confusion.

"There's a second boat," I clarify.

"Why is that?"

"I don't know," I say. "We've been gone much longer than I promised the rowmen. Perhaps they sent out a second boat to make sure everything is alright."

After kissing me fully on the lips one more time, she cups my short beard in her hands before pulling away. "Thank you, husband, for trying to capture my pygmy. I am sure you will be successful the next time around."

We slowly rise. The waters become lighter as my ears pop.

When we reach the surface, I drop the membrane, and Marine screams playfully as the waters drench us.

We're both laughing as the servants throw out a rope ladder and we climb aboard the pinnace. But when I see the second vessel, which is close enough to ours to climb aboard, my laughs are silenced, as are hers.

It contains five Northern soldiers in full regalia, despite the intense Southern sun. They are standing at attention.

"Master Voider Democryos," says one of them, stepping forward. He has four stripes on his shoulder patch.

"Yes, Commander?" I ask.

A rowman hands me a white towel and I dry my face. I step to the edge of the pinnace and look out at the other vessel with my hand over my eyes to shelter them from the harsh sun. Despite being on different boats, the commander and I could touch if we reached our hands out. But the waves make him rise and fall at odd intervals.

"You are needed back at the citadel," he says.

I shake my head in disbelief, looking back at Marine. Behind her are the glistening waters of Xi Bay and, far in the distance, the hazy, colorful shoreline of Winter's Baiou.

I turn back to the soldier in defiance. "I am on my honeymoon, Commander."

He takes a deep breath. "His Majesty, King Andrej IX, is dead."

# GIVING IN THE TENT

I wake up in warm darkness.

"It's okay," says a recognizable voice. "It was just a dream."

I turn to the curved silhouette next to me, barely discernible against the rustling dark blue. For an instant I'm still in Temberlain's Ashes.

*Chimeline.*

"It wasn't a dream," I say, my voice hoarse. "It was a memory."

Lying on my back, I lift my head slightly and make out my surroundings. For a moment, I am disoriented. I remember yesterday's bedroom with the thin pink drapes and briefly think that I am back there, in the mansion.

No. I'm in a small tent, the fabric around us not quite taut as it ripples in the night breeze, almost like the exotic waters of my dream. I half expect to see brightly colored fish swim past her.

Exhaling, I lower my head back down to the ground and then utter a moan of displeasure. Even though there are blankets under and around me, the ground is hard and uneven on my back, odd curves everywhere.

Chimeline's soft and warm body is the opposite. The curves of her hips press into my side like a long-lost piece completing a puzzle.

Just as these thoughts of contentment begin to seep in, Chimeline rises to a sitting position and pulls the blankets with her, demurely clutching them in one hand. We're wearing underclothes.

"I should leave," she whispers.

My body shivers violently without her warmth or the covers. It's the remnants of my latest brush with voideath.

She seems to sense this. After a pause, she nestles back under the covers with me, and I wrap my arm around her.

"Tell me about it," she says, after some time.

"About what?"

"Your dream."

"Memory."

"How can it be a memory?" she says, her face upturned on my shoulder. "I heard you in your sleep. You said that the king was dead."

"It was Andrej IX," I reply. "Not his idiot son."

"Oh."

"He was a great man."

She stays silent, and I hear the voices of Colu and Blythe beyond the tent. They seem to be arguing—Blythe's clear and high voice contrasts with Colu's, which is deep and gruff.

"Tell me about it," she repeats.

I sigh, feeling a desire to avoid all discussion about my past with Marine. The shipwreck of my life. But I want to keep Chimeline here next to me, and if this is what it takes, so be it.

"We were in Winter's Baiou," I answer.

"You dreamed of Winter's Baiou?"

"Yes."

"Because that's where we're going?"

"Maybe." I purse my lips in the darkness, wondering if there is a subconscious connection. "I've been there before. The place holds a lot of memories for me."

"With your Marine?"

I nod. "Although she's not my Marine anymore."

I crane my neck upwards toward the creased ceiling of the tent. "It was a memory of our honeymoon. A very happy time, until I acted like a fool by returning to the citadel prematurely."

"Why?"

"The old king had died. I had responsibilities."

She seems to be waiting for me to elaborate.

"I left Marine there with one of my submasters, planning to return a fortnight later. She was so desperate to capture a rare type of seahorse, and I knew that it would be a while before we would head that far south again. At the time, I thought it was a great thing that I was doing, not thwarting her dreams. A noble sacrifice. But I should have turned away that commander. I should have stayed in Winter's Baiou with my wife and ignored the new king. I had broken a very recent and important promise."

"But you are a man of principle," she says.

I shake my head. "Principles can be wrong."

Shifting, I weave my arm underneath her and try to get comfortable.

For a moment, the two of us lie in silence. Chimeline seems lost in thought, the hint of a wrinkle on her nose. It's so charming, I can't help but smile.

But this smile fades as I listen to Colu and Blythe argue outside the tent. I can't make out most of their words, but they seem to be discussing Prainise. And murder.

"What happened?" I ask quietly. "After I passed out."

"You were dying," she says, eyes suddenly wide. "Your body was shaking, and you were cold and gray."

"Voideath," I mumble.

"I was scared. I wasn't sure if . . ." She clears her throat. "After what you did in the road, we came back here."

"Where's *here*?"

"The campsite where we had dinner."

I nod.

"By then the fire was dead, and Colu said it would take too long to find more wood and get it warm enough for you. The wind was picking up, and then the effulgent—"

"Blythe," I remind her.

I see her smile in the darkness. "Blythe was very concerned. He said that we had to warm up your body using one of ours or you would die."

"He was right."

"I'm just glad you're doing better," she says.

"I'm not just doing better," I say. "I'm alive. You saved me from voideath."

"I did nothing but stay here with you."

A wisp of her dark hair falls across my face. With my free hand, I hook it behind her ear.

"Sometimes I think that's the only thing I really need."

I recall the moment on the balcony. When I felt myself slipping away—lost in the darkness of the void. The darkness that has become my life. And Chimeline was there, pulling me back.

Our faces are close enough that I can hear her nervous breaths. Her chest rises and falls on me.

"Someone's coming," she whispers.

There's a crunching of boots followed by a rustle beyond the thin tent fabric.

"Is the master voider awake?"

It's Blythe.

I can barely see his shadow on the rippling wall. He stoops by the entrance, where the two sides of loose fabric are tied together with a bowstring. His head is bent and his hand is on his chin. He looks as if he's praying.

"Yes," says Chimeline loudly. "He's doing much better."

"Blessed be the Unnamed. Tell him that Colu and I are preparing a meal now. We will break our fast with the sunrise. We have much to discuss."

I clear my throat and reply. "Thank you, Blythe."

His shadow nods hesitantly, before he stands up again and walks away.

Chimeline clears her throat as well. "Maybe if you get dressed and sit by the fire, you will stay warm?"

I nod.

She sits up again, bringing the covers to her while reaching for a small pile in the corner. I briefly look away to give her some privacy.

Gone is her recently repaired white-lace dress. It's been replaced with loose camel-colored pants and a white shirt that wraps around her waist with two long ties.

A clear voice calls out. "Master Voider," Blythe says, amidst the clanging of metal upon metal. "Breakfast is almost ready."

"Coming," I say.

I look for the rest of my clothes.

"Oh. Here, Dem. They were mixed with mine."

Chimeline reaches into the corner again. But along with my clothes, I feel something cold and smooth. It falls between the sheets.

She reaches for it, but I find it first.

It's the glass vial.

I bring it up between my thumb and forefinger. It's so dark in the tent that I cannot tell if the vial is full or not. But when I gently shake it, I can feel the liquid move about.

My heart sinks, all of my doubt returning. I had almost forgotten about the moonspit. Cleanthes' paranoia replaces my former peace of mind.

I glance past the vial to Chimeline, trying to read her expression in the darkness. It's almost impossible. A mix of sadness and concern.

"This, again," I mumble.

She lets out a nervous laugh. "While you were sleeping, I asked the effulgent to bring me my other clothes from the saddlebag. That must have found its way inside."

"You said it's jasmine extract?"

She hesitates and then nods once.

It's the pause that cuts deep. It's the pause that proves she's a liar.

"Back at the plantation, the skullmen found it in your belongings and asked me about it," I add, looking at the vial instead of her. Suddenly, I can't meet her eyes, a result of either anger or fear. "But they were confused as to what it was."

I hand it back to her and grab my shirt. The entire time I get dressed, I feel Chimeline stare at me.

The world around her trembles in blue, but she's a statue.

"I tried to explain to them that it was jasmine extract, but they were insistent that it was something else."

Because I cannot stand in the small tent, I pull on my pants awkwardly, waiting for an answer. Finally, as I finish lacing my boots, I glance at her and say, "They were insistent that *you* were something else."

We seem to switch places. Now, it is I who is motionless, and she begins to shift uncomfortably. Eventually she folds her arms and looks around the tent instead of meeting my eyes.

"So I ask you again. What is in that vial?"

"It's not what you think," she says softly.

"Probably not," I agree. "But I still want you to tell me."

Looking down, she shakes her head. Her face is downcast and buried in her black hair, but I can still see the slightest of flinches.

"Chimeline." I lean forward. I put my hand under her chin and raise it until her eyes meet mine. "I trust you. You could've killed me any number of times. Just tell me the truth. Were you hired by the king? Are you an assassin?"

She trembles underneath my touch. A single tear falls from her cheek onto my palm. Her face is a veil of conflicted emotions.

"Are you?" I repeat.

Her chin quivers as new trails form on her cheeks. "Please, Dem." She looks deep into my eyes. "Just let it go. None of it matters anymore. We're far from the citadel. We have a new life now."

I return the look, firmly.

"I just need to know if the king wants me dead."

She swallows. "You said that you trust me—and you can. Please—just continue to trust me. Just trust me."

Her plea is both maddening and moving. I believe her. I have no doubt that I can trust her. But her unwillingness to share the truth is the same wedge that was driven between Marine and me.

I pull away. "You'll tell me when you're ready," I concede. "But there will be no more secrets between us. I cannot bear falling in love with a woman and then losing her to lies. Once is enough."

Perhaps my words were too strong for her. She stares back at me, wide-eyed.

"Promise me," I insist.

She nods once and raises a hand to her mouth. "I promise," she whispers.

With that, I nod back at her solemnly. She still holds her hand to her mouth. After a moment, I turn toward the tent opening and skirt between the two loose panels of fabric.

The morning air hits me, smelling of burned wood and sweet plantains, and I can see the pink hint of sunrise upon the horizon.

A new dawn is rising.

# LE-SANTE

Blythe sets a steaming pot on the flaming logs, throws the rag he is holding onto the sandy ground, and rushes over to me. But he stops just before we meet, almost as if his excitement has been doused with fear.

I've seen this look before—when he pushed away from me in the road the previous night.

"You are recovered?" he asks hesitantly, behind the faintest glimpse of a smile.

I groan and arc my body with a hand to my back, noticing that the stars are still visible despite the approaching morning. The sky is familiar. O'Eridani, the End of the River, is directly above me. It must be just before sixbell. This was the time I usually awoke at the Royal House. I would leave Marine in bed and head to the university.

"We need to talk," he says quietly.

I bring my gaze back down. "About?"

"Last night."

I let out a deep sigh. Despite my thoughts being numbed by the closeness of voideath and the still-fresh memory of Chimeline's warmth, beauty, and lies, I understand Blythe's reference. There can be no other.

*The look he gave me in the road.*

He said that he heard voices in my stone, which is impossible. There are no voices. Although it is true that if one heard the wind, it would be natural for them to confuse it with whispers.

Except that voiders are the only ones who can hear the wind. To hear the wind is to be in the void. If a non-voider picks up a voidstone, it is nothing to them. A lifeless pebble.

That is the touch test we administer. The simplest of signals.

The man is clearly confused.

Besides, he wasn't even holding the stone. He was clutching my hand while I grasped the stone.

None of it makes any sense. But to explain all of this to Blythe is more than I can handle right now. The only outcome will be his eventual realization that he simply heard one of the buried men whimpering as they breathed in mud and water and confused it with something else.

"The plantains are burning," Colu shouts out from his seat by the fire, many yards away.

"We need to talk about your voidstone," Blythe adds urgently.

"About the voices you believed you heard?"

"Yes."

"It was a long night for us all," I say dismissively.

"You think I'm making this up?"

"No. I think you're confused."

"I am not a fool, Master Voider. If that's what you're implying," he says, his face taut.

I shake my head. "No, I don't believe you are a fool. I just think that the events of last night were traumatic for you and in the frenzy you became a little confused."

"The plantains are burning," Colu yells again.

Blythe reaches out and clutches my forearm tightly. "I know what I heard."

"Alright," I add, taken aback by his fervor. "We'll talk later, when we have some privacy," I say.

"Do I have your word on this?"

"Of course."

He hesitantly returns to the fire. I follow and pass Colu, who sits cross-legged with his elbows on his knees. The large Xian man is dressed the same as he was last night—

dark-brown leather armor and a chain-mail vest. His sword, scabbard, and baldric sit on the sandy ground.

He glances up and gives me a curt nod. The red skull is still painted upon his face, but it's smeared beyond recognition.

"Roasted plantains and maize," Blythe explains, picking up the cast-iron pan using a rag. "Colu packed the maize for us, and I found some plantain trees by the stream."

I nod in gratitude, taking a seat between them. Blythe sets the pan on the ground, flipping the plantains with a stick. They're blackened.

"As soon as we're finished eating, we must start making our way toward Winter's Baiou," I say.

Colu looks at me but says nothing. With his one eye and his paint-smeared face, he's impossible to read. Meanwhile, Blythe focuses on his cooking, but I detect some disagreement in the slow shaking of his head.

"What's wrong now?" I ask him.

"Why don't you ask the redskull?" he answers.

I glance between the two of them. "What's going on?" After neither of them answers, I add, "Are you concerned about the men buried in the road?"

Blythe just continues to shake his head.

"They'll be alright," I say. "There were a handful who got away, including the children you rescued. Prainise is not far from here. The survivors will surely return with shovels and dig them out. The fate of Prainise is in their hands, not mine."

Blythe looks to Colu with a piercing expression—something shockingly resembling hate. "Are you going to admit to him what you have done, or should I?" he says.

"The fate of Prainise is already sealed," Colu utters.

"What he means to say," adds Blythe loudly, "is that he murdered all of them."

"Fucking Temberlain. I will not have this argument all over again."

A rustle in the pastel darkness causes the three of us to turn toward the tent. Chimeline stands in front of it, wrapped in her patchwork blanket. She's looking at Colu with a concerned expression.

"Fine," he booms, arms out at his sides. "I repeat myself, but only for the master voider's benefit." He looks at me and nods as his posture softens. "Only because I am deeply in your debt. I would be dead if it were not for you."

I stay silent as Chimeline shuffles over and sits down next to me, rubbing her shins to get warm. She's barefoot.

Colu turns to the fire and leans in, red reflected in his eye. "After you passed out I carried you here, and the three of us figured out what to do with your convulsing body. By that time, probably a fullbell had already passed."

I wait for him to continue.

"Then I went back."

"To the road?"

He nods. "To finish what you started."

Blythe exhales as Colu continues. "The way this graycloaked fool makes it seem, I am some blood-crazed madman seeking revenge—"

"Slitting the throats of the defenseless can be no other thing!" Blythe interjects harshly.

I extend my hand. "Let him explain."

Colu blows air into his cupped hands and then folds them tightly into a fist.

"They needed to die," he says. "Despite what you may think, I am not seeking revenge. I'm seeking the quickest path to peace. Ensuring the least amount of death and suffering to innocents. And by my calculation, what I did last night was exactly that."

Blythe puts his hands on his bald head, and I shoot him a warning glance.

"Prainise only respects strength," Colu adds. "Brutal strength. Anything less, you may think it is a lesson, but it will be the opposite. Like pouring oil upon this fire."

I don't say anything.

"If I had let those men live," Colu continues, pointing north across the murky fields, "they would have regrouped and attacked our plantation. There still would have been a war, except this time there would be no prisoners. No mercy. Every man, woman, and child would be massacred in retribution for what you did. Tortured, even."

Blythe can't help interjecting. "But that is what you have done!"

"I stopped the bleeding. Those people cannot be reasoned with."

"You talk as if the people of Prainise are animals—"

"They *are* animals!" Colu yells. "And Cleanthes was no different. That is the way it works out here. And if you think anything different, you are a fool!"

Blythe turns away from Colu and looks at me. "Surely you cannot agree with this madness."

Suddenly, I feel the eyes of all three of them on me.

Turning to Colu, I nod slowly. "I understand that you had to do what you did," I say, my voice level. "I only wish that you had told me your intentions earlier. I risked voideath specifically to spare their lives. Killing them would have been far safer and easier for me. You have no idea how close I came to dying. If it were not for Chimeline . . ." I shake my head slowly.

"Would you have killed them, had I asked you to?"

"No," I say, without hesitation.

He extends his palms, as if my answer has just proven a point, and my brow furrows in suspicion.

"So your plan all along was to kill them? And that's why you wanted me here?" I ask, my voice darkening.

"No," he says, shaking his head forcefully. "Remember, I only asked you to stay a fortnight. To delay the inevitable. But when you showed up last night, things changed." He hunches. "I did what needed to be done, which is what any soldier would do."

"You are no soldier," Blythe says, as he spits onto the ground.

"Finally, you say something we can agree on."

Blythe grunts and begins serving breakfast. He dips large waxy leaves into a hot pot of water, cleaning them. Then he places the plantains and maize on the leaves and carries them over to us, starting with Chimeline.

"The Unnamed provides," he says, to each of us.

Chimeline and I offer our thanks. Then I watch Blythe serve Colu in the same manner. I'm surprised by this—given the man's obvious anger toward the other, I would think that he would make Colu get his own breakfast. But the effulgent seems content to serve anyone.

"I heard them in the night," Chimeline whispers. "The skullman plans on coming with us."

I look to Colu. "Is that true?"

He finishes swallowing. "Is what true?"

"You're joining us?"

"I can no longer stay here."

"What about being the new redskull?" I ask in surprise.

"I can't do it," he mumbles.

"Do what?"

He shrugs. "Growing the hilma. My heart is not in it."

"But the threat from Prainise has been removed."

He nods while chewing. "True. But another threat will eventually take its place. Comes with the territory."

"What about your promise to Cleanthes?" I ask, hounding him. "Your promise to all of his people?"

"They'll find another redskull," he grumbles.

"As good as you?"

"No," he says, shaking his head. "But good enough."

Chimeline adjusts her leaf-plate in her lap. "I see a piece of myself in what he's going through," she says softly. But when Colu leans in, obviously trying to listen to her words, she repeats them louder for him to hear. "I see a bit of myself in you."

"Is that so?" he asks. "Humor me, woman."

She presses her lips together in thought before speaking.

"You left your homeland to forget your past and to find redemption. But you didn't find any redemption. The only thing you found was the wisdom to know that you can never go home again. It exists in place only. Like a body without a soul."

Her words seem to penetrate Colu like the approaching sunrise, gradual and soft. Colu leans back, his shoulders relaxing as he blows air through his lips.

"You're right, girl from Scorpiontail," he says wistfully.

For a long time, we all sit in silence watching the embers rise into the morning air. The sky is light enough now for me to see the silhouettes of migrating birds flying overhead.

"I had a great love once, before I enlisted," Colu eventually says. "A beautiful woman—much like you, except Xian. She would have been home to me, but she's gone now. I lost her to the effulgency."

Blythe lifts his head and narrows his eyes.

"What do you mean you 'lost her to the effulgency'?" I ask him.

"No one is ever lost when they decide to follow the way of unwanting," says Blythe.

Colu flashes him a dark glance, but Chimeline speaks up, drawing his ire away. "Tell us about her," she says.

He shrugs his large shoulders. "We knew each other from childhood, but it wasn't until my apprenticeship that our relationship grew. She was the daughter of the mason."

"You're a mason?"

"Was."

I take my last bite of plantain.

"Just as our love was flourishing, she discovered the way of unwanting." He points across the fire to Blythe. "One of these fools came to Winter's Baiou and built a temple, sapping the mason's entire staff, including me. I never met the man, but soon my woman was reading from the white book and reciting its ludicrous phrases from memory."

Colu clears his throat before continuing. "Shortly after the temple was built, I proposed to her, but she gave me an ultimatum in return. I had to join the way of unwanting."

I raise my eyebrows. "She must have been very taken by it," I say.

He nods. "She had stopped calling me il-Colu by then. No names. She would not accept any of my gifts. But I still loved her." He grunts. "I thought it was merely a passing thing."

Colu leans forward, closer to the fire. "I didn't believe in the Unnamed, and she knew it. When I prayed to him, I felt . . ." He hunches. "Nothing."

"You are not listening to his voice," Blythe says.

Colu ignores him. "The night before we were to go public with our engagement, she begged me to pray. Afterward, she admitted to me that she'd prayed as well that night, harder than she'd ever prayed before. She begged for the Unnamed to reveal himself to me, to provide me with a sliver of grace." He smiles sadly to himself. "I remember those words, 'a sliver of grace.'"

He wipes his nose with the back of his hand, smearing more red paint away. "She loved us both—her cursed Unnamed and me. The problem was, her heart only had room for one of us."

"Did you hear his voice?" Chimeline asks.

I see the white of Colu's one eye as he briefly looks up at her before resting his gaze back on the fire.

"I'll tell you what I told her. I *did* try to pray. I *did* try to hear his voice, for her sake more than anything else. In that silence, I kept waiting for the spark of something to show me that there was more to all of this." He raises his hands to the shadows surrounding us. "But then, I realized that if I actually *did* hear something, it wouldn't be the Unnamed talking. It would just be my own stupid mind trying to force something that I so desperately wanted."

With these words, Blythe suddenly stands and walks away into the darkness, one of his hands on his bald head.

"What happened then?" I ask.

"Things got much worse between us," Colu says. "She couldn't accept my lack of faith, so our time was mostly spent fighting. It was unacceptable to her that I could not see what she saw."

"Surely she wouldn't leave you over such a thing," Chimeline insists.

Colu spits on the ground in disgust. "It was much worse than that. She didn't just leave me. She left me for *him*."

I exchange a confused glance with Chimeline. For a moment, both of us are too shocked to respond.

"You mean . . ." stammers Chimeline.

"The effulgent chose her," Colu answers.

I turn to Blythe, but he's a few feet away from the fire and his back is to us.

"Is that even possible?" I ask Blythe, raising my voice so he can hear me. "It was my understanding that the effulgency does not engage in marital relations."

But Blythe doesn't answer my question. He seems lost in thought.

"Oh, they don't," Colu booms, rising to his feet to stoke the fire. "Marriage is against the way of the unwanting. No man should own a woman, or the other way around, and marriage is apparently the equivalent of owning." He violently prods the fire with a branch. Sparks escape into the softening sky. Then he points it at me, the tip of it glowing red-hot. "But they have to maintain their hairless bloodline," he says. "There's no way around that. So this man chose le-Sante from Winter's Baiou."

"That was her name?" Chimeline asks. "le-Sante?"

He nods. "She believed that it was a privilege. An honor bestowed upon her from the Unnamed himself. Even her father, the mason—my master—even he was smitten. I was pushed aside."

Blythe suddenly turns around. He slowly walks forward, heading straight to Colu.

"I must not own the dark," Blythe says, his arms loose at his sides.

Colu snaps his stick in two and throws the pieces into the fire. "What are you talking about?"

"It was I. I was the effulgent in the town you call Winter's Baiou. I was the effulgent who chose the woman you call le-Sante."

Colu tilts his head but says nothing. He then smirks and flashes a line of white teeth before looking back into the fire.

I glance at Chimeline, wondering if I heard Blythe correctly. Her hand covers her open mouth, and then she inhales sharply.

I turn back just in time to witness Colu taking a swing at Blythe.

The graycloak doesn't flinch or attempt to get out of the way. He takes the punch right to his face.

Chimeline screams as Blythe stumbles backward, perilously close to the fire.

Colu follows, takes another swing, and punches Blythe a second time in the face.

Blythe goes down to his knees. Blood pours from his nose, but he doesn't seem to notice. He raises his head and smiles, his arms loose at his sides. It's not a devious smile. It's full of joy.

"The Unnamed blessed us with a girl. She is an effulgent now. A wonderful woman who helps others on the way of unwanting."

Colu positions his feet wide apart and brings his arm up, as if he's going to punch the man again.

"Colu," I say loudly, standing up.

But this time he doesn't follow through. For a moment, he stands there with his fist raised, looking down at the smiling Blythe as we all look on in silence.

Then his entire body relaxes.

"It's not worth it."

He walks away from him, back to where he was sitting before, on the opposite side of the fire. He picks up the leaf-plate and stuffs a large piece of plantain into his mouth. Then he brings his hand to his forehead, covering up his one exposed eye.

Chimeline stands and walks directly to Blythe. He's still kneeling by the fire while rifling through one of his pockets. He takes out a white handkerchief, which Chimeline places on his nose.

"Look upwards," she says. "There are no colored windows to look at this time," she adds, smiling.

"No, there are not. But there is the waking beauty of the Unnamed's creation. This lovely morning sky."

I shake my head at the coincidence of it all.

Colu was a mason's apprentice at Winter's Baiou, the very same place we are headed. Blythe was an effulgent there too, years ago. He stole this man's lover.

*Out of all the places he could have been from. Out of all the people he could have met along the way.*

Chimeline seems to be content with Blythe's condition. She walks around the fire and fetches the white rag Blythe used to hold the pan's handle. She dips it into the hot pot of water and then carries it back to the other side of the campfire, gritting her teeth in discomfort from the heat—I can see the drenched rag give off steam in the dawn light.

She approaches Colu.

"What the fuck are you doing?" he asks her.

He's sitting on a split log. Even though Chimeline is standing, they are almost at eye level with each other.

She carefully folds the rag in half and then lifts it to his face.

Colu flinches but allows Chimeline in. She delicately begins wiping the red paint away.

She takes her time and pays attention to the details—the sides of his face, his black eye patch, and even his hands.

She folds the rag again and goes over his face a second time.

Finally, nodding to herself, she tosses the rag back where she found it and sits down next to me again.

"What?" she asks, when it's obvious to her that we're all staring. "We can't have Colu looking like a redskull his entire way home, can we?"

Colu grunts.

"Home," he says into the fire, but it's only a hopeful whisper.

# PART FOUR

# THE MAN BEHIND THE VEIL

# THE FOUNDATION

By midmorning, southerly winds are bringing us the first hints of Xi Bay. Even though it's at least a good day's ride away, I feel as if I can already taste the salty waters on my tongue. With the rise in humidity, the sun seems stronger. All of us have taken off our outer layers—Chimeline's patchwork blanket, my black flaxen cloak, Colu's chain mail and brown leathers, and Blythe's gray-hooded cloak.

Wealthy plantations flank us every so often. They look remarkably similar to Cleanthes' mansion—gleaming white estates rising out of the greenery past glittering millionescents and moss-draped willows. Colu says that all the fields here are either sugarcanex or indigo. He calls them white gold and blue gold. But I'm sure that hilma plantations lurk in the distance as well.

We also share Xi Bay Road with more travelers than before.

Wagons full of field workers, burlap bags of raw goods, and wooden coffins stacked three high pass us from the opposite direction and turn down the sandy side roads that have become more numerous as well.

True to my word, I've been discussing the incident from last night with Blythe for the past fullbell. We talk in hushed tones as we travel. Colu and Chimeline ride ahead of us, speaking on occasion.

He's far more stubborn than I thought.

I've explained everything twice through, but he does not relent. He even tells me that he understood what these so-called whispering voices said to him. But when I press him to share their message, he becomes silent, which only adds to my suspicion that he's delusional.

"We must try again," he says.

I look at the man riding next to me. "Try what again?"

"I must listen for the voices," Blythe answers.

He extends his arm in my direction. "Give me your hand."

"Don't be ridiculous."

"Give me your hand!" he repeats, loud enough to cause Chimeline and Colu to turn and glance at us curiously.

I exhale and lock my hand into his.

"Now touch your stone with the other," he says.

"Nothing is going to happen, Blythe. This is foolish," I mumble.

"Then we are fools."

It's a good thing that our horses are walking and not trotting. I take my other hand off the reins and place it on the black surface of my stone, which hangs freely over my white shirt.

I enter the void.

The black wind is there to meet me, whipping around frenetically. Perhaps it's just my imagination, but it seems louder than usual. Faster, more urgent, as if the slightest voidance on my part would cause me severe pain. Colorless indivisibles glisten below. The horse. My hand grasping Blythe's. The dust in the air. A dragonfly hovering in the road in front of us.

And then something incredible happens.

The wind stops.

Complete silence. *In the void.*

Reflexively, I let go of the stone because I do not know what else to do.

Blinking away the sudden brightness of the day, I turn to Blythe. His grasp is too strong for me to escape from. His eyes are tightly closed in concentration. Beads of sweat fall down his smooth forehead and the tip of his nose. He's whispering something that I cannot hear.

Blinking open his eyes, he looks at me with an agitated expression. "Why did you let go?" he says harshly.

"I—" My mouth is slack. It has never gone silent in the void before. Ever.

"I was speaking to them!"

"To whom?"

"Grasp it again!"

The urgency in his eyes does not lie. So I do as he says.

The sunless world returns. I somewhat relax as I hear the wind. But then, just as before, it disappears as quickly as it came, and I must consciously refrain from releasing the stone in panic.

For an unknown reason, the silence is terrifying.

No. It's not completely silent. One current of wind remains, like a single viola string plucked and left to resonate.

The single current snakes around me—weak yet specific. I turn my head, looking for it, but of course I cannot see it. I can only feel it, soft and snug when I stay in control, cutting into me painfully if I don't.

*What is happening?*

Before, the wind was a monolithic, unchanging medium. It simply *was*. Always the same within a given stone, never capable of decomposition. The smaller stones were less powerful, and therefore the wind was softer there. In the larger ones, like the one around my neck, the wind was louder.

But now? This single thread is wind too. A strand of it. It is less of something more.

*Think, Dem.*

It is composed of something. Built of parts, just as a wall is built of bricks. Just as everything in this world is built of the indivisible.

*But what is the wind made of?*

Suddenly, the torrent begins again. A storm in the darkness, deafening, roaring, and I let go.

Sunlight.

I am out of breath, and so is Blythe. He drops my hand and turns to me. "It is unquestionable," he says loudly. "I spoke to them, and they heard me. They replied."

My mouth must still be open because he leans in, his eyes wide. "You heard them too, didn't you?"

"I did not hear any voices," I say slowly, as I organize my thoughts. "But something was profoundly different. Somehow, your presence altered the void."

"How so?"

"The wind . . ."

"What wind?"

I grab the reins tightly, as if they are the very principles of voidance and I am too scared to let them go.

"Normally, when I'm in the void, there is a howling wind. This time, I heard *silence* and then a single current. Which I have never heard before. It's usually . . . loud and consistent."

"You keep saying *wind*, Master Voider. Why?"

"Because it's what we teach," I snap. "It's not meant to be taken literally. It's an analogy."

"Analogy?"

I sigh. "We use an analogy of wind in a cave with our youngest students. Children who are learning about their gift for the first time. It *does* sound like the wind. It *feels* like the wind."

"Well, your analogy is wrong. Those sounds are voices. Voices that I can understand."

I look away from him, slowly shaking my head.

"Master Voider, you are so quick to dismiss the words I say, but they are no more fantastical than your analogy."

I don't reply.

"You pride yourself on being a man of reason. A man of numbers and slow repetition and facts. But at the end of the day, you do not even know what your so-called gift is built from. All you have are your childlike stories."

"That's not true. We have an entire college at the university devoted to the study of the origin of voidance."

"And what have you discovered?"

I close my eyes.

Blythe's claim is absurd. I've been in the void for more years than I can remember—many of those years as an instructor. I am adept at voidance. And at no time have I ever heard a voice. Much less someone speaking to me. He is leading me back to typical effulgent drivel. Souls trapped in stones. It's delusional.

The leather crackles as I loosen my grip on the reins.

But I don't believe Blythe is lying either. His conviction is unshakable. And something happened when he touched the stone. I could feel it.

"I need proof, Blythe," I softly reply, opening my eyes but not meeting his gaze.

"What more do you need besides what you just experienced?"

I nod in partial agreement. "True, something was different. But I did *not* hear voices."

"Then you were not listening."

I shake my head.

"You don't have faith," he adds, but his tone is not admonishing.

"No, I don't. I need something more than blind faith. That's your realm, not mine."

When I turn back to him, he nods and then replies, "Very well, then."

He begins speaking. But his words are not in the common tongue.

It's a whisperlike language, except deeper and from the lungs instead of the lips.

It is the sound of the wind.

My mind snaps back to Fiscarlo, when Blythe and his daughter were arguing in front of my student's grave. Although I didn't realize it then, they must have switched into this tongue in my presence, perhaps by mistake.

*The viola.*

"Was that you?" I ask. "Were you the one speaking in the void just now? The single thread of wind?"

"I'm not sure what you mean by wind," he says. "But yes, I was speaking."

"What were you saying to me?"

He smiles sadly and then shakes his head. "I was not speaking to you."

"Who else was there?"

But even before the words leave my mouth, Blythe's haunted look from the night before enters my mind. When he was crawling away from me in the mud.

*I heard my people! They are crying out for help!*

"Your people."

He nods.

"You mean the effulgency?" I ask.

"No. It was . . . you wouldn't understand," he stammers. "This revelation is just as complex for me as it is for you— but in a very different way."

I don't follow his meaning, but an idea suddenly comes to me and I act on it without hesitation.

I pull off my voidstone necklace and hand it to Blythe, who leans away from me on his horse and looks at me with wide, fearful eyes.

"What are you doing?"

"Try it," I say, dangling the necklace between us. "Grab the stone yourself and see if you can talk to them. Whoever they are."

He shakes his head. "I do not feel comfortable touching that thing."

"It's not going to harm you," I say.

"There is no need," he continues. "We have already established that working together—"

"I know," I say, cutting him off and giving the necklace another shake. "But I want to see if you can hear the voices alone. Without me."

He sighs and then tilts his head. "This is foolish."

"Then we are fools," I answer.

He flashes me a wry smile and then gives me the briefest of nods.

Blythe carefully reaches out and touches the stone. He does not grab the entire necklace. Instead, he squeezes the black shard between his thumb and forefinger while closing his eyes tightly. He stays like this for only a moment, and then he lets go, exhaling forcefully.

He turns to me and shakes his head.

"You couldn't hear anything?" I ask.

"No."

"Could you see the void?"

He shakes his head. "I don't know what you mean, but no."

"Alright," I answer. "That solves one thing."

"And what is that, Master Voider?"

"One moment."

As I put my necklace back on, I enter the void again— one final test while I'm not holding Blythe's hand.

Everything has returned to normal. The wind encircles me, constant, unchanging. I stay there in the darkness, just to make sure it doesn't disappear as before.

"Fascinating," I say, as I let go.

Blythe looks at me intently.

"Point one," I say, using my fingers to count along. "The voidstone is useless to you on its own. Which makes sense, since you are not a voider. The way the stone responds to you is how it would respond to any other non-voider during a touch test."

He nods.

"Point two. When I use the stone, the void behaves as expected. The wind . . . ." I press my lips together and then correct myself. "The sounds are constant and unchanging."

Blythe nods again.

"Point three is where it gets interesting. When we are connected, somehow the experience is changed for both of us. You can enter the void, whereas before you couldn't. You say you hear voices. You say you can *communicate* with your people, whomever they are. I can hear all of this as well, although I cannot understand it." I pause as the final thought comes to me. "It's because I don't speak your language."

I drop my three fingers and form a fist.

Blythe nods. "You do not speak the private language, but you speak the truth, Master Voider."

For a long time, we ride in silence.

My mind is a torrent of possibilities as I come to grips with what has just happened. Moments ago, I believed that Blythe was delusional. But he's obviously not. There is now proof that I cannot discount. His language. A *private* language. Something that's been kept a secret outside of the effulgency since before recorded history.

*Why keep it a secret?*

*Could this be the key to the origin of voidance?*

Blythe utters a groan of warning.

With a hand to his forehead, he looks down the road. I follow his gaze.

A trio of Northern soldiers are approaching us from the opposite direction, at a trot. No signage, plated armor, or draping cloaks like the ones we met last night. They are probably either deserters or mercenaries. As they near us, I pick out more detail. Their horses are so thin that ribs protrude sickly, and one is limping.

They eye Colu with sneers. "Fucking Xian," one of them yells, spitting in his direction.

Colu turns his horse and grabs the hilt of his sword. I sense that he's about to take their bait, but then Chimeline moves her mount in front of his, and the two exchange soft words.

While Chimeline douses Colu's ire, the soldiers pass Blythe and me. Their eyes go straight to my voidstone, which is glaringly obvious against my white undershirt, and their sneers evaporate in the harsh sun.

If it were any other day—any other moment—I would teach them a lesson in humility.

But not today. Not after what I've just discovered. There is a sliver of hesitancy within me. Something making me think twice before grasping the black surface of my stone.

As the soldiers pass us by in a cloud of dust, we stop our horses. I use the opportunity to focus all my attention on Blythe, instead of splitting it between him and riding.

"So what did you tell these voices? And what did they say in reply?"

He covers his nose and mouth with a hand and coughs. "Not much, I'm afraid. But it was enough to confirm beliefs. Their very presence is both the light and the dark within me . . ." He grasps his bald head. "Good Unnamed."

"What do you mean it 'is both the light and the dark'?"

"I need to pray on this."

"Dem! Are we moving on?" Colu shouts back at us, and I nod in reply, nudging my horse gently with my feet.

Soon we're moving again at a slow walk, and I look sideways toward Blythe. He seems lost in deliberation. I'm not sure if he's praying or just consumed in thought.

My patience reaches its limit.

"Blythe, tell me," I insist.

"I can't," he answers.

I exhale deeply before raising my voice. "You know, you have some nerve telling me I have no faith, when you keep the truth from me."

He looks at me sharply. "Yes, you have a right to know, but I need to start at the beginning. If I told you what they said, it would make no sense to you. Like trying to build a temple starting with the bell tower."

"Well fine, then. Start with the foundation."

He purses his lips and looks away. "I need your promise before we continue."

"What promise?"

"That what I am about to tell you, you will share with nobody. That this knowledge will die with you."

For a moment, the only sound is that of our horses' hooves on the road, which transitions from sand to red cobblestones. Far ahead, Colu says something to Chimeline and she laughs brightly.

"I give you my word," I reply.

After a pause, he continues. "There are secrets handed down from effulgent to graycloak, generation after generation. They are written down in a private language."

"That's the white book you carry around. Chimeline was reading it earlier."

"No. I am not talking about the Book of Unwanting. The white book that you refer to is meant for the people of this world. The secrets that I am about to tell you are not."

"What do you mean by 'people of this world'?"

"Non-effulgency," he says. "You, Colu, Chimeline."

I nod.

"The scripts that I am referring to are passed down through the effulgency—in our own language. The same language I just used, but its written form. None of you can understand it. Even the existence of this language is a secret."

I consider the void. "Are the voices the authors who wrote the scripts?"

"That is a good question, but no," he says, shaking his head. "Let me explain it another way. Do you remember the relic that I showed you? Back in the temple?"

*Twisted blue metal.*

"Yes."

"I told you it was from the ship that first sailed across the sea from the land beyond. It is how we—the effulgency—first came here."

"I remember."

He looks up to the cloudless blue sky and points.

"Our relic ship came from across *that* sea. Not from the waters of this world."

For a moment I simply stare upwards, squinting until sweat falls into my eyes, and then I bring my gaze back down and wipe my brow with my white undershirt.

Shaking my head, I quietly laugh to myself. "You mean to tell me that you fell out of the sky?"

"It is as I feared," he answers flatly. "You are not ready."

I quiet down, once it's obvious that he's not telling some sort of effulgency parable. He's being literal.

"Listen," I say. "You can't honestly say something like that and expect anyone to believe it."

He doesn't respond.

"Fine," I concede. "Just explain to me what happened. How did your boat fall from the sky?"

"It was not a boat. Not in the way you're picturing it," he says. "Think of it instead as a citadel capable of traveling great distances."

*A citadel?*

I look up again. "Where did it come from?"

"I don't know where, exactly. That is the problem with what happened. We lost much in the crash."

"Crash?"

He nods. "It was scuttled."

"There was a mutiny?"

"Yes. The survivors of the crash were the first authors of the scripts, which we continue to pass down, generation to generation. At least fifty times we have passed these memories down. Fifty times we have rewritten our ancient texts onto strong parchment with fresh ink. But I fear that with each generation, the scripts become less truth and more legend."

"What do you mean?"

"Well, for example, some effulgents centuries ago promoted the belief that all souls had been freed in the crash. That your voidstones, as you call them, were not axion. There was a schism in our ranks. They declared there was no proof of souls in soteria. We call them the Protherists."

For a moment, I pause in thought, trying to ground myself despite Blythe's confusing terminology. *Axion. In soteria.* But this schism is equally as confounding. How something so fundamental could be kept secret outside of their society I cannot understand.

But then again, they've been able to keep so much else secret.

"I had no idea," I reply. "I thought all of you believed in the same dogma."

"You would be surprised, Master Voider. Sometimes the way of unwanting has many roads that run in the same direction."

I offer a grunt of understanding. The university is full of disagreements as well. Conspiracies against master voiders by their own submasters. Ages ago, the university was destroyed, only to be rebuilt after much healing in our ranks.

"What the Protherists believe goes against what is written. Today they are finally proven wrong and the original text is proven correct. This is what I meant by the light and dark."

"I'm not sure I'm following."

"When I heard the voices of my brothers and sisters in your stone, I felt both vindication and sadness. Both light and dark. I was relieved that my faith was rewarded with understanding." He takes a deep breath. "But this is an understanding that I do not wish to own. I would give it away, if I could."

He finds a rag in his saddlebag and wipes his sweaty face and scalp with it. "Good Unnamed, I have no idea where to start. It's hard enough teaching this to a graycloak."

"Is that what the voices said?"

"No!" he says loudly. "Our discussion was the bell tower. I am laying the foundation for you, Master Voider."

"Well, I'm a quick learner. And I promise not to interrupt. Or laugh again," I add softly.

He grunts as he puts his rag back.

"We will start with the empowered and the enervated. It is as good of a place to begin as any."

"Empowered and enervated?"

He nods. "The empowered could harness the power of axion—the material we effulgents have presumed your voidstones are created from for ages."

"The empowered are voiders?" I ask sharply, before remembering my pledge. I bite my lip and summon my patience.

"Yes and no. In some ways, the empowered were no different from voiders. Like you, they were rare—only a handful in a generation were born. And also, like you, they were powerful."

I nod in understanding.

"The enervated were the rest of us," he says. "We were at the empowered's mercy. And they had none."

"None of what?"

"Mercy."

He closes his eyes and looks up toward the sun. "It is written that the relic ship was larger than one could comprehend. A flying citadel among the stars. At the heart of this city was the Axiondrive. A massive formation of axion that powered the ship across the stars. It was much larger than these wagons that pass us on the road. Larger even than the house your student was building. And just like the sails that move your ships here, the Axiondrive moved ours."

I furrow my brow. "That's not exactly true."

"What isn't true?"

"Sails don't move our ships. The wind does."

He smiles. "You and your wind."

I let out a short laugh.

"But you bring up an interesting point," he says with a nod. "Just as the wind hits the sails, and the sails move the ship, our vessel also depended upon two elements. The Axiondrive is comparable to sails—it has no power of its own. It is a container. A converter. It relies upon something else."

"The voices," I say, curiosity overcoming patience.

He looks sideways at me and narrows his eyes. "You are getting to the heart of the matter. A thousand years ago, it was the reason for the crash, and today it is the reason we are talking."

I look down at my voidstone, grasping the gold setting surrounding the black center. Blythe said that voidstones are made of axion. The same substrate that powered his relic ship. If what he says is true, the Axiondrive would have been a massive voidstone. Larger than a wagon. Larger than a house.

It's impossible to fathom. The largest voidstone ever recorded by the university was the size of a lemon.

A voidstone bigger than a house—I can't conceive of the power that would wield.

"Do you know the answer?" he asks me. I look up and see that he's studying me with glassy eyes. He's close to tears.

"The answer?"

"What powered the Axiondrive. What continues to power all axion."

I finger the edge of the necklace and think back to my recent revelation.

*The winds are voices.*

I cannot understand what the voices say, but that is inconsequential. They are speaking, regardless. I heard Blythe, and they heard him.

*The winds are voices.*

Voices are communication. Communication comes from intelligence. Thinking creatures, each one unique. Each soul carrying a message to a targeted recipient. Each one indivisible.

"People," I answer loudly, but despite my excitement, my brow is furrowed in confusion because I'm still lost. I believe it, but I don't understand it. Which is the opposite of my usual stance. I feel as if I'm drowning even though I know how to swim.

When I look to Blythe, I see a tear run down his cheek and a smile cross his face. Ironically, he is the only thing I understand at this moment. I read his face perfectly. He is both happy and sad at the same time. He is happy that I have come to partake in his sadness.

"Voidstones are powered by people," I say incredulously.

In some ways, these words are nothing new. I have heard them my entire life from judgmental effulgents, people like Blythe, whom I disregarded because they had no proof. Their faith was ridiculous to me.

But now, the thought of my building an entire life around voidance without understanding its very source— resorting to childlike allegories—this is the thing that is ridiculous.

"Souls of the enervated, to be more precise," Blythe says. "Their physical bodies died thousands of years ago, but their spirits linger on, trapped in the axion. And every time you use that fragment of yours, you abuse them."

With these words, my shock slowly turns into a complex mix of dread and revulsion. Guilt washes over me. I don't dare ask him how voidance hurts the ones trapped in the void. Not yet, at least. But the idea that voidance is built upon the backs of enslaved souls goes against everything that I stand for. It goes against the entire university.

Our charter is built of goodness and decency.

Despite what the young king has done in recent years— abusing voidance for his cursed war—we remain intent on this original charter. The university has always been about the powerful few helping the many and weak.

*But the ends do not justify the means. Creating good with evil is still evil.*

*So what now? What is the future of voidance?*

Despite the sunshine, a shiver courses through my body as I consider the consequence. It's as revolting as it is liberating.

*If this is voidance . . . then I must give it up.*

*But that would make me nothing.*

When I turn to Blythe, I see his tears flowing, and my guilt cuts deeper.

"I didn't know," I say weakly.

"How could you? Even some among the effulgency— the Protherists—they do not believe what I am saying."

"Why didn't you come to us earlier?" I ask, defensiveness rising from the bottom of my stomach.

"We did. We have always preached about souls in your stones. None of you would listen."

I shake my head. "I'm talking about your private language! We listen to logic, Blythe! If one of you had come to the university and laid all of this out logically, then we could have made this discovery years ago. Centuries ago!"

"I didn't know. None of us knew."

I'm about to go further, but I close my mouth, realizing that blame is a dead end. The university could have reached out to the effulgency as well. But we disregarded them as fools.

*We were both fools. The voiders and effulgency alike.*

"Dem!"

Chimeline screams my name, but there is no fear in it.

I look up. Colu and Chimeline are far ahead of us because Blythe and I have been riding much slower, consumed by our conversation.

She's pointing to a large wagon being pulled by two white horses. There's an elaborate green sign on the front of it that reads "Worchot's Wares." A trader.

She continues to excitedly point at it, and then yells back at me again.

"He found it!" she says.

A moment later, I understand. The wagon is full of all sorts of rabble, but toward its rear is a large basket that towers above everything else. In front of it are stacks of hastily folded fabric, painted black. Some of it has ballooned out through the wooden slats in the wagon's sides.

It's the airship.

# WORCHOT'S WORDS

I dismount, leading everyone else to do the same. Meanwhile, the trader pulls his large open wagon onto the side of the road. He turns past the bloodred cobblestones and onto the fine golden sand, sending up clouds of dust.

The driver is the only person in the wagon. A bone-white palehound sits at attention next to him.

He slowly stands. Springs in the seat let out rusty squeaks and the palehound flashes his red fangs at us.

"Good morning, fellow traders. Worchot is me," he bellows, a hand on his chest as he surveys the four of us below. He then looks to the sun, which is behind white-gray clouds. "It *is* still morning, Worchot believes. Worchot has a sunstone, if you wish to be precise about things. A sunstone that happens to be for sale."

Behind me, Blythe mumbles, "Good Unnamed."

The trader is an incredibly short, fat man with a gray-brown beard that could double as a bird's nest. He's wearing indigo trousers and a green vest over a white shirt—his vest matches the color of the garish sign hanging over his seat.

Worchot grasps one of the metal posts holding it up as he attempts to exit the wagon. As he does this, the railings fastened to the sign telescope out and suddenly a makeshift leather roof appears over him.

He lets out a curse.

"Pardon me," he adds, clearing his throat as he pushes the contraption back into place with a violent clang. Only then does he climb down, though he flashes a cautious glance at his two white horses.

"They're new to Worchot," he explains. "And Blood upsets them." He clears his throat.

"Blood?" I ask.

"Worchot's bodyguard," he answers, pointing to the palehound. "Worchot doesn't want the horses charging off. But then again, they're almost ready to be turned into stew meat. Probably couldn't charge off if their lives depended on it."

"Where did you get the airship?"

Worchot chuckles. The buttons on his green vest are perilously close to bursting. "Business, business. But we have not even introduced ourselves."

"You are the trader Worchot. I am Master Voider Democryos from the citadel."

He looks down at my stone and then to Blythe behind me. Too curious to wait for his response, I approach the back of the wagon to inspect the airship.

The basket has been placed on its side, so I can easily look into it from where I stand. I find nothing inside. Both the basket and fabric seem to be in good condition, and clean.

Which means it's unlikely that it crashed.

"It's for sale, Master Voider."

I turn around and face the trader. "I ask you a second time. Where did you get this?"

I notice him swallow and look at Blood and then back to me.

"At a farm not one mile from here. Worchot procured it from the owner."

I take a step toward him.

"Tell me what happened."

He wipes his clean hands on his green vest. "You see, Master Voider, even the story of this airship is for sale. And quite the marvelous story it is." He looks up wide-eyed, as if he's an actor on stage. "The way it came out of the skies, carrying two incredible Northerners. Even for a citadelian as yourself, you will be amazed at the tale."

I look back at my three companions. Chimeline's mouth hangs open. Colu's eye is narrowed, his thumb resting lightly on his leather sword belt. Blythe shakes his head.

"How much?" I ask him. "For the information. I don't need the airship."

He looks me up and down, fingering his tempest of a beard.

"One hundred," he says.

Colu grunts at that.

The Xian is right. We're being toyed with, but I don't care.

"Just give it to him," I tell Colu.

He swears under his breath but then storms off to his horse to retrieve the gold.

Meanwhile, Worchot kicks the bottom of the ladder on the wagon a few times. A wooden seat eventually pops out between the two bottom rungs, and he sits down on it with a groan.

"Come near!" he says, suddenly cheerful. He waves his pudgy hands toward himself. "All of you, gather around Worchot!"

I am already standing near. But Chimeline sits cross-legged on the ground next to me. Her pants are the same color as the sand.

Blythe remains standing as well.

Worchot slaps his palms against his knees, breathes out theatrically, and then begins.

"Worchot was at Farmer Owerjen's place, as Worchot was saying. Buying some fine golden honey. Worchot loves his bees, but they do not love Worchot back. See?" He cuffs his white shirtsleeve to reveal a trail of red swelling.

The trader then laughs to himself before his eyes get wide.

"Worchot was there, in the wildflower fields with Owerjen and his two sons, between stacks of bee houses taller than most men, when we saw something black in the sky. And it was growing."

He looks off to the horizon and points to nothing.

"Just like that, the black spot became larger and larger. Lower in the skies and directly toward us. The young one ran back to the house. He was scared. But the rest of us stayed, and to tell you the truth, Worchot was scared too. Nothing, in all of Worchot's travels, did this look like. That little master Owerjen had common sense, that he did."

"Who was in the airship?" I ask levelly, not appreciating his theatrics, although it seems that Chimeline is taken by them. She's resting her head on her hands, leaning forward.

"An effulgent and his consort."

Blythe steps forward and interjects before I can.

"Are you sure?"

Worchot nods. "By Temberlain's Ashes, he was wearing the white robes. And his head was just like yours—bald as a baby's ass. Not a single hair on his body, not even eyebrows."

"Did you speak to him?" Blythe replies.

"Yes. But like you, Graycloak, he was a man of few words."

Colu comes near and throws a bag of gold to Worchot.

"Worchot thanks you," he says, as Colu leans against a wagon wheel.

"Don't thank me," Colu says. "Ain't my fucking gold."

"The woman," I say. "Tell me about the woman."

He whistles. "Good Unnamed. If Worchot were younger and a few more inches, he would have asked that sprightly beauty for a dance, right in the middle of those wildflowers." He laughs to himself again. "Worchot is speaking about his height, in case you're all wondering. Worchot's manhood is not lacking."

"Did the airship crash?" Chimeline asks, ignoring his crude humor.

He shakes his head. "No, my fine lady from the archipelago. It was not a crash at all but a soft, delicate landing. Like the swans of Northinglight landing upon icy waters without even a ripple. The basket came down, and for a while it slid silently across the fields of wildflowers. Eventually, it toppled over, but by then the pair had deftly jumped out, hand in hand. They almost *floated* out."

"What did they say?" I ask.

He smiles. "The man wanted to know whose field it was. How far south we were. Owerjen stepped forward and introduced himself.

"Was there a veil surrounding his face?" I continue, motioning with my hand about my head.

His face wrinkles up. "Worchot does not understand."

"Was the man behind a veil?" I say, raising my voice.

"No," he answers. "What kind of pig's ass question is that?"

"Where was he from?" Blythe asks softly, before I can retort. "Did he mention a temple?"

Worchot shakes his head and spreads out his hands. "No."

"Do you know anything useful?" I ask.

"Worchot can see that you want this man's identity, but Worchot cannot give it to you. All Worchot can tell you is what happened next."

"Which is?"

"The lady wanted to freshen up at Owerjen's farmhouse, which was nearby, just over the hill. Owerjen rang his bell to call his wife out and she took the golden-haired beauty inside."

"Where were they headed?" I ask.

"Winter's Baiou," he answers, while pointing at me. "*That* much they revealed."

"But *where* in Winter's Baiou? It's a large city."

"Worchot does not know, for they did not say."

I nod slowly, somewhat disappointed.

"The effulgent wouldn't take gold for the black airship," he continues. "His revulsion to ownership. And Owerjen had no interest in it." He clears his throat. "It is the king's property. But that airship is right up Worchot's darkened alley, so we made a trade. The man and woman got Worchot's horses, which were in much better condition than these two," he says, a thumb pointed in their direction. "I gave them the horses, along with some goat clippings." He clears his throat again before continuing. "Worchot got the airship, and Owerjen got the thing off his property. Owerjen is a very lawful man."

I raise my head and look at him. "What did he ask for?"

"My good horses—"

"No," I interject. "The other thing."

"You mean the goat clippings?"

"Yes. What is that?"

He illustrates by slicing one of his hands with the other, and then doing the same with his nose. "Goat clippings. Muzzles and feet."

"Why would he want such a thing?" Blythe asks.

Worchot shrugs. "They're used for a great many things. Typically, one can make a very strong glue with boiled clippings. Used by painters, mostly. Saddlers and woodworkers, too. Worchot is asked for clippings once in a while. They are not as popular as honey." He extends his hands toward us. "By the way, would any of you care to purchase some fresh honey? Only ten gold per bottle."

"How did the two act together?" I reply, ignoring his question.

"Hmm?"

"The effulgent and the woman. Were they . . . friendly with one another?"

He takes a deep breath as he runs his hands through his beard again. A small piece of rubbish falls out and lands on the sand.

"If you don't mind Worchot saying," he says, "effulgents and graycloaks have always been a little strange to Worchot. Not very clear with their emotions. A tight lid over an empty jar is what Worchot says."

Blythe says nothing, and the trader laughs as he looks at me. "See what Worchot means?"

"Answer the question, please."

He grunts and shrugs again. "Worchot couldn't tell by the man. He was a statue. Like Worchot said before, a tight lid. But he held the woman's hand when they landed. And she put her arms around his chest. In a certain way, if you know what Worchot means."

I am silent as he adds, "Maybe she is going to bear him a graycloak. Gotta hand it to those effulgents. They get to pick the—"

"Is that all?" I say, cutting him off.

Worchot purses his lips. "That's about it. She paid ten gold to Owerjen's wife before leaving, for the use of their washbasin and also fresh honeybread. Worchot can't think of anything else."

"Then we're done here," I say, turning away from him.

I hear him groan as he gets up from his built-in ladder-seat. He kicks it back into place.

"Ah, Master Voider, there is one thing that Worchot forgot."

I look over my shoulder at him.

He taps his chest. "The effulgent had one of those, except it might have been bigger than yours."

I look down momentarily and then face him completely.

"A voidstone?"

He nods.

"That's impossible."

He shrugs. "Worchot says what Worchot saw."

I flash Blythe a worried glance.

"Tell us *exactly* what you saw," Blythe says.

"Worchot did not see the black stone as they landed. The effulgent had it in his fist. But after they floated down, he tucked it into an inner pocket of his white cloak.

Worchot has a quick eye for things like that, and Worchot saw the stone. Golden-haired beauty had one as well."

I bring my hand up to my temple and squeeze hard.

"Now Worchot has finished his story. Honest as mother's milk."

He wipes his hands across his vest again as he surveys the others. "Are you sure you don't want any honey?" He looks at Colu. "Worchot also has some fine weapons—and a kind warning. In the bay city, you will have a hard time finding an interested merchant. You being Xian and all. But me? Worchort's Wares is open to all."

Leaving the chuckling trader, I briskly head back to our horses, waving Blythe over.

"A voider-effulgent?" I whisper to him. "I've never heard of such a thing."

He stays silent, a hand to his chin.

"But the trader's story matches what Colu saw in the hilma field," I add.

Blythe nods.

"Do you believe it?" I ask him.

He brings a finger to his lips in thought. "The woman is a voider?"

I shake my head while darkly smiling. Blythe's thoughts are overlapping with mine.

"Not really."

"I thought you said she had—"

"Actually, yes," I say, interrupting. "She's technically a voider, but she's weak. There is no way she could power the airship all the way from the citadel."

Blythe narrows his eyes. "Are you sure?"

"Yes. I saved her from voideath years ago. She entered it just by touching my stone. It had to have been powered by him. The effulgent."

After a moment of silence, he adds, "Do you know what this means?"

"We're dealing with a paradox," I say, under my breath.

"More than that. We're dealing with an empowered."

We both come to a halt.

He closes his eyes and takes a deep breath. Meanwhile, I look to the others, who are still by the wagon. We're clearly out of earshot.

He looks up and swallows. "Which is impossible."

"Tell me why."

"All the empowered died in the crash."

"Which happened . . . when? A thousand years ago?"

Blythe extends a hand. "Please. I am thinking, Master Voider."

I sigh, looking back to Colu and Chimeline. They're talking to Worchot. He's brought out the honey and some other items as well. Chimeline holds up a bracelet that glitters in the midday sun. Colu inspects a dagger. Blood, the palehound, relieves himself in the brush, leaving a trail of pink urine. And far away, the clouds begin to darken.

"It is written that eleutheria was the goal of the mutiny."

"Eleutheria?"

"The process of releasing souls from axion."

I give a hesitant nod. I don't understand, but I don't want to interrupt either.

"But they were not completely successful," he adds. "The continued existence of voidstones is proof enough of this."

"So, your forefathers meant to free the trapped souls in the Axiondrive," I surmise darkly, "but they failed. And the result was the crash."

He nods. "And now I wonder, if they failed at that, perhaps they failed at something else."

I wait for him to continue.

"The enervated who survived proclaimed in their first writings that this world was a fresh start. Without the blemish of the empowered. But maybe one survived within our ranks. Maybe the empowered bloodline was carried forward to this time."

"Your people . . . the enervated . . . they became who we know as the effulgency today."

He nods.

"And an empowered among you would look no different."

"Correct."

"Then this man must have been an effulgent at the citadel," I say. "Which is why he sometimes hid his identity with a veil." I raise my hands and lower them against my sides. "Out here, there is no need to conceal oneself."

"Yes, yes," Blythe replies, finally looking up at me.

"How many effulgents are there in the citadel?" I ask. "I only know of the head effulgent and a few others."

Blythe exhales sharply through dry lips. "The citadel is one of the largest cities in the Northern Kingdom. It has over a dozen temples across the first and second rings, and probably over a hundred effulgents combined."

I utter a curse, kicking a loose red cobblestone that has found its way to the side of the road. "I thought that we were onto something."

But then my foot goes still.

"I never taught him," I say slowly.

"What?"

I shake my head quickly, back and forth, as if trying to dislodge my prior notions. "All this time, I thought that I was dealing with someone trained at the university."

"Why the university?"

"The man veiled his face. That's dynamic voidance. He designed a laboratory devoted to war. He powered an airship across the Northern Kingdom. All these things require advanced knowledge of voidance. It's just not reasonable to assume one learns these things on their own."

"I would not know but trust that you are correct."

"This is why I assumed that the man was a former student of mine. That would explain how Marine met him. But now, all of that's fallen into ruin."

"Because you don't educate effulgents."

I let out a single dark laugh. "No. I doubt that an effulgent has ever dared stepped through our front door. And if they ever did, I'm not sure we'd let them in."

Another span of silence ensues, until Blythe speaks up again. "Was the woman on the way of unwanting?"

"No, Blythe. Quite the contrary."

"How do you mean?"

I shrug. "She came from a wealthy Giriyan family, which was then dwarfed by the life of luxury I gave her. I think she owned more shoes than all the residents of Fiscarlo."

He groans. "I hope you are exaggerating."

"I'm not."

The bright, tumbling sound of gold coins causes me to turn toward the wagon. They're wrapping up.

"Master Voider," Blythe says. "I have an idea."

I look back to him.

"I'd like to speak to them again." He nods at my stone. "When?"

"As soon as possible," he says. "They may know about this empowered—if he is working alone, or if there are more of them out there. May the Good Unnamed help us all if the latter is true."

I feel my brow furrow. "How would the trapped souls in *my* stone know what this empowered is doing with his?"

Blythe presses his lips together tightly. "They are all connected, somehow."

"How do you know that?"

"They knew about the others."

"Others?"

"The enervated trapped in your stone knew of the other fragments of axion, all across this land. Somehow, they are one."

I open my mouth, but he extends his hand to silence me. "Understanding the extent of this evil is our first step. After that, I must get the word out, immediately. It is of utmost importance. Greater, I might add, than finding the empowered and the woman."

I bring a hand to my temple again in frustration. I am so close to Marine I can feel it. And now, more than ever, I need to know the truth. How could she fall in love with an effulgent, of all people? With a man who doesn't know the slightest thing about making her happy?

But after all I've learned today, it is hard for me to discount Blythe's words. There are more urgent things in this world than repairing a broken heart.

"How do you plan on accomplishing this?" I ask. "Getting the word out, I mean."

"There are temples in Winter's Baiou."

I look at him inquisitively.

"Every temple raises pigeons trained to fly to nearby temples. It is a network of sorts. I will send a message out in our private language—in all directions. And they will do the same. Within days, it will be carried across the entire land."

"Fine," I say, acquiescing. "We'll stop by one of your temples. But as soon as you're done, I'm going to find Marine and that bastard empowered."

He winces.

"What?"

"You're not thinking this through."

"I am thinking it through perfectly," I reply curtly. "I help you, and then I'm on my way."

"That's not what I meant. An empowered has arisen. He is a voider, but he is also an effulgent. Which means that if he's headed to Winter's Baiou, he might be going to the very same temple we intend to visit."

I see his point.

Blythe bites his lip, looks down, and then looks back at me. "Don't underestimate him."

With his words, an image of the veiled man appears in my mind. Except there is no darkness or blur about him anymore. All of that has blown away, along with my prior ignorance.

He's gleaming now. A nondescript, smooth face above shining robes. Painful white, like a needle in the eye.

And it makes me wonder: How could a man like this have gone unnoticed? How could a man who shuns attachments steal the greatest of mine out from under my nose?

Either he's brilliant or I am a fool beyond words.

"I won't, Blythe."

But when I look at him, he's smiling sadly.

"What is it?"

He presses his lips together again before answering. "All this time, *I* have been the one accusing *you* of seeking out danger. Now, look at me. I fear that I am stepping off the way of unwanting."

"Peace never begets peace, Blythe. Only justice does."

# WEEPING WILLOW

Blythe releases my hand as the storm outside overtakes the one within.

"Good Unnamed" are his first words after exiting the void. He sits up in the shadowed grasses, a torrent of rain only feet away.

He's whiter than a palehound.

The four of us have taken shelter underneath a weeping willow. It is so large and dense that it's almost enough to keep us completely dry. But every so often, the wind picks up and the rain goes sideways, finding its way in.

"What did they say?" I ask Blythe, sitting up straight.

Out of the corner of my eye, I see Colu and Chimeline lean in, captivated by our sudden awakening. Chimeline stretches and touches her toes. We've all taken off our boots to air our tired feet.

*Let them hear us. I have no secrets to keep.*

"What did they say? Many things. Some more troubling than others. It took time for them to trust me, given the betrayal they suffered at the hands of the empowered. A man with a heart as dark as axion."

"So he's working alone, then."

Blythe nods, forcing a half-smile.

"How can the voices be sure?"

"They know everyone who is in soteria. Everyone who enters axion," Blythe answers. "Just as we can recognize another by their voice in a darkened room. Except more so. To the enervated, every presence is special and unique. There is no concept of a name to a soul, which is why we have carried on this tradition in your land."

I don't fully understand the concept, but I take his word for it. "Meaning we can trust the other effulgents."

"Yes." His forehead is still deeply furrowed.

"What is it?"

Blythe looks at me. "They told me something else. Something far more troubling."

"What?"

"He found the Axiondrive."

A gust of wind sprays us with temperate rain, and I wipe the water from my face. The nearby willow strands sway in hushed whispers, as if they are carrying Blythe's words to sibling trees.

"But the Axiondrive was destroyed."

He shakes his head.

"Hold on. You said that there was a mutiny and your vessel was destroyed." I raise my voidstone by its gold chain. "And that these fragments were all that remained."

"That is what I thought too," he replies. "But it seems that the core of it survived. A very large core."

"How large?"

He looks up. "Based on their description, I calculate that it's nearly the size of this tree."

"But you said that the entire *thing* was roughly that size," I reply. "How could the remainder be the same, if all of these fragments exist?" I gesture to my voidstone.

His eyes go to my stone. "I would venture a guess that voidstones are but tiny fragments of the massive original. Chips around the edge, if you will. It is all relative."

Dropping my gaze, I pull a fistful of grass away from the damp ground and let the blades fall over my pants. Many of them stick to my palm. "So frustrating," I eventually mumble.

"What is it, Master Voider?"

"I just wish that I could communicate with the souls like you can."

"Why?"

I look up. "Because I think that they may be wrong, Blythe. Misled, somehow. But I can't help you get to the bottom of this if I can't communicate with them."

"Why don't you believe them?"

I shake my head. "I believe in their sincerity. But a voidstone that large is unheard of."

"Just because you have never seen something doesn't mean that it's not real."

I look up at him sharply. "Just because you've heard something doesn't make it real either."

Colu lets out a deep groan of agreement.

"It's buried underwater," Blythe answers, levelly. "Somewhere underneath Xi Bay."

"There is no way . . ." I begin, but then my mouth hangs open as a recent memory overtakes me. The rain-filled world of green, blue, and gray suddenly disappears. I see only flickering gold and red. A tense dinner conversation, seemingly a lifetime ago.

*What if we found a stone larger than you can imagine?*

I remember the way the candelabra flames looked in the king's eyes when he asked me the question. I'd thought he was drunk. And maybe he was, except it wasn't on red-currant wine. He was drunk on power.

*They'd be like gods, wouldn't they?*

"Master Voider?"

This image is replaced by a memory of the smug commander we met on the road. His red cape over polished armor glinting in the firelight. The news that the war had ended.

*The bay was always the objective. It was never about invading the south. It was always about taking control of Xi Bay.*

"Master Voider?"

"The war," I say, as the rain-soaked world returns. "This entire war has been about claiming a massive voidstone."

Colu leans in. My gaze passes over each of them as I tell them what the king said.

"How did your king find out about the stone?" Colu asks.

"The empowered must have discovered it and then sought out the king's help on the matter," Blythe says.

"But why?" I ask no one in particular.

"Because of Xiland," Colu says.

We all turn to him.

"Up until now, Xiland controlled most of Xi Bay," Colu says. "Which means this massive stone of yours would have been in Xiland-controlled waters."

"Then why didn't the voider-effulgent go straight to the Xian emperor? Gain his help instead of the king's?"

Colu blows air through his lips. "Maybe my emperor is not a puppet like your young king is."

I nod softly and then look at Blythe. "They said the voider-effulgent found the Axiondrive. But what does that mean? What are his plans?"

"He's in the process of raising it."

"Raising it," I repeat. "Because it's underwater."

"Yes."

"It would be incredibly heavy. Would you agree?"

He runs a hand over his glass-smooth head. "You are correct, Master Voider."

"Heavy?" Chimeline asks.

I raise my voidstone by its chain, feeling its weight. "Even small voidstones are heavy. We've always measured their power not by volume but by weight, and we've been conscious of the fact that they are far heavier than other substances the same size. Maybe it is simply that."

"Simply what?" Colu says.

"The voider-effulgent found the massive voidstone somewhere in the bottom of Xi Bay, but he couldn't raise it to the surface on his own. No voider could raise something that heavy. He would need help from—" I stare into the gray rain.

"What is it?" asks Blythe.

"Other voiders," I say slowly.

"You believe they are helping him raise it?" Blythe asks.

"It would make sense that they would. If there was ever a prize to be had, it's this."

I look down and pull out another fistful of grass as I collect my thoughts.

"I wonder how long he's known about its existence," I mumble. "Probably as long as the war's been going on."

"Much longer than that, Master Voider."

I look up. "How do you know?"

Blythe shakes his head, seemingly trying to put the pieces together himself. "He began speaking to them when he was just a child."

I lean backward in shock. "He can talk to the voices as well?"

"Of course," Blythe answers, as if I am a dolt. "He is one of us. He speaks our private language."

He continues. "Somehow he realized his power as a boy, when he was but a graycloak."

"How could he?" I ask.

"I should be the one asking you that question, Master Voider." He motions in the direction of my stone. "How could a graycloak stumble upon one of those fragments without anyone else knowing?"

I look down momentarily. "I suppose it's possible that he simply found one," I answer. "Voidstones are naturally present in the ground. Farmers have been finding them in their fields for years. They travel to the university and exchange them for a hefty sum of gold."

He grunts, as if dissatisfied with my answer, and then stares out into the distance. "They said that long ago, when he was a young graycloak, he discovered that he was an empowered. He began entering the void."

A sharp wind makes the hanging branches sway.

"Despite this, he was on the way of unwanting. He was even able to perform eleutheria."

"Eleutheria?"

"The freeing of souls in his fragment. But then something happened."

I wait.

"He stopped trying to help them. He stopped speaking with them."

"What do you mean?"

"He turned on them. He abandoned eleutheria. He somehow got access to another stone. A larger one. And then began using them." Blythe shakes his head.

"How many is *them*?"

"I do not understand your question," Blythe says.

"How many souls are trapped in an axion fragment?"

Blythe presses his lips together and looks down, running his palms gently over the blades of grass. He then looks at the clump of grass in my hand and motions with his head.

"Open your hand, and let the blades fall," he says.

I do as he says.

"That is roughly the number of enervated in that fragment of yours."

I look at the green blades scattered all over my pants, dark enough that they almost blend into the black. There are dozens—possibly hundreds—and as I wipe my damp palms together, more of them fall.

"What about the voidstone underneath Xi Bay?"

When I look back at Blythe, he's grazing the top of the wet grass with his palms again while looking out at the rain. For a long time, he's silent—to the point where I'm not sure he even heard my question. But then he answers.

"The number of souls in the Axiondrive is comparable to the number of blades of grass in this field we're sitting in. More than one can count."

"Good Unnamed," Chimeline says.

"It is a great evil," Blythe murmurs. "A great evil hidden in plain sight."

I shake my head forcefully.

"You don't agree?" Blythe asks sharply.

I clear my throat. "No, no. I agree. I just find it hard to comprehend how all of this was masterminded without my knowledge. Raising the Axiondrive. The war. Even the king being in on it. He may be a drunken fool, but I cannot see him willingly aiding this voider-effulgent. Or, for that matter, my . . ." I shut my mouth and look down.

"Or what?" asks Blythe.

"Marine," I add. There is a span of awkward silence, so I decide to fill it with honesty. "She may not have been a trustworthy wife, but she has a good heart. I cannot see her being part of something this dark."

"Perhaps she didn't realize what he was doing," Blythe says.

Colu grunts in approval. "Your woman was duped. Just like mine was. For some reason, effulgents hold sway over—"

Chimeline interrupts with a guttural sound.

We all turn to her.

She's convulsing. She closes her eyes and then puts her hands to her head.

Colu rises to his knees. "What the fuck?"

"Yes," she utters, her choking sounds becoming words. "Yes, yes, yes, yes, yes."

I crawl over the damp grass to her.

"I did it," she says. Her face is a balled-up knot of tension. "I did it. It's done."

"Master Voider?" Blythe looks at me warily.

I grab Chimeline's shoulders, as I did last time, and shake her. But it doesn't seem to work.

"This happened once before," I tell him. "In the airship. She was dreaming."

"This ain't no fucking dream," Colu says.

"He's dead. He's dead. He's dead."

I shake her again, harder this time.

She goes silent, her body relaxing in my arms. Her head falls backward and I have to catch it with my palm.

"Chimeline."

She opens her eyes and blinks rapidly.

"Can you hear me?"

After blinking a few more times, she then nods once. "Dem."

"Who's dead?" I ask her.

She looks around and sees Blythe and Colu.

"Chimeline, who's dead?"

"I . . . I don't know."

"Who were you talking to?"

She tightly shuts her eyes. "I don't know. Nobody."

"Master Voider," Blythe says. "Maybe she needs to lie down. Or have a drink of water. I have some in the saddlebag."

I ignore him.

*She was talking to someone. It wasn't a dream. It was a conversation.*

*With the person who wants me dead.*

The king started a war over a massive voidstone and simultaneously planned the murder of the one person who wouldn't go along with his plan.

Except the king doesn't have the power to do what just happened. Only voidance can explain it.

Her admission, in the cages of Fiscarlo.

*After a while, I could hear his voice in my head.*

*What do you mean?*

*Just like you're talking to me now. Except in my head.*

She opens her eyes.

As I stare into the brown darkness, her head cradled in my arms, the answer comes to me. There is only one person in the world who would want me dead besides the king.

"It was *him*, wasn't it?" I ask. My voice is barely louder than the driving rain.

"Who?"

"It wasn't the king who sent you. It was the man behind the veil."

Her lips quiver before she suddenly twists out of my embrace. She stands and runs off, through the curtain of willow branches and out into the blue-gray distance.

"Chimeline!"

I run after her.

Instantly, I am soaked through. But I am barefoot and not weighed down by my cloak—only my riding pants and white undershirt.

She is barefoot as well, and a good runner, but no match for me. In fifty feet or so, I catch up to her on the crest of a grassy knoll and grab her shoulder, spinning her around. We both trip on each other's feet and go down.

I fall against her legs and then madly climb over her, my hands pinning her writhing arms to the wet grass.

"Do you know who he is?" I yell over the storm.

She shakes her head violently, blinking as the rain seeps into her eyes.

"I need to know! You were talking to him!"

I let go, fearing that I may be hurting her.

She is crying. Her eyes are still closed and her face is wet with rain, but her throat is constricted, her usually light voice twisted with pain. She gasps for breath.

"I was the last one. The last one."

The last one?"

"He killed all of them. My three sisters."

It takes me only a moment to understand. The graves.

A gust of rain crashes into us with enough force to almost push me aside, and I shield her body with mine.

She clutches my rain-soaked shirt.

"He would voidspeak."

"Voidspeak?" I frown, having never heard the term before.

"He would tell me things, except not with his mouth. With his *mind*. That's what he called it."

"In the laboratory."

I pull away from her and stare down at her face. She's blinking rapidly.

"The place I burned down."

She nods. "In the beginning, yes. But then we would talk when he was far away. When I was in the harem house and he was . . . wherever. That is what he was using us for. His tests."

She swallows. "The other girls, they came first. They were unlucky, and he didn't value them. He treated me differently."

"Why?"

"Because of my past. What I was raised to do. He said he was saving me for something special."

I shake my head.

"When it came time for me to be part of his tests, it mostly worked and it didn't cause much pain. I could hear his voice. He could hear mine. There wasn't much bleeding."

"Bleeding?"

She takes a gulp of breath, as if she has just come up for air from underwater. "From the ears. Sometimes it happens when the conversation goes on for a long time."

I get off her and gently bring her up into a sitting position on the grass. I pull back her wet hair and check her ears—there is no sign of blood.

I turn around so her back is against my chest.

I wrap my arms tightly around her, as if to shelter her from the storm. It's impossible. We're completely exposed on the hilltop. But the rain is temperate, the soft hammering of flower petals instead of the stinging of nails.

*Breathe.*

Chimeline does. A low and slow, trembling feeling reverberating from her body to mine. It seems like the echo of contentment, the whisper to simply *be*. The world of gray holds only the two of us. A spun cocoon.

There are no more secrets. There is no more black-and-white. No more right and wrong. All of that is washed away.

"I am so sorry," I tell her.

"I'm sorry too." She sniffles, her voice level. "I should have told you. I just feared that you would send me away."

I hug her even tighter. "I will never send you away."

She clutches me tighter, and I am content to just hold her for a moment.

Eventually, she pulls back and swallows. Her eyes try to meet mine, but it seems difficult for her, as if she is feeling guilty.

"It was the night we met. His voice was weak, like someone speaking through a wall. He told me that he wanted me to seduce you. To use moonspit. You would be having dinner with His Majesty."

I nod.

"He terrified me. I . . . I was going to do it. But you rejected my advances that first night, and then everything changed."

She cranes her neck, looking back at me, and I loosen my hold.

"I lied to him," she adds, a nervous smile creeping across her face. It's a ray of sunlight.

"I know."

She wrinkles her nose.

"You were speaking out loud. You told him that you went through with it. That I was dead."

"I didn't know what else to say."

"You did the right thing."

She bites her lip.

"Do you think he'll leave me alone now? Do you think he'll just forget about me?"

She stares at me intently, waiting for an answer.

"Chimeline, I don't know who this man is. I don't know his name, or if he even has one. To me, he's the man behind the veil. The voider-effulgent. The empowered." I shake my head in thought. "But I know his dark soul. I have no doubt that he will continue to abuse the ones surrounding him until he is stopped."

She looks back out into the gray distance, her brief smile fading.

"I'm going to help you, Chimeline. I promise. I'm going to get him out of your head."

She nods absently.

"But I don't think you should come with us to Winter's Baiou. It's too dangerous."

She turns to me sharply, a hurt expression on her face.

"I'm going there to find and kill this man," I explain. "It's likely to be a very . . .unpleasant scene. And I don't want you getting hurt in the process."

She lets out a short breath of disbelief. "You just said you would never send me away. And yet here you are, doing exactly that."

I shake my head. "That's not what I meant. I'm not sending you away because I don't trust you. I'm sending you away . . ."

"Why?"

"Because I care deeply for you."

She seems to relax somewhat.

"Chimeline, it's for the best, based on what you just told me. The man behind the veil *knows* you. And if he sees you with me, he'll use you to get to me." I look back to Xi Road in the distance. "There are probably many safe plantations between here and the city—"

She grasps my hand. "I am *not* leaving you."

I sigh.

"I'm coming with you," she insists. Her voice is tight, either with tears or resolution. "After everything he's done to me and my sisters, I deserve to be there when it happens." She wipes her face with the side of her hand. "I deserve to help you. To be a part of it."

Inwardly, I cringe. I have no intention of including Chimeline in my hunt.

"Thank you, but I don't need your help," I softly say. "I need you to stay safe."

"You're forgetting something," she says.

"What?"

She looks away. "I'm an assassin."

"But you don't have to be."

"Just like you don't have to be a voider, now that you know the truth of what it means?"

Another gust of wind and rain hits us and I pull her closer.

"Sometimes you can't leave who you are," she whispers. "It's a part of you."

There is nothing I can say. I feel the heavy voidstone around my neck. I feel its wrongness mixed with its power, and I don't know which is stronger. The thought of overcoming the man behind the veil without voidance at my side seems ludicrous. And yet, if I destroy this man using the same evil that he espouses, what does that make me?

"Alright," I gently answer her. "Alright."

My reply is almost lost in the wind and the rain, and I imagine the millions of trapped souls encircling us. Souls I cannot see—listening, watching.

Waiting.

# THE EDGE OF A KINGDOM

Six guards stop us as we pass into the shadowed tunnel of Winter's Baiou's northern entrance. They seem in high spirits but are initially rude. Only toward Blythe do they show some respect, calling him graycloak and offering meager bows of their heads. One whistles at Chimeline until another sees me pull my voidstone out from underneath my white shirt and hits him in the side to quiet him. Then they fall into line.

A guard kindly asks us to dismount, citing safety orders from Commander Reddles, whom the king apparently appointed to run the city. No horses are allowed, due to the crowded streets.

They tag the four animals and a guard hands me a note with a number written on it, along with an address that states "Grenaden's Stables." Chimeline kisses her horse on the muzzle.

"Who's in charge here?" I ask the guard who handed me the note. He's the same one who prodded the whistling guard.

"I am."

"Have you been stationed here the past few days?"

"Yes."

I lower my voice. "Have you seen the Lady Marine?"

He narrows his eyes. "Sir Voider, we are not allowed to report on the comings or goings—"

I hold up the king's signet ring in front of his face. "I am Master Voider Democryos from the citadel. You are allowed to report anything to me."

Colu swears. Behind me, the soldiers confiscate his sword and daggers and give him another ticket with a number on it. They place his weapons in a small indentation built into the stone wall and lock them up behind iron bars.

"Your Grace," the guard says, bowing. "Yes, the Lady Marine came by here." His focus momentarily goes to the barrel-vaulted stone ceiling. "The day before last."

I nod. "Whom was she with?"

His face scrunches up a bit, as if, only now, he is realizing the absurdity of his words. "An effulgent."

"Where did they go?"

He shakes his head. "I don't know, Your Grace."

"Is there anything else you can tell me about their arrival? Anything at all?"

He stares into the distance while four of his guards walk away with our horses.

"No, Your Grace."

I exhale. "Alright, then. Let us in."


The unbridled revelry in Winter's Baiou is apparent even before we exit the other side of the shallow stone tunnel.

Its streets are flooded—not only with the remains of the storm, but the remains of the war. Women wearing brightly colored dresses are on the arms of Northern soldiers. These men walk around unarmored but still in partial uniform, the sleeves of their red tunics rolled up to their elbows. They carry canteens in hand, no doubt filled with sugarcanex.

Children dance and jump in puddles. Performers tower a dozen feet over them, on stilts. A firebreather hangs off a second-floor iron balcony by one hand, and a masked man juggles on the flat roof of the city wall.

"The commander was not lying," says Colu, squinting as we leave the shadows. "The war has indeed ended."

"Where is the temple?" I ask Blythe, as the distilled sunlight hits me. The storm clouds have gone, but wispy remnants remain. The late-afternoon light shines with a soft shade of lavender.

He points right, to the west. "There are three effulgency temples in Winter's Baiou, but I only trust one. It is not the closest, unfortunately."

"Why do you trust it?"

He glances over his shoulder at me. "I know the head effulgent—she's a woman."

"A woman," I repeat, staring at the cobblestones, before looking back up at him. "We can trust her because the voider-effulgent is a man?"

"Correct."

I hum in agreement.

Most of the crowd travels in the opposite direction, and we're pushed a bit before we find a slender current going our way.

I look around in all directions. I have the itching feeling that I'm being watched.

"Do you think we'll run into them?" Chimeline asks in my ear. She is very close to me, her arm tucked into mine.

I know who she's referring to. "With this crowd, the odds are unlikely."

"No effulgent would be out here in this debauchery," Blythe says. "It is one thing to quietly thank the Unnamed for a peaceful end to the war. It is another to reduce oneself to this . . ." He waves his arms nonsensically around his head and accidentally hits a passing woman in the face. She curses loudly.

"Don't forget, this isn't a normal effulgent," I point out.

As I say these words, I see someone.

Past the multicolored chaos of the moving crowd, a voider stares back at me with a furrowed brow. His black flaxen cloak is like the darkened center of a child's spinning pinwheel.

I mumble a curse and turn away, tightening my grip on Chimeline. "I don't like this at all."

"What don't you like?" she asks.

I let out a deep breath. "We're attracting too much attention."

"But you don't have your cloak on."

"I know. But my face is familiar to all my former students."

"Maybe you should try a little harder not to look like you're from the citadel," Colu adds.

"What do you mean?"

He shrugs. "It's just the way you carry yourself, like your shit smells like flowers. Try to hunch your back or something."

Chimeline laughs nervously and leans in, tapping my forearm with her hand. "You look fine, Dem."

A quarterbell later, still in the midst of Winter's Baiou, we reach the former edge of our kingdom.

It's the old demarcation—where, up until now, the Northern Kingdom ended and Xiland began.

Normally, this would be a subtle transition in this border town. White bricks inlaid down the middle of the street—a thin line. Clay tiles on buildings showing two languages instead of one.

But the war has changed all of this.

Wooden barricades still stand, some of them partially dismantled and strewn about, others used by the drunken crowd as places to recline. Stacked burlap bags and barrels lay strewn about in odd locations.

It's hard to believe that not too long ago, men were fighting here.

As we turn the corner, a large stone building comes into view. Or what remains of it.

Past a roped-off barrier, a soldier stands sentry. The walls have crumbled away at precise angles, as if they're made of gingerbread. All three stories are opened up, the rooms inside vacant and painted green. A wooden bed hangs lopsided twenty feet in the air, and a white sheet blows in the shadowed wind, caught on a ceiling joist. A ghost, left behind.

A plus sign remains etched into part of the intact exterior wall.

I stop.

"What is it?" Chimeline asks.

"This was a hospital."

She looks up at me in confusion and then back to the ruins.

"A place to heal the sick," I explain. "With help from voidance."

"Oh."

I shake my head. "We built this just before the war. My submaster, Herrophilus, and the Xian master voider Bartholu worked together on it. It was the first of its kind in Xiland."

"Whatever toppled these bricks must have been powerful, indeed," Colu adds.

"It was voidance," I add.

"Voidance?" Chimeline asks. "How do you know?"

I point at the destruction. "The way the walls fall away at precise angles. No battering ram would do that."

"Why would voiders destroy their own creation?" Colu adds.

Blythe groans. "Voiders do not create. They only destroy."

"Let's keep walking," I say softly.

After another block, we run into more Northern soldiers. They're markedly different from the ones by the city entrance. They're all sober and at attention, a few of them on horseback bearing the king's banner. With the north winning the war, they have come to occupy this section of the city, but their orders are obviously to maintain the peace. They stand mostly in the shadows, staying out of the way of the citizens, both Xian and Northern alike.

One of these groups of soldiers speaks to another voider, clearly discernible in his flaxen cloak. As we approach, the voider nods and walks away, passing us on the street.

I turn my head away.

Winter's Baiou slopes downward gradually toward the south. Just past the border, we all stop at a large park flanked by awninged shops. It looks like a play is about to be performed in the center. A wooden makeshift stage is set up, and people sit on the surrounding grass in all directions, many of them Xian. Past all of this, the city is sprawled out below and in front of us, narrow streets descending in angles. Xi Bay glistens in orange and pink far away over the slate rooftops, still wet from the passing storm.

"It's beautiful, isn't it?" Chimeline asks, as if reading my thoughts. But I don't look at her, since I know that any smile I give her would be a halfhearted one, and she's wise enough to know the difference.

I look out at the audience. It erupts in cheers and applause as the actors leave a nearby red-and-white-striped tent and arrive on stage.

Hundreds of couples and families recline on the grass on blankets, some wealthy enough to enjoy wine, cheese, fruit, and shellfish as they watch the production. They look as if a great weight has been lifted from them—the war is over. It is finally time for celebration.

But in reality, no weight has been lifted. Unbeknownst to this audience, a massive voidstone lurks in the bay, mere miles from here. *That* is the real weight, and someone in our midst just might be powerful enough to claim it.

"The temple is on the other side of this park," Blythe says.

I see it when he points. Between the treetops, its damp spire reflects the waning sun.

Colu laughs.

"What is it?" Chimeline asks.

"Nothing," he says, quieting down. "Life's fortunes playing a trick on me."

Chimeline charmingly wrinkles her nose in confusion as Colu shakes his head, as if to clear his thoughts. "This is where we part ways," he says.

"What?" Chimeline asks, her voice raised in shock.

He shrugs as he surveys all of us. "I told you that our destinations were not the same, only our paths, and even that was a momentary thing."

"Where are you headed?" I ask.

"The old Xian section of the city is near here," he answers. "It will be my first stop on my way home."

Everyone is clapping at something happening on stage, but I look only at the one-eyed, dark-skinned soldier in front of me.

I extend my hand to him. "This is farewell, then," I say. "I wish you safe travels, il-Colu."

He smiles wryly at my use of the *il* designation, something that he once said implies honor.

But before Colu can respond, Blythe interrupts.

"How about a dinner, first?" he says.

We all turn to him as he points again.

"We're practically here. I will arrange a sustaining meal for tonight, before you part ways with the company. It is the least I can do for you."

Colu looks down at my extended hand, then at Blythe, and then back at me. He finally nods.

"Alright," he says. "One last warm meal with you, and then I am gone."

So together we meander around the perimeter of the park, which is the only place with open ground.

Soon we're walking up stone steps to the temple, and Blythe opens the door, letting us all in. He shuts it afterward, and a warm echo reverberates through the lofty and empty space.

I would never admit it, but I am glad to be here, away from the noise of the crowd. It's been a long day, and even though I spent a quarter of it in the void, that time was not in the least bit restful.

This temple is the same style as the one in Fiscarlo, only four times the size. While the walls are curated stone, the ceiling is made of black-stained planks hung with massive iron circles. They hold candles that flicker in the early-evening breeze that came in with us.

The smell of incense and rain permeates the air.

"All of you, feel free to sit down," Blythe says, motioning to the many wooden benches, as he begins to walk down the center aisle toward the front of the temple, which is a good fifty yards away. "When I return, I will have a meal prepared for us, as promised."

"And where are you going?" I ask him.

"I am going to look for the head effulgent."

"And then what?"

"When I find her, I'm going to tell her what I know. So that we can warn the others."

"I'd like to come with you," I say.

"No," he says, in all his exhausting brevity, as he continues to walk away.

"What do you mean 'no'?"

"It's best if I go alone," he answers, over his shoulder.

"And I think that it's best if I speak to this woman," I say to his back, raising my voice slightly due to the increasing space between us. "To ask her about the voider-effulgent. She may know who he is. Or *where* he is."

Blythe pauses and turns around. "Patience, Master Voider. This is an effulgency matter. I will speak to her, and all of your questions will be answered in due time."

"In due time?" I reply. "What does that mean?"

"You really must learn patience," he says. "Think of the lifetimes the enervated have been trapped in that stone of yours, waiting to be freed. And then think of the brief moment that you've spent waiting to talk to this woman."

His perspective shocks me into silence.

I sit down on the wooden seat.

Chimeline sits next to me while Colu crashes down on the bench in front of us and puts his feet up, making a loud creak which echoes through the temple.

The commotion causes Blythe to turn around and stop in place.

"Please be respectful here," he says. "This is the house of the Unnamed." But he doesn't wait for a reply or acquiescence. He simply turns and continues walking down the aisle, his posture as straight as a board.

Colu lets out a deep laugh that sounds remarkably like the groaning wood we're sitting on. "That's what my le-Sante used to say before she left me for you."

Blythe pauses a few feet from a shadowed doorway near the front of the temple.

Chimeline leans forward and forcefully taps Colu on the shoulder. "We are guests here!" she whispers. "Put your feet down! You act like you built this place."

Colu laughs again. "I did."

Chimeline and I exchange a sideways glance.

"You built this temple?" I ask, leaning forward.

He nods, picking his teeth with a fingernail.

My gaze moves to Blythe, who blinks a few times before walking through the darkened doorway, a gray blur disappearing into the heart of the temple.

# A NEW PRESENCE

The head effulgent rushes into the lofty sanctuary where Chimeline, Colu, and I have been waiting for a good halfbell.

In the stillness of this space, her presence is striking. Her white robes flow and rustle behind her. The fabric shimmers subtly as it picks up the colored light from above.

She pulls back her hood, revealing a bald head, a gaunt, genderless face, and striking green eyes. With her hooked nose, she almost looks like one of the pigeons she keeps.

She looks directly at me.

"You," she says, in a high yet raspy voice, pointing as she storms down the aisle toward me. "Black arcanist. Get out of this temple."

A moment later, Blythe comes running through the same open doorway, steps behind her.

"Your Effulgency," he says. "Please let me explain."

"You *have* explained," the woman says, without taking her eyes off me. "And I have rejected your explanation."

She raises her voice. "Black arcanist, do you not understand the common tongue?" she snarls at me. "Why do you still sit when I have asked you to leave?"

I stay seated as Colu turns to me. "So much for dinner," he mumbles deeply.

Chimeline squeezes my arm.

"But Your Effulgency," Blythe says, catching up to her. "I can prove it. With the master voider's help, I have entered in soteria—"

She stops in place and turns to him, her white robes blossoming out like a giant flower in the shade of the forest floor.

"Do not speak of that in present company! I still cannot fathom your touching a voidstone," she says, her voice shrill enough to shatter the windows far above.

"I spoke to them!" he replies.

She shakes her head and points at me again, but this time she's looking at Blythe.

"This is what happens when you choose to travel with a black arcanist. You start believing the lies. The way of unwanting is as slender as a strand of silk. You of all people should know this!"

Blythe continues to argue with her in forcibly hushed tones while Chimeline leans close to my ear.

"You were right," she says. "She clearly doesn't believe him."

"I know," I say, as I stand. "She's going to have to experience it firsthand."

The two of them are so wrapped up in their argument that they don't notice me leave the bench in the back and approach them. Only at the last moment, when I am standing at their side, do they respond to my presence.

The woman takes a small step back. Her eyes are sunken in, and in the V where her white cloak reveals her upper chest, the form of her sternum protrudes underneath thin skin.

She shivers while looking down at my stone.

"Please leave," she says, then turns to the others. "All of you."

"You don't believe Blythe?" I ask.

Her lips pucker. "Who is Blythe?"

I point to the graycloak.

She turns to him. "Is this true? You have taken a name?"

He tilts his head. "I did not take it. The master voider was intent on giving it to me."

"Good Unnamed," she exclaims, her voice almost entirely devoid of tone. It's pure air.

She closes her eyes, perhaps in prayer, and I figure that this is as good a time as any.

Grasping my stone, I grab her skeletal hand in the other. It spasms, but I don't let go, and she doesn't have the strength to break free.

In the void, I hear the voices of the enervated again, only louder than usual, and then they go eerily quiet, just as they did when Blythe first grasped me.

*They sense her. A new presence.*

In the world outside, I may be smiling sadly.

Because even though I don't speak their language, for the first time I think I may understand them.

They detect the effulgent. They know someone new is here. Someone like them. And the reason they are quieting down is because they don't know if they can trust her.

Blind intuition is telling me this. A raw feeling in the dark.

Then, a whisper of wind.

*It's the woman speaking.*

Another current weaves into place, as if someone just opened a door and the breeze is singing through the gap. It's only slightly deeper, and I swear it seems familiar.

*Blythe?*

I let go.

When the world returns, I notice that Blythe is holding on to the woman by her other hand, and his eyes are still closed. So are hers.

She falls to the ground, her legs giving out. I've already let go of her, but Blythe has not. He catches her as he opens his eyes, letting her gently rest against his legs.

"Do you believe us now?" I ask.

"Yes," she whispers, almost to herself.

"We're looking for a voider-effulgent," I say, as her eyes flutter open. "Or as you call it, an enervated. This man has taken a consort. A blonde woman—"

"Patience, Master Voider," Blythe snaps, stooping and flashing me an annoyed glance. "Her mind is galloping."

"Right."

He speaks to her in the effulgency tongue, sounding similar to how he did in the void, except with less echo. A drier sound without reverberation.

Eventually, she looks up at me, her green eyes wide. And then she turns to the stooped Blythe, grasping his shoulders for support. "We must get the word out. The others must know. Everyone must know."

"Can you stand?" Blythe asks softly.

She nods.

Chimeline and Colu come near, and the woman looks at each of them before turning back to Blythe. She begins weeping.

"I am sorry for my offense. I give up my ignorance to the Unnamed. I do not own the dark."

He embraces her. "I do not own the dark."

Colu, Chimeline, and I stare at them in awkward silence.

Colu eventually clears his throat. "So we're going to send the pigeons now and then have some dinner?"

Blythe pulls away from her and nods. He places a hand underneath her armpit and attempts to lift her up. I assist, lending her my hand as well.

"Where do you keep your birds?" I ask her.

She motions with her head.

"The bell tower."

# THE BELL TOWER

The five of us proceed up a dark, circular stairway made of stone. Its center is completely open, save for the bell's thick rope, which extends all the way to the ground. Chimeline fearfully hugs the outside wall.

Every so often, thin slits in the wall offer a view of the outside. We're at least five stories up, and climbing. Everything else is below us—the rooftops and even the canopies of the grandest trees in the park.

"Did you build this part of the temple?" Chimeline asks Colu. She dares a quick glance at him, behind her.

"Yes."

"And you didn't think to put in a railing?"

He lets out a deep laugh.

"We are almost there," the head effulgent says, a few paces ahead. I am surprised—despite her gauntness, she leads us fervently and is not even out of breath.

Soon the stairway gets brighter, and we pass through an open square cut out of the wooden ceiling into the tip of the spire.

Chimeline lets out a rare curse and stops, hands splayed against the stone wall at her back.

A massive brass bell, glowing in the late-afternoon sun, hangs from a thick beam. Above this are smaller rafters. A few wild birds take flight as we step upon the wooden floorboards. They easily escape, flying through the four surrounding archways.

Each of the four walls is the same—a grand arch made of stone, through which is the open air. To the north and east, dark clouds cover the sky—the remains of the afternoon storm. To the west is the brilliant sun, low on the horizon, and to the south lies Xi Bay.

Neither Blythe nor the head effulgent stop to admire the view—they both head straight to a barbed-wire cage in the southeast corner, large enough to hold a grown man standing tall. The dozen pigeons inside begin to coo and flutter about excitedly.

Meanwhile, I furrow my brow and point to a gigantic ring of masted ships in Xi Bay, far from shore.

"What is that?" I ask Colu.

He puts his hand across his forehead to shield his one eye from the sun. "They're not Xian, that's for sure."

"It's a perfect circle," I say.

He grunts as he lowers his hand. "Formations usually indicate a blockade. To prevent other ships from leaving port. But . . ."

"But what?"

"Blockades are usually a line."

I nod. "I'm no naval commander, but that's what I thought as well."

"Almost looks as if they're trying to protect something," he says.

"You mean *inside* the circle."

"Yeah. Circle the wagons sort of thing."

"The Axiondrive."

Chimeline lets out a sound that is something between a sigh and a groan.

I turn to her, thinking that she's responding to my comment, but her hands are grasping her head, and she's looking at the rafters.

"What's wrong?" I ask her.

Her eyes flutter, and then she takes a step away from the top of the stairs and toward the open center of the floor, directly underneath the bell, where the rope descends over a hundred feet to the ground floor.

Cursing, I quickly run over and pull her away from danger and toward the northwest corner, where the floor safely meets the stone wall. She has no strength in her body—she collapses in my arms.

"Chimeline!"

I lay her down softly. She's shaking her head back and forth, her eyes shut tightly. Her body curls up into a ball against the dusty stone.

"It's happening again, isn't it?" asks Colu, coming near.

I place my hands on her, ensuring that she stays down. I don't want her moving toward the open center of the floor, nor down the length of the walls to the open archways. A few steps in any direction could be a fall to the death.

But soon, her body stops wrestling with itself and her breathing calms.

She passes out.

Standing up again, I remember the time that I had to coax her up on the stone wall in the citadel, before we jumped. "Actually, it might not be voidspeak."

"Voidspeak?"

"What happened earlier underneath the willow tree," I say. "I think she just might have fainted. She's scared of heights."

"Then why is she in a fucking bell tower?"

"I told her that she could wait down below, but she didn't want to be alone."

He shakes his head.

Behind us and on the opposite side of the bell, the effulgent steps into the birdcage and quickly closes the latched door behind her. She begins catching the pigeons, one by one, and tying a coiled note to each foot.

Next to her, on the outside of the barbed wire, Blythe meets my gaze and gives me a proud smile and a single nod.

Colu nods toward them. "She's even worse than he is," he says under his breath. "Stubborn and self-righteous."

"Blythe is alright," I say. "I think, deep down, he knows that neither he nor I have all the answers. Besides, he is helping me find the voider-effulgent."

"What about her? You think *she* knows him?"

I look at the birdlike woman. "No. She would have mentioned it by now."

"What's your plan, then?"

I look to the west, down at the canopy of trees covering the park. There are thousands of people down there, laughing and clapping at the performance on stage.

"I have to find Mander," I say distantly.

"Who's Mander?"

"A friend of mine and the best of submasters."

"He's stationed here, in Winter's Baiou?"

I nod.

"And you trust him?"

I furrow my brow without meeting his gaze.

"Ever since Marine left me, I have been running through the list of men she could have fallen for. Someone she knew well, who was a strong voider and was somehow involved with the war to the south. Mander is the only one who matches this description."

I turn to him. His face is contorted in confusion, as if the answer is obvious.

"It's not him," I say.

"Why?"

"First, he's not an effulgent."

"Ah."

"And second, if you ever met him, you would understand. The man is . . . peculiar, to say the least. The idea of someone like Marine going for him . . ." I let out a bitter laugh.

"So you trust him."

I ask a question in reply. "Have you heard of this Commander Reddles?"

Colu shifts in place, his leather armor making a crackling sound. "No."

"The king appointed him to be in charge of this city."

"So I heard."

"My hunch is that the voider-effulgent is working closely with Reddles, toward the same objective."

"Which is?"

I point to the circle of ships, and he nods.

"If I can find Mander, he might know of an effulgent who has been seen around Reddles."

"And?"

"That's our man."

The woman steps out of the cage cradling a single pigeon. I can see the coiled note tied to its foot with bright-red string.

She clasps the cage behind her, trapping the rest of the birds inside, as she steps toward Blythe.

She delicately places the single pigeon in Blythe's hands and then covers his hands with hers. They bow their heads, foreheads almost touching, until the silence is broken.

A flash in the air.

A gust of wind.

The bell rings.

It's so loud that I feel the reverberations course through my entire body. My bones shake. The dust on the floorboards hovers in the air, and if I tried to take a step, I would fall.

A few stones from an archway hit the wooden floor near Colu and then ricochet off, tumbling to the ground far below.

Instinctively, I cover my ears with my hands as I turn to Colu. He's done the same. It doesn't seem to help. The ringing in my ears doesn't stop.

"Why is someone ringing the bell?" I shout to him.

He must read my lips or have the same thought, since he gets onto his hands and knees and peers over the square hole in the center of the floor, where the rope descends.

He glances back up at me, shaking his head. "There's no one down there!" he shouts.

Yet, feet above him, the massive bell hanging over us swings wildly. I can see it vibrating, the edge of it hazy against the sky.

*What is going on?*

Another stone block from an archway falls.

Blythe and the woman have stopped praying. Her hands are over her ears, and Blythe takes a step back. He still has the bird in his hands, but he's peering intently through the archway, down at the crowds in the courtyard below.

Colu slowly stands back up, his feet spread wide for balance.

Dust falls upon us like snow. The dry kind, like when it is well past freezing.

"Something is wrong," I say.

Colu nods. "We need to get down now."

Before I'm able to respond, a wave flashes through the sky past the north archway. It originates at the ground and heads diagonally upwards, straight toward us.

It looks almost like a crest upon the sea, rolling and whitecapped, except it is instantaneous and mostly transparent. Nearly as faint as a membrane of dynamic voidance, but far stronger than that.

In less time than it takes to blink, the wave climbs and hits us at the top of the bell tower. There isn't even enough time to warn Colu, or open my mouth.

A buffeting gust of wind hits me as the bell rings again.

I am pushed back, my legs turned to putty due to the vibrations coursing up through the boards.

It's worse this time.

I lose my balance and fall to the floor.

Colu, Blythe, and the woman have all done the same.

The vibrations are not coming from the bell but from the wave. The bell simply reacts to it, as do we.

"Dem!"

It's Chimeline's voice.

I turn toward her.

She's awake.

She's still lying where I left her—in the northwest corner—with wide eyes, her body propped up on her outstretched arms, palms on the wooden boards.

I quickly crawl to her and kneel by her side.

"Don't move!" I say, loud enough for her to hear me over the ringing.

She grabs me with trembling hands, crying out in pain.

"Dem, he had a message."

My brow furrows. "What did he say?"

She grips me harder and I see her swallow. "I'm going to be buried alive. Along with the rest of you. Because I lied to him."

My hands cradle her head, and I feel wetness there. I pull them away and see blood on my palms. It's coming from her ears.

*He's down there, somewhere. And he's destroying the tower.*

I bring her to me and hug her tightly, speaking into her blood-soaked ear. "It's going to be alright."

Another shimmering wave passes over us, and the bell rings out a third time. Chimeline screams, her nails digging into my neck.

Then, a horrible feeling. A crumbling noise and the piercing, snapping of wood. I instinctively cover Chimeline with my body while the sounds around us deepen.

Turning my head, I watch as the southeast corner of the bell tower gives way.

One moment, the effulgent is standing there, next to the birdcage full of pigeons, her hands to her head. The next moment, she's gone in a flurry of white robes. The birdcage is gone. All of it falls away.

The entire corner section of floor and archway disappears, inches from Blythe. He is left standing on the severed edge, underneath the unsupported roof, holding a single pigeon.

"Blythe!" I scream.

He looks over to me in shock, his face like stone except for his blinking eyes.

Colu swears and rounds the bell, running over to him while the roof groans. He grabs his shoulders, pulling him back toward us.

The massive beam overhead starts to dip without the support of the corner, and this causes the bell to swing toward Chimeline and me as it rings again. Looking up, I can see into its darkened insides, black instead of gold, the open mouth of some hideous beast.

And then it falls.

Crashing through the wooden floor, it demolishes everything in its path, an enormous weight that pulls everything down with it.

The tower is falling, and we're falling along with it.

Chimeline is already in my arms, so I cup one arm around her waist tightly as we begin to tumble away.

I hear everything at once. Her screaming. The snapping of wood. The tumbling of stone. The ringing in my ears. The beating of my heart.

As I fall head over heels, the gray darkness of the stairwell becomes my up while the sudden sky becomes my down. Lines of light break apart in the darkness all around me, the mortar between the stones opening up.

My voidstone lifts from my chest. It's still tethered to the gold chain, but it's weightless now. As am I.

I grab it. All the noise is pushed away.

The wind returns.

*No. The voices.*

I create a sphere of air instinctively. Similar to when I was underwater with Marine, within the wreck of the ship. This is a wreck of a temple in the making. This is a wreck of a life already destroyed.

The forces are not static. There is nothing except graceful infinite falling. It reminds me of the blue of Xi Bay, but this is a brief illusion. The forces are coming.

Nothing is infinite. I must be ready. Trauma from below. Trauma from above.

In the void, I see the light of the living.

Shimmering, unlike anything else.

Past Chimeline, two other bodies fall over us.

*Or are they under us?*

Their indivisibles shine and move about differently than the dust and dead wood and dead stone. It isn't necessarily light. There is no light here—only gray. Only indivisibles. But it *feels* like light.

*Blythe. Colu.*

I extend the sphere as I fall, enveloping them, trapping them inside of the cocoon of safety, which is about to be hit from all sides.

The floor is coming as surely as death.

*It's time.*

I surrender to the voices. All of me. I am the enervated now, and they are my empowered. I scream to them, my voice wrapped up in the wind. It is only a dying wish. Maybe they understand me because I think I can understand them.

I plead with them—we cannot let him win. He will not kill my friends. The only ones I have left in this world. I know I am going to die, right now, one way or the other. Either by the thousands of stones that Colu laid years ago or by this singular black stone in my hand. But only the latter—only voideath—will save my friends.

The choice is easy.

# THEY BELIEVE IN YOU

It's so dark, I must still be in the void.

*Or I'm dead. I should be dead.*

No. Despite the absolute black, it's evident that I'm very much in the world of the living. I hear Chimeline's soft cries, Blythe's coughing, and Colu's heavy groans. Even the flapping of wings. The air is dusty but breathable.

*Air.*

My voidance is still in effect. I can feel the membrane, the enervated souls tethered to it, a kite on a string.

I grasp my voidstone in the darkness and suddenly see the shimmering forms of all three of my companions huddled around me—colorless in the void, and discernible despite the darkness of the real world.

Light doesn't matter here.

We're in a tight space, about ten by ten feet. Jagged stones and wooden beams surround us in all directions, forming a rough dome overhead. The honed-stone floor of the temple is at my feet.

Blythe still grasps the fluttering pigeon while Colu leans his body against one of the stones, trying desperately to move it. He's unsuccessful. And all around us, pushed into every crevasse and angle, is the shield of pressurized air that I created.

At the last moment before impact, I applied dynamics because I didn't expect to live. I remember the overwhelming feeling of it being too much for one to bear. I had accepted voideath as the price for wielding so much power.

But as I curl my fingers in the darkness, I realize that this is not the case. Not only do I live, but there is not even a trace of numbness.

In fact, there are no remnants of what I did. I'm not even cold.

*Impossible.*

I release the voidstone and reenter the darkness of the real world as Chimeline's hands gently touch my bearded face.

"Dem?"

"Yes," I answer. "I'm right here." I take her hand in mine and she grabs it tightly, her sobs getting louder.

"Are you alright?" I ask.

"Yes, I think so. Did the tower—"

"Collapse? Yes." I blink. My vision is not improving. There is not a sliver of light getting through to us. "We're buried in the wreckage."

"Blythe? Colu?" I ask, wanting to ensure that they're alright. I saw them in the void, but they could be hurt.

A moment later, I hear Colu clear his throat. "I'll be the fucking Unnamed," he answers. "Don't feel a scratch on my body."

"Blythe?" I call out.

Blythe coughs a bit but doesn't answer. After a pause, Colu speaks up for him. "He's right here next to me. Hey!" I hear a smack in the darkness.

"I am alive, Helmsman."

"Are you injured?" Colu asks.

"No."

"Well you should speak up, then," Colu replies.

"If I am silent, it is because I am praying."

He chuckles. "Well, it doesn't seem to be working."

"How can you say that? Don't you realize that we survived because of the Unnamed? My prayers that you interrupted were those of thanks."

Colu's laughter dwindles away. "You're kidding, right? It took us three years to build this fucking temple, and some jackass takes it down in an instant. You think the Unnamed willed that?"

"Yes, I do."

An awkward silence fills the dark, until Blythe continues. "But the violence is still here, around us. I feel the anger, but I do not succumb to it. It wants to crumble the towers of our beings. But I do not own the dark."

Colu grunts. "If you don't mind me saying, I think the dark is the one thing we fucking own right now."

"It is not a physical darkness."

"I know that, you hairless ass," he snaps. "I'm referring to this voider-effulgent. He destroyed this entire tower in order to kill us. But we survived." He laughs crazily and then grunts loudly in the darkness. He must be pushing upon a stone. "Assuming we can get ourselves out of here, that fucker is gonna get what's coming to him."

"There it is," Blythe says quietly. "The owning of the dark."

Colu continues straining. "I'm not being dark, I'm being realistic. We're lucky. Somehow got trapped in a pocket of air on the way down."

"The Unnamed saved us, soldier," Blythe replies. "He, the master voider, and the enervated worked together. We are not *lucky*, as you so crassly put it. We are *indebted*."

"Dem, is that true?" Colu calls out.

"Yes," I answer. I'm not sure about the first part concerning the Unnamed, but I'm too overwhelmed to dispute it.

"So you used voidance to shield us?" Colu asks.

"Yes. Except what I just did expended more energy than anything I have ever done in my life. I should be in voideath right now."

"Then why aren't you?" Chimeline asks.

"Because of the enervated," Blythe says matter-of-factly. "Because they believe in you."

I turn to him, even though I cannot see him.

"Do you know this to be true?"

"Of course."

"How?"

"We spoke about you," he answers.

"When you were in the void?"

"Yes." After a pause, he continues. "I vouched for you. I told them about the lesson."

I sigh at his cryptic answer, remembering him speaking about a lesson as we left Fiscarlo.

"But there was no need for my vouching," he adds. "They were already familiar with your presence. They know you. They know your pain. They know that you seek to stop the empowered. So they helped, under the authority bestowed upon them by the Unnamed."

I hear another deep groan. "Well, can they help you a little more to get us out of here?" Colu asks.

*They helped me. Can it be true?*

Chimeline presses into me, shaking my arm and whispering, "He might still be around."

I know who she's speaking of.

"Has he voidspoken to you again?" I ask.

"No."

"What about your ears? Are you still bleeding?"

"I don't think so."

"Are you in pain?"

"No."

I exhale. "He probably figures that you are dead. That we're all dead."

"But what if he's staying around, just to make sure?"

"Actually, that's what I hope," I answer. "Because I intend to kill him."

I hear her inhale sharply. "Dem, please, he is very dangerous. You don't know him like I do. What he's capable of. If he's waiting out there, he will kill us all."

I think about what Blythe said. The voices kept me alive.

The idea of being protected from voideath is fascinating. Voideath has always been the consequence of using too much power—it has always kept voiders in check. Without that consequence, the power I can yield is nearly unfathomable.

The possibilities make me dizzy.

I find her face in the darkness and cup it with my hands.

"It's *he* who does not know what *I* am capable of," I whisper in her ear. "He can knock down the tallest tower in Winter's Baiou, but he's not going to lay a mark on you."

Then I grab my voidstone and switch my attention to the souls across the stars.

*I need your help one more time.*

Within the colorless landscape, I begin to extend the pocket of air.

Since I cannot sense light, nor hear the crumble of rock, it's hard to gauge progress. But I do see the indivisibles slowly move up and out in all directions. Fine dust, smaller fragments, and larger pieces of wood and stone—they all follow the curvature of my membrane. Nothing penetrates the space we inhabit below. I even see the immense bell, lying upside down above us. As the curve of my sphere gradually grows, the bell is cast aside as if it were made of gilded paper.

The voices swirl around me. I am in the middle of a cyclone. They tear into me, but the feeling is subdued. There is no pain. No numbness.

It feels as if I am being carried.

*Thank you.*

Once the work is done, I let go of both my stone and the membrane and am immediately shaken to the ground. There is a loud booming sound. My eardrums pop and my hearing is momentarily muted. The ground trembles and the sound echoes, like a rolling thunderclap.

I shut my eyes against the light.

The other three are similarly in shock, hands covering their faces while lying on the hewn-stone floor of the former temple. I glance at them when I can, seeing that they are not even covered in dust or grime. Only a little sweat.

Then I look up and around.

A wide ring of debris surrounds us, at least ten feet tall. My vision on all sides is blocked by it. Past the stones and rising dust are the treetops in the park and, further away, the slate rooftops. Everything casts deep shadows in the setting sun.

I hear screams. Past the mound, the entire park sounds as if it is in chaos.

"Stay here," I tell the other three, as I start climbing the ruins, but Blythe scrambles forward.

"You are going after him," Blythe says. It is not a question.

"Of course I am."

"But you are seeking vengeance, not justice."

I turn back momentarily, about to say that there is no difference between those two—the result is the same.

But as I look at him standing at the foot of the rubble, staring at the fluttering pigeon in his hands, I am reminded of the reason we came to this temple in the first place. To send out the message.

*We failed.*

"That's the only one left, isn't it?" I say.

"Yes."

He unfurls a short and weathered piece of paper tied to its foot.

"This bird is trained to fly to Fiscarlo," he says, without looking up. "I was saying a prayer before I released him. That prayer saved his life."

"Fiscarlo?" I say. "That's your temple."

He shakes his head. "It was never my temple, Master Voider. One does not own a temple."

I roll my eyes and begin to turn away. But Blythe interjects.

"My daughter is the effulgent now."

I'm too shocked to reply, but Blythe doesn't seem to be waiting for one. He opens his hands, and the pigeon immediately flies up and to the north. I follow it as far as I can through the pink and orange sky, until it's blocked by the gray rooftops.

"Master Voider, please, do not own the dark."

I lower my gaze back to Blythe.

"And what would you have me do?" I ask. "Just let him continue doing what he is doing? Ask him to stop?"

"No. You can bring about justice or you can bring about vengeance. Only one is on the way of unwanting."

Pressing my lips together, I turn from him and resume climbing.

"Do not own the dark!" he says to my back.

Soon, I reach the crest, and the madness becomes apparent.

In the center of the park, the stage is torn apart—painted murals and fabric banners ripped to pieces. The massive tent, further away, is lopsided, as if a pole or two have been knocked away. People are running to the corners of the large square, but the alleys weren't designed for this much foot traffic. Bottlenecks have formed. Soldiers on horseback ride in, attempting to regain control and prevent a stampede.

Much closer, a few bystanders are covered in grime and tears. One woman kneels, leaning over the body of a small child who must have been hit by a stray stone. His body is lying motionless within a pool of blood.

Rage rises within me as I look around in all directions. All I can think of, besides finding the bastard who did this, is how Blythe is so impossibly wrong. He thinks that somehow having a natural reaction to this attack legitimizes it. That anger spreads the violence, makes it stronger. Fulfills it, even.

No. Anger ends it. Right here and right now.

*There. A patch of white.*

I stop turning in place.

*It's him.*

The bright effulgency cloak is not the only thing that gives him away. It's his absolute stillness. He's the only one standing on the grass within a flurry of people going in every which way. He's the eye of a hurricane.

Underneath a white hood, he's looking at me with a slightly open mouth, his hands at his sides.

For a moment, all I can do is look upon him in awe.

The man behind the veil.

*Somehow, he looks familiar.*

All this time, he's been a blur. Cast from something that I don't even know. My own heartbreak, my own regret, my own failures. And only now has the blur taken on the form of flesh.

*A blur I cannot kill. But a man? Yes. That I can do.*

He turns and runs, his white hood lowering.

"Not so fast," I say, as I grab my voidstone and float above the rubble.

# A WALK IN THE PARK

I voidsprint as hypocrisy fills me. But I push it back down.

What I'm doing is a trick that many young voiders inevitably attempt at the university. The faculty, under my guidance, have always frowned upon voidsprinting, even take disciplinary action when it is witnessed. The reason for that is it is wasteful.

Generations of voiders have taught us to respect the craft and apply it only when needed. If my gifted students began using it to run faster, then when would it end? Create a brighter light. Reach a higher shelf. Clean the room faster.

Voidance is not an excuse for laziness. Overuse is a road to addiction, which leads to voideath. This was a tenet even before we knew about the enervated.

But this is not laziness. This is necessity.

I grasp my stone every other instant, letting a torrent of air push me forward as my feet touch the stones every few feet. It requires dexterity, being able to quickly switch from the twilight skies into colorless forms, back and forth, time and again. I need to see where I am headed, in ways the void cannot offer me.

In this manner, I cover over fifty yards of the courtyard in an instant.

But soon I step off the stones and onto the soft grass of the park. The crowd becomes dense further away from the wreckage of the temple. I've halved the distance between the voider-effulgent and me, but now I am reduced to simply walking again, pushing people aside and weaving between them. I step over blankets and plates of discarded food and bottles of wine.

He's only twenty yards away, stuck within the same mess as I am. Actually, it seems even worse for him. Many strangers, seeing that he is an effulgent, approach him and pull upon his robes with tear-streaked faces. They're seeking the Unnamed's intervention, or simply solace and reassurance.

He gives them neither. Those surrounding him are pushed outward and to the ground.

He cranes his neck backward and sees me. His browless eyes go wide. There is no mistaking it.

*He's afraid.*

Turning forward again, he presses on, stepping over the ones seeking his help, his cloak a white beacon that I follow through the madness.

We're getting deeper into the shade of the park, underneath the tallest of trees. I cannot see the dusk-lit sky. In front of me is a multitiered stone fountain at least ten feet high. The voider-effulgent rounds it, and for a moment I lose track of him in the shadows. I curse, pushing around a much larger man and jumping over the body of an elderly woman cowering on the grass.

As I near the fountain, the voider-effulgent reaches its other side.

Suddenly, he comes to a standstill, facing me while grabbing a voidstone in his lowered hand. His head is angled slightly downward and his face is taut, teeth showing. Tendons protrude above the V-shaped neckline of his cloak.

I have no time to react. No time to grab my voidstone or even slide to a halt. My momentum carries me.

Instantly, the fountain explodes as a cone-shaped wave of light flashes past me. The tip of it originates at his head, and it fans out on all sides—left, right, above, and below.

An incredibly loud *boom* reverberates throughout my body.

All of this happens within the time it takes to blink.

The delicate details of the fountain become shards of stone that emanate outward, while the larger pieces break away from one another. The water is turned into a wall of spray. Everything comes in my direction, following the same angles of the flash of light.

But none of it touches me.

I am not quite sure what to think. The same seems to be true for the voider-effulgent. He lets go of the voidstone by his side. It slips down a bit, but he still clutches it by its chain.

His mouth is open in shock.

Again, there is something about him that seems familiar, yet I am sure I've never laid eyes on him before. The man is shorter than I am. His eyes are a striking blue and his nose is angular—as if it were broken when he was a child and it never properly healed.

He closes his mouth, his thin lips pressed together in confused frustration.

I look down. The ground between us has been ripped apart. The blades of grass have been blown out, leaving only soil. But there is a distinct circle that curves around my feet. Within this circle, the grass is deep green and untouched.

Screams erupt behind me.

I turn and see a few people on the dirt, bloodied and nearly naked. They lie within the cone-shaped area that the wave took. A few others have come from the nearby grasses and are kneeling in panic and anguish.

The man I previously pushed aside is behind and to the left of me. His entire body is red, his clothes and outer layers of skin gone except for his leather belt. A jagged piece of stone is lodged in his skull. His body is still twitching, a gurgling sound coming from his open mouth.

Gold millionescent leaves flutter around me.

I look up. A branch of a nearby tree has been stripped bare.

This is undoubtedly the same technique he used to bring down the tower. But at this close range, it's far deadlier. The force of the air is enough to blow apart cultured stone, strip branches of their leaves, and disintegrate clothes and skin.

Yet I'm standing in a perfect circle of grass, untouched.

I didn't create a membrane, nor work any voidance. I didn't even grasp my voidstone. There was no time.

*They believe in you.*

Narrowing my eyes while Blythe's words fill my mind, I look to where the fountain used to stand.

The voider-effulgent is gone.

I mutter a curse, looking around in all directions.

Almost immediately I find him again, thanks to his white robes and the sudden absence of others—the consequence of his actions.

He rounds the far side of the stage, which is about waist height, a good twenty yards in the distance.

I run after him.

The red-and-white tent is on the other side of the stage. It's twenty-five yards square and capable of holding at least a hundred people. The sides are covered in the same striped fabric as the sloped roof. The panels blow in the breeze, as well as from people frantically coming and going. The entire structure hangs somewhat lopsided, one of its three peaks deformed.

As I round the stage, he ducks between two side panels and heads inside.

I am briefly tempted to grab my voidstone and do something creative. I have him trapped now. I could set fire to the tent. I could mend the seams closed, sealing him inside. I could turn the ground into mud, as I did on the road to Prainise.

But there are innocent people inside this tent as well.

I decide to do nothing. I run to the same gap in the panels and step inside.

And then mumble another curse in frustration. It's entirely crammed with people and props.

They're mostly actors, fearfully clustered around circular tables full of makeup, wigs, and mirrors. They must believe that they are safer in this tent than outside, where the destruction has occurred. They have no idea that the author of that destruction is now in their midst. A few men hold gaslights on tall iron poles—a dangerous thing in a closed fabric tent that isn't structurally sound. The combination of the gaslights and the weak evening light from outside the fabric create a dark reddish hue that permeates the space.

I don't see the voider-effulgent.

I weave through the tight space, walking around tables and folded privacy panels, apologizing to a woman changing behind one. I move faster, panic rising within me. A bright light enters the space as someone either enters or exits. I peer into the distance, looking for the telltale sign of bright white there, but it's someone else, in brightly colored clothes and with a head full of hair.

"You're a voider," says someone behind me.

I turn around. It's one of the men carrying a gaslight. He leans the pole toward me, bathing me in overhead light.

I nod while frantically looking around.

"You're a Northerner."

"Yes."

"Some are saying that a Xian voider is loose in the city, and that they brought down the tower."

I ignore him. "Did you see an effulgent pass by here?"

"An effulgent?"

"Yes! In a white robe."

He peers at me, leaning forward further. The lamp dangles over my head. "You mean the actors?"

I push his pole back toward him and narrow my eyes. "What do you mean?"

"There's a comedy act about them. It's called *You Don't Own Me*."

He's pointing to a far corner of the tent, but it's blocked by stacked painted boxes. "You'll find all the effulgents over there."

I leave his side. He still speaks to me, but I am not listening. All I hear is my heart beating through my chest as my mind explores all possibilities. If I lose him, then I've lost the upper hand. He knows that I'm alive and that I'm onto him, but I still don't know who or where he is. I had him in my grasp only moments ago. I could have trapped him in here with the rest of these people. Would that have been worth the cost? Would that have been justice or vengeance?

I fear the answer to that question.

A flash of white glimmers through the red-tinged throng.

Stepping around the boxes, some chairs, and a rolling cart of hanging clothes, I near another circular table surrounded by a close-knit group of sitting effulgents.

Spinning each one around, I pull off their white hoods.

They're all actors. They're wearing skullcaps over their hair. Tape covers their brows. One woman is crying, her eyeshadow smeared.

I let out a scream of anguish.

They all look at me as if I'm crazy.

"Did another effulgent come by here?"

"You're not from the troupe," one of the men says, ignoring my question. "How is it out there? They're saying it was a Xian—"

"Did another effulgent come by here?!" I scream, and they all jump in place. The crying woman shrieks and grabs the shoulder of a fellow actor.

"No," he says slowly. I look at the others, and most are shaking their heads.

I swear again, taking another look around. I'm in the very corner of the tent. Far away, one of the large poles meant to keep up the tent has been shattered, which is causing the roof to sag. Nearer to me is the stack of painted boxes. I contemplate climbing them to give me a better vantage point.

But then my gaze scans something on the floor, directly next to them.

There's something white lying behind a vertical folded screen.

I run over to it, lean down, and grab the piece of clothing. I hold it up in front of me.

It's a white effulgency robe.

As my heart drops, I quickly head back to the table of actors, holding it up for them to see. "Is this yours?"

They look at me with confused expressions, and I throw the garment in the center of the table. "Is that cloak one of yours?" I scream.

"How should we know?" the crying woman says. The man whose shoulder she's grasping takes it, analyzes the material, and then shakes his head slowly. "This is much finer. Do you know—"

I quickly round the table, rip the cloak out of his hands, and head to the nearest gap between the panels.

When I exit, I'm facing west—toward the destroyed temple and setting sun beyond, weak and half-hidden under the slate rooftops. The breeze hits me. It should feel refreshing after being in the tight confines of first the rubble and then the tent, but I don't feel anything but dread.

Somehow, despite everything being in my favor, I failed.

*He's gone. I can feel it.*

The wooden stairs leading to the stage are directly in front of me, so I climb them. The boards creak under my weight—this stage has seen better days. It's empty of people, but there are wigs, props, and boxes of other miscellaneous theater gear strewn all over the place, hinting at the panic that ensued when the bell tower came down.

With a groan, I sit down on the edge of the black-painted platform and look out onto the park.

I'm right above eye level of the slowing crowd, giving me an elevated view. It's all I can do, at this point. Watch them move about. They look as though they're in a dream, and I feel the same. We all seem to be thinking the same thing. There is no more danger here. It has passed.

I'm no longer looking for an effulgent. I don't know what I'm looking for. He's back to being a blur again.

Almost without thinking, I grasp the voidstone around my neck and enter the void. Not to perform any voidance, but to offer an apology.

*I don't know if you can even understand me. But I am sorry. You saved my life and I repaid you by failing. He got away.*

Their voices seem to quiet down, as if they're listening. But if they reply, I cannot understand them. It's as if a frosted pane of glass is between us.

*Can you show me the way back to him? Give me a sign of where the voider-effulgent went? Or who he is? Blythe said you don't have the concept of names. But I need his name.*

There is nothing but the wind.

Eventually I let go.

When the world comes back to me, it is darker. I glance west and notice that the sun is gone. Lavender hues bathe the park.

A woman's blonde wig lies next to me on the stage. I put down the balled-up effulgency cloak and pick up the wig. It smells like cheap perfume and sweat, so I toss it aside.

A few glass vials roll toward me, coming to rest against my thigh. They had been trapped underneath the wig.

I pick one up. It's rouge paint, something Marine would put on her cheeks when there was a formal dinner. I slide it across the stage and pick up the other. It's labeled "Goat Clippings Glue."

I'm about to slide this across the stage as well, in an attempt to hit the other, when recent words come to mind.

*I gave them the horses, along with some goat clippings.*

My hand freezes before I can let go of the vial. I take another look at it, turning the handwritten label around.

It reads, in finer print, "Royal Theater Supply, Winter's Baiou."

"Goat clippings," I mumble out loud to myself, as I think back to what that odd traveling salesman said to me.

*They're used for a great many things. Typically, one can make a very strong glue with boiled clippings. Used by painters, mostly. Saddlers and woodworkers, too. Worchot is asked for clippings once in a while. They are not as popular as honey.*

"Is that what you wanted it for?" I ask nobody in particular, as I pick up the blonde wig again and analyze its underside. An amber residue lines the edges. Most of it is gummy to the touch, but in a few places it's dry enough to flake off as I run my fingers over it. "A wig? To blend in with the rest of us?"

Soft footsteps on the stairs draw my attention upward.

A small Xian girl no older than ten stands on the stage with me. She's wearing a fancy yellow dress and decorative beads in her hair, but one of her puffy sleeves is ripped, and she's barefoot. Most likely she was in the park watching a performance on this very stage when the tower collapsed.

She looks at me hesitantly, her chest heaving as if she has just been running.

"Are you lost, child?" I ask, trying to keep my voice pleasant despite my bitter mood. I drop the wig off the side of the stage while stuffing the vial of glue into my pocket.

She shakes her head. "Are you the master voider?"

I straighten my shoulders. "Why, yes. How did you know that?"

She takes a few steps closer and extends her hand.

"I have something for you."

"You do?" I ask, looking down to her hand. There is a note clutched in it.

"It's for you," she says, motioning with her hand.

I take it.

"Who is this—"

Before I can get the question out, she turns, jumps off the stage with a deftness only a child could possess, and runs east through the park. I follow her with my gaze until she disappears into the dusky shade of a cluster of willows.

"What is this?" I mumble, as I unravel the small parchment in my hands. I nearly drop it in shock.

The handwriting is painfully familiar. There is no mistaking it.

I look up again, back to the willows, to see if I can spot the Xian girl, or the person who sent her. But nobody is there. Just moss swaying in the breeze.

Bringing the paper up to my nose, I take in the scent. Fresh ink. It was written very recently, but the ink is dry to the touch. Within a halfbell's time, most likely.

I read it again, not quite believing the words that are in front of me. But I have to because there is nobody else in the world who could know such a thing.

You should not have come.
It is dangerous for both of us.
Meet me tomorrow. Sunrise.
In Temberlain's Ashes.

The Lady Marine

# ELEUTHERIA

I sit on the empty stage and stare at Marine's sparse note in my hands until it is dark. I'm not sure how much time passes—it could be an instant or a fullbell. Such is the magic of twilight and broken dreams.

Chimeline's voice pulls me back. It's raspy and urgent, and when I turn my body to face the wreckage past the trees, she stands in the flickering glow of torchlight. She cannot see me yet is calling out my name. A soldier on horseback is nearby, looking down on her from his high perch.

After stuffing the note into my pocket, I put my palms on the black stage and jump onto the grass.

On the way through the park, I look ahead. Blythe, Colu, and Chimeline, with torches in hand, are looking for survivors amid the rubble, while a handful of nearby soldiers treat the wounded and collect the dead. The wounded lie nearer to the wreckage, where most of the soldiers are huddled. Ten yards from them is a row of bodies. Two dozen, perhaps—children and adults alike.

I cross from grass onto stone, from tree cover to starry skies.

"Dem!" Chimeline cries, once she sees me. She drops the torch onto the rubble and scrambles down the hill, arms out, crashing into my arms.

She's full of dust and smells of burned oil, but I pay no mind. I embrace her tightly, wrapping my hand around her head and bringing it into my shoulder.

Blythe and Colu slowly follow, torches in hand.

"Did you—?" she asks, pulling away and looking up at me as the words fail her. She shivers, either due to the evening air or fear. I continue to hold her. Blythe has the courage to comment.

"Your countenance tells me everything. You lost him."

"Everything was in my favor, yet I still failed," I tell him.

He steps forward and briefly puts a hand on my shoulder. "Do not take on the yoke of blame. Do not own the dark."

"They helped me, Blythe."

"Who helped you?"

I gesture to my voidstone.

"The *enervated* helped you?"

I nod and point to the park. "Did you see?" I ask. "He destroyed the fountain. I was standing directly in front of it, yet I was untouched."

Blythe's smooth face peers into the darkness. "I did not see it happen, but I saw the damage. We brought the bodies back here."

I grit my teeth. "I saw him, Blythe. He was right in front of me. Almost as close as you are right now."

He gives me a look of sympathy.

"After that, he went into the tent, and then . . . ." I run a hand through my short hair. "I found his effulgency cloak. He has another disguise. He uses a wig or something to blend in with the rest of us."

"A wig?" Colu asks.

"Like the actors," I reply. "Eyebrows too, most likely."

"So he doesn't look like a hairless ass anymore?"

"Exactly," I say. "Do you remember the trader?"

"Worchot?" Chimeline asks.

I nod. "He bought goat clippings from him. To make glue."

Everyone is silent for a moment. Then Blythe speaks up.

"You see?" he says, his voice bright yet strained, as if he is trying too hard to convince himself of something. "It was the Unnamed's will that this happened. Instead of achieving vengeance, you discovered something important."

Colu loudly clears his throat and spits to the side.

Meanwhile, the soldier on horseback slowly ushers his mount in our direction, the *clip-clop* sound of hooves over stone echoing out into the night.

"You are the voider," he says. "The one who was in the tower when it collapsed."

I look down and see my necklace still hanging about my neck.

*So much for anonymity.*

But it doesn't matter now, anyway. We've lost the element of surprise.

"Yes," I say, annoyed that he's here asking questions and that I have to look up at him. Underneath his open-faced helmet, I see a large mustache and a fat nose. "I am Master Voider Democryos."

He leans back slightly in shock and then nods.

"Do you know what happened?" he asks me. "People are saying it was a Xian voider that brought down the tower."

"No," I say, shaking my head. "He wasn't Xian."

"So, a Northerner, then?"

"Not quite."

*His kind is from another world.*

As he narrows his eyes, I am stuck between wanting to tell the soldier the truth, so he can aid me in my search, and knowing that his comprehension is an unattainable goal. Any further discussion on the matter will be time wasted. How am I supposed to explain the concept of a voider-effulgent to this soldier when I barely understand it myself?

"Where is my submaster?" I reply. "There are complexities in this attack that demand his immediate attention."

"Submaster?"

"Mander," I say, raising my voice.

"He's probably meeting with Commander Reddles at the Union."

"The Union?"

"The city center."

"I don't understand. Your commander is having a *conversation* while his city falls apart?"

He straightens his shoulders and the leather on his saddle creaks. "I do not presume to speak for either my commander or your submaster."

I can feel my temper getting the better of me as I realize that the tragedy in this park is a microcosm of what has happened over the years.

"I will speak for my submaster. There should be a dozen voiders here tending to the wounded," I say, pointing to the ones in the distance. "But where are they? All out to sea, most likely, doing something with that massive voidstone underneath the bay. And Mander is as spineless as the fish he studies, prioritizing what Reddles wants over the safety of these people. This is madness."

The soldier seems to weigh his words carefully.

"I'm sure this attack is horrific to you," he replies. "But our city has seen enough violence for several lifetimes, and its people have been through many hardships. Today is no different."

"No," I say, taking a step toward him. "Today *is* different."

He blinks rapidly underneath his open-faced helmet.

"Go now," I continue. "Put that horse to work and find my submaster."

For a moment, his eyes narrow. Then, as if he's either taunting me or deliberating, he aimlessly guides his horse around me. More *clip-clops* echo out. The soldiers helping the wounded briefly look up from their patients.

Without a word, he makes up his mind, straightening his course and leaving the square through a narrow street bordered by darkened shops. I watch him go.

"We never ate dinner," Blythe says, by my side. I almost jump in place.

"I'm not hungry," I mumble, without even wondering if it's true.

"The others might be. They have been exerting themselves and may need sustenance. Sometimes a full stomach calms the nerves."

After a moment, I nod. "Actually, I could eat. But I don't want to leave the square until Mander gets here."

"You are angry at him."

"Yes. He's not doing his job."

"How so?" Blythe asks.

"Because he's nowhere to be found when this city needs him the most."

"And why is that?"

"He's easily swayed."

"We're all easily swayed, Master Voider. Just by different things."

I utter a groan of agreement.

Chimeline and Colu have joined the soldiers in taking care of the wounded. Colu tears a bandage into two with his teeth. Chimeline sits nearby, next to a child. She gives him a wide, genuine smile while gently combing his hair with her fingers.

There is a kindness in her heart that is unequaled. I could never see Marine doing this. She would think it below her. She would be more concerned about wiping the dust from her face or preventing the hem of her dress from becoming soiled.

"We should be taking all of them to the hospital," I say. "But it's destroyed."

"I heard one of the soldiers mention that more of their ranks are coming with stretchers," says Blythe. "There is a temporary hospital set up on the other side of the city."

"Good."

"In the meantime, may I have a word with you?" Blythe asks, pointing to the intact remains of his temple.

I turn to him but cannot discern much in the dimness. Just that he seems more somber than usual.

I acquiesce, following him around the rubble. There's a lit torch on the ground, which Blythe picks up.

A few feet later, we enter underneath the remains of the sanctuary. A short span of vaulted ceiling is still intact, the edges of it exposed like the ribcage of a whale. On the walls are two anchored candlestands, which Blythe lights using the flame in his hand.

The half-room is cast in flickering shades.

I sit down on one of the few benches, which is covered in a thick layer of dust. Both it and I let out a deep groan— I am far more tired than I believed. Almost deliriously so.

Blythe throws his torch back into the rubble and sits down next to me as I crane my neck and look up. The vaulted ceiling ends in jagged shards directly above me, the candlelit wood giving way to the deep-blue star-studded sky.

"How many fragments do you carry?" he asks me.

I look back at him. "What?"

"Fragments of axion." With a puckered expression, he adds, "Voidstones."

"Oh," I say. "Three. Mine, Anaxarchis', and Cleanthes'."

He seems lost in thought. Flames reflect in the curves of his eyes.

"Why do you ask?" I say.

"They wanted me to try something with you, but I am not sure that you will be receptive to it. And I am not sure if this is the right time."

I lean in. "What is their idea?"

"It's called eleutheria," he says.

My brow furrows as I repeat the word. "You've mentioned it before. But I don't understand. What does it mean?"

He turns to me. "Liberty."

I swallow.

Suddenly, without any further explanation on his part, I understand perfectly what he means.

And, in some way, this idea—this fear—has always existed in the back of my mind, from the very first moment I learned about the true nature of voidance.

*If voidance is built upon the backs of trapped souls, its end is centered upon their freedom.*

"You know what I speak of," he says. "I can see it in your eyes."

I nod. "How?" I ask, turning to him. "How do we free the souls?"

He takes a deep breath. "I'm not sure."

"You're not sure?"

He shrugs. "Eleutheria has always been somewhat of a mystery. Part of our writings, handed down, century after century."

"But the souls told you, didn't they?"

"Yes," he says. "They did."

"And?"

He purses his lips, as if he's recollecting a memory. "It must be done one fragment at a time. We would need to work together, like before."

"You mean, in contact with one another."

"Yes."

"And?" I ask.

He squints. "This is hard for me to explain. They said to enter the fragment itself."

I think upon his words, but they don't make sense. He seems to see the confusion on my face.

"It is what I feared. I will have to talk you through it. When we have left this world—together."

I dig into my cloak pocket and fish out one of the extra stones, grabbing it tightly by its gold setting. It feels heavy in my hand.

*Raw power.*

"What will happen?" I ask.

"To the fragment?" Blythe answers. "It will enter stasis, I imagine."

"Become useless, you mean."

He nods. "As it should be."

I look down at the voidstone in my hands. I cannot contest his words, even though I want to.

"What you speak of—it is the end of voidance," I say weakly.

"Yes."

All I can think of is how priceless the object in my hand is. When poor farmers bring us fragments half this size, we give them more gold than they would earn in a lifetime. And when a voider dies, we take their stone from them before burial. It is an elaborate ceremony. Beautiful, even. The voidstone has served a voider, and it will serve another in the future. This stone happens to be Cleanthes'. It was a different voider's before him. And before that, another's.

After centuries of use, the thought of turning it into something useless is impossible for me to fathom.

But then I think of what's inside of it.

"Look at your hands."

"What?" I turn to him as he pulls me out of my thoughts. He motions with his head. "Look at your hands."

I look down.

"They are closed so tightly."

He's right. Cleanthes' stone is clutched in my right hand, which is encircled by my left. My knuckles are white.

"That is your problem, Master Voider. You approach life with clutched hands. Always taking. Always using. Always objectifying. You've done it with your profession, and you've done it with the one whom you've proclaimed that you loved."

I remain silent.

"I've heard you repeatedly talk about your wife. You speak about her as if she's one of your stones. As if she is something beautiful that you clutch in the night.

"You need to let go. Of her, of the black arcana. You need to let go of everything you know.

"The tighter you grasp, the smaller the chance that you receive."

"Receive what?" I ask.

"Gifts from the Unnamed."

I open my hands and see the black stone in my upturned palm. It does not reflect anything. And for a long time, I only stare at it, recalling a life that may not reflect anything either.

I think about Cleanthes, his lifeless body resting upon his piano, abandoned by me. I think of the poor souls I cannot even see. I think of black sand. What Aphelime called tephra, the love of destruction.

*Liberty. From all of it.*

Placing Cleanthes' voidstone in my left hand, I extend my right to Blythe. "This isn't an end," I say. "This is a beginning."

The last thing I see in this world is his eager yet guarded smile.

# THE WEIGHT OF A SOUL

*Look down at your fragment.*

It's Blythe. Over the muted and wispy voices of the enervated, he's speaking to me in the void. I call out to him.

*Are you here with me? Do you see what I see?*

*Yes, Master Voider. We are one.*

Instinctively, I look in all directions. Colorless indivisibles are everywhere. There he is, sitting next to me on the bench in his destroyed sanctuary, shimmering. I can tell from his shape that he's facing forward, and his body is perfectly still except for the blood coursing through his veins and the air filling his lungs.

I look down at myself and then back at him.

Everything is synchronized. The pumping of our hearts, the cadence of our breathing. Two orchestras playing the same symphony.

*Look down at your axion fragment.*

I do as he says, after noticing that his lips are not moving.

It looks the same as in the real world. Only voidstones have that quality. Black and seamless. Everything else is colorless and made of indivisibles.

*Closer!*

I move through the void, slowly descending into Cleanthes' stone. I see the shimmering indivisibles of my thumb—the pores and crevasses of my skin, ripples like wind-battered dunes.

*Go inside it.*

The black expands.

I move down through my thumb until I am surrounded by blackness. Quite literally, I am inside the voidstone while using the voidstone.

No.

*Blythe, this isn't going to work.*

*Why do you say that?*

*It's a dead end.*

*How would you know?*

*This is called Delving, and its practice is strictly forbidden. Men and women have lost their minds trying to penetrate the voidstone by using voidance. There is nothing but endless emptiness in here!*

*Trust in the enervated.*

I am silent.

*Have they not proven themselves to you?*

*Yes.*

*Then push on, Master Voider. Against all reason, follow them.*

It's impossible to tell from my vision that we're even moving. But it's like walking through a perfectly dark room. I can feel it. The sensation is similar to that of a passing breeze.

And then I stop.

*What's wrong?*

*This is dangerous.*

*Why do you say that?*

I spin in place, looking in the direction we came from. Far away, the colorless indivisibles are in the shape of an oval. My stone has become a doorway.

*We will get lost in here.*

*No, we won't. The enervated are giving me directions.*

*But the way back—*

*Let go of your doubt, Master Voider.*

I pause. What Blythe is asking for is much more difficult than he understands.

*We must keep going. They are relying on us.*

*Alright.*

I turn around until Blythe tells me to stop, and then I begin moving again through the absolute blackness.

My fear rises the further we go. It is pure irony, the master voider scared of being in the void, clinging to the faith of an effulgent. I have never experienced anything like this. I am surrounded by nothingness. Pure nothingness. I will never find my way back.

This place is evil.

*You are doing fine.*

*I'm not fine, Blythe. This is not right. It feels wrong, like we should not be here. Maybe we should turn back and try another—*

*Look!*

Up ahead, I see something. The tiniest pinprick of light. It's radiant.

*The black will become white.*

*You remember.*

*What is it?*

*The inner place. It's where they're being held. We're close, now.*

I stop a second time. The white spot is barely larger than when it first appeared. Larger than the brightest star, yet smaller than the moon.

*We're going to become trapped in here, like the rest of them.*

*No, Master Voider. I will not let that happen, and neither will the enervated. We are all in this together.*

The most intense urge comes over me. I want to run away from the light, but I know that if I turn around, I will no longer see the way we came, and this makes me even more afraid. The doorway back to the indivisibles is gone, I am sure of it. I will be trapped here, forever.

*Let go, Democryos! Do not fear!*

I wish I could shut my eyes, but there are no eyes here. Nothing to hide behind.

*Even in the void, you grasp on to things. Your mind is clenched like your fists were. How can you expect to free the enervated if you are not even free yourself?*

I try my hardest.

*Good.*

I move toward the light.

Soon it grows, so much so that the black is now in my periphery. There are things moving in the white. Floating clear circles. It is a room. Three walls, a floor, and a ceiling, all perfectly white. We are the fourth wall.

*Stop here!*

I do as he says.

*Why?*

*If you go inside, we'll be trapped.*

*You see!? I was right. We need to—*

*Relax, Master Voider. I am here with you. Just let them come through us.*

*You mean to us, right?*

*Not exactly.*

They look like glass spheres, perfect in every way. Except there is no reflection on their curved surfaces. No place the light is coming from. It is everywhere and nowhere.

The spheres are coming toward me.

*Are these the souls, Blythe?*

*Yes.*

*There are hundreds of them.*

*I know.*

*Good Unnamed.*

The first one floats into my vision, coming closer until it fills everything.

It passes right through me.

Color.

I feel struck down.

There is no breath here, but it is knocked out of me anyway. No legs, but I stumble to the ground.

Then, the visions come.

A child playing on the beach. Two suns on the horizon. Her mother laughing, a red pail in her hands.

In an instant, the image is gone.

*Blythe, what is happening? Did you see—*

Before I have a chance to react, another clear glass sphere passes through me.

Green trees, pillars rising above the clouds. A strong man swinging from one to another, a girl with orange eyes laughing in his arms.

*Do not be afraid. They are introducing themselves to you.*

And then, another.

Damp streets. Driving rain. An older woman carrying a loaf of bread and pulling open a metal grate. A man covered in silver looms in the distance behind her. His visor is blue light.

These images hit me, flash upon flash, building into a stream. I cannot keep up. There is one for every sphere.

A memory from each life?

As quickly as it began, it ends. Before I even know what is happening, all the spheres have passed through me. The room in front of me is empty.

*Master Voider, can you hear me?*

*Yes.*

*We can go now. But be careful. Back up slowly.*

I do as he says. The white shrinks in front of me, the corners becoming rounded, resembling a circle again.

*Turn around.*

Part of me doesn't want to, since I know what I'll see. Pure blackness.

But I steel myself and do it nonetheless. I don't see the spheres anymore, but I know that they are here, floating all around me. I can feel them sing. I can hear their silence.

*Turn slightly to the left. You are going a ways off. There, that is better.*

*How much further?*

*Not long. If it helps, just think of the centuries the enervated have been in here. Our time left is a heartbeat.*

Soon, I see it. Another pinprick, but this one is not white. It's nonblack. Simply colorless.

It's the glorious world of the void. Indivisibles.

Back to safety.

At first, I am disoriented, since I don't know what's in front of me. As the black is left behind, all I see through the oval door are jagged shards and shimmering points of grayness. Then I realize that I am looking upwards, at the broken ceiling of the temple and the stars beyond.

Meanwhile, the sounds around me are getting louder, like the wind whistling through an open door. It is almost a screaming. The glass spheres quickly float past me, through the oval and into the colorless night.

As this happens, the outside world and the indivisibles go darker.

We're losing light.

The voidstone is weakening.

And then nothing.

Perfect silence.

*Blythe?*

It is so quiet. There is not one iota of sound.

*You can let go of the stone now. It is finished.*

This is a foreign thought. My body.

I have a body.

Remembering this, I think of my arm. My arm has a hand. My hand has fingers.

*Move it.*

As I do this, the void disappears.

The world never seemed so beautiful.

Glorious night. Vivid orange glow against luxurious blue velvet.

Blythe grabs me by the shoulders. He's smiling wide.

"We did it, Master Voider. Eleutheria!"

His happiness seems strange to me. It's misplaced. The flashes of color are all I see. The beach, the cloud-trees, the heavy grate, the man in silver with the blue face. And hundreds more. They haunt me. Through tears, I close my eyes and they're still there. Their phantom trails follow me. Blythe is shaking me and patting me on the back, but I feel unworthy to be here.

"I'm sorry, Blythe."

"What are you sorry about? No grander first steps on the way of unwanting have ever been made."

*How can I explain to him that my entire life has been a lie?*

"I'm so sorry."

Opening my eyes, I see Cleanthes' voidstone in my hands. I'm clutching it by its gold setting. It's no longer heavy. It's nothing. It's absolutely nothing.

Instinctively, I weakly push it away. I want nothing to do with it.

And then, something strange happens.

It ricochets off the wooden bench in front of us and then slowly spins in midair, its delicate gold chain fanning outward.

It's floating.

I reach out and touch the stone from below, giving it a gentle push upwards with my palm.

And watch as it rises into the night sky.

"What is happening?" I ask Blythe.

But his mouth is open and his neck is craned, just as mine is.

"It's in stasis," he whispers.

"Did they tell you that this would happen?"

"Not exactly."

He wipes his eyes with the back of his hand.

My energy is gone. My body slinks down sideways across the back of the bench, until I am lying on my back on the wooden seat. I watch Cleanthes' voidstone rise into the night, mere feet from the jagged edge of the vaulted ceiling. Only the sky above is its limit, and then I realize that even this is a falsehood.

There is no limit to what we have done here tonight.

"How is this even possible?" I ask nobody in particular.

"You mean that it's flying away?"

"Yes."

"Axion is weightless," Blythe answers. "There are no souls to weigh it down, my friend."

# MANDER AND REDDLES

The softest thunder wakes me.

I slowly rise from the temple's wooden bench, groaning in pain. My back aches.

It's still night. The torches have all gone out. The world is cast in shades of blue. Looking up past the shattered vaulted ceiling, I expect to see storm clouds, but the sky is as clear as can be. Stars glitter in every direction.

*That's not thunder. It's the faraway sound of horses' hooves.*

I look across the square to see if anyone is approaching but find it still empty. A weak fringe of orange down an eastern alleyway gleams past the silhouette of a shop's awning. It's not coming from torches but from the sun.

*Meet me tomorrow. Sunrise. In Temberlain's Ashes.*

"Shit," I mumble. I don't have long if I'm going to meet Marine.

"It *is* a shitty morning," booms Colu, causing me to jump in place. Turning in my seat, I see him sitting on the bench behind me, arms out at his sides.

I clear my throat and twist my fists into my eyes, trying to clear them. Colu drinks out of a suede wineskin then holds out a piece of dried meat.

"Want some?"

"Where did you get that?"

"In the park."

"You scavenged it?"

He shrugs as he takes a bite from another piece. "If that's what you want to call it."

I look to the darkened trees in the park behind him. Dozens of people huddle in the shadows, heads down as they scrutinize the ground for anything of value. Some pick up blankets and dump out baskets on the grass. I hear the crystalline sound of glass shattering in the distance.

"Beggars started coming in a fullbell ago, while you were asleep. Meanwhile, the injured were asking for water and food. So the hairless ass and I went into the park and brought in what we could find, before all the pickings were gone."

He takes a swig from the wineskin. "Take, for instance, this excellent Xian wine. Care for some?"

"Are you sure there's any left?"

He laughs, sober enough to catch my dig.

There's a larger skin next to him on the bench. "Is that water?" I ask.

He nods and tosses it to me.

I open the stopper and let the stream of clean water quench my dry mouth. After drinking my fill, I give it back to him and ask, "Where's Chimeline?"

"Sleeping," he says, pointing to the ground nearby, under open stars. She's buried in a flurry of blankets, which I assume were taken from the park as well. "She was afraid to be under the roof," he adds.

I nod. "And Blythe?"

He motions with his head. "Hairless ass has been speaking with the wounded all night about his fucking Unnamed. Talk about a captive audience."

I look over to Blythe, about fifty yards away, sitting cross-legged next to a person with a bandaged arm. Behind him, soldiers sit against a low stone wall, most with their heads resting on their folded arms.

The thunder of hooves and wagon wheels gets louder. The echo makes it impossible to tell which direction they're coming from.

One of the soldiers stands and starts kicking the others awake. They obviously don't want to be caught dreaming.

*Caught dreaming.*

I blink rapidly as recent events catch up to me.

It seems impossible. Only a dream. Entering a voidstone while using voidance. Delving. Eleutheria. The white room. The souls floating through me. Flashes of memories from other lands. And then the stone rising into the night sky.

None of it seems true.

In a flurry of hand movements, I count my voidstones. Mine is still hanging around my neck, outside my white shirt. In my pants pocket is a second one. Anaxarchis' stone.

The third one—Cleanthes'—is missing.

*It wasn't a dream.*

"She loves you, you know."

Shaken out of my thoughts, I turn around and face Colu again.

"What?"

"Your girl. She loves you."

"Chimeline?" I ask.

He lets the breath out of his nose and rolls his one eye. "Who else?"

I look in her direction. Her curled-up body faces away from me underneath the blankets.

"She doesn't think that she's worthy of you," he adds loudly.

"Will you keep your voice down?" I whisper forcefully. Despite the sound of approaching horses, I'm worried that she'll overhear. But after another glance in her direction, I can tell that she's still asleep.

"Did she say that to you?"

"More or less."

"That's ridiculous."

He takes his arms off the bench and leans forward. "Come on. She's a harem girl. Or an assassin. Or both."

He belches. "Actually, I don't know what the fuck she is, but it doesn't matter. The fact remains."

"What fact?"

"She's not a good match for you! You're the master fucking voider."

"Lower your voice," I urgently whisper again.

He reaches out and touches my arm—the action of a man not fully sober. "You know, you should just tell her. Rip off the bandage. She's a nice girl. She doesn't deserve you stringing her along."

I bring my hand to the gold setting around my necklace. It's *this* that I need to rip off me. *This* is the bandage. I feel its heaviness. It used to remind me of power. It used to fill me with self-confidence. Now it makes me nauseous.

"I am no longer the master voider," I mumble. "I am nothing."

He laughs, despite my somber tone. "You've been hanging around Blythe too long," he says. "Now you talk in riddles."

*The time for voidance has ended.*

The echoing, ubiquitous sound suddenly becomes staccato and directional. Bright orange light bleeds into the square from the perimeter.

One after another, horse-drawn wagons bearing torches enter the square from the corner road, soldiers on horseback riding alongside them. Three of the wagons head directly to the rows of dead bodies, while another three approach the wounded and Blythe.

A carriage arrives last. It's made of polished wood. Red velvet curtains line the windows, and the driver is dressed in black-and-white semi-formal attire. He's not a soldier like the others.

"There's someone important in there," Colu mumbles.

I stand and begin walking. I pass the wounded, Blythe, and the chaotic mix of soldiers who have just arrived. I pass the dead, already being lifted and placed into the wagons. I pass the soldier with the large mustache and the fat nose—the one I sent away fullbells ago. My destination is the carriage. Its curved wooden surface glows in the torchlight.

The driver gets off his perch, walks around the side, and opens the door.

A flaming torch is mounted next to it, but through the opening and red velvet panels I see only darkness.

"Ah, the master voider," says a clear voice from the shadows.

A large, muscular man with an angular face leans into the firelight. He's wearing the gray-and-red formal attire of a commander. His hair is short, grayish-blond, and damp—perhaps from an early-morning bath. And a star-shaped gold medal hangs around his neck on a red ribbon. It clangs against the pins on his chest as he deftly works his way out of the relatively small opening.

"You must be Commander Reddles," I say.

He nods distantly, already looking past me to the dead, the wounded, and the rubble, his face slowly caving into what looks like worry and frustration. "This is worse than I thought," he says levelly.

"Mander, you need to see this," he says, slightly louder. "Nearly the entire temple is destroyed."

"Yes, um, certainly, Commander," replies a soft voice that I recognize instantly.

My submaster climbs out of the darkness.

He's wearing a traditional black flaxen cloak over gray silken pants. His wild and curly brown hair is even more unkempt than I remember, and his brass-rimmed glasses reflect the torchlight. He grabs the doorframe in three different places before speaking up.

"Um, driver, can you, um, move this flame. It is perilously close to the opening. With the, um, wind and all."

The driver steps forward and grabs the gold handle of the torch next to the door, pulling it up and out of its anchor. He takes a few steps away from the carriage with it.

"Thank you, kind sir."

Finally, he exits the carriage with sounds of exertion and then flashes me a weary smile before closing the door behind him.

"Greetings, my dear friend."

I let out a breath, realizing that in nervous anticipation, I had been holding it.

Despite everything, I return his smile.

Here stands Submaster Mander—another voider whom I once taught. He is alive, and just the same as when I left him. He's not rotting in a well as Anaxarchis was, nor is he consumed with hilma, like Cleanthes. He's just the same clumsy and spineless man I've always known.

I'll take this over the alternative.

I step closer, arms out, with the intention of embracing him. But he holds out a palm.

"Dem, have you seen yourself? You are covered in, um, dust and grime. I would embrace you, but I have just showered and dressed for the day. And I have appointments after this. Xian merchant dignitaries. I am assisting in the discussions around the, um, new trade embargoes."

The scents of soap and sandalwood drift my way. It's the smell of a man who has been well taken care of, despite being in the very epicenter of a war. A man who sees only the perfect places.

*The way I used to be.*

Reddles continues to survey the damage as Mander clears his throat and continues. "When I heard that you and Marine were, um, here in the city, I was elated. It warms my heart to see you, although I wish it were under better circumstances."

I take a step closer. "You've seen Marine?"

"Um, yes. Of course. Yesterday morning."

"Who was she with?"

He pushes his glasses up the bridge of his nose. "Nobody. She was, um, alone. Walking through the Union.

She was in a hurry. I said my greetings, and, um, she continued on her way."

I utter a groan, and he points to the rubble.

"You were involved in this, um, this horrible undoing."

I nod.

"I trust that your lady was not—"

"No," I interrupt. "She wasn't present."

Reddles takes a step closer, his hawkish face looking down at me. "What happened here?"

I pause before I reply, deciding how honest I should be. Reddles may be working with the voider-effulgent. He may know everything and simply be playing along.

*But I can play along too.*

The commander must sense my reluctance. "Master Voider, if you know something, you need to share it with me. It's imperative that I get to the bottom of what happened here." His voice is more pleading than his words imply.

A strange emotion rises within me. A tinge of hypocritical resentment builds and even overshadows my distrust.

"If it is that important to you, Commander, then why did you wait until nearly sunrise to arrive?"

I turn to Mander and raise my voice. "And there should be voiders here helping here with the wounded. Not assisting in matters of trade."

Mander opens his mouth, but the commander replies first. "I have spoken with my cadet about the delay. He didn't think the attack was important enough to wake me. His judgment is clearly lacking."

"Yes, um, Dem, I was not informed until—"

"The important thing is that we're here *now*," interrupts the commander with an outstretched hand. "And I *am* concerned. I have finally been able to secure peace in this city, but it is a fragile peace." He flashes another worried look at the remains of the tower, shaking his head in thought. "Two days ago, I dispatched some of my men north to relay the good news to the king that we've taken the city and an accord has been signed. But *this*?" He points while taking a deep breath. "This could shatter our peace overnight. This could make me a liar in the eyes of the king."

His concern regarding the king's perception of him over the well-being of the people in the city seems almost too subtle to contrive.

*He doesn't appear to be acting.*

Briefly, I look to the flurry of soldiers behind me in the square. Most of the dead and wounded have been loaded onto the wagons—already one of them is pulling away. Near the remains of the temple, Blythe, Chimeline, and Colu stand together, looking at me. Past them and down the same narrow alleyway I spied before, the orange light grows.

*Sunrise is here.*

I remind myself that all this conjecture is meaningless. Only when I see Marine will I know the truth. Who is the voider-effulgent? Is Reddles working with him? All of it.

Turning back to the contrasting pair, I decide to play things out.

"The man we're looking for is the greatest of traitors," I say.

"A Xian voider," Reddles says, narrowing his eyes. "I knew it."

"No," I say sharply. "*Not* Xian."

"A Northerner, then? Some Xian sympathizer?" He quickly looks between Mander and me. "One of yours from the university?"

"This has nothing to do with north versus south. It's much more complicated than that."

"How so?"

"Have you been approached by an effulgent in the last few days? Or in the recent past?"

Reddles shakes his head. "An effulgent? No. Why?"

Taking a deep breath, I begin to relay my story.

I explain that there is an effulgent who can also work voidance. Someone who may be in disguise. His general appearance in the park when the fountain blew to pieces. His goal of gaining control of the massive voidstone underneath Xi Bay. I leave it at that. No mention of the empowered or enervated. No mention of eleutheria or Marine.

Mander replies first.

"Why would this voider-effulgent, um, traitor, destroy one of his own temples?"

"Because I was in it."

His mouth hangs open in confusion.

"He was trying to kill me," I add. "Because I am close on his trail."

"Tracking him is why you are, um, here?"

I shake my head. "Killing him is."

Reddles raises his voice. "No. We must take this voider-effulgent alive and transport him back to the citadel. Based on what you said, the king will want to question him personally. We stay out of the details." He fingers his star medal. "I only wish we knew how to identify and apprehend him without further destruction to the city."

"This is ridiculous," I say, turning away in frustration.

A shattering sound comes from the temple ruins.

Colu is throwing rocks at the stained-glass windows. Blythe yells at him to stop.

Reddles frowns. "What is that fool doing?"

Ignoring his question, I turn back and address both Reddles and Mander. "You two should already know who this effulgent is. He's been under your nose this entire time!"

I start ticking off the items on my fingers. "One, he's a voider. Two, he is known to use dynamic voidance to blur his face from others. Three, he's an effulgent. Four, he's used goat clippings, like the actors on stage here do, to wear some type of disguise. Five, he'll have been seen with Marine."

"Your wife?" Reddles says.

I once again ignore his question and point south, as if I could see the bay from where I stand. "Narrow it down! Find out who has been out there on those ships."

"It is, um, a fine idea, Dem."

The commander's eyes dart back and forth, focused on nothing, and then he lifts his head slightly, opening his mouth as if he has just remembered something.

"There is a problem," he says.

"What?"

"Gaining control of the voidstone is *my* primary objective. The king himself ordered it. From what you say, this traitor's goal is the same."

"That's true. The traitor is using the king."

The commander leans back. "Master Voider, do you know what you are implying?"

"I'm not implying anything. I'm full-on declaring it. The young king is being manipulated."

The commander extends a hand and begins whispering. "Keep your voice down! If you are questioning His Majesty's competence, this is treasonous talk."

"It is not treason to state the truth."

He shakes his head. "We are not having this conversation," he says forcefully.

I look away in frustrated understanding. This is precisely the type of self-preservation that has enabled Reddles to rise through the ranks. He is savvy. There's a soft and slimy politician underneath all those hard medals.

"Fine," I say. "Let's just stick to the facts. How do you get your orders?"

"I send a carrier squad to the citadel weekly, via Xi Bay Road. It is less risky than by the wing. That is now how I receive all my orders, and how I communicate my status back to His Majesty."

I nod. "So the king mentioned the stone in one of his letters."

"Correct."

"When?"

Reddles pauses. "About a month ago."

"What else did it say?"

Reddles looks to Mander. "Up until then, my orders were to secure the bay. When we gained control of it and pushed the Xian navy out, the focus changed. The letter instructed me to coordinate my efforts with the submaster. The way it was written alluded to him already knowing of its presence. But Mander may have received letters from the king that I was not privy to."

I turn to Mander.

"Is this true?" I ask him.

"Yes, Dem." He nods nervously. "I have known about the stone for a very long time. Since shortly after Andrej IX passed on."

I narrow my eyes without taking them off my submaster. "You knew about it for *five years*?"

"Nearly. Um, yes."

I take a step closer and have the urge to grab his clean clothes with my dirty hands. "How could you keep something like this from me?"

He looks at the ground between us while keeping a finger on the bridge of his glasses. "I, um, could not divulge it, Dem. His Majesty specifically, um. Specifically said *not* to tell you. He was very clear on that. Very clear. He knew, um. Knew of our closeness."

I raise my voice almost to a shout. "Why would he keep something like that from me? I'm the master voider! I'm the one person in the kingdom who *should* know!"

"I do not know. It is not my place to question, um. To challenge His Majesty's orders."

"What happened years ago is of little relevance now," the commander says levelly.

"Yes, it *is*," I say, turning to him. "Because if you want to identify this traitor, you must follow the stone. *He* was the one who knew about it first."

There's a moment of silence as the thought sinks in.

"Dem, um, how do you know this?"

*Because the enervated told Blythe, that's how.*

There's no way that I am going to divulge the full truth to these men. At least not now. So I simply shake my head. "I just do."

Another shattering sound echoes in the square.

Far away, Colu raises both of his hands above his head in drunken victory. Directly behind him is an eastern alleyway—his body is a silhouette against the beginning of the sunrise.

I shake my head.

I was going to ask Colu to watch Chimeline and Blythe while I met with Marine. To take them somewhere safe until I returned.

But he's in no condition to help.

"I need to ask you both a favor," I ask.

"Um, certainly."

"Name it," Reddles adds.

"Look after my three friends." I subtly gesture to the ruins with my thumb. "For a few fullbells."

Mander positions his glasses, gazing into the distance. "They are your, um, friends? They look like, um, trouble."

"It's a long story. But, yes, they are."

He shrugs his meager shoulders. "I can take them to my estate, Dem. If that is, um, satisfactory?"

I nod. "That's fine. But don't tell anyone."

I glance at Reddles and he nods.

"As you wish."

I give Mander a pat on the shoulder, and he jumps in place.

"I'll see you soon."

"Where are you, um, going? To the Union?"

I've already turned to leave, but I stop and look back at the pair over my shoulder. "Not quite."

Mander furrows his brow. I walk away.

I pass by the soldiers and the three remaining wagons.

Blythe sees me coming and runs to meet me before I reach the rubble.

"The one-eyed helmsman is mad drunk," he says, out of breath. "He stole wine from the park."

"I know."

"He's destroying the temple!"

I turn to him and briefly place a hand on his shoulder, trying to quell his anger. "Listen to me. I want you to go with Mander. You, Colu, and Chimeline."

He lowers his voice. "Why? Are we in danger?"

Chimeline walks up briskly to my side, curious as to what we're talking about, so I repeat myself.

"You're not coming with us?"

I shake my head. "I have somewhere I need to go, but I'll be back by midday."

"Can I go with you?" she asks.

"The safest place for you right now is with Blythe and Colu, at Mander's estate," I say.

"The safest place for me is by your side."

"Is this more vengeance, Master Voider?" Blythe asks. "Now that you have spoken with those two, you know where the enervated is—"

"No," I say, alternating my gaze between them. "To both of you, the answer is no." I turn to Blythe. "I'm not going after him—at least, not yet." And then softly to Chimeline, "And you're not coming with me."

A creaking sound nearby draws my attention. Colu is talking to himself while lying down on one of the benches. An orange falls out of his hand and rolls across the stone ground, coming to rest against a pile of debris.

"Why not?" Chimeline asks, in an innocent tone.

"Because," I say, "this is something I have to do on my own."

She nods once, her eyes glassy in the torchlight. I feel that in some way I have upset her. That because of my non-answer, she thinks that I still don't trust her.

So I stuff my hand into my pocket, dig out Marine's note, and hand it to her.

Despite the approaching sunrise, it's still so dark that she needs to bring it right up to her face. Her nose scrunches up before she realizes who wrote it—and where I'm headed. Then her face becomes placid, devoid of any emotion whatsoever.

"I am happy for you, Master Voider," she says. "You have found what you were looking for."

Then she hands me back the note.

I sigh in frustration as my attention is drawn by the sound of the remaining wagons pulling away. I turn and watch Reddles shouting orders to his men while Mander looks upwards at the brightening sky, as if imagining how it once looked with the bell tower standing there.

I leave Blythe and Chimeline and walk around the remaining half-wall of the temple, over shattered glass and strewn blocks of stone. Within a few breaths I am behind the sanctuary, out of sight. A slender alleyway in the shadows leads south.

But I hesitate.

Through a tall and narrow opening in the wall, where a stained-glass window used to be, I see Chimeline. Past the benches and torn ceiling, she walks away from Blythe and sits alone on a pile of rubble under the early-morning stars. Her back is to me.

In the shadows, I feel torn. Part of me wants to walk down the alley to Temberlain's Ashes. The other part wants to stay here.

Am I running to my past or to my future?

In the end, I choose to slip away.

# TEMBERLAIN'S ASHES

The waterfront lies only ten blocks from the crumbled square. I don't even have to ask for directions. I keep the rising sun to the left of me, and each step I take is on a decline.

Soon I reach the beach.

As white sand swallows the gray cobblestones, I look in both directions underneath endless rows of palms. To my surprise, scores of fishermen are present, despite the early fullbell. They mend their linen nets and stretch them out in the sand. At first, I assume that they are preparing for a day of work but then realize that it's possible they've been out to sea all night and only now is their work done.

They all ignore me.

I take off my boots and carry them as I walk down the length of the beach. I reach the closest pier.

Small fishing boats are lined up so closely that they're almost touching. The waves make a gentle slapping sound against the hulls. This is punctuated by the exertion of men hoisting wicker barrels full of fish out of their ships and carrying them down the pier, their loads dripping as they go. None of them speak to each other, which is probably a testament to their exhaustion.

A wrinkled, shirtless man in a floppy hat sits in a flat-bottomed rowboat at the end of the pier. It's so small that it doesn't even have a mast.

As I approach him, he looks up from his work. Despite his age, he has strong hands. Half of his fingers are wrapped in white tape. He's fishing a line through a hook.

For a moment, his eyes narrow as he scrutinizes me, and then he seems to laugh to himself. He drops his gaze and continues to work on the hook.

"Is this boat for hire?" I ask.

"Been out all night, landy."

I wait, but he doesn't say anything else.

"I need someone to ferry me into the bay."

Again, silence.

When I take out three gold coins from my pocket, he suddenly looks up again.

"Ain't going to no ring."

"What ring?"

He points a white-taped finger to the south. "No gold worth that trouble."

I peer into the darkness and see it.

The barricade.

Silhouettes of the three-masted ships are barely discernible against the misty gray horizon. It's the same formation I saw from the bell tower.

"I'm not headed there," I say.

"Then where, landy? Know you're an arcanist, so if not ring, then what?"

"Have you heard of Temberlain's Ashes?"

He hesitates and then nods.

"That all you got? Three gold?"

"No," I answer. "This is for you to ferry me there. I'm going to need you to wait for me, and then I'll give you another seven when we're safely back to shore."

He smiles, revealing more gaps than teeth.

"Hop the bow, landy."


For a long time, the fisherman rows in silence, and I am content to simply be an idle passenger. I sit in the front, up high due to the angle of the boat hitting the water. The only sounds are his oars cutting into the sea and the dripping water as he pulls them back out, time and time again. I'm facing backward, looking down at the fisherman and, behind him, the receding shoreline. It's come alive with lanterns in the small windows of the buildings that rise into the hilly, gray-pink distance. Above them, more palm trees dangle over rooftops, but the tallest thing, by far, is the bell tower. It rings five times.

It seems this effulgency temple was spared destruction from both the empowered's wrath and the war.

The beautiful city is waking up, but in some respects, its occupants are still asleep. They have no idea what is happening in their midst.

Turning in place, I look at something far more menacing and distant and decide to pry.

"Tell me about the ring of ships," I say.

"What's to know?"

"Why are they there?" I ask. I feign ignorance since I don't want to influence his answer.

"Heard about underwater stone. Black arcanists trying raise it. Not supposed go near."

"Why are they trying to raise it?"

"In Blackscar."

"Blackscar?"

"Trench, landy."

*The trench.*

For what seems like a quarterbell, I am lost in my thoughts again. What the fisherman says makes sense. If the Axiondrive is somehow in the trench underneath Xi Bay, that would explain why nobody discovered it before. Countless voiders explored the trench throughout history. Many died trying to reach its bottom.

Until the voider-effulgent came along.

The shoreline becomes distant as the sun engulfs the morning sky in reds, pinks, and oranges that give way to a soft blue. It is almost cloudless.

"Another hot one," the man says, looking at the sky with me.

A short time later, the fisherman sets both oars inside of the boat, spraying my legs and my boots, which I'm still holding. For a moment we sit in silence as our small boat rocks gently in the waves.

I look around. Another small rowboat bobs in the water about fifty feet away. Its insides are painted white, and a rope on its edge descends into the water. Besides that, only the open sea surrounds us. The barricade looks as distant here as it did from the shore.

"Meeting someone?" the fisherman asks, motioning toward the empty white boat.

I nod.

"You arcanists strange sort. You be gone long?"

"A fullbell at the most."

"Fullbell?" he says, spitting over the side. He looks to the east and nods.

He turns in his seat, picks up an anchor that looks like a rusted, oversized cowbell, and drops it over the edge with a groan. The coil of rope at his feet starts to disappear.

Dropping his tan hat over his eyes, he lies crosswise on his seat, his legs dangling over the side of the boat. In one of his taped hands is one of the gold coins I gave him. He twirls it over his fingers.

I look sideways and down at the dark waters, and then at the voidstone hanging around my neck.

Guilt consumes me. I need to use it to meet Marine. I need to use *them*.

The worst part about it is that I am not about to save a life. I'm not about to kill the empowered—only identify him.

I hope that this is enough for them.

Turning to the misty horizon, I briefly survey the white rowboat floating there, fifty feet away. The paint inside is not as fresh as I thought—it's peeling in places, exposing darkened, rotting wood underneath.

Swallowing my shame, I grab the voidstone, creating the first of two membranes of dynamic voidance as I jump off the edge of the boat and into Xi Bay. The transparent sphere is slightly larger than my body—ten feet in diameter—and is centered on me. The ambient sound of the waves hitting the boat becomes muted.

Not a drop of water touches me.

When the light of the morning sky turns a glowing shade of blue, I add the sphere of weight.

An anchor, dragging me down into blackness.

The water is murky here.

It almost seems like a different place from the one I knew. Above the water's surface, the sun barely stretches over the horizon, reducing the light below. When I was last here, the sun was high in the sky and everything below was turquoise and clear. I could see for miles.

It's hard to believe that five years have passed.

A weak light guides me. A shimmering, golden-yellow cloud. Like someone holding a lantern in a dense fog.

As I descend in the sphere, my heart tightens.

I can't help feeling I should be more excited. From the moment Marine's letter dropped from my hands onto my bedchamber floor, I have been searching for her. From the stain of black pitch to the secret laboratory by the riverbank. From the dizzying heights of the airship to the muddy cages in Fiscarlo. I have taken so many steps to get here.

But I don't *feel* as if I've arrived. I feel homeless. I am a husband without a wife. A voider without voidance. A teacher without students. And this rendezvous is not going to change any of that.

It's getting darker.

Past a coral reef and a field of sea life either unaware of or untroubled by my presence, the massive stern of the Xian galleon wreck soon rises before me. It tilts on the seabed. Its three stories of arched windows and elaborate wooden railings stacked on top of one another resembles the facade of a tall building perilously close to tipping.

The topmost array of windows—the level directly underneath the deck of the ship—glow with soft yellow light.

Below all this, and just above the former waterline—where, in its prime, the hull must have met the surface of the water—immense letters, beautifully etched and painted into the wood, are still quite legible.

They read *Temberlain's Ashes*.

I float downward, past the deck and toward the top railing of the stern. I reach one of the golden windows and know from prior experience that the fine glass was shattered ages ago.

Only a membrane of Marine's voidance exists there now.

Touching my stone briefly, I delicately penetrate it. My sphere merges into the vertical plane, which deforms before suddenly dissolving like a massive soap bubble. By then, I have stepped through the window, from blue into gold. The tiny hairs on my skin flutter with the motion.

In the captain's chambers, the water has been pushed out completely, but it still drips periodically from the decor, sounding like a light spring rain.

Slowly, I walk into the middle of the room, around a large wooden table bolted to the plank floor. It's the same table we made love on years ago on our honeymoon.

It's tilted and distorted like everything else.

An oversized gray tapestry map of Xiland, mostly decomposed, hangs on the dark-plank walls. Over this is a faded oval-shaped oil painting of a bearded Xian man in uniform—undoubtedly, a portrait of the captain himself. Mounted to the wall on each side of it and between each arched window are iron-and-glass lanterns that house a dozen thick white candles. But since they're attached via chains, they don't follow the tilting lines of the room. Instead, they hang straight down. More than half are lit.

When I turn around, Marine is already standing there, waiting for me.

Even with the table between us, I can see she's wearing a strapless white cotton dress that ends above her knees. Her blonde hair has been pulled into a ponytail, revealing diamond earrings that fall into black teardrops. Her feet are bare. Her lips are painted coral pink.

With her pale skin glowing in the candlelight, she's as stunning and flawless as ever. I notice her, but no fire is sparked inside of me. Only ashes are left now. She's a map that takes me nowhere. She's a painting in an abandoned room.

A large voidstone necklace hangs about her neck. The stone is surrounded by diamonds.

It's revolting. There must be fifty diamonds in the setting, each one worth more than what a villager of Winter's Baiou earns in a lifetime. This display of wealth and power straddles both this world and the next. Over bodies and souls, she has climbed a horrendous ladder.

I shake my head to clear both my vision and my thoughts. Then I get straight to the broken heart of the matter.

"Who is he?"

Her anxious expression turns into one of confusion. "Don't you know?"

"Of course not. How could I?"

"Then how . . . What brought you to Winter's Baiou?"

"I tracked you."

She stares at me with an incredulous expression.

"Who is he?" I repeat, louder this time. "An effulgent from the citadel? Or from Winter's Baiou? I know it must be—"

"It's Mander."

When she says the name, it is almost a whisper, but it's loud enough that I know I didn't mishear it.

*Mander.*

Suddenly fearing that I will fall to my knees, I press my hands on the table, but it's awkwardly tilted with the ship. So I turn away and stumble across the room, at a slight decline, until I can face port side. I brace my hands on either side of an open window, the transparent buzzing of Marine's membrane and the vastness of Xi Bay less than a foot from my face.

I stare into murky grayness.

*I've known Mander for years. Longer than I've known Marine.*

He came to the university as a young man. Around ten years ago. I was only a submaster then. He was a shy orphan, full of peculiarities.

*He is no effulgent.*

Marine comes near. She leans her body against the slanted, damp wall and faces me.

"It can't be him," I say, shaking my head slowly. "The man I'm looking for is an effulgent."

"Dem, he *is* an effulgent."

I turn to her, but it's the black stage that I see in my mind. The glass vial that rolled toward me and came to rest against my thigh.

"The clipping glue," I say.

Marine nods. "The Mander you knew was nothing more than a disguise," she says. "The hair and glasses, the way he speaks. Everything. It's all a ruse. He's been planning his entire life for this moment."

I run a hand through my short hair as a harrowing thought comes to me.

"Good Unnamed. What have I done?"

"What?"

I straighten up.

"I need to go. My friends are in danger."

"What friends?"

I grit my teeth and look to the murky waters as I realize my mistake. I've broken the promise I made to Chimeline. I told her that I would protect her from the man behind the veil.

Instead, I handed her over to him.

"Dem?"

I face her. "Three people I met during my travels. I placed them in Mander's care."

"Voiders?"

I shake my head.

She shrugs. "I'm sure they're fine. Whatever you think of him, he's not evil."

My breath catches in my throat—I cannot believe what I am hearing, and one look in her eyes tells me she's not lying.

"That's *exactly* what he is . . ." I run my hand over my hair and point upwards. "He just murdered dozens in the park, Marine! When the tower collapsed. You must have seen it." I fumble in my pocket and retrieve her note. "You were there."

She nods, but her jaw is set, full of conviction. "What I saw was two headstrong men fighting with innocents caught in the wake."

"You think this is about *you*? How typical." I drop the note and begin walking away from her and the wall, toward where I entered. "You know what? Believe what you want. I don't have time for this. I need to go."

When I reach the slanted table again, I pause. The slow dripping of water is the only sound.

"I just need to know one more thing," I say, and turn back toward her. "Why did you leave me?"

Marine looks down and nervously draws lines in the wet floor with her bare foot.

"I'm sorry, but when Mander told me about the lost voidstone, I had no choice. It's going to change everything. It was either go with him or be left behind."

"So you threw away an entire life with me for some sunken treasure and an elusive promise."

She looks back up at me angrily. "*Who* gave *whom* the elusive promise? Our marriage was already over. You just refused to see it."

I don't answer.

Her face softens. "He found it, Dem. The voidstone. He's going to be the new master voider. With that stone, he will be more powerful than all the voiders in the world combined. And the king is behind him."

I shrug. "Master Voider is a dead title. It means nothing. All the kings in the world can be behind him and it won't change a thing."

She drops her head back and forces out a breath. "You've changed."

"And you haven't."

"What is that supposed to mean?"

Again, I don't answer, and this seems to goad her.

"Things are going to change, Dem. Voiders will no longer be servants to the poor. We're going to put *ourselves* first, where we belong. We're going to create wonders with voidance that you can't imagine. And soon, we will rule this land."

I shake my head slowly. "How do you sleep? How do you justify such evil for the sake of your so-called wonders?"

"It's not evil, Dem. It's just the way the world works. A kingdom has rulers and those who are ruled. The roles haven't changed. Just the people who inhabit those roles."

I narrow my eyes in suspicion. "You're talking about the people of this world. You only know about the abuse of the *seen*. What about the abuse of the *unseen*?"

Her brow furrows. "The unseen?"

"The dark underbelly of voidance. Those in soteria. The enervated."

"I don't know what you mean."

I utter a grunt of understanding. Mander kept her in the dark, and it's no wonder why. If he had revealed the truth, he would have risked losing her. The truth destroys all of it.

I head toward the window I came in through and grab the setting of my voidstone. I remind myself that once I create the membrane, she won't be able to hear me.

"The effulgents were right, Marine. All along, they were right."

She stands half-leaning against the slanted wall, hands splayed out, almost as if she's falling into Blackscar.

"About what?"

"About everything," I say, not having the time to explain it all to her. "Just stay away from him. You don't want to be caught in the middle of what's about to happen."

"Dem, no. Whatever you are about to do, don't do it. You don't know how powerful he is. Just please go away. Disappear somewhere. You should never have come here."

I shake my head. "I'm going to kill him, Marine. If it's the last thing I do."

Reaching out, I gingerly touch the membrane in the open window with my free hand. It ripples in rainbows.

"That's impossible," she insists. "He's raised the voidstone, Dem. That's why he came for me, days ago, and why we fled the citadel. The time has come for something wonderful to happen."

"Something wonderful? What are you talking about?"

"A new kingdom."

I nod, not doubting it for a second.

"Well, I'm going to tear his new kingdom down."

Before she has a chance to reply, I grab my voidstone. A moment later, the curvature of my creation surrounds me.

I break through Marine's rainbow and head out into the storm.

# ON THE WAY

When I break through the surface, the daylight is far stronger than before. Through the curvature of the membrane, I see the fisherman almost fall off his seat in surprise, floppy hat in hand. He scrambles to the rear and grabs the anchor's rope.

I float over the boat and set myself down. Then I dissolve the voidance. Beads of saltwater fall like rain from a wind-shaken tree after a storm has passed.

I take a seat in the elevated front.

"Unnamed, landy! Nearly gave me a grabber!"

"You can start rowing back to shore," I tell him. "The faster you go, the more gold you'll get."

He positions his hat down over his forehead and pulls up the anchor. When he's done, he grabs the oars and turns us around. Because I'm sitting in the front facing backward, I'm looking out to sea.

Directly at the ring of ships.

They are still very far away, but the rising sun has burned the mist away, and now details emerge.

The anchor chains of the impressive galleons all descend at an angle into the middle of their circular formation. Almost like a massive spiderweb with something dark at its center.

*The Axiondrive.*

Marine wasn't lying. Mander's actually done it. But how does he plan on using the massive voidstone? What is the next step on his dark path toward this new kingdom?

Touching the setting around my voidstone, I contemplate using voidance to channel water around our hull to speed our return. But despite my friends' peril—in truth, the entire *world's* peril—I can't do it. It would make me a hypocrite. It would make me just like him.

I turn around to watch the approaching shoreline.

Above the beach and slightly to the west, the land rises via sandy cliffs. The largest mansions perch there, above the city, adorned with clay roofs and sun-warmed painted stucco. Outdoor terraces are lined with statuary and lemon trees.

There. The white one, the furthest on the plateau.

*Mander's estate.*

For a long time, I study it, listening as the oars hit the water, the fisherman grunts with exertion, and the seagulls cry.

When the pier is close, the fisherman stops rowing. He throws the oars in with a clang, and then we glide silently to the side of the pier, kissing it with a brushed sound. Once he has tied us up, I take out my bag of remaining gold and hand it to him. It's more than ten, but I don't count it, and neither does he. Covering his face with his hat, he collapses in the boat, clearly exhausted from the rowing.

Meanwhile, the rest of Winter's Baiou is finally waking up.

I leave the beachfront behind and walk up winding streets.

More people are about, most of them house servants, though a few soldiers patrol the area. After seeing my necklace and cloak, they offer respectful nods.

A few blocks in, I come to a market half the size of the park that contains the destroyed effulgency temple. Dozens of green-and-white striped tents cast shade over the merchants and their wares. Smoke trails from charcoal pits rise into the sunlit square.

As a result of the gradual incline, the strengthening sun, or the fact that I didn't sleep last night, I break into a sweat and suddenly feel weak. I'm ravenous. It's been far too long since I've had anything decent to eat, and with the smells of the market, my stomach grumbles with dissent.

Despite the urge to get back to my friends, I know I will be useless to them if I can barely stand.

A man with elephantine skin cooks fish and eggs over a charcoal pit. I am out of gold, so I offer him my cloak as payment. It is worth at least one hundred such breakfasts, and he knows it. There is nothing as black as this in the land—no squid ink or iron filings could match it. With raised eyebrows, he grabs it from me the moment I take it off and hands me a generous helping.

Standing under the green-and-white tent, I have my fill of fish and eggs. I eat with my fingers. With the morning breeze coming through my white undershirt, everything feels extraordinary. My strength returns, and not just from the food.

The giving of my cloak, while spontaneous, could not have been better planned. Without it, I can be anyone. I could be no one.

In some respects, nothing is new. Before we entered the city, I hid my cloak in the saddlebag. But its absence had been a disguise. Now it is my new skin. What was once temporary is now permanent.

I smile to myself. If Blythe were here, he would say that I am on the way of unwanting.

*And in my own way, maybe I am.*

Only the heavy necklace and the other stone in my pocket identify me in the way I never want to be identified again. But I need these voidstones to deal with Mander. Then, eleutheria.

There is no denying it. The end of voidance is near. The souls will soon have rest. His kingdom will never come.

As soon as I'm done eating, I take a narrow eastern road on the opposite side of the market. It follows a steep incline, but I keep my pace brisk.

The stone-and-stucco buildings on each side of the street rise two or three stories. Most of them press right up against each other. Every so often, a narrow alleyway populated with stray cats and dipping clotheslines provides separation. Windows are open everywhere, and I hear calm conversations as I pass.

This is a rich part of town and getting more so with every step I take. Nearly everyone on the street is a servant. I recognize their simple dress, putty-colored tunics, and unadorned sandals. They carry wicker baskets or clay pots, undoubtedly headed toward the market to bring back fresh food and wine—today's supply for their masters.

Once the ground levels off, the buildings and people begin to clear. There is no other way down into the city.

On the great plateau, without any buildings to cast shadows, the waxing sun hits me. Tall palms and low lemon trees dot the landscape. Only a handful of private estates remain nestled within this dead end.

It's oddly peaceful. There's no one about. It is almost a kind of wilderness, but what has grown wild here is wealth. The soft silence of luxury.

I stop as a memory surfaces.

Through the trees, a low stone wall sits to my left, and past that, the sandy cliffs drop down to the beach hundreds of feet below. Xi Bay glistens in splendor.

During our honeymoon, Marine and I sat on this wall. She would throw lemons off the cliff, each one a wish, and I would use voidance, throwing them back to her in jest.

I shake my head at the thought. Even before I knew the dark truth of voidance, I espoused its limited use. The idea of heinously wasting it by tossing fruit through the air is preposterous to me now. But that's what love does. It turns even the wisest man into a fool.

*It wasn't love. It was tephra. Black sand.*

I push the image of Marine away. She is lost to me. But these bitter memories do serve a purpose: they remind me that I continue to be a fool. My three friends are in danger because of me, and I can only hope that I'm able to somehow pluck them away from this place before Mander realizes that I am onto him.

A deep, repeating sound breaks the wispy silence, emphasizing my sense of dread.

*A galloping horse.*

Turning away from the wall, I look up the road.

Patches of Mander's white-stucco estate gleam in the sun a half-king's mile away. It lies shrouded behind lines of trees and within the vanishing point of the immaculate gold-tinged road.

A single soldier on horseback heads in my direction, leaving behind a cloud of dust.

Before long, I see that it's Reddles, riding alone. His star medal glints in the sun.

I remain motionless in the middle of the road, my hand ready to grasp the voidstone about my neck.

*Commander Reddles. Where do your loyalties lie?*

Has Mander been weaving webs of deceit since the sunrise? Does Reddles know the truth about him? Have they been working together all this time?

As he pulls the reins and dismounts, his angular features twist in concern. I'm glad to see that his hand is not on the hilt of his sword. As the dust cloud passes over me, he approaches and extends his hand in greeting, but it's shaking. This in itself answers most of my questions.

"Master Voider," he says levelly. "Are you aware of what's happening?"

"What do you mean?"

"It's your submaster."

My heart tightens.

"Tell me."

"I stopped by a halfbell ago. To discuss our report to the king. I thought you would be there." He clears his throat. "Anyway, I could see that Mander was not himself. He was annoyed by my presence. He said he was busy." His eyes dart from left to right. "We got into an argument."

"About what?"

"He wanted me to leave. He *ordered* me to leave, actually. Which he has no right to do, of course. Then he just . . ."

He shakes his head.

"What?"

Reddles puts his hand up to his mouth. "He used voidance against me. For a moment, I couldn't breathe. Like the air was pushed inside."

"He's the traitor, Commander. The man we're looking for."

Reddles looks down the road toward the half-obscured estate, as if he can see Mander from this far way. Then he turns back to me and nods.

"I feared as much. Standing there in the Celestium, unable to breathe . . ." His brow furrows. "I trusted him. *You* trusted him. You thought he—"

"I thought many things. But they were all wrong."

He fingers his star.

"Did you see my friends?" I ask.

He looks past the sheer cliff to the open sky then shakes his head. "No."

*Then where in Temberlain's Ashes are they?*

"I'm headed there now—to get my friends to safety. Why don't you come with me?"

"What?"

"I can't do this alone. We need to take down Mander. Right now."

Reddles points to the estate. "I am *not* going back in there."

His fear surprises me.

"Gather your men, then. The ones you trust with your life. We can take him down together."

He shakes his head. "I am sorry, but there is nothing swords can do against that man."

He bites his lip and blinks his blue eyes rapidly. I can tell that he's torn. He knows he is abandoning me, and his guilt is as obvious as bearing the king's banner.

"Master Voider, I have ridden into battle surrounded by the enemy, with the scorching sun beating down on me, my body drenched with sweat that blinded me behind my helmet. With the scent of blood everywhere, making my steed tremble under my legs. There is no battlefield that I fear." He swallows. "But this is not a battle of steel. There is no strategy to be had. That man raised a single finger to his stone, and I was powerless."

"I will protect you and your men."

He shakes his head as he walks away from me, and I run my hand through my hair.

Reddles climbs back atop his horse, the leather saddle creaking.

"The truth is, you are the only person in Winter's Baiou who can stop him," he says. "And if you fail, we're all doomed."

"Where are you going, then?"

"I need to warn the king."

The horse stomps its feet and moves slightly about in anticipation, whipping its tail. Reddles looks around warily in all directions, as if he doesn't trust a single thing left in this world. Then he turns back to me.

"May the Unnamed or luck be on your side. Because I don't know what else is."

*The enervated are.*

With a kick, he gallops away.

For a moment, I watch the billowing dust cloud he leaves behind. Then I turn and begin my long approach to Mander's estate.

Along the way, as the breeze off the sea hits me, I keep thinking of what Reddles said.

*If you fail, we're all doomed.*

I can't argue with his logic. It's just that I don't feel it.

I'm not thinking of everyone else.

I'm only thinking of Chimeline.

A quarterbell later, the patches of white have grown into a full facade. The vanishing point has become a front door as red as blood. But I don't go in.

*Reddles mentioned a Celestium.*

Instead, I take a narrow set of stone stairs nestled between hedgerows. It curves gracefully upwards around a fountain, up to a southern-exposed terrace lined with onyx statues of dead Xian heroes and potted tongues of fire.

A pair of glass-paned doors are open on the north side of the terrace.

*He must be expecting me.*

Cautiously, I step through into a massive empty ballroom lined with windows and mirrors. But I don't see any sign of voidance.

It's dimmer than outside, but not by much. My boots let out a single squeak on the parquet floor, which is so glossy that it looks wet.

Next, the ceiling draws my attention. The entire expanse is painted a deep shade of something not quite green and not quite blue. It reminds me of an emerald ring that Marine sometimes wore.

Against this field, the ceiling glitters with countless gold-leaf stars. In truth, I have never seen anything like it.

"Welcome to my Celestium," says an echoing voice, as the doors behind me close.

# THE CELESTIUM

I bring my gaze back down from the lofty, star-studded ceiling.

Mander stands all the way against the far western wall of the Celestium—at least one hundred feet from me. Maintaining the lie that has existed for as long as I've known him, he wears his cursed wig, but not his flaxen cloak. Instead, he has on a silken shirt and pants—nearly the same vibrant blue-green color as the ceiling. He's barefoot, and a voidstone on a thick gold chain hangs around his neck.

My three friends are in front of him. Colu, Chimeline, and Blythe all sit motionless on simple wooden chairs spaced about ten feet apart from one another. Their hands are behind their backs, presumably tied. Their faces are raised, and I can see the whites of their wide eyes. Their mouths look gagged.

In front of all of them—about a quarter of the way into the room from the western edge—a subtley shimmering membrane extends wall to wall and floor to ceiling.

"Star painter," Mander says loudly, his voice echoing. "Leave us."

At first, I don't know who he's speaking to, but then I hear creaking above me.

Bamboo scaffolding in the northeast corner rises thirty feet into the air. At the top, a wiry man with a paintbrush in his teeth looks down at us. The area above him is not emerald but a faded yellow—apparently the original plaster ceiling of this converted ballroom.

The painter descends with ease as I check my rising anger.

I can only surmise that Mander is theatrically displaying the three in a bound state on purpose. Everything in front of me seems calculated. Perhaps to elicit my emotions, or to prove that he is smarter than I am. Even though I had the enervated's help, he somehow found a way. He identified my only weakness and then exploited it.

The desire to call out to my friends overwhelms me. To calm them, especially Chimeline. To say that everything is alright—this would quell the emotion burning in my chest. But this would only prove to Mander that his plan is working, which I refuse to allow.

Mander paces back and forth, one hand scratching his wig, the other in his pants pocket. I try to read his body language as he waits for privacy. Is he scared or confident? It's impossible to tell.

The voidstone hangs heavily upon my neck, reminding me of my options.

I don't fear him. The scene in the park is proof enough that I don't need to. But I fear what he could do to the others. There is no guarantee that the enervated will help Colu, Chimeline, or Blythe. They let the effulgent in the bell tower fall to her death. I don't know the rules to this macabre game.

The painter reaches the parquet floor. He quickly shuffles past me, and I breathe in the pungent smell of fresh paint that accompanies him. Departing through the same door in the southeast corner that I came through, he closes it behind himself with an echoing *thud*.

"I have to be honest with you," Mander says, the moment the painter leaves, walking casually between Chimeline and Colu. He approaches his side of the membrane, both hands now in his pockets. "When I found out that the whore failed, and that you somehow trailed me south, I was shocked, to say the least. But now I understand. I should have foreseen your doggedness. This is you, Dem. This is all so very *you*."

As he speaks, something doesn't seem quite right, but I can't place my finger on it. I look around instead. My eyes follow the silver edges of his membrane.

It's possible that I could destroy it, but this would take precious time—time Mander could spend killing Colu, Chimeline, and Blythe.

And there is always the chance that I can simply walk right through it.

*Too many unknowns.*

I focus on the southern wall, to my left.

The door that the painter went through is not the only one. There are at least ten sets built into the southern wall, along the span of one hundred feet. Their bronze handles and hinges repeat against the white-painted trim. Each of them leads out to the terrace, but they are all closed.

Between all these doors are windows. My view of the terrace is almost as clear as if I were standing outside.

Past a cluster of potted tongues of fire and right up against the bronze-statuary-filled edge of the terrace, where the cliff drops to the shores of Xi Bay, something catches my attention.

A large cylindrical device rests on a brass tripod. Glittering in the strong sun, it looks identical to the one in the rogue laboratory.

"It's beautiful, is it not?" says Mander.

I turn back to him. He must have noticed my gaze.

"I call it my starglass," he continues. "It took me years to perfect the lenses. You wouldn't believe how meticulous a task it was. Even with voidance."

I refuse to reply, despite my curiosity.

"Don't you want to know what it does?" he asks me, playfully.

I don't answer.

"Of course you do, Dem. Your inquisitiveness is outmatched only by your stubbornness. Do not fear, I will tell you without you having to stoop so low."

He takes a deep breath and looks upwards. "It helps me find my way home."

I raise my head to gaze at the ceiling. It's a map of the night sky.

"You're a fool," I tell him, as I walk across the pristine parquet floor. "Your home is here, not somewhere across the stars."

He smiles. "Ah, you know part of the truth, then. But knowing *part* of the truth is more dangerous than knowing nothing at all."

"I know more than a part."

"Really."

I nod. "You are a descendant of the empowered."

He narrows his eyes. "How do you know that?"

"Is that what all of this is about?" I ask, approaching the center of the room while I reflect on everything that Blythe has told me. How Mander must have been born to an effulgent parent and somehow learned that he had the gift of voidance. He began speaking with the enervated in the void, but then something changed. A dark seed was planted before I ever laid eyes on him.

"You have lived a life of constant lies," I say, as the full realization comes over me. "Pretended to be one of us, studied at the university, became a submaster." I glance left as I walk, past the windows and terrace and toward the ring of ships barely visible in the glistening waters. "You created a war in order to raise the stone underneath Xi Bay. All just to get home?" I ask incredulously.

"No, Dem. Home is coming to me."

Clearly, he's not going to reveal more. My footsteps soften as I tread onto a circular handwoven rug. It's Xian-made—angular patterns and striking, contrasting colors amid the black and white.

A massive unlit chandelier hangs from the ceiling above me. An impressive desk with dozens of haphazard rolls of parchment and one large tome lies before me. Numerous candlestands. A brown leather chair. More sheets of parchment on the floor, weighed down by finial weights.

Running my fingers over a parchment and glancing at the writings, I realize that they are not in the common or Xian languages. They've been written in a script I do not recognize.

*The effulgency language.*

"What are your plans with the Axiondrive?" I ask, looking up.

His face is emotionless. "You answer my questions, and I'll answer yours."

"Alright," I answer. "What do you want to know?"

"For starters, how do you know all of these things?"

I press my lips together tightly and then look at Blythe. I nod in his direction.

"The *graycloak*?" Mander asks, his voice rising in surprise.

He spins and addresses Blythe. "You divulged secrets from the sacred texts?"

Behind the membrane, Mander walks over to him while shaking his head. "I am shocked, Graycloak. This is not on the way of unwanting. Not at all."

Blythe raises his head as Mander approaches, but he does not say anything—something seems to be stuffed in his mouth.

"Oh, that's right," Mander adds theatrically. "You're incapable of rebuttal at the present moment."

I take a few steps around the desk to get a better view.

No ordinary gag is in his mouth.

The same is true for the other two.

What immediately comes to mind are the black garden spiders in the hedgerows outside the Royal House. I can always see their webs in the early-morning dew. They're built on a level plane and, in the shape of a cone, descend into the dark greenery, where the hunter waits for its prey.

I step closer.

The sunlight coming through the windows interferes, causing a subtle radiance. A ripple of light. Only when I move can I see its design.

Directly in front of each of my friends, the surface of the membrane curves inward, like a massive cone whose point terminates in their open mouths.

Momentarily closing my eyes, I take a deep breath and tell myself not to fall into his trap. I will not be the prey of this spider.

Mander turns away from Blythe and faces me again.

"What else did he tell you?" he asks, his voice strong and level.

"Your people have been imprisoning the enervated for generations," I answer.

He brings a hand up to his curly hair and scratches it while cocking his head to the side. "*Imprisoning* is the wrong term. It's too . . ." He scratches his hair furiously. "Overdramatic."

"What term would you use?"

He purses his lips and then hunches his shoulders. "They are soulservants, Dem. It's their place in the nature of things. Our kind could not have crossed the stars without them."

"But to trap—"

"They're not trapped," he says, cutting me off. "They're preserved."

I fight the urge to laugh at his ridiculous statement. "Preserved?"

He nods. "The body is a cage. When the cage dies, we save what's inside before it has a chance to disappear. If anything, the enervated should be thanking us. We give them something close to immortality."

He sighs, perhaps with impatience. "If given the chance, Dem, what would you choose? To help a great people do great things forever, or to become nothing?"

Flashes of eleutheria enter my mind. The spheres passing through me. *A child playing on the beach. Two suns on the horizon. Her mother laughing, a red pail in her hands.*

When we briefly became one, I had the sense that they were going home.

"They don't become nothing," I answer.

He lets out a sharp laugh. "You sound like an effulgent."

"Is that a bad thing?"

Mander groans in annoyance. He scratches his curly wig again, more forcefully this time, before suddenly ripping it off. He plucks off his eyebrows.

"My, that feels better," he says.

One hand still grasping the wig, he rubs his suddenly bald head with the other. It's redder than the rest of his body. I see flakes—presumably dried glue—catch the sunlight as they flicker to the wooden floor.

I'm too shocked by his sudden change of appearance to say anything.

Mander walks between Chimeline and Blythe. He approaches the only other piece of furniture in the room, which is behind the membrane and pushed up against the north wall. It's an ornate vanity—similar to something Marine had in her bedchamber. Various bottles and supplies rest upon its marbled surface.

He flings the wig and eyebrows onto it and grasps his voidstone. Almost instantly, steam rises out of a white bowl on the vanity.

He picks up a nearby white towel, dips it into the bowl, and then wrings it out. The sound of dripping water fills the room.

"You don't know how good it feels to be myself again. After all this time. That ludicrous wig and stammer. I don't know which was worse."

*Stammer.*

That's what was off this entire time—Mander's speech. The words come out of his mouth fast and clear. His charade was fuller than I ever imagined.

While he's busy wiping his head with the damp towel, I step forward and study each of my friends.

It's amazing what their eyes convey. From Blythe, I pick up nothing. He is relaxed, taking even breaths and not looking at me. Chimeline looks petrified, her eyes reddened with tears. Colu's facial muscles ripple under his skin, and he blinks constantly. He's furious.

Mander neatly folds up the towel and places it on the table.

"Alright," he says, walking back up to the membrane. "Time for more questions and answers. This is why we're here, is it not?"

I mirror him, until I am inches away from my side of the membrane.

"It's my turn," I say. "What are you doing here?"

He smiles. "Restoring things."

"How?"

"If I told you, you wouldn't understand."

On the other side of the shimmering curtain, Mander looks both oddly familiar and utterly alien. An overwhelming desire comes over me to reach out, through the membrane, and choke him to death.

He smiles, as if reading my thoughts.

"I wouldn't touch it, Dem. With either body or voidance."

"You think I care what happens to me?" I sneer. "I would gladly end my life if it meant ending yours too."

He raises his hairless brow. "Oh, I know. But it's not you who will be torn apart." He motions to Colu, Chimeline, and Blythe. "It's them."

Mander takes a deep breath and then lets it out. The curtain between us ripples. He runs his palms over his breasts. "Do you feel that? The capacity to breathe?"

I don't answer him.

"My membrane is woven deeply into their bodies," he continues. "Where the throat divides and spreads out like the finest of tree branches, entering two spongelike cavities." He moves his hands from his chest and puts his palms together, fingertips toward the ceiling. "Do not worry your simple mind. My voidance still allows your friends to breathe, as long as you don't disturb the membrane. If you do, the entire membrane will snap back to the plane. If you use voidance to counter it, it will do the same. It will, quite literally, rip their insides out."

I lean to the side slightly, so I can see the light hitting the surface of the funnels where they enter their mouths. "It would have taken you fullbells to construct this," I say. "To weave the indivisibles. You wouldn't have had the time."

He smiles darkly. "It may have taken *you* fullbells, Dem. Not me."

"You're bluffing."

"Am I, now."

He separates his palms and raises his finger until it's a hair's length from the membrane, and I cannot help but breathe in sharply.

He laughs.

"That's what I thought," he says, lowering his hand. "You don't know what you believe. You're like this one-eyed soldier. Only seeing the half you wish to see."

As frustration builds within me, I grab my necklace and enter the void.

*Careful.*

The enervated are speaking to me, but I cannot understand them. Maybe they are saying that I have nothing to be worried about. *Destroy the membrane and then destroy Mander! End this now!*

Or maybe they are telling me that I am a fool.

Within the void, I cannot see through the membrane, nor can I penetrate it. It is an impervious wall, but I can follow its surface. I see the curvature of one of the depressions. Chimeline's, I think. I follow it down, descending into the cone, and then stop once I am deeply inside. The indivisibles are in front of me, branching as if I am buried within the trunk of a millionescent. Threads are stitched with a different kind of indivisible here, tiny knots similar to what comes forth from a weaver's loom.

Mander's membrane has literally become one with Chimeline's body, in all directions.

Slowly, I back myself out, feeling nauseous.

In despair, I ready myself to let go of my stone. Mander is right. His voidance is sound. The only way forward is to gamble, and if I'm going to gamble, it's going to be with *my* life. Not theirs.

I turn away from the cone and cross the smooth vertical surface of the membrane. But it is not vertical to me. There is no *up* here. I am a Northinglight falcon flying over a frozen lake.

I see something else, in my peripheral vision.

There's something in the north wall.

It's on my side of the membrane. Everything on the other side is smooth and colorless. Imperceptible. But on my side of the membrane, I can see everything. The dust in the air. The layers of paint on the north wall. The panes of mirrors. The smudges on them. Further and deeper, the lathes of plaster, the millions of nails, the wooden studs that frame the building.

There is someone standing behind the wall.

The shape of a person is indisputable. Glistening indivisibles. Light that is not light.

Inhaling sharply, I release the stone and return to the mirrored and sunlit world, but I make sure that I am not facing the north wall. I keep my head down for a moment as a bead of sweat falls down the bridge of my nose. I wipe it with my white shirt and then face Mander.

He nods to himself in smug satisfaction—as if he knows his voidance was so well-executed that I cannot unravel it. "Wise choice to leave it alone," he says.

"What do you want?"

"I want many things. But let's start with some information."

"Let them go, and I'll tell you anything you want."

He laughs. "I am no fool, Democryos. Even your dogged moralities are no match for the hatred that you must have for me." He sighs as he runs a hand over his smooth head. Already, it has broken out into a sweat since he toweled off, and his scalp is still as red as it was before.

He looks down at the perspiration on his hand and frowns.

Meanwhile, I risk a glance to the north wall, just to my right.

At first, I don't notice anything. No door. No handles or hinges. Only white-painted trim and mirrors.

But then I see it.

There is a slender vertical crack in the wall, between the white-painted trim. A single handprint upon a mirror pane. The parquet floor, slightly less polished. Dusty footprints leading into the wall.

*Someone is hiding behind it, listening to every word we say.*

I quickly turn back, before I give my thoughts away. But my mind still races.

"What information do you want?" I ask him.

Mander looks up from studying his hand. He leans forward and glowers at me.

"I want to know how you're still alive."

# THREE LIGHTHOUSES

Mander's green eyes glare at me from beyond the yellow-shimmering membrane as he waits for me to answer his question.

But I don't want to tell him the truth. It could be a strategic misstep to reveal the source of my power. It's the only thing giving me the upper hand.

The problem is, I cannot think of a lie that would fool him. And my friends' lives hang in the balance.

Eventually, my thoughts lead back to his twisted justification, and this is what allows me to make up my mind.

Mander said that the enervated are soulservants.

*If given the chance, Dem, what would you choose? To help a great people do great things forever, or to become nothing?*

There is no injustice in his world. Only privilege, and an ancient ruin that must be restored. A cryptic way back home. This is why I must speak the truth. Because the truth is the only thing capable of shattering these notions.

"The enervated are protecting me," I say.

He narrows his eyes even further. The ripples are pronounced, given the absence of hair. His head seems even redder than before. Droplets of sweat form everywhere the wig used to be.

Mander slowly shakes his head. "You're lying."

"No. I'm not."

He sighs as if he still does not believe me. "The enervated would never help a voider—they do not trust people like you. Besides which, you can't even speak their language." He smiles darkly and then begins laughing softly to himself. "You fools at the university thought that the enervated were winds in a cave. How could you possibly hope to commune with them?"

"We commune because we have a common enemy," I say.

His smile fades as he wipes his hand over his scalp. It comes away dripping.

Mumbling a curse to himself, he quickly steps over to his dressing table and grabs the same white towel as before. He touches his stone, and this time the rag begins to freeze and crackle. Steam emanates from it, but it falls instead of rises.

He gently drapes the towel over his bald head, exhaling in comfort.

"They're protecting me because what you're doing is wrong," I continue, while his eyes are shut. "They're helping me because I'm helping them."

"You have no idea what I'm doing, and you speak nonsense." His eyes are still closed underneath the edges of the towel.

"You asked the question, Mander. If you don't like the answer, that's your problem," I say. "Now, release my friends."

For a moment, he's silent. The steam dissipates around his face. Eventually, he opens his eyes, peels the cold towel off his head, and sets it back on the table, though not as neatly as before.

Then he walks back over to me, extending his hand through the membrane. It flexes around his fingers, like a glove of sunlight.

"I'm more than happy to," he answers. "Just hand over the two stones in your possession, and they're free to go."

I take a step back in surprise.

*How did he know that I have two?*

"I *feel* them, Dem," he says, as if reading my mind. He bares his teeth. "They belong to me."

"Let my friends go first."

"No."

"Then I won't give them to you."

He raises a hairless brow. "Are you sure you want to play this game? You know as well as I do that with a mere thought, I can paint this wooden floor with your friends' insides."

"Perhaps," I answer. "But your membrane will collapse. Which means that your insides won't be far behind."

He blinks rapidly, lost in thought, before grabbing his stone.

He doesn't even turn to face my friends, but all three cones of membrane begin to change. The shimmering funnels unravel so quickly that they seem to disappear, translucent threads fraying, snapping, shrinking back toward the vertical plane, like raindrops upon a still lake.

The remainder of the membrane still exists, but it is only a wall now. Ripples of yellow light cross its surface, moving back and forth from floor to ceiling and side to side.

Chimeline hoarsely cries out while Colu spits blood on the floor. Blythe only opens his eyes and takes a rattling breath.

"Dem!" says Chimeline. "Don't trust him—"

Mander grabs his stone again as Chimeline's eyes go wide. She nods and closes her mouth and eyes tightly, tears running down her cheeks.

"There," Mander says, releasing his stone once again. He unbuttons his sleeves and begins cuffing them up to his elbows. "As you can see, I am a reasonable man."

"That's not enough. I want all three of them out of here," I demand.

He shakes his head. "I can't do that yet, Dem. One step at a time. A stone for a life."

My eyes dart to my friends behind him as I ponder whether I should comply. He seems to want my two stones enough that I could demand anything.

"Don't do it," blurts out Blythe, staring straight ahead at nothing. "Think of the souls."

"Shut it," spits Colu, before meeting my gaze. "Just give them to him so we can get out of here."

I study Mander. His green eyes are bloodshot, which I hadn't noticed before. "If I give them to you, you'll let them go?"

He nods.

"Do I have your word?"

"Of course."

I lift my voidstone from around my neck and remove Anaxarchis' stone from my pants pocket.

"Dem, don't," says Blythe. His use of my name takes me off guard. He's looking at me now. "Please. You hold hundreds of lives in your hands. If you turn them over, you'll be condemning them to an existence of torment."

Both stones shift in my upturned palm. I bounce them gently a few feet from Mander's outstretched hand, deciding to use what bit of leverage I have for more information.

"I suppose you're going to use these to continue to raise that massive stone underneath Xi Bay?" I ask.

He removes his hand from the membrane.

"No, Dem. I've already done it."

I glance to the left, past the windows, at the ring of ships far away.

"It took over five hundred voiders. We fused anchors to the Axiondrive in all directions and hoisted it up."

"Out of Blackscar," I say, looking back at him.

He delicately touches his sweaty scalp again. It's almost beet red, but he seems to have no idea—he must not have looked yet at his reflection in the mirrored wall. "Damned clipping glue. That charlatan Worchot sold me rubbish," he mumbles to himself before looking up from his wet hand. "Yes. It was at the bottom of Blackscar," he says, wiping his hand on his pants.

"How did it get there?"

He looks at me with an expression somewhere between confusion and disappointment. "It crashed."

"I know," I say. "But what are the chances of, out of all places, it landing in one of the deepest trenches known to humankind? Unless it was put there for a reason."

He scowls, disappointment taking over. "No, Dem. The crash *created* Xi Bay. It *created* Blackscar."

This silences me, and he begins softly chuckling. "There is so much that you don't know."

"But why?" I ask, ignoring his insult. "It's not like you can build a new ship around it and sail back home."

He nods. "Correct. But I can *voidspeak* with it, over very large distances. That's why I had to raise it to the surface. When it was buried in the trench, the thousands of feet of water above it dampened the voidance. Made voidspeech impossible."

My eyes flash to Chimeline, and he notices this. "Yes, quite like I did with the whore. It's also how I communicated with Marine. But this voidspeech is different. It is across *the stars*. Only the Axiondrive makes that possible."

I stay silent, pondering the possibilities. Voidspeech is new to me. I cannot even comprehend doing it over the span of this room, let alone across the enormity of the sky.

"And this is the result of our discussions," Mander says, raising his voice while extending his arms toward the ceiling in beaming pride. "My map. My starglass. My people have been guiding me. Teaching me. Helping me look for what they call *pulsars*."

"Pulsars?"

"Lighthouses of the night sky."

I look up.

"This world is a rocky shore," he continues. "And they are lost at sea. Amidst the fog of history. The location of the pulsars is critical to my people finding me. Locating this *world*. They needed three of them."

I squint, picking out the details in the emerald-and-gold ceiling, so many feet above. Among the hundreds of painted stars, precisely three are much larger than the rest. A single gilded candle lamp hangs from each of them, unlit yet shining with burnished sunlight.

"A pulsar is a star?" I ask.

"Yes. A *type* of star," he answers. "And, while I would love to educate you on the makeup of the night sky, it's time that we get on with this. Hand over the voidstones."

Looking back down, I see that his hand is again extended past the membrane, clothed in shimmer.

"Let one of them go," I say.

He nods quickly, as if he'd been anticipating this.

With his other hand, he grasps his voidstone, and Colu's hands are freed from behind his chair. Colu lets out a deep groan and rubs his wrists, standing slowly.

"One for one," says Mander. He doesn't even turn to meet Colu's gaze. "You may leave."

Colu glances at me with his one eye. He cocks his head sideways, as if to ask if it's alright.

I give him a subtle nod.

Spitting once more onto the parquet floor, he looks around and then finds the patio doors to his right. Heading straight toward them, he leaves without a backward glance, shutting the door behind him. There's a deep echo. In my peripheral vision, I see his dark form walk the length of the patio, out of sight.

I throw Anaxarchis' stone to Mander.

The necklace flies through the air, passes through the membrane with a sound similar to wind chimes, and falls into his outstretched hand.

"Good. Good. Now the other one," he says.

"Let the others go," I say.

He bows his head while putting Anaxarchis' necklace around his neck, carefully laying the chain around his blue collar next to his other one. He puts his palms together, fingertips touching his lips and pointed toward the ceiling.

"You are a man of your word. It was always your greatest weakness, but perhaps now it is a strength."

He grabs one of the voidstones, and Chimeline and Blythe are instantly unbound in similar fashion.

Chimeline cautiously stands, but Blythe shakes his head.

She walks toward Blythe and places a hand delicately on his shoulder.

"I am not leaving," Blythe says.

"Blythe," I yell. "Get out of here. Take Chimeline with you."

He shakes his head. "I am sorry, but I cannot go."

"Neither can I," Chimeline says.

I grit my teeth. "You both need to leave!"

She looks down at the floor and shakes her head quickly.

"Chimeline . . ." I shake my head.

"What about you?" she asks, looking up at me with fearful eyes. "I'm not just going to leave you here."

"Stay then," Mander says calmly to her. "If you don't want to depart the Celestium, by all means, stand by your man. My membrane will not hinder you."

Breaking down into sobs, Chimeline runs over to me, creating yellow ripples as she passes through the translucent wall with the sound of wind chimes. She crashes into my arms, and I look over her shoulder at Blythe, who follows her reluctantly. He stops briefly and peers at Mander with a detached expression.

"Dem, your last fragment," says Mander, wiping away beads of sweat from the corners of his eyes.

I am about to throw my necklace, but Blythe, coming near, stands in my way. "Think about what you are doing."

"I'm saving your life," I say. "That's what I'm doing."

"A life is neither yours nor mine to save."

"Blythe, move aside."

I gently push Chimeline's body off me. Then I step around Blythe and throw my last voidstone through the membrane to Mander in a graceful arc. As he catches it, the entire membrane, from floor to ceiling, collapses like a golden waterfall hitting rocks.

As the sound of chimes fades away, the hazy shimmer between us is gone. I am left standing in front of a perfectly clear Mander bearing three voidstones around his neck. He seems suddenly taller, but something about him looks sicker as well.

"Get behind me," I softly tell Blythe and Chimeline.

Mander begins to chuckle. "I gave you my word, Dem. I won't kill them. But I'm sorry to say that the same doesn't hold true for you."

"The enervated will protect me."

The words come out strong, full of conviction. But deep inside, there is a sliver of doubt.

It's probably because I now bear no voidstone. The feeling of having no stone around my neck is one similar to that of being naked in a crowd. But it's liberating, too. I am no longer complicit in an ageless injustice.

My hope is that the enervated can still help me without it.

*May the Unnamed help all of us if I am wrong.*

He tilts his head in curiosity. "Still, you maintain the lie. Why?"

"Because it isn't a lie. And I want you to know that you will lose."

Mander laughs deeply, the sound echoing off the mirrored walls. "I'm the one holding the voidstones, you idiot."

"We performed eleutheria," I say.

His laughter abruptly stops.

"What did you say?"

"Eleutheria." I pronounce all five syllables.

Mander takes a deep, raspy breath, his chest rising and falling beneath the smooth fabric of his shirt. I hear the gold chains softly clang against each other.

"Where did you hear that word?" I notice his gaze move subtly from me to Blythe, who's standing behind me. "From the graycloak?"

I don't answer him, and neither does Blythe.

Chimeline grabs my hand from behind, and I gently squeeze it without breaking his gaze.

When Mander looks back to me, he flashes a snarl but then covers his mouth with a clenched fist. After a moment, he drops it.

"The one thing I will give you credit for," he says, "is your gift of voidance. For someone who didn't even know what it was, you were very good at it." He nods to himself. "So you discovered eleutheria. Without that tart of a wife to run after, your head must have been buried in your books. Even more so than usual."

I glance to the right, at the mirror-paned wall in the distance, wondering if the spy is still hiding there. Now that I don't have my voidstone, there is no way for me to tell for sure.

"What happened to the stone?" Mander asks.

I face him again.

"The stone?"

He nods.

Now it's my turn to smile, as I reflect on what Blythe and I accomplished in the ruins of the temple, underneath real stars instead of painted ones.

"Dem?" he asks, apprehensively. "What happened to my stone?"

I furrow my brow. "It wasn't your stone. It was Cleanthes'. He was one of my most talented—"

"They're *all* my stones!" he screams hoarsely. The red on his scalp has spread to his face. "Every single one of them."

I look at him curiously. "By what right are they yours?"

"They belong to the empowered. They were created for us."

I shake my head, not wanting to argue with him or delve into ancient histories. "Well, to answer your question, it rose," I say. "It floated away."

He lets out a guttural moan that turns into a scream. "You wasted an axion fragment, you fool! It is the most precious element in the universe."

I pause at the strange term, *universe*.

"No, Mander. What's *inside* of them is what's most precious. And what I did was only the beginning. When I'm done with you, I am going to free them all. Starting with the Axiondrive."

His face contorts into pure rage. Ripples form on his red, glistening forehead, creases extend from his eyes, and his thin lips stretch around gritted teeth.

He slides his hands down the gold chains and then grabs all three of his voidstones with both hands, over his heart.

The room begins to shake.

# A CIRCULAR RIFT

First comes fine dust, like snow from the Northern Kingdom.

I look up toward the painted ceiling.

Hairline cracks cross it from star to star.

Larger sections of the ceiling begin to fall, the brilliant blue-green replaced with patches of yellow-white. When they hit the floor, loud noises like a hammer against stone echo in the space. Clouds of white dust rise and billow in the still air.

Candles lean and topple from the gilded lanterns—the three lighthouses Mander mentioned. Then, a moment later, the bronzed lamp housings separate from the ceiling within the span of a breath. They fall thirty feet and crash onto the wooden floor, their metal panels and chains ringing out in the Celestium.

The ground vibrates so strongly it's hard to stand.

A staccato sound. The snapping of branches.

Between Mander and us, and from wall to wall—the very same place where the membrane used to be—the parquet floor buckles.

I turn and raise my arms protectively around Blythe and Chimeline. The enervated may protect me, but not necessarily my friends. I have no voidstone. I cannot weave a membrane around us. All I have is my body and my faith in others—two things that I am not used to relying upon.

I'm not sure what type of voidance Mander is mustering, but its scale is extreme. Any other voider would be close to voideath. Being empowered must make him immune to that check. Thinking back to how he knocked down the tower with ease, I know this is not an unreasonable notion.

*This Celestium is going to be destroyed.*

"Let's go," I say loudly, over the crackling and rumbling, while pointing to the southeast corner. "Over there. Stay as close to me as possible."

As a unit, we begin to leave the same way I came.

After a dozen steps—before we reach the center of the room—I look over my shoulder. Mander looks straight at us with his hands over his heart, clutching the stones.

A shiver courses through my body.

"Come on," I urge, turning back to my friends.

We've almost reached the center of the room when the chandelier falls from the ceiling.

Putting my head down, I pull Blythe and Chimeline toward me while trying my best to cover them with my body.

The thing is so massive—roughly ten feet in diameter—that when it crashes into the desk a few feet away from us, the desk splinters into pieces, sending parchments, dust, and shards of crystal and wood in all directions.

A cloud rolls over us. Even though I cover my nose and mouth with my white shirt, I begin coughing with the others. The pockmarked sounds of destruction surround us. Hundreds of crystals hit the floor and walls. The brief sound of hail.

I quickly gauge the three of us. Grime and plaster dust cover every inch of our bodies. Chimeline's hair is more white than black. Blythe's chest is cut—there's a small rip and a spot of blood on his light-gray shirt, but since he's not complaining about it, I don't bring it up.

The back of my neck burns. I reach back there, and my fingers come away red.

*There are limits to the enervated's protection.*

Chimeline looks at me with concern. "Are you okay?" she asks.

I nod.

"Turn around," she says softly.

"I'm fine. We need to go."

I urge us on. We stand and resume the path toward the exit.

"Dem," she says, her eyes flashing to my bloody fingers. "You're bleeding."

"It's fine."

While we stumble through the dust cloud, she snakes a hand underneath my shirt, and I feel her lift it away from my skin. It's damp and clingy.

"You need stitches," she whispers quickly. "This is not a small cut—"

Suddenly, the three of us are knocked to the ground as an earsplitting sound rings out, then a deep groaning.

When I fall to my hands and knees upon the Celestium's round center carpet, I happen to be looking west.

Over fifty feet from me, Mander is on his knees as well.

The ground between us falls away.

A dark rift, at least ten feet wide, cuts between Mander and us.

But unlike the membrane, this one seems curved.

And it continues to grow.

In my peripheral vision, dark lines are being drawn on the floor. Narrow, then widening.

Turning my head, I follow them as the ground continues to fall away in all directions.

He creates a wide circle around us, and its diameter is just short of the width of the room.

"He's trapping us!" I call out to Blythe and Chimeline over the deep rumbling. They're looking in all directions too.

Looking to the southeast, I see the rift hasn't formed there yet.

"We need to make a run for it!"

But before we can act, a new sound comes forth. It's treble filled. A high-pitched whistle.

The north mirrors crack into cobwebs. The entire wall, from floor to ceiling, from east to west, instantaneously shatters.

"Get down!" I scream.

Chimeline kneels next to me, oblivious. I grab her shoulders and pull her roughly to the ground.

Blythe covers her other half with his body, pushing her into the floor with me, as the crystalline whistling becomes louder and louder.

In my prone position, I turn my head past the tendrils of her thick, dust-covered hair and watch in dread and awe.

Every pane of mirror on the north wall. Every pane of glass on the south, east, and west walls. They're all the same now. All shattered and vibrating. Singing.

All at once, they launch at us from all directions, like a sunburst of sunlit daggers.

The high-pitched noise is deafening.

Instinctively, I close my eyes and bury my head over Chimeline's as I wait for the pain.

But nothing connects with my body.

Yet, I feel movement. The dance of air. An itch that I cannot scratch. My hairs stand straight up. My body breaks into a sweat, and then cool air washes over me, making me shiver uncontrollably. My body knows that every inch of it should be bleeding now, but it isn't, and it doesn't know how to react.

There is only so much glass in the room, so after a while, the vibrations cease. The hairs on my skin relax. The floor no longer shakes. The only sound I hear is that of chunks of plaster and panes of glass falling, like thunder and lightning in a departing storm.

I raise my body off Chimeline's, and Blythe does the same.

"Are you alright?" I gently brush back her mangled hair. Shards of mirror and glass like priceless diamonds fall away, revealing her face. It's covered in dust, but besides that, she looks untouched.

She opens her eyes and gives me a quick nod.

*We're fine. All three of us are fine.*

"Thank the Unnamed," I say, and I embrace her tightly, my hand on the back of her head.

Looking past her, I see that the field of glittering debris covers the entire floor except for the space directly around us. The sunlight coming through the south wall is reflected in it so strongly that I must squint.

I let go and rise to my knees, carefully grasping a handful of the pea-sized shards. They're razor sharp.

A gentle gust of wind hits me, and I look around.

There is no more glass on the walls. No more mirrors. No more plaster.

*No more wall.*

Even the delicate wooden trim is ripped to pieces. Only thick wooden beams remain, still standing straight. They are probably the only thing keeping the ceiling from toppling.

With the walls mostly gone, the wind comes through the room off the cliffs to the south. The breeze carries with it the scent of the sea: salty, musty, and bright. I hear the faraway cries of gulls.

Turning my palm over, I let the pieces fall. They hit the floor with a tinny, granular sound.

To my right, a woman inhales sharply.

When I turn around, no reflections greet me. Only unfinished wood and strips of dried glue against the remains of raw plaster.

And Marine.

She's standing in the Celestium, just beyond the circular rift, near the damaged periphery. She's still in the same white dress she wore in Temberlain's Ashes. Its color is in sharp relief against the dark hallway behind her, fading out of view.

Our eyes connect briefly, but her mouth does not close. I'm not sure who is more in shock.

I stand. A few shards of glass are stuck in the folds of my white undershirt, and I gently brush them off.

Mander makes a sound barely loud enough to echo throughout the space—something between a whimper and a groan.

I turn to him.

Half the room away, he still kneels, but his hands no longer grasp the three voidstones. They hang loosely at his sides. His head is as red as blood, and sweat pours from it. Drops hit the parquet floor. The wetness reflects the sunlight.

He puts his palms on the floor, his head bent downward.

"What's happening to me?" I hear him say.

Chimeline grabs my hand, and I glance back at her. She attempts to stand, so I pull her up. I brush her hair over her ear. Then I brush back her bangs to make sure that her forehead is uncut. The bangs fall back into place. She shivers, so I put my arms around her and hold her tightly.

"Your neck is still bleeding."

"I know."

Then, a moment later, she lowers her voice even further. "Who is that?" she asks into my ear.

Pulling back, I turn to the right. Marine stares at us with a blank expression. Her blonde hair is undone, and the makeup around her eyes is slightly blurred with tears, making her look disheveled and lost.

"That's Marine," I say.

She wrinkles her nose. "Why is she here?"

I shake my head. "I'm not sure."

Blythe stands with a groan.

When I face Mander again, he's still on his hands and knees, but he looks up at me, and I am taken by his eyes. Bloodshot white holes within dark recesses.

At first, I think that he is near voideath—he certainly created enough voidance to kill himself. But his symptoms don't match. His skin should be grayish-blue. He should be shivering uncontrollably.

What's happening to him is the opposite.

"Are you alright?" Marine asks him hesitantly, from her position near the north wall.

Mander barely glances in her direction, as if she were a servant.

"Mand?" she utters in almost a whisper, as she takes a few careful steps in his direction. She's barefoot, and some of the shards have made it past the wide rift.

*Mand?*

"No, I'm not alright." He spits. It looks like blood.

"Your face . . ." Marine adds with an outstretched hand, coming to a stop roughly ten feet away from him. Even though she's on the same side of the rift as Mander, she seems equally as severed from him as we are. Fear, uncertainty, doubt, sadness, opportunity—I have no idea what her dark chasm is made of.

"What is happening to me!?" he screams to the ceiling.

Chimeline lets go of me and takes a step forward. Pieces of glass crunch underneath the thin soles of her sandals.

"You deserve it, you monster!" she says.

Mander looks at her, his eyes narrowing.

Chimeline's hands have formed fists at her sides. They're shaking uncontrollably.

"Chimeline, what are you doing?" I ask softly, reaching out to grasp her arm, but she shakes me away.

"There is no antidote!" she screams.

Mander puts his hands on one of the three nearby chairs, trying to hoist himself up, but the chair begins to slide away from him.

"Antidote," he repeats. "Why would you say that?" he adds softly.

The chair continues to slip away.

"Help me," Mander loudly barks. He's obviously speaking to Marine, but he's not even looking at her.

Marine flashes us a dark look and then hastens over to him on tiptoes, weaving between shards. She puts a hand underneath his arm and helps him stand, but she arches her upper body backward, as if trying to stay away from him as much as possible.

And through that subtle stance of hers, I can see that whatever was once between them is now gone.

*It's all about the power. It has always been about the power.*

Marine never loved Mander. And she probably never loved me. She loved power and influence. Whoever held it, held her.

*But was I any better?*

My former self lived a life of entitlement. Lord Democryos, the master voider. I cringe when I think about the hideous title. When Marine sought me out, I took advantage of her, just as I took advantage of the enervated.

As I look at Chimeline standing in front of me, I see a woman who doesn't love me for my power. I see a woman who loves me in spite of it.

Marine screams.

Mander runs a palm over his head. Something comes away with it, along with the sweat. Because he's standing a good fifty feet away from me, I can't tell for sure, but it seems like a layer of skin.

Marine is barely holding on to him. She takes a step back, her arms stretched away from his.

As he studies the translucent film, his wince turns into a grimace of rage.

"Moonspit," Mander hisses, dropping his layer of wet skin on the floor with a soft splatter. "You put it in the glue."

"Yes!" Chimeline says loudly. "And I hope you rot from it!"

"Is that true?" I ask her in a hushed voice.

She gives me a distracted nod.

"How did you do that?"

"He was preoccupied with Colu and Blythe—making his membrane. When he wasn't looking, I poured it in his vial. Then the commander showed up."

Pushing Marine away, Mander stumbles toward his vanity, where he left his wig, bowl, and towel. Careening into it, he clutches its edge and peers into a hanging shard of mirror there.

"Mand?" Marine utters behind his back.

He ignores her.

Marine then pivots to us and approaches her side of the rift.

"What have you done?" she demands, her voice high-pitched and tight.

"What have *I* done?" Chimeline answers, taking another step forward. "I've given that monster the death that he deserves."

Marine's mouth is half-open, as if preparing to speak, but no words come out. Instead, she looks down into the darkness of the rift and then back to Mander.

"It will be slow and painful," Chimeline adds. "Just like what my sisters had to endure."

I step to Chimeline's side, gently grasping her shoulders. "You shouldn't be doing this," I whisper into her ear. "He still has the voidstones."

"I don't care," she says, tears falling down her dusty face. "I want him to know that it was me."

Mander takes the white bowl, full of water, and dumps it over his head.

It completely drenches him, turning his emerald shirt a darker shade of midnight.

"You're wrong," he snarls, turning back to her.

This seems to catch her off guard. She turns back to me in reticence. The only sound is the dripping of water onto the floor from his body.

"My power is the ultimate antidote. It can undo the damage you have done."

Mander then grasps his three voidstones.

Instinctively, I reach for mine and find only a soiled white undershirt.

Suddenly, Chimeline is pulled out of my hands and glides through the air like a marionette on a string, arms ahead of her and head tilted back. Dust trails off her body.

With a cry of surprise and protest, her body flies toward the rift and Mander.

I sprint after her, toward the edge, but she crosses it and then passes Marine's side before I take even a few steps.

In a heartbeat, she's in Mander's arms.

# IN SOTERIA

"I think a little retribution is in order," Mander says. "Wouldn't you agree?"

He lets go of all three voidstones, but he still absently touches the gold settings around his neck with one hand. He stares at the space where the southern wall used to be, as if contemplating his options.

In his other hand he squeezes Chimeline's writhing wrist.

I ignore his taunts and spin toward Blythe. "How is that even possible?" I say under my breath.

He blinks rapidly, but no word come forth.

I grab his shirt with both fists, getting his attention. "Blythe," I say, through clenched teeth. "How did Mander do that? I thought they were protecting us."

"The enervated *are* protecting us."

"Then explain what just happen—"

"You and I were both in the void together," he interrupts, his voice maddeningly calm. "We performed eleutheria. Chimeline was not there. They do not know her name."

"Her *name*?"

"Think of it as the signet ring of her soul."

I push him away.

"It is only a guess, Master Voider," he adds. "They have no reason to protect her in the way that they protect us."

"But she's *with* us," I protest.

"Not according to them."

Shaking my head, I turn back to Mander. He's regarding us in silence, probably content to see us quarrel.

"Let her go," I command.

But he holds on tight as Chimeline continues to struggle.

"Or what, Dem? Are you or the graycloak going to call down the enervated on me? Or maybe the judgment of the Unnamed?"

After I don't reply, he lets out a short laugh. "Your place in all of this is as a witness. You have no say in the matter."

*The bastard is right.*

The rift lies before Blythe and me. It's at least ten feet wide. Too far to jump across, even with a running start. There's a fleeting chance that a soldier like Colu could make it, but he's gone.

Looking down, I study the splintered midsection of the subfloor. Massive wooden trunks have been split cleanly apart, as though they were kindling. Below this is a maze of stone blocks—the foundation. And then soil, sand, and rock. Layers upon layers of natural rock continue into the darkness below.

Sounds of struggle draw my gaze back up. As Mander wipes his sweaty face with a shoulder, Chimeline lashes out in a frenzy, tearing away from his hold.

She's able to take only a few steps, toward Marine.

I know it's voidance at work, even if I don't catch him quickly clutching a black stone near his black heart.

A tunnel of wind snakes into the room, clearing a path through the glass shards that litter the ground, sending them in all directions.

Chimeline is knocked forcefully to the ground, and a moment later, Marine's dress flutters like a storm.

"I never should have given them up," I mumble to myself.

Blythe grabs my shoulder, turning me to face him. There's a cut on the bridge of his nose that I hadn't noticed before.

"Don't say that. It was the absolute right thing to do."

I extend my hand to the rift and whisper urgently, "But I can't do anything, Blythe. I'm useless."

"If you had them now, what would you do?" he asks with a raised brow.

"Isn't it obvious?"

He's nodding quickly as I speak. "Yes, but where does it end?"

"It ends here."

"No! There would always be another evil stain that you'd try to wash away with more evil. And *that* is the real trap."

I shake my head forcefully. "Not like this. If I had known that she was in danger, I would have never done it. I would have waited." I exhale in disgust. "Why are they allowing this?"

Mander yanks a screaming Chimeline off the floor. Blood gushes from her nose. He inquisitively picks up something next to her. A small dark object—perhaps a shard of glass. Then a second one.

"It is the Unnamed who allows evil to happen, not the enervated," Blythe whispers. "And if he is allowing it, then there is another way."

"Well, I'm going to find it," I say, walking away from him.

I follow the curvature of the island almost at a running pace.

I'm searching for anything to help me. A part of the chasm that is narrower than the rest. A wooden beam that hasn't fractured. Something to walk across. Roots to jump to and climb. Anything.

But there's nothing. The chasm is ten feet wide, no matter where I go. It's perfectly symmetrical and consistent in its design. We're trapped on an island within the center of the Celestium.

I quickly make my way over to the destroyed remains of the writing desk and chandelier. I rifle through collapsed drawers looking for a spare voidstone. But again, there is nothing. I could throw an iron finial weight at Mander, or perhaps spear him from afar with a wooden fragment of the desk. That's it. These are the options I am reduced to. Sticks and stones against a madman with inconceivable power.

As I storm back to Blythe, my eyes meet Marine's.

"Do something!" I urgently tell her.

She looks away.

"You have a voidstone!" I add, but my plea falls upon deaf ears.

Mander notices her dismissal, and it seems to fill him like wind in a sail. He stands up straight while grasping Chimeline again.

Then, holding up something between his thumb and forefinger, he speaks to me, almost absently, while studying it.

"Your ex-wife is smarter than you, Dem. She knows the difference between a nobody and a conqueror. She knew it the night she left you, and she knows it now."

Against the sunbathed western wall, I clearly make out what he's holding.

It's a large floorboard nail, longer than a finger.

Mander nods to himself, lets go of Chimeline, and then grabs his voidstone again.

The nail leaves his hand, flies through the air, and then darts downward, into Chimeline's foot.

A second one follows.

Her scream pierces the broken Celestium. It's a mix of pain and confusion. But all I hear is abandonment.

Chimeline's head is cast downward. The blood from her nose drips down her white shirt and dusty tan pants. She slowly squats down to the floor, her hands out to her sides, fingertips splayed wide to balance herself without moving her bound feet.

Marine turns to Mander, a look of shock on her face. "What are you doing?"

"Keeping her in place while I get to work," he answers, letting go of the stone and then wiping his reddened scalp once again, flicking the blood and sweat away.

Chimeline's screams momentarily subside. A lull between two cresting waves. She takes a few panicked deep breaths, as if she has been holding her breath underwater.

But then she tightly shuts her eyes and shifts her knees. Her squatting legs are in an awkward position and seem to be giving out. This forces her to check her balance again with her hands. Her sharp cries return.

There is nothing I can do.

"You're mad," I say, my gaze on Mander unflinching.

"Embracing the natural order of the universe is not madness," he says, while calmly regarding Chimeline. "It is common sense."

I shake my head, both confused by his continued use of the strange term and repulsed by his justification of such cruelty.

"Have the enervated taught you nothing?" I ask.

His chuckles turn into coughs.

"You laugh, but you know the truth," I add. "They would not protect me without cause."

When his coughing spasm ceases, he purses his lips and puts his two hands to them, almost as if he's praying.

"You are right. They *are* protecting you. Even without your voidstones. You would be dead by now a hundred times over if they were not. But their protection can only go so far." He drops his hands and points a finger at Chimeline. "This whore, she does not seem to share that protection. Apparently, she's nothing to them. A nobody in this world and the next."

"Mand?" pleads Marine. "Let's just go. You need to heal yourself."

He drops his finger. "Yes, I do. But this will all be over in less than a quarterbell, when I have opened up a doorway."

"What doorway?" Marine asks.

"A doorway of retribution. They stole from me, and now, in return, I will steal from them."

Marine furrows her brow and motions to Chimeline's feet with a look of revulsion. "But this is unnecessary—"

"This is what she deserves!" he snaps. Pointing to me, he repeats, "They stole from me!"

I close my eyes in disbelief once I understand what he's referring to. "One cannot steal what is not owned," I say.

"Well said," mumbles Blythe at my side.

"You will come to learn how wrong you are."

After carefully taking off one of his voidstone necklaces, Mander places it on the floor. It's stone-side up, a good ten feet from his side of the rift and only a few feet away from the weeping Chimeline.

Then he backs away, nodding to himself, and slowly settles down to the floor, legs crossed.

"This is something I planned on teaching you one day," Mander says to Marine, who stands many feet away. "But now is as good a time as any."

She takes a step closer while Mander looks to Blythe and me.

"In soteria," he says.

Blythe inhales sharply.

I glance curiously at him before looking back to the sitting Mander.

"You promised that you would let my friends go," I say.

"I did," he replies. "But that was before you revealed your indiscretion." He slowly shakes his head. "Eleutheria, Dem. How could you?"

Blythe falls to his knees. "Not this," he mumbles. "Anything but this."

I look to Blythe, my gaze lingering this time. "What is he doing?" I ask him.

Blythe doesn't answer.

Mander grabs one of the two remaining voidstones around his neck. The one on the ground instantly glows a soft white. It almost resembles the butter-yellow sunshine beyond the western wall.

"Blythe, what is Mander doing?" I ask, under my breath.

"I am sorry, Dem," he answers. He closes his eyes and bows his head. "I am so sorry."

I step even closer to the rift. The tips of my shoes hang over the abyss. Glass shards and dust fall away into darkness. "Mander!" I shout.

His smile deepens as he puts a finger to his lips with his free hand. He looks toward me but not at me, like some blind beggar from the Second Ring. "Time to concentrate."

A deep rumbling begins.

"Mander!" I repeat, my voice a roar.

But the bastard doesn't answer.

When the echoes of my shout fade, only the deep rumbling remains. It grows stronger, although I find it strange that the ground at my feet is not shaking. There is no feeling to match the sound.

But across the rift, the wooden floor *is* reverberating. Glass shards dance upon its surface, Chimeline cries out anew as she struggles to stay balanced, and a small section of floor near Marine falls into the abyss.

Squinting, I look back at the white voidstone.

It's grown in size.

No—it's changed shape. Flattened.

*It's done both.*

The gold setting and chain are half buried underneath its surface, which has turned into a liquid about one foot in diameter. A thick white gold, rippling and pulsing, as if it were being poured out of some blacksmith's crucible.

*The voidstone has melted.*

Then, another sound from behind me. Above the deep rumbling. It's high-pitched. Squeaking and dragging.

I turn around.

It's Colu.

He's in the northeast corner pushing the painter's scaffolding across the floor with all his might. His body is bent over, head between his arms.

I slowly raise my gaze, following the scaffolding toward the Celestium's ceiling.

It must be thirty feet tall.

*Thirty feet long.*

"Blythe!" I say. I put a hand on his shoulder and give him a shake, but he's lost in prayer.

Leaving him and the western rim, I run east, past the rug and destroyed desk and chandelier, to the opposite side of the island.

Across from me, Colu has already pushed the scaffolding a good twenty feet away from the corner, in my direction.

He stops with an exhale.

Raising his grip on the bamboo stalks to a spot above his head, he begins to rock the entire contraption back and forth in slow and smooth motions. It follows his movements in a series of cascading creaks and groans. The hanging rope and bucket jangle wildly.

After five or six repetitions, Colu suddenly puts all his weight into it. The easternmost legs rise from the floor.

He squats, feet wide apart.

Grabbing the base from underneath, he lifts the edge with a deep scream, the veins on his neck rippling.

*He's doing it. It's going to fall over.*

I back away and to the side as the entire tower of bamboo and wooden planks leans perilously and then topples through the air.

It easily crosses the ten-foot rift and crashes into the island with many feet to spare. The sound reminds me of the chandelier falling—it's earsplitting, and it takes a long time for the echo to fade and the dust to settle. The bucket had been filled with emerald paint, which splatters across the parquet floor. Most of the large wooden planks on the scaffolding fall into the rift, but the bamboo shafts remain.

*It's a bridge. A shaky one, but a bridge nonetheless.*

"Come on!" Colu says to me over the rumbling. He's on the other side, motioning me forward with a waving hand.

I look back.

Blythe is still kneeling, head in his hands, oblivious.

Past him, beyond the western rim, are Mander, Chimeline, and Marine. Mander sits with his legs crossed, lost in the void. His face, still red and glistening with sweat, is awash in white light. But shockingly, an impervious calmness permeates it despite the chaos all around him.

The melted voidstone in front of him is brighter and larger, as if it's thinning even more. It's become a puddle of pure light. I need to look away. And once I do, a phantom black spot floats in my vision.

"Dem!" Colu shouts at me from behind. "What are you waiting for?"

Blinking the spot away, I squint and look at Chimeline, holding a hand out to shelter me from the light. The air is distorted.

She's still huddled on the floor, head cast downward. Despite the radiance mere feet away from her, her face is hidden from me, concealed behind a curtain of dark hair. But then she looks up at me with an expression that breaks my heart. She mouths a single word.

*Go.*

Gritting my teeth, I turn back to Colu.

"I'm not leaving her," I tell him.

Before he can reply, another deafening crack pierces my ears above the rumble, and Colu's mouth opens wide. He looks past me and above.

I spin around and catch something unbelievable.

The southern wall splits in two.

From floor to ceiling. Even the ceiling tears apart where it meets the wall. Sunlight from above pours in. It's like dusk compared to the intensity of the melted voidstone.

The encircling rift cracks open further and a line juts southward, a black canyon, a rushing river to the sea.

The patio falls away.

Mammoth squares of slate and bronze busts of men long dead topple to the beach hundreds of feet below. Entire lemon trees lean and disappear. The entire area past the southern wall collapses.

Only blue sky remains. And Xi Bay beyond.

"We don't have time!" Colu yells above the roar.

I turn back to him. "I'm not leaving her."

"Then you're going to die with her!"

"Just go!" I tell him.

"I came back for you, you stubborn son of a bitch!"

Everything becomes silent.

Absolutely silent.

The reverberations cease, and the only remaining sound is the wind. It comes off the sheer cliffs, peeling through this husk of a room. A few birds flutter in the jagged opening above us, perching on splintered beams. There's a rustle outside as more bushes give way. Another shaving of bluff meant for the sea.

"It's time," Mander says.

Chimeline lets out a short and meager scream.

In the stillness, I hear the bright rattling of nails on the floor. I catch Mander briefly clutching his stone once again.

Chimeline fully collapses, letting her feet finally stretch out, now that the nails are gone. She brings them into her chest in a fetal position as she whimpers softly.

The melted voidstone sits directly between Mander and her. It's just as bright, but undulating now, casting white-tinged moving shapes in all directions, as if we're underwater. It resembles a glowing tide pool two feet in diameter.

Mander remains sitting on the floor. He looks exhausted—whether from the moonspit or voidance, I cannot tell.

He glances curiously at Colu and the scaffolding and then at me, as if all these new developments are of no significance at all.

Unaffected by the strong light, he extends both hands toward the glowing pool in front of him, looking upon it in beaming admiration.

"Come close and look, Marine. It is most beautiful now, when the doorway is first opened. While it is stable."

She doesn't move forward.

A few steps behind the huddled Chimeline, she wears an expression that is not one of admiration. Her face is turned away in revulsion, brow furrowed, neck pulled back.

Mander glances at her, sees her reticence, and then exhales.

"So be it. It is your loss."

"I *am* interested," she answers.

She looks up to the destroyed ceiling, as if searching for the words. "Just not like this."

Mander's grunt is the only acknowledgment of her reply. "It will lose stability soon and will eventually collapse back into its natural state. But for now, the doorway is wide open. In a fragment this size, we could fit countless souls." He shakes his head. "It seems that it will be only one today. Such a wasted opportunity."

"You shouldn't be doing this to an innocent woman," Marine says.

"She's hardly innocent," he snaps. "She tried to kill me."

But Marine clenches her jaw. "This is wrong."

"This is *necessary*," he replies harshly. "Where do you think your power comes from? Your place of privilege in this world?" He points up at her from his sitting position. "For you to say that this is wrong, you are like a queen refusing her throne. And what a stunning queen you would be, if you only had the courage to envision it."

A groan echoes throughout the room.

"Quickly, now," Mander adds. "Push her in."

"She's in pain."

"Then remove her from it! Pain is only of the body. Pain is only of this world."

I watch as Marine cautiously steps forward. She stands over Chimeline and then stoops, grabbing her limp arm with one hand while seemingly caressing her black hair in the other.

I almost can't bear to watch.

Marine whispers something in Chimeline's ear.

Meanwhile, the area around the pool seems to be darkening.

At first, I think it's the undulation of the white light. A trick of the eye. Simply moving shapes, underwater shadows.

But then, I realize that the area surrounding the pool *is* darker than the rest of the room, even though it should be the opposite. It should be bathed in light, but it's cast in shade.

Directly above the glowing pool, the air is hazy and curved. Translucent tendrils, almost imperceptible, are being pulled inward from every direction.

*The voidstone is swallowing the light.*

Another groan fills the room, and this time the ground shakes violently. Even I can feel it on the island.

Marine stands up straight. She's visibly shaking. "No," she says, her voice surprisingly level and confident. "I won't help you in this."

She wipes her face with the back of her hand. In the shadowy light, I see a tear fall down her cheek. It looks like a droplet from her diamond earrings.

Mander lets out a guttural sound. He tries to get up from his cross-legged position, but he can't seem to stand on his own. So he begins crawling around the pool, across the floor, to Chimeline.

"Dem!"

I turn around.

It's Colu.

Across the rift from me, he points to the bucket of spilled paint at my feet, tied to the thick rope. It's caught within the bamboo stalks that cross the rift, all the way to his side, where it's wound and knotted up.

He's untying it from his end.

*The rope.*

I pick up the wooden bucket. It's coated with wet blue paint that covers my hands as I grab it. There are holes set into each side of the thick rim, where the rope is bound.

I pull hard.

The rope snakes around some of the bamboo scaffolding, getting caught, but it comes away once Colu unties the knot on his end. Within no time, I've got a coil of rope in my hands—about the time it takes for Mander to reach Chimeline.

He grabs her thick black hair, pulling her toward the glowing pool.

Chimeline screams hysterically while fighting back, blindly clawing at Mander's face and body. Her hands find purchase on one of his blue shirtsleeves—it rips clean off at the shoulder and falls off his arm.

It's sucked sideways, into the pool. As it connects with the liquid, it disappears in an intense flash of light.

Her protests aren't working. Despite Mander's fatigue, he is still stronger than she is and is dragging her toward the shimmering white.

It's only a few feet away.

"Stop it!" Marine yells, hands to her head.

I stand at the edge, ready to throw the bucket, but there's no way Chimeline can grab it. She's fighting for her life.

Minor flashes of brilliance are happening now, like staccato pinpricks of lightning in a darkened storm cloud. It's from the smaller bits of glass lying nearby. They're all being pulled in. The two dark nails that were driven into

Chimeline's feet slide across the floor and disappear in two pulses of white.

Surrounding all this are countless tendrils of black.

With a pang of exertion, Mander again pulls Chimeline's hair with both hands. His head is bloodred and glistens with sweat and reflected light. Her straight black tendrils are sucked toward the glowing pool—they look almost like the dim contrails, only more vivid and opaque.

One of Chimeline's hands is on his face, fingers clawing at his eyes. Her other hand is on the floor.

It touches the pool of light.

She immediately turns white, a flash of lightning. And then she begins to scream.

But this scream is different. I've heard it before. It's muted, higher-pitched, distant. A voice in a cave through the storm.

*Good Unnamed. It's the wind. The sound in the void.*

As I drop to my knees, the room snaps in two.

The entire western side of the room—the section where Mander, Marine, and Chimeline are—drops away from view, sliding down about ten feet. It suddenly lurches and stops with a painful and drawn-out cracking and splintering sound. The ceiling is rent perfectly down the middle, separating the two sides of the Celestium.

I've lost sight of the three, so I stand and run forward to the edge.

They have all been knocked to the floor, which is now at an angle. The southern, left side is higher than the right.

Chimeline's hand no longer touches the pool, nor does she glow white. She lies on her back, mouth open, one hand clutching the other hand over her heart. It looks as if she's struggling to breathe.

Next to her, the undulating white pool of voidance begins to spread, turning from a circular shape into an oval.

It's following gravity, as any pool would.

Headed away from Mander and directly toward Marine.

The room shudders again.

*Now.*

"Chimeline!"

Her wide eyes lock on to mine as I swing the rope.

"Grab it!"

The bucket acts as a perfect weight. As it leaves my hands and I loosen my grip, the rope snakes through.

The bucket crosses the ten-foot rift and falls at least the same distance until it hits the parquet floor on the other side, perilously close to the shimmering pool of voidance.

It skitters a bit, just out of Chimeline's reach, and starts to slide and spin to the right.

Marine lunges for it, dropping to her knees to grab hold of the bucket before it has a chance to fall back into the rift. She then shoves it into the hands of Chimeline, who is still prone on the floor, as if in shock.

Mander grabs one of the voidstones around his neck.

"I said *no!*" Marine shouts. She grabs her own necklace as she steps between them.

But Mander is too fast. His voidance arrives first.

It must be the same technique he used before. A violent gust of air, forced from above, toward Chimeline.

Only this time, Marine is standing there instead.

Instantly, she's pushed to the ground and forward. Right onto the elliptical puddle.

Her body goes in. Underneath. To her lower waist. As if she's washing her hair by the riverside, only screaming while doing so.

For the briefest of moments, time stops.

As Chimeline's did, Marine's body turns a painful white, but it's more than just a flash. Eventually, I need to look away, and when I do, her black figure haunts me.

The cracking and splintering sound returns.

It's cleaner. Not drawn out. A ripping note of finality carried in it. Such silence afterward, as if there is nothing left to fight for.

"Chimeline!" I yell in my blindness. "Grab hold!"

*Please.*

Before the words leave my mouth, there is a weight in my hands. A weight that makes my soul lift in ecstasy.

But the paint makes my palms slippery, and the rope slides through my burning palms.

I fall to the ground and begin sliding off the edge.

Someone grabs hold of me.

*The enervated?*

*No. Colu.*

*Blythe.*

An arm over my shoulder.

Hands on my feet.

"Pull!"

I am blinking, frantically trying to see, but the only thing in front of me is Marine's haunted silhouette. A black shape against blue sky.

My hands burn, but I keep pulling. The pain is all I have to give. I keep pulling until the weight is lifted.

A void.

An indivisible in my arms.

*Sunlight.*

There is nothing but sunlight.

# FAITH IS WRAPPED IN SILENCE

I don't take a breath until we cross Colu's bridge, which happens not a moment too soon.

The center island breaks apart and falls away toward the beach in a similar fashion as the western side. The Xian rug, desk, chandelier, even the remains of the scaffolding—all of it snaps off and disappears from view the instant we climb off the bamboo.

As I listen to the ensuing distant rumble, I can't help but think of the timing of it all. The Celestium's collapse and our return to safety. It seems too close a call to be coincidental.

The others seem to be thinking the same thing. Blythe immediately gets on his knees. Like me, Colu sits on the floor. He adjusts his black eye patch. "If that's not kismet, I don't know what is."

Against the blue sky, Marine's burned-in silhouette is replaced by the living form of Chimeline, who collapses in my lap. The smell of her sweat and lingering orange perfume comes over me. Her skin is slippery, making me clutch her even tighter, as if she still dangles perilously over an abyss.

"I'm so sorry," I whisper into her ear. The wind blows her hair around me, so I pull back. "I didn't know they wouldn't protect you. When I gave the voidstone away—"

"It's alright," she answers, placing a hand on my cheek. "They know now. They know my name."

Her cryptic answer takes me by surprise. "The enervated?"

In the middle of her nod, her skin begins to glow like pale moonlight.

"Chimeline?"

Her eyes roll into the back of her head and her mouth opens slightly, as if in ecstasy. Her body goes slack in my arms, and I quickly adjust my grip to prevent her from falling backward.

"Chimeline!"

I grip her shoulders tightly and give her a shake.

Her head bobs forward, black hair glowing white.

"What the . . ." Colu says, standing up in panic.

My heart tightens. She seems lost to me again. After everything that transpired in this room, I was beginning to hope that she was safe.

My only solace is that she's not in pain. This is not Mander's voidspeaking at work. It's the opposite—she seems incredibly at peace.

I slowly lay her down.

"Blythe," I call out. He's lost in prayer, so I nudge him in the side, which gets his attention. "Do you see this?"

He raises his head, eyes fluttering. "Good Unnamed."

"What's happening to her?"

He shakes his head. "It looks like soterian light. Only not as strong."

"She touched the pool," I add. "Briefly. With her hand."

"I saw." Blythe crawls forward, squinting while analyzing her. He runs his fingers down her arm and then her body. When he reaches her bare feet, he touches them delicately. "They have healed her," he whispers.

I look at her feet. He's right. The wounds from the nails have vanished.

"Is that what the glow is from?" I ask. "They're healing her?"

"I don't know."

"Hey," Colu says loudly.

I look up.

He stands at the edge of the cliff, peering west, out to sea.

We both look at him.

"That fucker is getting away." He spits into the open sky. "Somehow he survived the fall."

"The empowered?" Blythe asks, his head lifting.

Colu nods and points. "He's on the beach."

"Let him go," I say. I cup Chimeline's ghostly face with my palm. "He can only run so far."

Tears are in my eyes. Maybe it's the brightness.

Blythe is correct—her glow is not as strong as the pool's. I can make out the details of her body. Her eyebrows. Lips. Clothes. Fingernails. When Chimeline momentarily touched the pool, she turned into a pure silhouette of white. The same thing happened to Marine, except Marine's body sank. And then the island broke off.

*This is somehow the same yet different.*

I want to slap her across the face to try to force her out of this stupor, but I can't bring myself to do it.

It doesn't even look as if she's breathing.

I bring my face very close to hers, to check. I can feel her warm exhales on me, and then I part her bangs and give her a soft kiss on the forehead.

She stirs.

Her eyes blink rapidly as her body reawakens. She sits up suddenly, putting her arms around me and clutching my back with her fingernails. They tear at my wound there, but the pain is pure joy to me.

She has returned. The moonlit glow has vanished.

"We must hurry," she says, pulling away while biting her bottom lip.

Her face is soiled with dust, sweat, and dried blood. But I cannot help but stare into her dark eyes, another abyss, captivated by the fairness of her flaws. It rips my heart open that I let so much damage be done to her, and yet she doesn't blame me. She has never once blamed me for anything.

"Hurry where?" I ask.

She puts her hand back on my cheek. "They say you must jump."

"Jump?" My eyes dart toward the edge.

We're on a sheer plateau facing west. Under the open sky. White gulls circle above, perhaps as shocked as I am.

Behind and above us is the Celestium—or at least the eastern remains of it. A pinnacle of Winter's Baiou's splendor, split straight down the middle. In front of us is Xi Bay.

"You mean off the cliff?"

She nods. "Yes."

Chimeline rises to her feet and urges me to stand, which I do. Together, the three of us approach Colu by the precipice.

Far below—at least a few hundred feet—is the beach, littered with ruins. The emerald paint speckles the shore like colorful rocks, its gold flecks reflecting the midday sun. Splinters of wood have already been dragged out to sea. Dust rises from it all, like smoke from a dying fire.

A gust of wind buffets the shoreline. The cloud of dust is torn apart into miniature cyclones that curl while fading away. This reveals a small untouched area of beach. It is perfectly clear, devoid of any ruins. Pure-white sand.

And a pure-white dress.

*Marine.*

My three friends must see her at the same time as I do, as I hear everyone take in sharp breaths.

Chimeline turns into my chest.

I furrow my brow, doubt and hope colliding.

The way the area of beach underneath Marine's body is unblemished indicates that she was contained in the same membrane of voidance that safely held Mander. Her body touched down upon sand as soft as a feather.

"She might still be alive," I whisper to no one in particular.

"No," Chimeline quickly says, her voice muffled against my chest. I feel the meager shaking of her head. "I'm sorry, but the cage has been opened."

"She was in Mander's membrane." I point downward. "There is not a mark on her."

She keeps shaking her head. "I was going to tell you, but she says that the time for mourning is not now. She wants us to hurry."

*She?*

"Did Marine voidspeak with you?"

After a moment of silence, I gently raise Chimeline's head in my hands and make eye contact with her. "Did Marine speak to you?"

Chimeline nods once, very subtly, almost as if she's embarrassed.

"How?"

"Dem," Blythe interjects, leaning in. "Did you not see the woman fall into the white pool of axion? She must have been pulled into soteria."

My eyes lock on Chimeline's. "So were you, but you're still alive."

"I barely touched it," she replies, blinking once. "I was lucky. Marine was not."

I exhale deeply and bow my head. I bring Chimeline's head to my chest again as I stare at the distant body.

"Was she dead before she hit the ground?" I ask, swallowing hard.

"It would seem so," Blythe answers. "Putting anyone in soteria would kill them immediately. This is a horrible act of wanting. Her mortal life was never his to take. But the continued enslavement of her soul is the far greater crime."

I sharply raise my head. "You mean that her soul is now in one of his voidstones."

"I'm afraid so."

It takes me a moment to comprehend what Blythe is saying. It's the most obvious conclusion, but it still doesn't seem real.

When I learned about the enervated, they were strangers to me. A distant people. During eleutheria, I saw through their eyes when their shapes passed through me. Memories in the white room. Flashes of their short mortal lives prior to being placed in soteria.

That experience changed me forever, but the souls were still strangers to me. Like how a child in the womb must be to an expectant father—priceless, yet unshaped. Unknown and certain.

But now? The idea that Marine—someone I loved for years—is trapped inside one of Mander's voidstones seems too cruel to be true.

A gust of wind hits me.

I become enraged by both the sight of her body and the absence of what remains. Two crimes, one visible and one unseen.

It's not a burning rage, as when Chimeline was tortured and I could do nothing. This is a rage of loss—something frigid, bruised, and empty. My wife left me for Mander because she was following something that was not quite love. She had thought that Mander would lead her to greater things. Gilded heights.

And now her dead body lies in the sand. An opened cage.

When I met her, her youth was an attractive quality. Her beauty could have taken her anywhere. Now, all I see is the other side of that hideous coin. Gullibility. An innocence exploited.

The tide rises slowly. The waves start to reach her, pulling her away to a place she always loved.

My gaze eventually leaves Marine and follows a set of footprints down the length of the shoreline. It looks like a trail of ants.

Even though he's hundreds of feet away, there is no mistaking Mander. His bald head is visibly red, and his brilliant blue shirt and pants are torn to shreds. The way he's walking is even clumsier than what sand would impose. As I watch, he falls to his knees and then scrambles back up again, arms flailing.

*He's in a hurry.*

Colu points further ahead. "He's headed for that sloop."

Far in the hazy distance, a red-painted pier juts out from the beach like a congealed scar. There are a few smaller fishing vessels tied up there, and a single-masted ship.

"He's moving slow, but we can't get to him before he reaches it. Unless you have one of those stones left on you."

"I don't," I answer. "Nor will I ever again."

My gaze continues westward, out toward the bay.

The cobweb of ships and anchor chains lurks in the distance, with the Axiondrive in the middle.

"Dem?" Chimeline says softly.

I turn to her.

"I know this sounds crazy, but you must jump."

My rage is doused with sadness as I touch her shoulder. She is surely thinking back to when we were in the citadel, in front of the Royal House. The night we first met. In the moonlight, we jumped off the stone wall together. It was when I was still following a man in shadow and the stain of black pitch.

"I wish I could, Chimeline, but I can't do what I did in the citadel. I don't have a voidstone."

She looks down, past the precipice.

"No. But *she* does."

I follow her gaze. Marine's body is so far away, I can't make out that level of detail. I doubt that Mander would have forgotten to take her stone, but it makes no difference.

I turn back to her. "Voidance doesn't work like that. I need to touch the stone in order to work it. By the time I reach it, I'll be dead from the impact."

She shakes her head forcefully. "No! Not *you*. *Them*."

"Them?"

Chimeline flickers into a glow again. Blythe, Colu, and I all frantically grasp her, pulling her away from the edge as she collapses to the ground. But by the time she's lying down, the glow has already faded.

"Aim for Marine." She exhales. "The voidstone. We will slow your fall."

"Are you speaking to the enervated?" Blythe asks.

She glances distractedly at him and gives a quick nod.

"How is that even possible?" I ask.

Blythe looks unsure. "Perhaps her brief touching of the pool changed her in some way."

"Is Marine there?" I ask her.

"Yes. She's with them now."

Colu laughs darkly and raises his hands to his head. "This is insane."

I lend a hand to Chimeline as she scrambles back to her feet. She grasps my shirt with her fists.

"I know this is hard for you to understand, but please believe me. It is the only way."

I'm paralyzed until she shakes me with surprising strength.

"Please, go now! The waves are taking her body out to sea!"

I peer over the edge once again.

She's right. Marine's body is now facedown and floating free of the sand, the gentle waves rolling over her.

"Do you trust me, Dem?"

Briefly, I close my eyes.

*May the Unnamed help me.*

"Dem, do you—"

I take Chimeline's face in my hands and kiss her deeply on the lips.

When I pull back, her gaze is built of matching conviction.

"I trust no one more."

Then, without another word, I step backward a few paces.

Colu and Blythe look on in shock. The Xian still has his hands on his shaking head.

"Dem? Are you sure about this?" Blythe asks.

But there is nothing left to say. Reason is tangled up in dialogue, but faith is wrapped in silence.

With a running jump from the edge of the broken Celestium, I cross into open sky.

# OWNING THE DARK

This is the first time that I have fallen without a membrane.

It is terrifying.

I look down to make sure my aim is true. The ruins quickly pass under me, replaced by shallow turquoise waters.

Marine's body.

It comes too quickly.

Currents of hot and cool air rush around me, howling. It's almost like being in the void. My white shirt lifts over my head, obstructing my view of the blue sky, but it doesn't matter. I decide to close my eyes anyway.

Then, perfect silence.

An abrupt slowing down. Nausea. My heart in my throat, my body spinning forward.

I hit the water with enough speed that it stings. I am submerged. My boots and clothes are instantly soaked. The wound on my back stings anew.

*The bottom.*

I blindly grab a handful of rocks and seashells on the seabed while swallowing saltwater.

*If I can do this, I can stand.*

Waist-high waters.

Regaining my balance, I spread my arms and legs wide, coughing out the sickening taste of salt.

I turn around in all directions.

Marine is a few feet from me, facedown in deeper waters, floating away.

I rush over, splashing in the shallows. I grab her arm and begin dragging her back to shore.

I try not to look at her.

There's a noise from above. Colu cheering, from the sound of it.

I look up at the sheer cliff, my free hand sheltering my eyes from the harsh sun. The three stand inside the shadowed, open Celestium.

I wave once.

So much debris blocks my way that I need to walk north, down the length of the beach in the direction Mander went, before I reach a clear section of sand. I spy a flat and smooth boulder at least five feet long.

*Here. She will be safe from the rising tide.*

Kneeling by Marine's side, I turn her body around so that she faces upwards. Arms under her, I gently lift her body and lay it down upon the large rock. A makeshift altar.

I remove a string of blackish-green seaweed from her face. One of her pale breasts is visible, and I pull up on her white-lace dress to conceal it, spreading the waistline out at her side. Then I see her glassy eyes reflecting the sky.

I force them closed with a gentle hand.

That's when I see it.

Her voidstone.

The gold necklace still hangs around her neck. The heavy stone lies off to the side, hidden in the tangles of her blonde hair.

*She's trapped inside.*

*No. Not this one. She's in one of Mander's. The voidstone that turned white.*

It must still be taken for eleutheria. There are thousands of souls in this voidstone alone.

Following the chain, I carefully separate it from the tendrils of hair and then rip it off while looking away.

That's when I see him.

A hazy black ellipse on the sandy horizon.

Careful not to touch the stone itself, I stuff Marine's necklace in my pants pocket and then force myself to look at my wife one last time.

I wipe the sand off her face and kiss her on the forehead. She broke my heart, but she didn't deserve this. Nobody deserves this.

"I promise I'm going to find you," I say, even though I know she can't hear me. "I'm going to set you free."

I rise to my feet then take off my boots and socks, both of which are saturated with saltwater. They will only weigh me down. I curl up the ends of my pants to midcalf and orient myself.

The sheer bluff is to my right, Xi Bay to my left.

And through my tears, I see Mander far in front.

I begin to run.

Almost immediately, the lure of voidance is in front of me, as if it were a second set of footprints in the sand to follow. As I put one foot in front of the other, my frequent warning to my former students runs through my mind.

*Never use voidance to move faster, to carry heavier weight, to attain something out of reach. Never use it to assist you in everyday activities. This is the surest way to voidance dependence and addiction, a certain path to voideath. If you must use voidance to run faster, it should be a life-or-death situation.*

*A life-or-death situation.*

There has never been a greater need than in this moment, right here and right now.

*No.*

I will test the limits of my body instead. I am done using voidance.

The dark form slowly becomes larger. Blue, not black. I step in Mander's footprints when I can. Two of his for every one of mine.

My legs soon burn, pleading for rest, but this burning is nothing compared to the screams I heard when Chimeline and Marine touched the pool. The souls plead for rest in every moment of voidance, but these pleas go unheard.

Sweat drips into my eyes, causing me to briefly lose sight of Mander. I rip off my sodden shirt and use it to wipe my brow so that I can see. Then I throw it away.

I'm slowly catching up to the bastard.

The red pier lies five hundred feet in front of him, and he's half that distance from me.

When I'm about two hundred feet away, Mander sees me.

He spins around then looks back over his shoulder at the crimson pier, a rickety structure seemingly dipped in blood.

*You're not going to make it.*

He seems to reach the same conclusion. He faces me fully, shoulders hunched, legs spread and shaking.

I slow my pace to a brisk walk.

One hundred feet now.

He grabs his voidstones, holding one in each hand.

Between us, the sand begins to divide in a perpendicular line, from sea to bluff. He forms another rift.

It widens as it deepens. Two feet. Then three.

Instantly, the waters from Xi Bay fill it.

I pick up my pace to a sprint. By the time I reach the edge, the rift is five feet wide and still growing.

I take a running leap.

But my legs are tired. They are wet clay, hot ash.

I hit the water. My hands barely reach the surface of the beach on the other side.

Sand crumbles under my fingers, and for a moment I go under. The saltwater burns the cut on my back.

When I rise to the surface, I try again. Sand crumbles.

And again.

The fourth time, my clawing hands find purchase, and I use all my strength to pull myself up. I cry out with a voice that burns my lungs.

Slowly, I rise to my feet as he backs away.

He's less than twenty feet from me—close enough for me to notice that sweat and blood have darkened his silky shirt and pants.

Bent in exhaustion, he looks up at me with a murderous gaze, fear and hatred grappling with each other.

He grabs his voidstones again as I walk toward him.

This time, it isn't a rift that he's creating. Instead, the sun slowly dims. A bronze cloud of sand rises and swirls.

A few steps later, I am in the middle of a buzzing sandstorm, tall drifts on each side of me. The gusts stream constantly from him to me. A shaving of bluff to my right collapses in the shadowy air. The speed is deafening.

I shield my eyes with an outstretched hand, but I don't need to.

The sand doesn't hit me.

Between us, sunlight barely flickers through a narrow tunnel of phantom twilight, as though filtered through swaying heavy branches. Beyond it, in all directions, a torrent of sand and wind.

He's doing what he did in the park. The violent gusts that brought down the bell tower and destroyed the fountain. They would have killed me as well, if it weren't for the enervated's help.

*And they're still helping.*

Within our tunnel of air, Mander and I lock eyes as I continue to walk slowly forward. Even though I'm not being buffeted, I still feel resistance. I lean in with my body, as if pushing a heavy weight, legs behind me, using the deep tracks in the sand as leverage. He blinks rapidly, and I see the struggle within him wash away. Hatred has lost. It's only fear in his eyes now.

He spins around as the sandstorm shifts.

I catch my balance as the resistance disappears. The wind begins to fly in the opposite direction. It now comes from behind me and toward him. But the tunnel of emptiness between us remains the same.

*He's trying to use voidance to move faster.*

But it's not working. The currents of air snake around him. Drifts fan out to the left and right, but not where he stands.

In a hideous scream, he gives up.

The storm instantly dissipates. The brown air collapses to the beach as the sun returns.

He cuts left, out to sea.

I follow, cutting in on an angle to head him off.

When he's up to his knees in water, he dives forward.

A shimmering sphere appears. The shallow water around his body cuts away in a perfect negative curvature.

I reach him, pounding the membrane with my fist, a hammer to the anvil.

I'm met with resistance. The same pressure that prevents the water from entering the sphere also prevents my attack. As I hammer on the membrane with my fists, it gives slightly—almost like flesh. Rainbow-colored ripples form, creating the look of oil on water.

The sphere is too large and heavy to lift. I step around it so that I'm between the sea and him and then push the sphere with all my might, back toward the shore. I'm not going to let him get to deeper waters.

I continue hitting the clear membrane with my fist, over and over, feeling the pressure give and seeing the iridescence darken.

Mander floats within its center, looking at me with a face that seems to be melting.

The skin underneath his eyes resembles a beeswax candle left out in the wind. Additional layers peel off his scalp, revealing a patch of skull. When he grimaces at me, his gums are tinged red with blood.

I hit again with my fists, which are already numb.

He shouts something at me, but I can't hear him. No sound penetrates the membrane. Bloody spittle from his mouth hits the inside of the bubble.

Finally, with what must be my twentieth blow, it disintegrates in a syrupy splash.

I fall onto him as we both go under the knee-high water.

My strength is sapped. I have nothing else to give. But he has less than nothing.

Our arms flail and our necks crane. I find his wrists and push him down into the coarse sand. He tries to reach his voidstones, but I hold his wrists down. A wave comes over me, and I take a shallow breath, going under.

Rotating my body, I pin one of his arms underneath my foot. This frees up my hand, which I put on his face, pushing him down below the water while I go up for air between waves.

As I take a gasping breath, the skin of his face slips off and I lose my grip. He rises.

"You're too late!" he screams.

I grab his face again—what's left of it. And push it down.

Mander says something else, but his words take the form of bubbles.

I fall to my knees as he writhes under my weight.

*You're too late.*

His strength slowly leaves him. Tears and saltwater blind my eyes, so I shut them briefly as I wait for the end.

It comes within three waves.

I face the shoreline. The water slaps my back and stings my wounds, and the crests roll over my shoulders.

His body remains underwater but is now lifeless. I search blindly for his voidstones and then rip them off his neck, bringing them above the surface.

There are only two.

*He had three.*

My mind flashes back to before the collapse. The one that turned white—it melted. It separated from the gold setting and chain forever.

I rise to my feet.

*Could he have left it back on the beach?*

*No. Marine is trapped inside it. He would have taken it with him.*

Gripping his thin shirt, I pull him out of the water. His head falls backward, toward the bluff.

He's too heavy to hold, but when I set him back down on the churning surface, he floats on his own.

I clutch his shirt with one hand to stop the waves from taking him while searching his body with the other.

*His pants pocket.*

There's something heavy in there, dragging the thin fabric down.

A larger wave crashes into my back and I stumble, falling onto Mander. I pull him back out again.

My hand digs further, ripping open the seams of the wet pocket.

As I grasp what's inside, the sunlit world disappears.

*Blackness.*

I am in the void.

But this time the sounds are different. There is a voice being carried above the wind.

*Dem. Can you hear me?*

I let go.

For a moment, all I can do is stand there in the harsh sunlight. Then I release my grip on Mander's shirt and fall back to my knees. The rolling waters come up to my shoulders.

*Marine.*

When I'm able to blink away the sweat, tears, and confusion, I see the voidstone directly below me, looking exactly as it did before. It's on the seabed, blacker than any other shell or pebble could be.

*Good Unnamed.*

Only the waves reply as I stare down through the glittering waters.

I knew that she was in soteria. I came here for her soul as much as Mander's death. But now that I've accomplished both, I am more uncertain than ever. I don't feel as if I've won.

Mander's dead body slowly floats away. I know that his soul has moved on, to whatever dark place it deserves. But in some way, he still feels *here*. The sun is prying. The waters battering. The gulls taunting. Nothing seems private.

I lunge for the body and pull it toward me before it's out of reach. Pulling hard upon Mander's shirt, I rip a handkerchief-sized section of it away.

Lowering my hand below the water's surface, I pick up the voidstone with the fabric, reverently folding it within layers of emerald.

I carefully place Marine's prison into my pocket and then stumble back to shore.

As for Mander, I leave his body for the sea.

# SHE IS BOTH HERE AND THERE

I make my way back to Marine's altar and sit beside it on the sand. The sun has started its slow decline in the west, hovering over the waters with heaviness. The slab of stone casts a shadow, and I rest inside this darkness. My shirtless back rests against the cold tableau. Marine's elevated head lies directly behind me, and past that is the sea and the sun. Her hair brushes the bare skin of my neck and shoulders. I know that it's only the wind, but I imagine that she's fidgeting with it—something she always did for attention.

I assume Blythe, Chimeline, and Colu are on their way. The long way around will take them down through the crowded streets of Winter's Baiou to the crimson pier. Then they will make the trek along the beach.

I am content to wait. The prying world is far away here, and the two of us need to speak.

Four voidstones lie in the sand before me, between my bare feet. They are various sizes—from cherry to plum. The leftmost three are in gold settings. The fourth one rests free, the most priceless of the collection.

I reach for it, and the void takes hold.

One voice—louder than the others—speaks to me in words that I can understand.

*Dem, is that you?*

Even though I was expecting this, it takes me a moment to reply. I have never spoken in the void. It isn't the same as speaking with the body.

*Yes.*

I hesitate. *Mander's dead, Marine.*

More silence. Then the wind in the cave picks up.

*We know. They thank you.*

*It is I who should be thanking them. The enervated protected me.*

*Yes.*

Another hesitation, as if both of us are circling a fountain. I think back to the moment that she fell into the pool, screaming out, white on black.

*Are you in pain?*

*No. Not any longer.*

*Because your body died?*

*No. Because Mander died. He forced us to do things that we didn't want to do. We had to fight it.*

*Like the sandstorm?*

*That, and other things. It felt like when I was alive. When I had a body, only much worse.*

*What do you mean?*

*Do you know how it felt when we used too much voidance? How the enervated ripped into us?*

*Yes. The first sign of voideath.*

*It is how you know you must stop. That you must let go of the stone. The body knows its limits. Do you remember the time I set your room on fire? I didn't know any better.*

*I remember.*

*Inside here, when you fight it, the feeling is the same. But there is no voideath because the body is already dead. There is nothing to let go of. So the pain never ends. The feeling of being ripped apart by the voider is endless. I dreamed of having a body again only to be able to let it die.*

I stay silent, thinking about the horror these poor souls must have endured. And for how long?

When Marine continues, her words come to me slowly, perhaps because this is all new to her. Or maybe she is simply numb or exhausted.

*What any voider does in here is a command to us. But sometimes we can subtly affect things. Like a horse under the whip, we can change direction, but then the pain gets even worse. We have to be smart. Rebel when it matters. It is a contest of wills.*

*I'm so sorry, Marine. I didn't mean for this to happen.*

The other voices, which sound like the wind, have quieted. The enervated seem to be listening.

*I'm sorry too, Dem. For everything that happened between us.*

A heavy pause in the colorless world.

*I was wrong. Leaving you for him.*

The words emanate from my mind before I even think them.

*Marine, I forgive you. And I hope you can forgive me.*

A gentle funnel of wind builds around me again.

*Dem, forgiveness is the only thing I can give you. It is the only thing left.*

Despite her words lifting this weight, overwhelming sadness washes over me. In a few moments, I will let go of the stone, perfectly able to walk away from this muted place and continue my life in the sunlit and star-studded world.

While Marine is trapped here with the enervated.

*Very soon, I'm going to free you. When Blythe returns. We're going to perform eleutheria.*

*I know. But . . .*

*What is it?*

*I'm afraid.*

*Eleutheria is not painful. We've done it once before, and the feeling was . . . It is wonderful, Marine.*

*That's not what I'm afraid of. I'm afraid of where I'll go when I leave this place.*

*I don't understand.*

*Don't you want to be free?*

Silence.

*I fear that I'll go to a void beyond the void.*

Then it dawns on me what she means.

*You're afraid that you'll be punished for the choices you've made?*

No answer.

*What about Chimeline? You saved her life. And in doing so, you've redeemed yours.*

The sound of wind in the tunnel picks up so rapidly I have the sensation of being gently lifted, even though there is no body to lift. And then it dies down again.

*I wish we could understand what they are saying.*

*They are pleased with us, Dem. They say that we do not own the dark. Except for my fear, which they say is not mine to own.*

A thought hits me.

*Wait. You can understand them?*

*Partially.*

*How?*

*I don't know. I hear their words. What we always thought was the wind—there is meaning inside of it now. Like one of those hidden-picture drawings where you see things only after staring at it for a long time. But many things I still do not understand. There are strange concepts. Like what happened to Chimeline.*

*What do you mean?*

*She was in soteria, but then . . . not.*

*I saw what happened. She touched the pool but then got pulled away from it when the room dropped.*

*She is not the same.*

Her abrupt response shocks me into silence. The recent memory of Chimeline flashing white and going slack in my arms adds to my dread as Marine continues.

*What happened is very rare. There is a name for it that I do not understand. Axionlighter. I can feel her—even now. We all can.*

*What are you talking about?*

*She is connected to us, yet her soul is still within her body. The cage was not fully opened. In a way, she is in the void with us right now, just like any voider.*

*Chimeline is here?*

*I know that it's hard to believe, but in some ways, she is the most powerful voider to ever walk the land.*

Marine's words make me pause.

I don't doubt them. Marine would know, being trapped in here with the shared knowledge of the enervated. Still, it's beyond comprehension that Chimeline could live her entire life untrained in voidance to become the most powerful voider in the land.

*I'm lost, Marine.*

*She is both here and there.*

*But what does that mean?*

*She doesn't need to touch an axion fragment in order to work voidance. She only needs to be near one.*

*How can you enter the void without touching a voidstone?*

*She doesn't have to enter the void because she's already in it.*

I pause in thought, considering that idea.

*I know that it's hard to believe. She didn't believe it either, when I explained it to her.*

*Wait . . . You talked to Chimeline?*

*Yes.*

*What did you say to her?*

*I relayed their message.*

*Whose message?*

*The enervated's.*

I pause. *You mean you translated for them?*

*Yes.*

Another hesitation. *What was their message?*

*They wanted her to slow your fall, so you could destroy Mander.*

*No. It was Chimeline who told me to jump. She said that the enervated would protect me.*

*Well, that is true.*

I wait for her to explain.

*Mander was getting away. You were the only one who could stop him.*

*That's why I jumped. And the enervated saved me.*

*Yes, except the enervated can't create voidance on their own.*

*What do you mean?*

*We need a bodily actor to use us. A voider. Voidance can't just happen on its own. You know that.*

Good Unnamed. She's right.

I am quiet as the logic connects, piece by piece. It was voidance that stopped my fall on the beach and saved my life. And voidance always requires a voider. Marine was already dead.

*It was Chimeline.*

*Yes. When you jumped, it was Chimeline who worked the voidance. She used my stone. I talked her through it.*

I stay silent.

*But there is a problem, Dem.*

*What?*

*Chimeline. She's in danger.*

*What danger?*

*She's near voideath. Creating the membrane was too much for her.*

The indivisibles seem to close around me.

*How do you know this?*

*As I said, she is both here and there.*

I don't have time to try to understand Marine's cryptic explanation. Instead, I am wondering how to help Chimeline.

*Can the enervated save her?*

*Only through you. You need to start a fire.*

*A fire?*

*To raise her body temperature. Just as you did for me, so long ago . . . Although I'm ashamed to admit that I was trying to get your attention at the time. Chimeline did it for justice. When we asked her, she didn't think twice.*

*How close is she? To voideath?*

*I can feel her pain and confusion. Her coldness. She doesn't have much time.*

*No. This can't be happening.*

I begin to panic. The void now feels like a prison to me as well, as if I were an enervated. I cannot—I *will* not—let anything happen to her.

*I told her to hold on, Dem. Not to let go of the body and the outside world. I told her that you saved me once before, and you can save her now . . . I think in some way . . . she is holding on for you.*

The winds slowly return, overtaking Marine's voice, making her seem distant.

*She is strong. And she loves you. Start a fire, Dem. She is coming.*

*Marine?*

*Use us. It is alright. They say it is alright.*

*Marine!*

*You must save her!*

The windlike voices are so loud that when I drop the voidstone back onto the sand, their chorus melds into the sound of crashing waves behind me.

Despite my sitting in shade, it takes me a moment to adjust to the light.

Turning to my left, I see a small group of people far away, walking down the beach near the crimson pier. Dark, hazy shapes in the afternoon heat. I cannot even count their numbers or tell who they are, but I don't need to. I heard what Marine said.

"Build a fire," I mumble to myself, frantically looking around.

I place my palms on the stone altar and push myself up.

Pain shoots through my right hand. I quickly take the weight off, letting it hang uselessly by my side.

I most likely fractured it from ceaselessly battering Mander's membrane earlier. If that's true, it was a cost worth paying.

*Wood. I need wood, and lots of it.*

Directly next to the altar and up against the bluff are a few tree trunks, twisted and gray with sun-bleached decay. They look like the remains of lemon trees that fell from the sandy cliffs years ago. Their branches are still attached, the finer ones covered in cobwebs and dune grass.

I bend down to grab one of the voidstones.

And pause.

My good hand hovers over the stone I recently used. The one containing Marine.

Instead, I choose another, pulling it up by its golden chain.

"I'm sorry," I softly tell them.

Grabbing the stone, I reenter the void and begin my work without taking a single step.

First, I strip all the finer branches from the trunks, making a giant pile of kindling. I spread the dry dune grass as well, creating a circle ten feet in diameter and a foot high.

Then I cut the trunks into pieces and drag them away from the sheer bluff.

*I'm sorry.*

Over the mound of kindling, I place the moderate-sized sticks. I put the largest logs on top. I clear the area around the campfire of all debris, ensuring the cleanest bed of white sand.

Moving between the indivisibles in the air, I float toward the density beyond. The center of the pile. Within the heart, two sticks in a dry bed of dead dune grass.

I begin moving the indivisibles together. Faster and faster.

Before long, they change. Old ones die and new ones emerge. Rising.

*Enough.*

When I let go, I must shield my eyes with my left hand due to the sun and smoke. I toss the voidstone next to the other three.

The fire already snaps with fury.

I take a few steps away from it and head to the water. The waves hit my feet as I look north, toward the pier. The people are much closer. Only a hundred yards away.

Only two of them are walking.

Colu is carrying Chimeline. Blythe is at his side.

They're both running.

"Dem!" Blythe yells out in the distance. "She needs your help!"

"I know," I answer quietly.

# SOMEWHERE

Colu approaches carrying a trembling Chimeline. Her head tilts back toward the sea, eyes closed and lips blue.

In his large arms, she looks like a child.

"How long has she been unconscious?" I ask, as I step forward to meet him.

He talks as he runs. "Since you jumped. We came as fast as we could."

I let out a deep breath. "Alright. Lay her by the fire."

Colu blinks away sweat and plows through the sand, crashing to his knees. He sets her down then stays near her side, bending over her body while he catches his breath.

The man seems near exhaustion.

I follow in his footsteps, kneeling next to him by Chimeline's side. The fire burns almost painfully warm on my face.

"Thank you for carrying her."

He nods, wiping his forehead with his shoulder.

"She's been flashing white," he says.

I turn to him. "Again? Since I jumped?"

He nods.

"When's the last time it happened?"

He shrugs his wide shoulders. "The pier, I think." He pauses. "No. It was after that. When we passed that fucker's body."

Blythe arrives. He stands a few feet away from us, where the water hits the beach. The bottoms of his pants are sodden, and he leans over, his hands on his knees. But his head is tilted up.

"Did the empowered perish from the moonspit?" he asks.

"No. It slowed him down, though. Allowed me to catch up."

"Did you use black arcana?"

I shake my head. "He drowned."

Blythe doesn't say anything. He looks down at the sand.

"Well done, by the way," Colu says, slapping my back near my wound, which makes me wince.

I glance back at Blythe and our eyes connect briefly. I expect a look of judgment. Some oblique comment about me owning the dark. About seeking revenge instead of justice. But he only nods.

Turning my attention back to Chimeline, I touch her cheek with my palm. It's frigid.

Colu stands, rips off his shirt, and walks into the sea, passing Blythe along the way.

"Will the fire save her?" Blythe asks me.

"Yes. It should."

"Is there anything that I can do to help?"

For a moment, I study the unconscious Chimeline. Then I look at Marine's dead body behind me on the stone altar. Finally, I turn back to Blythe.

"Pray," I tell him. "For them both."

He tilts his head, perhaps wondering if I am being snide. Which, surprisingly, I'm not.

Blythe presses his lips together and gives me a meager nod.

Then he falls upon his knees. The fringe of waves nearby causes them to sink into the sand. A small puddle forms around him that reflects the light almost to the point of whiteness. It reminds me of what happened hundreds of feet above us, in the Celestium.

"Dem?"

It's Chimeline.

I immediately turn to her.

Her eyes flutter open as she tries to lean upright.

Quickly, I position myself behind her, placing her head on my lap. The fire radiates against my left side. Which is good. Chimeline needs this.

Smoothing her dark hair down the sides of her face, I give her a gentle kiss on the lips. It seems fitting that I am upside down. My life has become completely untethered. There is no clear direction anymore.

"You d-d . . . did it," she says.

"Please, don't talk," I say calmly. "Conserve your energy."

"It makes me warmer when I speak."

I nod.

"You k-k . . . killed him."

I look up at the fire and nod. A breeze comes in off the water and stirs the flames.

"Marine told me. She said I am d-d . . . different now."

"You're an axionlighter," I say softly.

She wrinkles her nose. "How do you know?"

"I spoke with her in the void," I answer, motioning to the altar before realizing that Chimeline probably can't see it from her angle. "Her body is over there. So is the stone that has her in soteria."

"And the one that I used to help you jump from the cliff."

I nod.

She smiles. "She s-s . . . said that you would look after me."

I continue to gently smooth her hair. "I will always look after you."

"I'm sorry to cause you trouble. I did what she said . . ."

"Shh," I say. "You have nothing to be sorry about. Voidance is new to you. That's why you're cold. It happens to all of us."

She nods with a confused, accepting expression that warms my heart more than these flames ever could.

"You're going to be fine," I tell her. "I promise."

"Maybe now I'll be useful to you."

I furrow my brow. "What do you mean?"

"Marine says that I'm s-s . . . special now. That I can d-d . . . do things if I can l-l . . . learn."

I look up to hide my tears, but the smoke from the fire makes my eyes water more.

"Chimeline, I want you to know something," I say. "It's very important."

When I look back down, I see that one of my tears has fallen on her cheek.

Moving to her side, I cradle her in my arms. Her brown eyes bloom orange in the light of the flames.

"You were always special," I say. I place my hand on the back of her head, preventing it from falling backward. "And I was a fool to not see it earlier."

She wrinkles her nose again.

"But I am nothing," she adds. "And you are the m-m . . . master voider. Maybe if I am an axionlighter—"

I shake my head. "I'm not a master voider anymore. That life is over. And your importance has nothing to do with being an axionlighter."

"But—"

"Do you remember what the effulgents say?"

She looks up. "Be nothing?"

I nod. "In nothing there is everything."

She blinks.

I kiss her again, and this time the kiss lingers. Her lips are cool to the touch, but soft and receptive.

She shudders in my arms, so I pull back.

Her skin flickers a pale white brighter than the fire.

"Chimeline? Can you hear me?"

Her mouth opens slightly, teeth unclenched, and her face relaxes. The light turns from a flickering to a constant glow.

"Blythe?" I call out, glancing in his direction. "It's happening again!"

Despite being in prayer, he hears me. He scrambles over and kneels by my side in the sand while studying her. The light from her body cuts through her clothes like sunlight through gauze. His outstretched hands briefly hover over her, as if he's too scared to touch.

"The enervated are speaking to her."

"Marine is," I answer.

Blythe rubs a hand over his bald head, looking away in confusion as I continue.

"Somehow, Marine can understand the enervated. Maybe because she's in soteria? I don't know. Regardless, Marine is translating everything that—"

Blythe draws in a sharp breath. "Dem. Look."

He points to the shadow of Marine's altar, where the four stones lie.

They all glow white.

Just as quickly as it came, the light radiating from her skin disappears. Simultaneously, the four voidstones turn from white to black.

Her eyes snap open, and she weakly grabs my wrist.

"There is a book," she says, jaw clenched.

"A book?"

"In the r-r . . . ruins. Halcyon . . ."

Before she can respond, her eyes roll backward, like two burned-out suns setting on the horizon. Then they shut completely.

"Chimeline!"

I give her a gentle shake, but she doesn't stir.

Putting my palm over her heart, I make sure that it still beats. It does, but panic still sets in. I shake her again.

"She's fine," Blythe says. "You have done what you can. It's time for her to rest."

"Are you sure?"

He nods.

Looking up, I see that the flames are at least five feet tall. Logs hiss and crack, and black smoke rises in a thick column.

Trusting Blythe's advice, I turn around and face the sea. Shortly thereafter, Blythe follows suit, keeping his legs crossed.

Colu is in the deep, washing himself. Only his head and shoulders stick out of the undulating surface. His black eye patch is off.

Far away and behind him, rain hides the ring of ships. The spiderweb of anchors. Above it all, a dark storm cloud approaches, the palest purple and green. Flashes of lightning push at the edges.

"We'll need to find shelter soon," I say. "And fresh water to drink."

"The Unnamed will provide."

I look back at him curiously.

"Is he really listening?" I ask.

"Is *who* listening?"

"The Unnamed."

Blythe smiles but says nothing, which I find maddening.

"How can you be so smug?" I ask.

Continuing to smile, he slowly shakes his head. "I am not being smug. Your question made me think of how far the two of us have come." He clears his throat and brings his pressed hands to his mouth, as if in prayer. "Days ago, I could not have foreseen a voider and effulgent freely talking about such things. Performing eleutheria and questioning the Unnamed. Now, the two of us are stripped of our stature and dogmas, but in less we have become more. I would not have it any other way."

He looks at me, and I nod. "Neither would I, Blythe."

Dropping his hands, he looks at the storm in the distance. "You are more than just a lesson to me, Dem. You are what one calls a friend. But I still struggle with this. The way of unwanting is absent of friends, since it is owning the light."

"I've never understood that saying. Owning the light."

"It's the words that we choose."

"As in how?"

"*Having* a friend. What you have, you own."

"It's just a stupid saying, Blythe."

He nods. "On one hand, you are correct. Words are just the sounds that we make. In that regard, they mean nothing more than do leaves rustling in the wind. But the context that comes with them is important. The hidden weight of history." He clears his throat. "Just like when one lover says to another, 'You are mine.'"

I think of Chimeline.

"Despite this," Blythe continues, "I cannot see how it is wrong, given that the Unnamed has brought us together."

I lean back in the sand, stretching out. "We were both wrong about so many things. You didn't know that we could perform eleutheria together. You didn't know about the Axiondrive. About an empowered being alive. I didn't know the true nature of voidance. That my own submaster was capable of such evil. That my wife . . ."

"We were both lost in our own dogmas."

The next words exit my mouth without caution. "But what if you were wrong about the Unnamed too?"

He bites his lip, and for a moment I fear I've offended him.

"It is a possibility," he says softly.

My neck snaps in his direction. "What?" I ask, genuinely surprised. I expected the most zealous of defenses.

He purses his lips. "The truth is, I have no proof the Unnamed exists."

A gentle rumble sounds from far away.

"But you pray to him. You've spent your entire life—"

"Where do you think they go, Dem?"

I furrow my brow. "You mean the souls?"

He nods.

"After eleutheria?"

He nods again.

"I . . . I guess they move on."

"What does that mean?" Blythe asks.

"I have no idea. That question is void-destined."

"Void-destined?"

"Incapable of being answered objectively. That's what we used to call it back when I ran the university. Meaning, you cannot prove it in a lab. Not by repetition, not by analysis of data, or observation. Therefore, it is a question not worth asking."

I turn to him. "But I would have thought that the effulgency would have all of this worked out. The unanswerable is your domain. Your temples and holy books."

"I led people on the way of unwanting. Notice that it is a *way*. Not a *destination*."

For a moment, neither of us says anything. I listen to the gentle surf and snapping fire.

"Marine," I say, more softly. "She was fearful of where she would go. That there would be . . . judgment."

"Hmm," he groans, a finger to his lips.

"She seemed just as lost as me." After a moment I add, "One would think that with her being dead, she would know more. About the Unnamed, I mean."

He pauses before replying. "There are really only two options, aren't there?"

"Either he exists or he doesn't. You're either right or you're wrong."

"No. I mean there are only two options regarding where the souls go. After eleutheria."

I look out at the storm as I ponder my reply. There is blue sky above us, yet the sun is masked behind a bruise-colored anvil. It makes the day haunting.

"They either go to a good place or a bad place?"

He shakes his head. "No. They either go *somewhere* or *nowhere*. That is the more important mystery."

Suddenly, I see his point.

"If they go nowhere, there cannot be an Unnamed," I say. "There is no creation without a creator."

"Correct."

"So where do they go after eleutheria?" I ask.

"I don't know."

I let out a laugh. "You're exhausting, Blythe."

After another set of waves comes in, he quietly adds, "But I have an idea."

"What?"

"I've always thought of it like this. Being trapped in soteria is evil."

"Sure."

"So, after a lifetime of enslavement, do you think simple disappearance is the natural next step?"

"Meaning, they deserve rest?"

"No. Rest implies life. Consciousness. Rest is not destruction. And did you see how they moved through us? They moved on, willingly. I did not sense fear."

"No. Me neither."

After a pause, he continues. "I guess that is why I believe. That is why I have always believed. In life, given the choice between nothing and something, I have always chosen nothing. Except when it comes to belief. An eternal hope. That is when I choose something. Because nothing is even worse than being in soteria."

I don't answer him. It is hard to argue with his logic.

"There is something else," he says.

"What?"

He scoops up a handful of sand and lets it fall slowly through his fingers.

"When we did eleutheria, I saw through your eyes. Before we completely entered the axion fragment. The indivisibles. Everything in this world is made of them— even these grains of sand."

I wait for him to continue.

"But in soteria, all was black."

"We were inside of the fragment."

"Yes," he says, brushing his palms together. "And then we traveled through that lost place. To the white room and the souls."

I nod.

"Did you notice it?"

I furrow my brow.

"The souls. They were not made of indivisibles."

He picks up another handful of sand. I watch, hypnotized, as the grains fall.

"You're right," I say. "The souls. The spheres. They were . . ."

"Beautiful."

"Yes."

"They were not made of indivisibles," he adds.

"No."

"Perhaps, in that place, they *were* indivisibles."

I turn and meet his eyes, and then I give him an ironic smile. I've been in the void since I was a child. When we performed eleutheria, I should have picked up on this fact immediately. But it took a man of faith to see it.

A rumbling clatter rolls in, but it's weaker than the storm, and higher-pitched. It comes from the north.

Turning in that direction, I see dozens of people by the distant crimson pier. Over a mile away, they fill the beach, from sea to bluff. Despite the ominous sky, their armor glitters with light.

"Reddles," I say, with a sense of relief. "He came back."

"What do you mean 'back'?"

I turn to Blythe. "I met the commander on the way to the Celestium. He was visibly shaken. Mander used voidance on him."

"So he knows the truth?"

I nod. "Some of it, at least. I asked him for help, but he refused. He told me that he was going to warn the king."

"He must have noticed the Celestium fell into Xi Bay."

"No doubt."

"What will he think of all of this destruction?" Blythe asks.

"It's not the destruction of the Celestium that will concern Reddles," I say. "It's the destruction of his dogma."

Blythe looks at me, confused.

"Soldiers have dogma too. A simple framework of rules with the king at the center."

Blythe doesn't look convinced, so I continue.

"Reddles' world has been shaken. He ran away from a fight for the first time in his life because voidance was used against him. And his blind faith in the king . . ."

"What about it?"

I sigh as I think back to my dinner conversation with Andrej X. "The king will probably not let the Axiondrive go just because Mander is dead. He'll exploit the situation and will lean on Reddles and his army to defend it."

"Then we need to perform eleutheria on it while we still can."

We both face forward to look at what's lurking in the rain.

"Can the two of us do that on something that large?"

"I don't see why not."

He balls his hands into fists.

"What is it?" I ask.

He turns from the storm to me. "What about the rest of them?"

"The voidstones?"

He nods.

"We'll do the same thing. Eleutheria for all."

"Your fellow voiders will not freely give them up."

I dig my heels into the sand, feeling the damp coolness below. "They'll listen to me. I was once their leader. As far as they know, I still am."

Blythe brings his folded hands to his lips, looking forlorn.

"You don't agree?"

He shakes his head. "I have dedicated my life to trying to influence your former kind. I have tried to educate you all on the evilness of these stones. But my words have always fallen upon deaf ears. Voiders only worship what can be seen and understood. The unseen are swept aside like children's tales."

"You got through to me, Blythe. And if you can get through to me, we can get through to the others."

"I admire your optimism, but you speak without experience. You've never been on the opposite side of power."

He briefly looks at me and swallows before turning back to the anvil-shaped cloud.

"It's not an army of soldiers that we have to fear," he says. "It's an army of voiders."

# HALCYON ROADMAP

At least a hundred men stand before us under overcast skies from sea to bluff. Reddles is in the rear. His soldiers hoist a large white tarp above him, anchored in the corners by tall rods of bamboo.

The entire company droops with an exhaustion that needs no explanation. Most of their helmets are off, their heads matted with sweat.

The white tarp advances, floating over the throng. It's about ten feet square. Reddles is in its shadow, along with another young, bald Xian dressed in white. By the way the person is walking, I can tell she's a woman.

*An effulgent?*

Reddles is barefoot, his gray-and-red pants cuffed at the calf. A nearby soldier carries his boots and sword. Another carries his folded suit. But the golden star still adorns the commander's neck—it's hung upon a bloodred ribbon against a sweaty white undershirt.

Blythe and I have already risen to our feet. Colu steps out from the deep, ties his eye patch, and picks up his sword up from the sand, attaching its belt around his hips.

The shadow cast by the white fabric crosses my feet at an angle. In the shade, Reddles combs his wet blond-gray hair with his fingers as he looks at me, unblinking and pensive. The effulgent is hidden, eclipsed by Reddles' wide shoulders.

"I imagine congratulations are in order," Reddles says. "I saw his body, though it looked nothing like Mander. If it weren't for his tattered clothes, I would not even believe it was him."

"The Mander we knew was a disguise," I say. "There was a monster behind that veil."

Reddles nods. "Well, he certainly played me for a fool."

"He played us all for fools. He fooled me, and he fooled my wife." I purposely pause before saying the next charged words. "And he fooled the king."

Reddles winces subtly. One of the soldiers holding up the tarp breaks from his stoic forward gaze to look at his commander in shock.

"I thought you were on your way to warn him," I say.

"I was. But there were two things awaiting me at the Union that changed my mind."

The wind picks up. Shadows slowly disappear as the clouds thicken. There is no more light and dark. Only shades of gray.

As I cock my head in curiosity, Reddles moves aside.

"This effulgent was one of them."

She looks down at her bare feet. Her dress is a shining white that makes the tarp's canvas look drab.

Then she timidly raises her head. Tears have formed trails down her cheeks.

I inhale sharply in recognition.

"My daughter," Blythe gasps, at my side. "My daughter," he repeats, louder this time.

Blythe steps forward, walking right underneath the tarp and past Reddles, as if the commander were not even there.

He wraps his arms around his daughter.

Her head is tilted upward, over his shoulder, locked in his embrace. For a long time, her mouth hangs open in shock. Then she says something into Blythe's ear, and he nods.

Blythe pulls back but stays at his daughter's side. As he turns back to me, a smile crosses his face. "Thank the Unnamed. She received the message."

She adds, "I copied the note and sent more pigeons on their way, in all directions. Then I came as fast as I could."

The first drops of rain begin to fall. They are loud upon the taut canvas. In the distance, they hit the soldiers' armor like wind chimes in a garden.

"Anyhow." Reddles waves his hand. There's something clutched inside of it. "The other thing waiting for me was much more—"

I give Reddles an apologetic look. "Excuse me for one moment."

I walk out from under the tarp to the campfire beyond. Chimeline is still unconscious, the first raindrops on her skin not enough to wake her.

Kneeling, I touch her hands and forehead. Her skin is noticeably warmer than it was, but being out in the elements is the last thing she deserves.

I try to pick her up but let out a short cry of pain. With my fractured hand, it's impossible.

Colu sees what I'm trying to do. He comes near, easily lifts her, and carries her underneath the shelter of the canopy. He sets her down upon the dry sand near Reddles' feet.

Reddles looks at her with curiosity. "What happened to her?"

"Mander tried to kill her," I say. "Thankfully, he was not successful." I sigh heavily. "I cannot say the same for my wife."

This is the second time since Reddles has appeared that I have said the words *my wife*. Inwardly, I don't believe them. But the two of us went through so much pain together. The rift. The loss of love and trust. In this last moment, I refuse to acknowledge it. Maybe it is a sign of forgiveness. Maybe it is a small act of rebellion in the face of death.

Reddles glances over at Marine's body on the altar, exposed to the wind and rain.

"I am sorry."

After a moment of silence, he shakes what's in his hand. It's a wrapped scroll that bears a broken red waxen seal.

He hands it to me.

"This was the second thing awaiting me."

I take and unfurl it, starting from the bottom. The instant I see the king's signature, my heart drops.

To my most loyal commander, Reddles:

My master voider, Democryos, has dishonorably abandoned his station. I have reason to believe that he is heading south toward Winter's Baiou with ill intent.

Apprehend him and secure his voidstone. I am appointing Submaster Mander as the new master voider. Have him assist, if necessary.

Personally escort Democryos back to the citadel, where he will await justice. If this proves too difficult, his head will suffice.

Your Majesty of the Northern Kingdom,
King Andrej X

Slowly and tightly, I curl the parchment up and then hand it back to Reddles.

"So, what are you going to do, Commander?"

"If the king wants you brought to him, that leaves me with little choice."

"We all have choices."

He takes a step forward and forcefully whispers into my ear. "What would you have me do? If I disobey the king, it will be my head being delivered to him, not yours."

I don't reply, since he's right.

"Just come back with me to the citadel," he adds, his whisper a little less urgent. "I will vouch for your innocence. You have my word."

*I'm never going back to the citadel.*

"I can't do that, Commander. I am sorry."

"Why not?"

"Because there's a much bigger problem."

He waits for me to explain, so I point out to sea.

"Mander has been excavating that massive voidstone from beneath Xi Bay. That voidstone has been the reason for this entire campaign, and what happens next is of critical importance—not just for the Northern Kingdom, but for this entire realm."

"How so?"

"Voidance is at a crossroads, if you will," I explain. "Suffice it to say that it's a matter for voiders to resolve—ourselves. And the last thing we need is the king trying to abuse a power he has no understanding of for his own benefit."

Reddles looks out to sea, fingering his star. "Be that as it may, I took a vow, Master Voider. A *vow*. To serve and obey. I am a soldier, not a voider."

Reluctantly, I nod. "But you saw what happened here. The darkness that is at risk of being multiplied."

He swallows.

"It is the *kingdom* that you serve—it and its people. Do you really think that taking me back to the citadel is best?"

For a long time, Reddles is quiet. The storm grows. The sound of rain on the tarp drowns out the crying gulls.

An intense brightness draws our attention.

It's Chimeline. She's glowing again.

Reddles takes two steps away. "What is going on?" He unsheathes his sword with a shimmering sound. The metallic rattling extends across his company as other soldiers snap to attention.

I extend my hand to him. "It is alright, Commander."

"That voidance?"

I nod. "But not harmful."

Chimeline leans up, gently extending a hand in front of her. Her eyes are open but fixed on something far away.

"What is she doing?"

"I don't know."

She stares at the mound of debris underneath where the Celestium used to be.

I follow her gaze.

There is movement. The sound of ruins being sifted through. New dust rises, beaten down with heavy rain.

The storm is so strong now that it comes in sideways, getting most of us underneath the tarp wet. The fabric undulates violently. The four soldiers grasp onto the bamboo tightly, arms and legs bent.

Beyond, the waves grow in strength, pushed by the arriving storm. They're taller than a man standing, relentlessly crashing into the ruins by the bluff, pulling more and more debris out to sea.

A perfectly round hole emerges from the side of the mound of debris.

Iridescence. Oil in water.

A perfect sphere flies in our direction.

It collapses in a syrupy splash before it reaches the canopy. The large book that was inside slides across the wet sand, coming to rest at my feet.

The light goes out, leaving us in gray darkness.

I turn back to Chimeline. She's collapsed, and her eyes are closed again.

Reddles sheathes his sword but still looks perplexed. "I am confused, Master Voider. Why are we reading a book in the middle of this storm?"

*There is a book in the ruins.*

*She was trying to warn me. Or the enervated were.*

"Because they want us to," I answer.

"Who does?"

I shake my head. There is no way I can fully explain this to him now.

"Mander had a journal on his desk, in the Celestium."

Bending, I attempt to pick up the book with one hand, but it is too heavy. With a groan, Blythe takes it from me and sets it within the center of the shelter, where it's mostly dry. I open its umber leather cover and brush off a strand of seaweed.

"It looks intact," I say to the others, sitting. I take a moment to riffle through the hundreds of pages. I can't read the writing, which is in black ink, but for a different reason than I feared. Except for the edges, there are no smudges or areas of wetness. The book is dirty, and the binding is loose—pages are even falling out—but besides that, it's in good condition.

Blythe kneels in the sand next to me.

"What does it say?" Reddles asks impatiently. He begins to pace.

"It's written in the effulgency language," I explain. "Only Blythe can read it."

I move aside and let him in.

"My daughter can, as well." He puts his fingers on the first page. There are only two words—large, centered, and elaborate. His fingers trace them.

"*Halcyon Roadmap*," he says. "It seems to be a title."

"Where is Halcyon?" Reddles asks.

Blythe looks up at him and then at me with a confounded expression.

"Halcyon is not a place," says the daughter. "It is a state of being."

"Yes. Of course. A time of great peace and prosperity," Blythe adds.

"What?" Reddles asks.

"That's what *halcyon* means. A time of great peace and prosperity."

He grunts. "So, you're telling me that Mander wrote a diary on how to reestablish peace and prosperity within the kingdom?"

Blythe turns his attention back to the book, so the commander looks to me for an answer.

I don't know what to say.

Perhaps the first two words of this book shine a light upon the twisted nature of Mander's world. Inside of it, he didn't view himself as evil. He was trying to do good—his distorted definition of good. By raising the massive voidstone, he would bring about a new era of voidance. With such power at his fingertips, he could do whatever he wanted.

Somehow, he was able to justify his actions as peaceful. The enervated were not souls to him. They were resources. They were not an end but a means to it.

"That does not sound condemning," Reddles says.

"Do not be deceived, Commander," Blythe says levelly. "This is a black mirror that we are looking into. Nothing is what it seems."

"I don't know what that means, Graycloak."

But I do. I put a hand on Blythe's shoulder. "When do the writings start? Are there any sort of dates written down?"

He turns the page and begins reading. Leaning over the book, he shakes his head.

"The script is very small. I wish there were more light at our disposal. Maybe a torch?"

I can empathize. We're in the thick of the storm—the sky is a deep gray that mimics dusk. The canopy makes it even darker.

"Father, let me," says the daughter.

"Ah, yes," he says, sitting back up and pushing himself away in the sand. "Come close, Daughter. Young eyes see the world clearer. You carry a sun within you."

She doesn't even need to lean over or trace the lines with her finger in order to read it. She points to the upper-right corner of the page.

"The date is four hundred twenty. Late harvest season."

"Six years ago," I say slowly, as I do the math. "That's two years before the war."

I look up and see Reddles nod. A flash of lightning appears out at sea behind him.

When I look back down, the daughter is already scanning the page. She raises her voice to be heard over the rolling thunder and driving rain.

"He is committing to writing down daily thoughts in this journal, as part of his new station."

"New station?" Reddles asks.

She flips the page. "It appears that he just moved here from the citadel. He is unpacking as he writes this. Into a Xian estate on the hill overlooking the bay."

I look up at the destroyed remains. "The Celestium."

She shakes her head. "He does not mention that name. But he mentions Winter's Baiou being a city that straddles both the Northern and Southern kingdoms." She continues to scan, and then opens her mouth.

"What is it?" I ask.

"He mentions you."

"What does he say?"

She looks sideways at me. "It is not in a kind light."

I wave her ahead and she clears her throat.

*"I cannot believe that I've finally been able to wear down the master voider. That man is as stubborn as an old mule. I had to write up over two dozen voidance applications of sea life before he even considered sending me here. I had the overwhelming urge to just tell him that the largest voidstone in the world is hidden in Blackscar. But, of course, I cannot tell him that. He would wonder how I knew such things.*

*"No. For now, I am on this journey alone, as I have been for quite some time. One more secret is but another leaf of camouflage."*

Both she and Blythe look at me.

"What is he talking about?" Reddles asks, continuing to pace.

I shake my head in thought. "I sent him here. To Winter's Baiou. He was my submaster."

"The man told you he was studying sea life?" Blythe asks.

I nod. "It was his specialty. His lifelong passion. But apparently, it was just a ruse, like everything else."

"There are maps," the daughter says, flipping the pages.

I lean in. "The Northern Kingdom."

"He must have drawn them," she says.

"They're quite good," I say.

She turns the page. There is a detailed map of Xi Bay, heavily annotated.

"What do the words say?" I ask.

"Coastal towns. Here is where we are." She points.

"What is that circled area in the middle of the bay?" Reddles asks.

"This must be Blackscar," the daughter says, running her finger down a dark jagged line right through the center of the circle.

"Most of Blackscar was in Xian waters," Colu says.

I look out to sea, wondering if I can see the ring of ships, but it's too far away, and masked by the storm.

"Can you please tell me what is going on?" Reddles asks.

I stand and point at the book. "Mander is mapping out where he thinks the massive voidstone is located. And he's coming to the realization that it's probably not in Northern territory. So, he has two choices. Either switch sides and cozy up to the Xian emperor or find ways for the Northern navy to gain control of the entire bay." I give Reddles a knowing look. "This is where the idea of the war was born. Right here, on this page."

Reddles stops pacing and brings his hand to his chin.

"He mentions the king," she says.

I look back down. She's already onto the next page.

Reddles steps closer.

"But he's writing about the father," she adds, her voice full of confusion. "Not the son."

"King Andrej IX?"

"Yes."

Blythe's daughter clears her throat. "Shall I continue?"

"Yes, go on," Reddles says with a wave.

"*I wasn't planning on executing this part of my strategy so soon, but the opportunity is slowly presenting itself. Here I am, after only one season, back in the citadel. Due to Dem's ill-timed wedding and honeymoon.*"

She pauses and looks at her father. "What is a honeymoon?"

"It is not on the way of unwanting . . . I think it is best to let Dem answer," he says.

I address the daughter. "After two people are married, sometimes they go on a vacation to spend some private time together."

She raises her hairless brow. "Oh."

"Marine wanted to come here," I explain, pointing down at the sand. "I had asked Mander to effectively switch places with me. Travel north. To represent me in the citadel while I was away. Marine and I used his accommodations and house staff while he stayed in the citadel."

Reddles and Blythe nod while his daughter keeps scanning.

"*Despite the chaos this will surely create, I am convinced it is the right decision. The current king is not pliable. The son, however, is a lazy and arrogant fool.*

"*I have concerns, though. Not about getting caught, but about convincing Dem to let me return to Winter's Baiou after the deed is done. With the ensuing political turmoil, his instinct will be to pull all submasters back to the citadel. That is unacceptable, of course. The search must continue.*"

My mouth hangs open as a terrible thought comes to me.

"What is it?" Reddles asks.

"Andrej IX would never have started a war over a voidstone. And Mander knew it."

"What are you saying?"

"What if Mander murdered the king?"

Reddles grunts. "I think your imagination is running away with you. His Majesty fell to his death. It was a tragic and very public accident."

The daughter turns the page. Her eyes dart back and forth quickly.

"There's more," she says, leaning in.

"*Finally, some good news. The king sent messengers this morning to the Royal House. I am to represent the university in the wintertide celebrations. I will be in the king's presence, and the only voider, at that. Tomorrow is the day.*"

She takes a deep breath.

"Oh, no," she says. "He is owning the dark."

"Keep reading," Reddles says, his arms folded and his legs spread apart.

"*Andrej IX was full of wine before the first course of Xian squid was even served. By the time dinner was over, he could hardly stand on his own. The queen had already left the room—she was livid. Before dessert and smokes, the servants opened the balcony doors to let the king wave to the commoners, out on the square, five stories below. The cold wind blew in from the north so strongly that it extinguished some of the candles in the candelabrum. I had a second fragment hidden underneath my cloak, which I used to weave a subtle membrane. Nobody saw the shimmering in the darkness on the balcony.*"

I collapse to my knees in the sand.

"What does that mean? A membrane?" Reddles asks.

"He used voidance to push him over."

Reddles bares his teeth. "Then this is all the proof we need," he says, staring off into the distance. The muscles in his jawline clench.

Suddenly, he steps around the book and Chimeline, leaves the shelter of the tarp, and approaches the campfire. Despite the rain, it still rages.

Reddles throws in the king's coiled parchment. For a moment, he stands in the rain, watching it burn.

When he returns, he rubs his palms on his thighs, as if this subtle act of treason has left residue. But he doesn't say a word. His face is still coiled with rage.

I am moved by his display of both logic and courage.

"There is a gap in time," says the daughter. "A few days."

"Most likely due to all the chaos," I add.

"Or traveling. The next entry, he is back in Winter's Baiou."

Reddles clears his throat. "You sent him back here?"

"Yes."

"A lot of these entries are about his searching," she continues, flipping the pages. "He's using something called a membrane." She looks up. "Wasn't that how he murdered the king?"

"Same, but different. This type of membrane is used to breathe underwater."

She turns back to the book. "He's using a makeshift buoy as a marker. Some piece of painted wood tied to an old anchor. He moves it every day, as his search progresses further from shore and down Blackscar."

She utters a murmur of surprise. "The Lady Marine is mentioned here." She glances at me curiously. "You left her here?"

"I did," I answer with a sigh. "I had to return from my honeymoon when the king died."

"But your wife remained?"

"I didn't want her trip cut short. She had many dives planned. She wanted to find her cursed pygmy seahorse."

"What?" Reddles asks.

I wave the thought away. "It doesn't matter. All that matters is that I chose the university and the king over

Marine. Right after I promised her the exact opposite. It was a profound mistake. One of many."

She turns the page and freezes.

"Oh, my."

"What?"

"*An interesting development*," she begins. "*Dem's wife witnessed me today, in my true form. Underwater, fifty yards down within Blackscar. I cannot believe that she was going that deep. Brash for someone of her limited power. I was in my membrane . . .*"

She pauses.

"What?" I ask.

She looks at me with a worried expression, her brow furrowed.

"Whatever is written there, you can read it out loud."

She swallows, turning back to the book.

"*I was in my membrane, completely naked and undisguised. I had assumed that my dives were the only times when I could be myself completely, without the prying eyes of this world. Such was not the case.*"

She glances at me before continuing.

"*My first instinct was to kill her. She had seen too much. But then I realized that this would only draw more attention to me and my work. Dem would come back here looking for answers. The man is exhausting.*

"*Besides, the young beauty seems like a climber. It's why she pursued Dem in the first place. Well, I can make her climb a bit more.*"

"Why don't you move on to the next page?" Blythe softly advises.

The daughter nods and complies.

I look away, into the rain, almost wishing I were in it.

"These are more passages dealing with Marine," she says. "He told her that he was an empowered. He told her about the Axiondrive. She is agreeing to keep silent. To search for it with him."

"Just move on," Blythe says.

I'm still watching the storm, barely able to hear the daughter flip multiple pages.

She clears her throat.

*"It is exactly as I feared. The stone is massive. At least ten yards wide and twenty yards long. It's at the very bottom. So far down that it's in complete blackness without voidlight. When I try to move it, with either voidance or brute force, it doesn't budge.*

*"It is the most frustrating feeling in the world to float next to it. On one hand, I can feel the enormous power at my fingertips, through the membrane. There must be billions of resources inside.*

*"The problem is, I cannot tap into the stone's power in order to raise it myself. It's so heavy that voideath would occur. I need other voiders. I must think on this. Break up a large problem into smaller problems and solve each individually."*

The daughter shakes her head while turning the page.

I interject.

"Thus the war. Once it began, the king forced me to send almost all voiders south. They weren't being used on the field of battle. They were being used to raise the Axiondrive."

"He keeps visiting it," says the daughter. She's about halfway through the tome. "Every day he dives down."

"For what purpose? Is he trying to raise it?"

She shakes her head then looks back at me in confusion. "What is voidspeaking?"

I sigh. "Mander was able to somehow speak to people within their minds. Using voidance. He did it with both Marine and Chimeline."

"Well, he's voidspeaking to others using the Axiondrive," the daughter says.

"What is this Axiondrive?" Reddles asks.

The daughter points out to sea.

"It's just their word for it," I explain, and then I turn my attention back to the effulgent. "Who is he voidspeaking with?"

"I . . ." She whispers something to Blythe.

He replies in a whisper. As their voices escalate, I realize that they are conversing in their effulgency language.

"What is it?" Reddles asks loudly, cutting them off.

The pair looks up at him and then to me. "He's speaking with other empowered," the daughter says. She looks petrified.

"I don't understand—what other empowered? I thought he was the only one."

"He's the only one *here*," she says.

"Remember I told you that the Axiondrive powered a great ship?" adds Blythe. "A very long time ago? It crashed here in Xi Bay."

"Right," I answer. "It came from across the sky."

"Across the sky?" Reddles asks, ducking slightly to look out past the white tarp and into the storm. "Are you mad?"

Blythe flashes him a look that flirts with impatience.

Colu laughs. "Get used to it."

"Please keep reading," I say to Blythe's daughter.

"*The problem is the lack of clarity. There is a delay. Not quite a fullbell. It makes it very hard to communicate. The voices are muffled, as if they are coming through a wall. They say it is the water. It acts as a dampener. I barely hear enough.*

"*They were waiting for this glorious day. The moment of first contact by one of their own kind. My own kind. Someone who is awakened. The halcyon days are near.*"

"What does all of that mean?" Reddles asks, but I hold out a hand to quiet him.

"*Our ship fell out of a field of time into stars, and from them onto this world. But the original field of time is so immense that they don't know where we are. They only know* when *we are. They need my help.*"

The daughter looks up, her petrified expression growing. "He's promising to help them find us."

"How?"

She flips the pages, and suddenly the words are replaced by dots and lines.

"What is that?" Reddles asks.

"Stars."

"It's the painted ceiling in the Celestium," Blythe adds.

"*They tell me that I must find three pulsars. Special stars that rotate and emit a beam of energy, like a lighthouse. This energy can only be seen when the pulsar faces us. If I locate and measure the three of them, they can find me.*"

"The three lighthouses," I murmur.

Blythe and his daughter begin feverishly talking in their language again, while Reddles kneels in the sand and grabs my forearm.

"Tell me what is going on."

"There are others," I say.

"Others?"

I shake my head and try to simplify my thoughts for this man, who knows nothing of the empowered or the enervated. "Even though the stone was buried underwater, Mander was somehow able to use its power to speak to his kind. They come from very far away."

"Who are they? What do they want?"

Blythe addresses the commander. "They are evil," he says. "And they want everything."

The daughter begins to cry, and Blythe puts his arms around her. Beyond them, a bolt of lightning pierces the turbulent waters, and the canopy ripples in a chorus of crackles.

Her mouth is open. She's riffling through the book, turning the pages frantically.

"The rest are blank," she cries. "This is the last entry. It's . . ." Her finger touches the corner. "It's from two weeks ago."

"It is alright," Blythe says softly to her. "The Unnamed will provide. Remember, he always provides."

"What does it say?" I ask her. "The last entry."

She looks up at me with glassy eyes that reflect the storm.

*"They're coming."*

552

TO BE CONTINUED . . .


TEMBERLAIN'S ASHES


AGE OF AXION
BOOK TWO


FALL 2022

# A NOTE FROM THE AUTHOR

Reviews are gold to authors! If you've enjoyed this book, please consider rating and reviewing it on the following platforms:

Amazon.com, Goodreads.com, and BookBub.com.

# SIGN UP FOR MY MAILING LIST

Sign up for my mailing list to get access to author updates, including progress on upcoming books, deals, giveaways, and much more.

www.dmwozniak.com

# OTHER WORKS BY D.M. WOZNIAK

**The Perihelion: Complete Duology**
A newly combined edition of the critically acclaimed duology *The Perihelion* and *An Obliquity*. Also contains the prequel novelette *The Rue Cler Decommission*.

It is Thursday, January 3, 2069: the eve of the perihelion. Night is upon Bluecore 1C (what used to be known as the city of Chicago, before the riots). Snow is falling, plans are being made, and within hours, everyone in 1C will be changed forever.

Narrated from the vantage point of six residents of 1C, The Perihelion: Complete Duology is a work set against the dystopian backdrop of near-future events. As the modern trappings of their bluecore fall apart, each must strike his or her own separate path toward salvation. Their interlaced stories become a compelling exploration of moral deviation and ultimate redemption.

**The Perihelion (The Perihelion Book 1)**
"Literary, character-driven science fiction at its best."
- Self-Publishing Review

"It's clear that D.M. Wozniak's future in science fiction shines bright."
- IndieReader Discovery Awards

**An Obliquity (The Perihelion Book 2)**
"An intelligent, superbly written, creatively unique and complex, supremely imaginative story."
- Readers' Favorite (Five Star Review)


"One of the more innovative literary dystopian sci-fi novels you'll ever read."
- Self-Publishing Review


**The Gardener of Nahi**
Since the mysterious closed timelike curve appeared above the world of Cassidian, nothing has come in or out of it. So when an innership emerges from the celestial cloud and crashes on the beaches of the Still, a Hunion courier named Anon Selfe is sent to investigate. When he lands, he finds the blood and footprints of the only survivor leading away from the wreckage. But inside there is someone else awaiting him in the darkness: his own dead body.

What follows is Anon's desperate chase up through the tiers of Cassidian to find the survivor of the crash – a young woman named Myria who is unyielding in her belief that she knows Anon from her past.

The only problem is that she claims to be from a world called Nahi, which is not known to exist.

# ABOUT THE AUTHOR

Born and raised in the west suburbs of Chicago, D.M. Wozniak discovered his passion for software at St. Lawrence High School, where he joined the computer lab as a ploy to get out of gym class. By the time he graduated in 1993, D.M. knew that he wanted to code for a living. But his senior-year honors-English teacher took him aside on graduation day and said, "Never stop writing. It's your true calling."

Four years later, D.M. graduated from the University of Illinois at Urbana-Champaign with a degree in Computer Science from the College of Engineering. After that, he started a family and a career in software. He didn't have the time then to consider that true calling.

But he never forgot.

D.M. Wozniak is the author of two two-volume speculative fiction epics: The Perihelion: Complete Duology (The Perihelion, An Obliquity) and the Age of Axion (The Indivisible and the Void, Temberlain's Ashes). His first novel was The Gardener of Nahi. He lives in Raleigh, North Carolina.

www.dmwozniak.com

www.ingramcontent.com/pod-product-compliance
Lightning Source LLC
Chambersburg PA
CBHW031043110726
47900CB00003B/792